MERCHANTS BRIDGE

DARK RIVER SERIES, BOOK ONE

J.D. TRAFFORD

ALSO BY J.D. TRAFFORD

To my mother for all of her love, patience, support, and completely unbiased opinion of my ability and intellect.

—J.D.

I was neither living nor dead, and I knew nothing.

— T.S. Eliot, The Waste Land

CHAPTER ONE

Their solitude was disrupted by the roar of an engine as they crossed Chestnut Street. It was late, and downtown was empty. Gray looked up and saw a Chevy Tahoe round the corner. Its backend fish-tailed in the fresh snow, and then straightened only to swerve twice more, cross over the centerline, and hop the curb.

It stopped just five feet in front of them. A door flung open. The driver jumped out and walked toward Virgil with purpose. He was a stocky man, leather jacket and a hood. The driver didn't seem drunk at all, forcing a revision to Gray's initial assumption when he had noticed the vehicle barreling toward them.

Then Gray saw the gun. Three quick shots and Virgil went to the ground. It happened so fast that Gray didn't even notice that a passenger had also gotten out of the Tahoe or maybe he came from behind on foot. Wherever he came from, Gray wasn't expecting it.

The handle of a gun whipped his face. It dropped him hard. Gray's head snapped back against the sidewalk. Then he was rolling, one kick to his side after another as he tried to get away. The wet, frozen ground soaked through his clothes.

A pause, and then two hands grabbed hold, flipped Gray onto his back, and emptied his pockets. When he tried to move, again, the response was swift. Two punches to the head, maybe three. Then a foot came down on Gray's chest. Air left his lungs. He was pinned, each breath a struggle.

Unlike the moments e was no montage of childhood *memories or signif*ts flashing before his eyes. No past *or future. There* ead, simply a heightened awareness of *the immediate* The everyday distractions of a middle-*aged man's life* ple hours, petty disputes with his ex, emails *needing repli* kid's soccer schedule, laundry, and bills—*disappeared* nothing besides that present moment.

There The *The* crete beneath Gray was covered by one large slab of ice. Sha pains coursed from his ribs and head. Gray couldn't see him but he knew that Virgil was in trouble. Even in the midst of a snowstorm, the air around them hung heavy, not easily pushed. Gray had smelled that same scent as a boy, hunting with his father on the edges of a vast Missouri prairie. It was a deep, earthy musk, that of an animal in distress. A combination of blood and bodily fluid that could only mean that death was close or had already arrived.

Gray's attacker looked down. He couldn't have been much more than seventeen. His face still rounded like a boy, but wary. Gray saw every feature: the tiny mole on his cheek, the wispy mustache, one chipped front tooth and the other wrapped in gold. Then there was the knife, a crude neck tattoo with the initials BMP on the handle.

Without turning away, Gray's attacker asked a question. To the stocky man who had just killed Virgil, it came out in one slurred burst of words: "Whatchuwannnadonaw?"

The response that came back was devoid of emotion. In contrast to the kid, his diction was clear. "Just clap him."

Nodding, the young man tightened his grip on the gun. Gray thought there was hesitation, but that may have only been in Gray's own mind. Desperation often created hope where none existed, and this was, without a doubt, a moment of desperation.

The trigger was pulled.

The barrel kicked back once, then a second time. The sound of shots broke through the storm, but only for a moment. The echo off the buildings was muffl. ray gasped as the tw lets hit his chest. His eyes widened thered air, as if he was about to jump into a deep pool of w It was a breath that he gathered air, as if he was was sure would be his last.

Then there was nothing.

The kid walked away. He and the other n drove off in the Tahoe, and Gray remained on the ground. He v shot and bleeding. With this understanding, one would assume at Gray would exhibit terror, screaming or crying, but there was one of that. Gray was quite calm as his body began the process of shutting down.

His mind wandered.

As he lay on the sidewalk, Gray couldn't help but think that being shot felt a lot like getting hit by a bottle rocket. When he was a kid, his buddy Mike would bring a bunch of bottle rockets to Boy Scout camp and they would run through the woods shooting them at each other—this being an era of loose supervision, before the invention of liability forms and permission slips—the obvious goal of the game was to hit another kid in the nuts, which they all thought was hilarious. There was nothing funnier to a boy than a good old-fashioned nut shot. Anyway, the bullets initially felt a lot like getting hit by one of those bottle rockets.

As the bleeding continued, Gray's lips curled into a tight smile at the memory. He'd read somewhere that the brain knows when organs are failing. Chemicals are supposed to be released into the body to make the final moments less painful. Maybe that was what was happening. Maybe that was why he was smiling as he lay on the sidewalk, losing blood, growing tired, and thinking about running through the woods with a lighter and a handful of Silver Tails.

The respite from the pain, however, didn't last forever. A burn grew. That was the difference. When a bottle rocket hit, it was like a pellet or a small rock. When the bullets had entered Gray's chest,

there was that same qui_ but, unlike the bottle rocket, the discomfort didn't fade. I_ the opposite. There was a slow build.
Although tolerable a_ _, heat began to spread and intensify.

Gray still did_ _anic. There wasn't any rolling around, but
his breathing gr__arder. He went in and out of consciousness
as time passed _d more blood was lost. What happened next
was a series of _agments. A narrative creates a false impression of
coherence an_ linear thought, of which there was none. So, here's
what Gray _emembers, not necessarily in this order:

Siren in the distance,

fade to black;

A horse in the backseat of a station wagon, head out the
open window with tongue dangling like a dog,

fade to black;

Gagging on his own blood,

fade to black;

A woman with long orange dreadlocks wearing a nightgown
and slippers with a pigeon on her shoulder, feeding it McDon-
ald's french fries,

fade to black;

Putting his hand on his chest where the burning was the
most intense and feeling his finger dip into the bullet hole,

fade to black;

A Santa Claus with an Irish accent holding him in his arms
and telling him that it'll be okay as an elf waved down a coming
ambulance,

fade to black;

Two flashes of lightning and a clap of thunder,

fade to black;

An EMT putting an oxygen mask over his head and lifting
him onto a stretcher,

fade to black;

Rolling through the hallways of Barnes Jewish Hospital as
one nurse says to another, "this guy got really jacked,"

fade to black.

There may be more. In BRIDGE
remainder was sand in Gray's re was much more, b
shape into anything recognizable, too fine and too dry to
colors, scents, and sounds. ncoherent scrambles of

CHAPTER TWO

As Gay woke up, air didn't come easy. He struggled to breathe. His heart raced. His vision was cloudy. He didn't know where he was or what happened— that would come later—but for now it was as if he'd been teleported through time and space from the familiar to the strange.

Before total panic, his ex-wife whispered to him. "It's okay." There was worry and concern in Kendra's eyes, but her voice was reassuring. "You'll be fine, Gray, just calm down." She leaned in, repeating the mantra. "It's okay…You'll be fine…just calm down."

His body relaxed. Knowing that he wasn't alone staved off total panic, as his mind tried to process the pieces through the flood of narcotics being pumped into his system. A few of the memories came back and then a few more.

Gray tried to say something, but his throat was dry.

"Hang on." Kendra took a large plastic mug with a lid and straw off a nearby table with wheels. She leaned over and put the straw in Gray's mouth. "Here you go."

The cold water mellowed his throat. He tried to speak, again. "Did they get him?"

Kendra's eyes narrowed and Gray could tell that she was thinking about how to respond. It was like when he had asked his mom whether the Easter Bunny was real. She wanted to tell the truth but didn't know whether it was in his best interest. If, as a parent, you concede the fiction of a giant bunny delivering

6

candy and hiding eggs for m.
in one night, certainly it open children all over the
related to Easter, like rising from uncomfortable questions
cave enclosed by a giant stone. It w ad after three days in a
ppery slope.

"The kid who shot me." Gray ma ained, but ultimately
unsuccessful attempt to lift his head. He k further back into
his pillow, exhausted by the small attempt ove. Softly now,
Gray repeated the original question. His tong vas thick, causing some of the words to slur.

Kendra began to answer but stopped.

"I think you should just focus on getting better." She turned
to the door, as if expecting someone to appear. Then Kendra
turned back to him. "Let other people worry about that stuff."
She stood up and walked over to the far side of the bed. There
was a plastic box on the end of a thick cord. She picked up the
box and pressed the button, calling the nurse's station. "You're
safe now, Gray. Focus on getting stronger."

A few minutes passed, maybe more, and then a nurse and
doctor arrived. The doctor was tall and thin with the intensity
and look of a long-distance runner. "Can you tell me your
name?"

"My name?" He looked at Kendra, and then back at the
doctor. It was a simple question. He knew the answer, but it took
more effort than it should to force the words to come out of his
mouth. "Graydon." He paused, suddenly even more tired than
before. "Graydon Wendt, but people call me Gray."

"Alright." The doctor took a step closer. "I'm Doctor Craig
and this is Nurse Bailey. You've been in the hospital for a few
days now, Mr. Wendt." His eyes narrowed as he studied Gray's
injuries. "When you came in, you were in pretty rough shape, so
we had to put you under some heavy sedation." His inspection
continued. "How old are you, Mr. Wendt?"

He hesitated. "Forty-four....Born on Halloween, October
31st and please... call me Gray."

"That's good." The... removed a small flashlight out of his pocket and turned ...I'm going to touch your face, now. There's still a lot of s... and bruising, but it's not as bad as the night when you... ere." Dr. Craig put his hand on Gray's forehead, and the ...ed the light in Gray's eye. "And do you know who the P... ent of the United States is?"

Gray notic... the nurse at the small desk in the corner. She tapped infor... ion into a computer, making a record of their conversation... His eyes narrowed. "Are you testing my cognitive abilities?"

Dr. Craig smiled. "I most certainly am." He spent a few more seconds examining Gray's eyes and face, and then turned off the flashlight as he took a step back. "Do you have an answer to my question?"

Gray nodded, and then told the doctor who was currently overseeing the dysfunctional circus, otherwise known as American democracy, and then continued to answer a few more of Dr. Craig's inquiries. On the whole, Gray thought he did pretty well.

Doctor Craig, then, asked him the current date and month.

Gray remained silent, thinking. "I don't know." He, then, remembered lying on the cold sidewalk, snowflakes falling down around him. "Winter?"

"Sure feels like it." Doctor Craig looked out the window. There was snow covering the ground, a foot deep. "Looks like it, too." He smiled, again. "It's November 7th. Thanksgiving is just a couple weeks away, but it feels more like February out there." He shook his head. "We used to be able to count on a nice 60 or 70 degree day for Thanksgiving, maybe some rain in a worst-case scenario, but not so much anymore." He laughed, and Kendra and Nurse Bailey laughed along with him. Any attempt, however lame, to lighten the mood seemed appreciated.

"Snow." Gray looked toward the window himself, although only a wall of clouds was visible from his angle. "I remember it was snowing." Gray turned back to the doctor a little too fast. It was a slight movement tha[t] grunted. "When do you thin[k] have hurt, but it did. He thought, and then picked up the ...," Gray lost his train of "When do you think I'll be out of here?"

"I'm going to hold you for a few days," Doctor Craig said. "You've got some fractured ribs, a[nd] took some really bad hits to your head. It's too soon to deter[mine] the severity level of a brain injury, if any, but it's important t[hat w]e keep a close eye on it. There was significant swelling." He co[nti]nued talking as he walked over to the computer in the corner [of] the room where the nurse had been working. "We had to cut a [sm]all hole in your skull to drain the fluid. I know this sounds stra[n]ge, but the cold weather actually may have saved your life, it slowed the swelling down just enough to get you here."

Over the nurse's shoulder, the doctor reviewed her notes, and confirmed their accuracy. Then, his attention returned to Gray. "Unfortunately we won't know until you start getting back into your old routine the extent of it, but there's a possibility that you'll have headaches, lose track of tasks, become irritable, or find that you have forgotten how to do some things. Obviously, right now, it's unknown."

Gray's breathing was shallow. As the doctor talked further about follow-up appointments and specialists, Gray tried to take deeper breaths, but the pain was too much. He felt his eyelids grow heavier, and he was having a hard time staying awake.

Dr. Craig noticed, and so he stopped what he was saying and decided to wrap it up. "I'll also give you some more medication to manage your discomfort when you're home. It'll take several weeks before your ribs begin to really heal and you can move around. It'll be slow. Just take it easy." The doctor nodded, signaling to everyone that his job was done. Other patients were waiting.

There was a rack near the door, and inside was a clipboard with a pen attached. Dr. Craig picked it up. He wrote the date and time and signed in the appropriate boxes, documenting this

9

J.

stop in his rounds. The ~~put it back, an attractive nurse~~
walked by in the hall said hello, and it was enough of a
distraction that Dr. ɔropped the clipboard and it clattered
on the floor.
    It was nothi ɔ Gray, however, the sound of the clip-
board hitting th ɔr was an explosion, transporting him back
to the shootin ɔ Chestnut Street. He felt his chest rip apart.
He screame ɔ pain. The various monitors attached to Gray's
body emitt a high-pitched warning, causing Doctor Craig and
Nurse B.ey to rush to his bedside. Kendra, eyes wide and
scared, tepped out of the way. Her back to the wall.

"t's going to be fine." Doctor Craig was just a few inches
from Gray's face, forcing Gray to look at him. He whispered.
"Calm down, man. Calm down." To nurse Bailey, "Up the
pento."

Nurse Bailey pressed a button that released Pentobarbital
into the IV attached to Gray's arm. Within seconds, the panic
subsided. Gray's heartbeat slowed. His breathing eased, and the
machines went silent.

"That's it, Gray, just relax." Dr. Craig stepped back. "In a
minute or two you'll be sound asleep."

Gray felt his eyelids get even heavier than before. There was
tingling in his fingers, and he began to float. Gray closed his eyes
and put his hand on his chest. Under his breath, he said, "Getting shot is no fun."

Dr. Craig looked down at his patient. The corner of his
mouth curled up, a little amused. "Shot?"

Gray's eyes were still closed. His breathing even slower, but
much to the doctor's surprise, Gray nodded.

Dr. Craig turned to Nurse Bailey, and she shrugged her
shoulders. He, then, looked back down at Gray. "*You* got shot,
huh?"

"That's right." Gray's speech was slurred. There was a pause,
then a declaration, "In the chest…it hurts."

Dr. Craig nodded, cautiously. "I'm sure it does." Then, with care, the doctor pulled back Gray's loose-fitting gown to look. Eventually, he was able to see what was there or, more accurately, what was not. Except for some bruising, there were no bullet wounds or any other similar injury. He put the gown back in place, and stepped away. "Sometimes in a traumatic event like this—an assault in combination with a head injury—the brain has trouble processing things. It's nothing to be alarmed about, and I'm sure that with time, hopefully, the physical and mental injuries will heal."

Agitation stirred. Gray fought the drugs and managed to force his eyes to open, just a little. "I was shot." Through gritted teeth, he pushed. "I know what happened." Then Gray drifted. He couldn't keep his eyes open any longer. "That kid... he...gun..."

Doctor Craig put his hand on Gray's shoulder, gentle. His tone sympathetic. "It's hard. Memories can sometimes be tricky." Then he turned and walked away.

CHAPTER THREE

Two men stood at the door that evening, both wore cheap suits that didn't quite fit. Without the protection of doctors and nurses and with Kendra gone in search of decent coffee, they walked into the room and over to the bed, unfettered.

"Hello." The tall, thin one held out his badge. "I believe you are Graydon Wendt, true?"

"Please call me Gray." Despite the pain, he leaned over and examined the identification, not because Gray disbelieved that the man was a law enforcement officer, but rather it seemed like what people were expected to do in such situations. After he'd given it a few seconds, Gray nodded and leaned back, trying hard to mask his discomfort.

The tall and thin detective put his identification away. "I'm Sergeant Anthony Bird and this is Detective Richard Doles." Unlike Sergeant Bird, Doles was shorter and never offered up his badge for examination. He was muscular with a prominent, dimpled chin. The two of them together looked like real-life versions of Woody and Buzz from Disney's Toy Story movies, minus the cowboy hat and spacesuit.

"Mind if we talk?" Bird located a chair in the corner of the room, slid it next to the bed, and sat down, all while riffing on whether the Blues had any chance of making the hockey playoffs, again. After unexpectedly winning the Stanley Cup a few years back, everybody in St. Louis was suddenly an expert.

Gray tolerated the obligatory small talk, despite a headache, because he thought he might finally get some answers. Kendra had always changed the subject whenever he asked, and the doctors claimed that they didn't know the details.

"Did you catch them?"

Bird held out his hand, cutting off the question. "We can and will talk to you about that, but I'd like to get your statement first." Bird, then, took a digital recorder out of his pocket, and he held it up. "Mind?" When Gray didn't object, Bird pressed a button and set the recorder down on the tray next to the hospital bed.

"This is a statement from Graydon Wendt." Bird further delineated the preliminaries, date, and time as well as who else was in the room. "Mr. Wendt, before we begin, I'd like to give you a Miranda warning." He tried to be reassuring, but it was obviously superficial, an act. Casually, he said, "As a lawyer, I'm sure you understand your rights, but you know how it is. We do it with everybody. Just part of the procedure."

"We don't really have much information about what happened last night," Doles said. "We want to make sure that we have a good basis to begin the investigation."

"Begin?" Gray was confused. "You haven't caught them? You haven't even started?"

"We've certainly started." Bird exchanged an annoyed look with Doles, and continued, ignoring Gray's question related to whether anyone had been caught. "Shall we begin?"

"That's fine," Gray said, "But I don't know how long I can do this."

"Give us what you can," Bird said. "Anything will help." He ran through a paraphrased version of Gray's rights, and then began the interview by asking for basic biographical information.

Gray adjusted himself as he responded. He told Bird his age, address, and employer. He tried to concentrate, but it wasn't easy. Scattered memories of that night rushed through his head, and, as he tried to collect them, the pieces often slipped away. He started to talk about the dinner at Tony's with Jack Durell, but the image of Virgil laying on the ground near him came forward. The sounds and the smells.

In the middle of talking about Jack Durell's plans to develop a vacant triangle of land wedged between the highway and entrance ramps, Gray stopped. "Virgil's dead, right? I mean...I know that, but..."

"Yes, sir." Bird confirmed what nobody else had been willing to confirm. "I'm sorry to tell you about that." He waited a few seconds for the information to settle, then continued. "Let's back up and start at the beginning, again?"

Gray hesitated, but it wasn't really presented as a choice. "Okay." Gray, then, repeated his story. "When the dinner was done, we needed to get back to the parking garage at our office."

Doles chimed in. "That's Met Square?"

"Yes," Gray said. "Virgil wanted to get a ride and I wanted to walk."

"Why did you want to walk?" Bird's eyes narrowed. "The weather was pretty bad at that point."

"It's not that far." Gray remembered the conversation about calling a cab and his own stubbornness. He was 100% German and grew up poor. Thrift was hard-wired in Gray's brain. His dad had worked for the post office, cleaning a government warehouse off Vandeventner Avenue. His mother cooked lunches at the neighborhood high school, back when schools served kids real food and not glorified microwave dinners. Even after making partner, Gray wasn't going to fritter his money away on some guy driving him four city blocks. It was, in hindsight, a decision that likely cost Virgil his life.

"So we walked," Gray said. "Downtown was abandoned. Nobody was around, and then this car came out of nowhere."

"Was it a car?"

Gray closed his eyes, and then told Bird that it wasn't. "An SUV or something, I think, but maybe not."

"Do you remember the color?"

"No."

"Light or dark?"

"I really don't remember. Light maybe, maybe cream."

"And then what happened?"

"It jumped the curb. A guy got out and shot Virgil, and then somebody hit me in the head." Gray stopped talking, lost in his thoughts. After his conversation with Doctor Craig, Gray decided it wasn't in his best interest to continue insisting that he too had been shot, even though that memory was the clearest of them all. He also decided not to share his memories of horses, women in nightgowns feeding french fries to pigeons, and Santa Claus or his elf.

"It's pieces," Gray said, "There was a short stocky man—I didn't get a real good look at him— and then there was a younger kid, baby face." He described the young man who stood over him with a gun, the mustache, and the neck tattoo. "That's pretty much all I know."

"And that's good information." Bird appeared to be encouraged. He leaned forward, now speaking in a softer voice, as if anything loud might scare Gray away. "Let's go back to the beginning, go through it another time. I want to slow it down even more, take it apart. We need as many details as you can provide." Bird looked over at the digital recorder, sitting on the table. The small red light was still on. "From the beginning."

Doles hung back while Bird continued to interview Gray. They must've gone through the story another eight or ten times. With each telling Bird focused on different parts.

When it seemed like Bird was going to ask Gray to go through it, yet again, Gray stopped him. "I have to rest." He held up his hand. "I'm sorry. I don't feel good." He closed his eyes. "I'm just repeating the same things over and over. My head really hurts and I feel like I'm getting sick to my stomach." After taking a few breaths, Gray opened his eyes.

Bird nodded. He acted like he understood the situation, but Doles was less sympathetic, annoyed. As Bird stood and began to move the chair back to the corner of the room, Doles stepped forward. "If we were to put together a photo lineup," his tone strangely confrontational, "you'd be willing to take a look, right?"

Gray held out his hands. "You know where to find me."

"And we appreciate that." Bird put his hand on his partner's shoulder, regaining control of the interview. "I just wanted to let you know that we got a warrant for your cell phone. When you were first admitted to the hospital, you didn't have a wallet or phone. We figured they were taken. I think a judge is reviewing the warrants now or he will first thing in the morning, but that should be set up soon."

"My phone?" Gray didn't understand. "Why do you need a warrant for my phone?"

"Every phone has a GPS inside that's constantly pinging off cell towers. We can use that information to find your phone, and, hopefully, find the people that shot and killed your friend."

Doles, tired of being silenced by his older partner, added, "But cell phones are sold pretty quickly. That's why it's important for us to know anything you remember about the people who did this. That's why I asked about the photo lineup."

"I understand." Gray looked down at his hands. They were shaking, slightly. "I'll do my best."

CHAPTER FOUR

Doctor Craig did not want Gray to go home alone. Every morning he'd schedule another physical therapy session and promised to reassess in the afternoon. This went on for four days, during which he must've asked whether there was someone Gray could stay with at least a dozen times, but Gray's answer remained the same.

Kendra was not an option. She'd moved on with her life, dating before their divorce was even finalized and remarried within a year. Gray's older brother, Patrick, lived in California. His mother passed away a few years prior and his father long before that. There were no women in the picture. Being single at 45 was not something he'd planned for. Dating apps and websites scared him. The bar scene made Gray feel even older than he was and trying to date someone he met through work seemed like a good way to get sued for sexual harassment.

"My neighbors will keep an eye on me." Thinking of Midge and her wife Haley, Gray thought it sounded better than telling the doctor to call his legal secretary with concerns. Gray wasn't feeling that much better, but he wanted to get home. "I'll give them your number. If there's any difficulty getting in touch with me, they'll call you right back. It's not a problem."

There was a long pause, then Doctor Craig sighed, acknowledging defeat. "Fine," he relented, "but those headaches concern me. You need to take this slow. You need to schedule follow-up visits."

Kendra had been sitting in the corner, looking at her phone and working hard not to get involved. Doctor Craig looked at her for support, but she offered nothing. Kendra had come to the hospital, because she was a decent person. She'd waited at Gray's bedside, because there was nobody else, and she was now giving the father of her children a ride home. That was all she was going to do, and Gray wasn't going to ask her to do more.

It didn't take long once Doctor Craig made his decision known. Forms were presented by Nurse Bailey and signed. There were final visits from the occupational therapist and a few other specialists. Then, finally, all that needed to be done was to get dressed.

Since everything Gray wore on the night of the shooting was now in a police evidence locker, Kendra had borrowed some of her current husband's clothes. She gave Gray a paper bag. "I think these will fit."

Gray took the bag and looked inside. "Certainly better than wearing a hospital gown in this weather, but I'd get out of this place even if I had to wear the gown. There's no shame in letting the world see my sunshine if that's what needs to happen."

Kendra held up her hand. "I think I've seen and heard enough." She turned to the door as Gray pulled out the pair of sweatpants. "I'll give you a little privacy."

"Thanks." He removed the remaining clothes from the paper bag and slowly edged off the bed as Kendra left the room. He hadn't been connected to tubes or wires for two days, and the only thing impeding his movement was pain. Gray had now been in the hospital for almost a week. Although his discomfort had lessened, it wasn't gone.

Alone in the hospital room, he slipped the flimsy gown off his body and it fell to his feet. He, then, grabbed the pair of boxer shorts and bent over, but he couldn't bend far enough without a shot of fire ripping up his side. He stood up. His heart raced, his breathing shallow. Then he tried, again.

This time he was prepared.

Gray forced himself to get his feet through the holes. He stepped once, almost lost his balance, and then stepped, again. A bead of sweat rolled down his cheek, or maybe it was a tear.

Another try, and he finally had both feet through the openings and pulled the boxers up. Out of the corner of his eye, Gray saw his reflection in the window. *Who was this old man?* His hair hadn't been properly combed. His bruises had turned an awful dark purple, yellow on the edges, and he'd lost weight, mostly muscle.

He touched his chest, where the bullet wounds should have been.

It didn't happen, he reminded himself as the image of the baby-faced kid came into his head. He pushed it away. *It didn't happen.* Maybe he could pretend that none of it happened. Maybe that's how survivors go forward. Maybe it was better to just put it all in a box, and shove it away, deep where it could be forgotten.

He decided to give that a try.

They didn't talk much during the ride. Kendra drove Gray from the hospital to his narrow brick house on Hartford Street in almost total silence. Built in 1910, just a few blocks away from Tower Grove Park, the house was Gray's declaration of independence after their divorce. Although she never came out and said it, Gray knew that Kendra hated the house and where he now lived. Perhaps that's why he chose it, a rebellion from the life he'd felt pressured to live.

Kendra had been all about open floor plans, fancy schools, and copious amounts of free parking in front of every store. The city offered none of that. In her mind, the city didn't even have a decent church. Early in their marriage, it had taken a year of church shopping before Kendra finally settled on Mosaic Life in Chesterfield. Gray couldn't tell the difference between Mosaic Life or the dozen other places they had visited. They all had names that sounded like yoga studios and offered a theology rooted more in Dr. Phil and Oprah Winfrey than John Calvin, Martin Luther, or Soren Kierkegaard.

In the moment, Gray hadn't complained. His job was to shut-up and make money. That's what Kendra wanted, and he thought that was what young married couples were supposed to do, but that life in suburbia was suffocating. Every day Gray lost a little more of himself. It got harder to get up in the morning and more difficult to fall asleep at night. The commute transformed him into a zombie. Gray didn't realize how depressed he'd become until Kendra handed him the divorce papers. He remembered looking down at them at the dining room table and feeling nothing.

Now, the imperfections of his house on Hartford Street were healing. The floors squeaked. Some of the doors didn't shut right or shut at all. Lights often flickered for no apparent reason. Each quirk lowered expectations. The house wasn't perfect and neither was he.

"The streets are still terrible." Kendra slowed and turned right off of South Grand, going west. Her SUV bumped and rocked through ruts of ice and snow. "Doesn't even look like the plows have been down here." She pulled over to the side of the street and stopped. She started to rant about the mismanagement of the city, a favorite activity for those that didn't actually live there, but Kendra cut it short.

Gray hadn't made any move to leave, nor had he said a word. He simply stared out the window at his house.

Now wasn't the time for a diatribe about high taxes and substandard services. Kendra gave him space to process. Then, she put her hand on his, gentle. "I'm glad you're okay."

He looked down at their hands. Gray couldn't remember the last time they'd had physical contact like that. For years it

number. I told him that you'd report anything weird, like if I start roaming the neighborhood in my bathrobe or something."

They both smiled, kindly.

"We'll get the number when we come back for your shopping list," Haley said. "And you're also invited to Thanksgiving dinner with us."

"Thanksgiving?" Gray shook his head. "I almost forgot."

"No excuses," Midge said. "You're coming to our place for dinner. It'll be filled with misfits and losers just like you."

"I'm not a misfit or loser."

"Sure you are. Embrace it." Midge put her arm around her wife. "We all are." Then she went up on her tiptoes and pecked Haley on the cheek.

The two were an odd couple, and not just physically. Haley was a proud supporter of Missouri Public Radio and Democracy Now. Midge had hair that was buzzed high and tight, former military. On Midge's forearm there was the logo for the Republican party, a blue and red elephant with three stars. Together they sold real estate, primarily in south city.

"Y'all are very cute." Gray couldn't think of a reason to decline their invitation. "I'll be there. Just tell me what I need to bring."

"Bread." It was requested without hesitation, as Midge pointed at the brick oven in the corner of Gray's yard. "Bring copious amounts of gluten, please."

Haley added, "We can help you fire it up, if you want, and you promised me that you'd teach me how to use it, anyway."

"I think that would be good for my soul." Gray smiled at the thought of standing in front of an 800 degree oven on a cold night.

They finished their goodbyes, and Gray entered his house.

Closing the back door and walking into the small eat-in kitchen, it didn't take long for the emptiness to hit him. After days of nurses and doctors poking and prodding, machines beeping, and constant activity in the hallway, the silence seemed louder than anything he'd heard during his stay in the hospital.

The house was just as he had left it, but different at the same time. As he walked through, the gears stuttered in his head. Nothing was automatic. Memories took a fraction of a second longer to come forward, as if he'd been gone years, not days.

With each room, Gray reacquainted himself, opening drawers and closets. When the inspection of the upstairs was finished, he walked back down to the main living room and over to the fireplace. He looked at himself in the mirror that hung over the mantle. It was a large beveled mirror framed by substantial pieces of oak, intricately carved.

Usually clean shaven and hair neatly parted, the person in the reflection looked nothing like the ambitious young man who had dutifully married his college sweetheart over twenty years ago, worked his way through law school, and now spent his days and nights at Daniels & Bloom. A once precocious kid always surrounded by people waiting for his next joke or quip about a politician or celebrity in the news, now alone. His friendships and even his marriage had been largely, if not entirely, sacrificed to the billable hour. His children loved him, but did they know him?

Gray ran his hand through his hair, a movement that sent a sharp reminder through his body of everything that had happened. Like his face, his hair was different than before. Maybe it just appeared different because it was untamed by the hair product he usually applied each morning before work or maybe he just hadn't been paying attention. Gray noticed that there were more speckles of white above the ears. He knew it had been turning, but not that much.

Gray took a step back, hoping for a kinder, broader view. Luckily the hair on top remained thick, curls and waves running in every direction. Generations of Wendt men had all benefited from a genetic predisposition that prevented hair loss, and, in that moment, Gray realized that he could've been looking at a picture of his father.

His father never owned a comb. He let it go wherever it wanted. The people in the warehouse where he spent his days didn't care.

Gray closed his eyes. A tear ran down his cheek as he took a shallow, jagged breath. Emotions running quicker and more unpredictably than they had ever come in the past. *What's happening to me?* He wiped the tear away, trying to regain his composure, but the memories of his father weren't brushed aside as easily.

Gray missed the old man. His father never saw him graduate high school or marry or have children. He died too young, never taking advantage of the retirement he had earned. He opened his eyes and, once again, moved close to the mirror. Gray ran his hand along the top of the old oak mantle as he studied himself, thinking about how close he'd come to being just like his father. His life was almost cut short, a future of beautiful moments unrealized.

He stepped back from the mantle, turned, but didn't go very far. Virgil Hawthorne was on the floor, wearing his suit and long wool overcoat, convulsing. Half his face was gone. The remainder pulp.

Gray looked around in a panic, as blood spread across the floor and Gray the contents of his stomach roiled up. Sirens drowned out his screams. Blood now soaked through the ceiling as well and flowed down the walls. It surrounded him.

Gray looked for a way out, but the doors and windows had disappeared. He was trapped in a red box that grew smaller. There was nowhere to go. It kept coming. The walls closed in and the blood rose higher, rising from his ankles to his knees. The raw, metallic smell filled his nostrils. When he tried to lift his feet, it was as if they were in concrete. He struggled against it, splashing, trying to rip them away from whatever held his feet to the floor. Finally, one foot broke free, and Gray lost his balance.

As he fell into the pool of blood, two shots were fired into his chest.

CHAPTER FIVE

Old Betsy was the only other living thing in his house. Gray didn't have a dog or a cat or even a fish. After his two kids, Nick and Zoe, had advanced past diapers, Gray swore that he would never be responsible for cleaning up the feces of another. Old Betsy, however, was different. She was the sourdough starter that lived in a crock on his countertop.

The daily practice of feeding and caring for her was almost a form of meditation, and, at that moment, he needed Old Betsy more than ever. Gray needed her to help collect himself, sort out what was real and what wasn't, because everything had become unsettled. One moment he was looking at himself in a mirror, the next he was drowning in pool of blood and screaming in pain. After blacking out, Gray awoke and it all had reverted to normal. Except it didn't really revert to normal, because the monster had escaped from its box. He couldn't control it, and that knowledge was more disturbing than anything else, to lose control of your own mind.

Gray turned on the faucet, thinking.

This was something he should tell somebody. Dr. Craig had specifically warned him, and Gray knew that he should call him, but he didn't want to. Such a revelation would surely have consequences. Gray ticked through various scenarios in his head, possible outcomes, including being institutionalized. He could lose everything.

Gray's hands shook as he washed them under the stream of warm water. He took deep breaths, trying to center himself.

Then Gray dried his hands, filled a bowl with room temperature water, and was about to remove a few scoops of Old Betsy from the crock when the doorbell rang. The unexpected sound made him jump, but he didn't scream and no blood flowed down from the walls. Progress? Perhaps.

It's just the doorbell, Gray assured himself as he slowly walked toward the front entryway, *not a big deal*. When he opened the door, there was a woman in a dark suit.

"I'm Investigator Amy Wirth from the St. Louis Police Department. Are you Mr. Wendt?"

Wirth wasn't much taller than five feet, athletic, with short brown hair and sharp features. A badge hung from a lanyard around her neck.

Gray felt an overwhelming urge to slam the door in her face. The reaction surprised him. It was strange, seemingly coming from nowhere. He knew how he was expected to act, which was to welcome the police, answer their questions, and fully cooperate. Yet, he didn't want to. He was making bread— trying to forget, keeping the monster in the box— and this woman would likely want him to remember.

"Call me Gray." He forced a smile, revealing nothing of his irritation. He opened the door a little wider and stepped aside. "Are you taking over for the other two? The ones who came to the hospital."

Wirth shook her head as she stepped across the threshold. "Detectives Bird and Doles are still assigned to this matter. I came here to administer a photo lineup."

A photo lineup, Gray thought. This should've made him happy. It was a sign of progress. If there was a photo lineup, then they must have suspects. This was a good thing, but he still wanted her to leave. Not much below the surface, he was still irrationally angry at her mere presence.

"That's fine," Gray glanced back at the kitchen, "but I'm sort of in the middle of something. If you're not in a hurry, do you mind waiting while I finish up? Won't take too long."

It was a small act of defiance, and it made Gray feel better, like he was a little more in control.

Wirth didn't mind. She followed Gray to the kitchen and sat down on a stool.

"I like to bake," Gray said, "and I've had this starter going for almost ten years." Gray took the lid off of the clay crock, and then he showed it to Wirth.

She scrunched up her nose. "Smells like something is rotting."

"In some ways it is," Gray said. "But that's because it's been neglected while I've been…" His voice faded. Gray felt a threatening rise of the memories and emotions, but shoved them away.

Gray set the crock down, and then he stuck his finger in the bowl of water. It needed to be warm, not hot. Then he scooped about three tablespoons of the starter into the bowl. "Have you arrested somebody?"

"I don't know," Wirth said. "I'm not specifically involved in the investigation at this time." She watched as Gray mixed the starter with the water until it turned into a creamy tan bath. Then she reached down and opened her briefcase. Wirth removed a thin board. It looked like a clipboard, only slightly thicker and wider.

"It's part of the protocol," she said. "The person administering a photo lineup isn't supposed to know much about the case and nothing about the suspects. It eliminates the chance that I accidently lead you in one direction or another."

"Which would give defense attorneys an opportunity to poke holes in the identification."

Wirth nodded. "Sergeant Bird told me you're an attorney."

"I am." Gray took a bag of his special flour off the shelf. It was an organic heritage grain called Turkey Red. His neighbor, Haley, claimed his bread was easier to digest than loaves made from commercial flour sold in grocery stores. Gray just thought it tasted better.

He looked at the board that Wirth held in her hand, and then turned his attention back to tending to Old Betsy. "I do real estate law not criminal, but every law student is required to take criminal procedure. So I know enough to trick myself into thinking I'm smarter than I am." He was trying to sound nonchalant, but the entire act was exhausting and he wondered if Wirth was being fooled by any of it. He was obviously in pain. His mind was dulled by painkillers, and Gray felt a migraine coming on faster and faster.

He poured flour into the bowl of creamy liquid, mixed, and then repeated the process until it was the consistency of thick pancake batter.

"Law school was a long time ago," Gray said to himself as he studied the batter, waiting for a sign of life. When nothing happened, Gray looked up from the bowl and pointed at the board in Wirth's hand. "I assume there are photographs behind each of those doors."

"There are."

Gray, then, turned back to the bowl. He studied it, again, hoping. Then, after a few seconds, he looked up with a smile on his face. This one was genuine. "It's still alive." He picked the bowl off the counter and showed it to Wirth. "See the bubbles. That's a good sign. The starter isn't as strong as she was before, but she's still alive. In a day or two, she'll be back to normal. I might be able to bake some good Thanksgiving bread after all, assuming I can get my oven up to temperature in the cold."

"Don't you just turn it on?"

"No." Gray pointed out the window at the oven. "After I bought this place, I built a wood-fire oven in the backyard. Some divorced guys go out and buy a Porsche or a boat. I built an oven. I slightly modified a version of one built by Alan Scott in the 1960s. He's considered the master among the bread heads."

Gray finished mixing the dough, and then they went back into the living room after he'd cleaned up.

"We'll go through each photo." Wirth sat down on the couch and held the board with doors so that Gray could see it. "You aren't required to identify anyone in this line-up, because the perpetrator may not actually be anyone presented here. Understood?"

"I understand."

Wirth opened the first door. "Let me know if you recognize any of these men as the person who attacked you or Virgil Hawthorne."

Gray studied the first photograph. After a minute, he shook his head. "No."

Detective Wirth closed the first door, and then opened the second. Gray, again, didn't recognize the person in the photograph. The third door opened, then the fourth, and then the fifth.

That was the one.

Gray stared at the baby-face, and he felt his whole body shake. The command of the stocky man rattled around in his head: just clap him. Gray turned away, unable to look anymore.

Wirth concerned. "Are you okay?"

Gray didn't respond to the question or even look at her. Instead, he said, "That's him. That's the man who shot…" He stopped himself. Gray promised himself that he'd ignore the false memory of two bullets being fired into his chest. He reminded himself that it wasn't real, talking about it would only make people think he was, at best, unstable. "…I mean the man who robbed me. I recognize him, and he was with somebody else."

"And you're sure that this is who robbed you when Virgil Hawthorne was killed."

"I am."

"How certain? Like what percentage?"

Gray forced himself to look at the photo, again. The fifth door was still open with the picture. It was him. The neck-tattoo, the mole, and the wispy mustache was all there. Gray took a breath, and then looked at Wirth. "100%," he said. "That's him."

CHAPTER SIX

Victor Morales watched her leave the house from a distance. A briefcase was in one hand, a "six pack" was in the other. That was the nickname he and other officers used to call the photo line-up board, since there were typically only six photos for a witness to choose from. As Morales watched her get into the un-marked squad he thought about the six-pack. It indicated that the investigation was going forward. Enough information had been gathered to have a specific enough description of the per-petrator to identify at least one or two suspects.

This was not anticipated and unwelcome.

His phone rang, and Morales knew who was calling. He considered letting it go, but that wasn't an option. He was paid well to answer, regardless of when the phone calls came or whether the conversation was going to be good or bad.

When he pressed the button and put the phone to his ear, there were no greetings or small talk. The caller wanted an up-date, whether needed or not, and Morales knew better than to play games.

"An investigator was at the house for about an hour," he said. "Nobody else has come or gone. No feds."

Morales considered whether to withhold the information about the six-pack, but knew it was better to come clean. His employer had better contacts and a lot more money. He probably already knew.

"She had a photo line-up with her." Morales paused, waiting for a reaction, but nothing came. "I'll find out whether the guy fingered someone or not, then I'll let you know."

The man asked for additional details, which Morales did his best to provide. If his employer knew or didn't know the information relayed by Morales, he didn't express any surprise at anything that was said. There was, however, an intensity in his voice that hadn't been present before: a mess had been made, and Morales needed to clean it up, fast.

The call ended, and Morales removed the phone's battery and SIM card. He kept a small nail clipper in the center counsel of his van, but it wasn't for a quick manicure. He picked it up and clipped the SIM card in half, and then tossed the tiny pieces out the window. Then he looked back at the house, and tried to understand how the lawyer was still alive.

CHAPTER SEVEN

Kendra arrived early in the morning. Gray had been watching for her from the window, while Nick and Zoe were eating their freshly baked pretzels on the living room couch. "Looks like your mom is here." Gray pointed at the coffee table where there was a cloth bag filled with another three pretzels. "Don't forget to give her one."

The two agreed, and then fetched their backpacks. Gray gave each a gentle hug, longer than usual, and then sent them out the door. He had savored every precious second with them, each growing too fast. Zoe was right on the cusp of becoming a teen, and Nick wasn't that far behind his big sister. Being with them over the past two days, Gray had felt moments of lightness that he hadn't felt in a long time, but it didn't last.

This was his first day back at work. It was intended to be an easy one. That morning, he decided to wear his best suit and tie. In his imagination, Gray pictured himself entering the firm's lobby like a conquering hero, stronger and better looking than he ever was. The ladies would swoon, and he'd modestly brush away the many compliments. "No, really," he'd say, "the recovery wasn't half as bad as the doctors made it out to be." He'd shrug. "I was bored, to be honest, couldn't wait to get back."

Gray, in truth, struggled to even get his clothes on without intense pain and, eventually, gave up on the tie. Driving through downtown, he pulled to a stop at Pine and waited for the light to turn green. Gray was lost in his thoughts, wondering about his kids and how he could become more present in their lives. Then he thought of Virgil Hawthorne.

Hawthorne was shot dead just a few blocks away, dominating the news for a few seconds and then forgotten. If he would've been the one who died, Gray figured it'd be the same for him. There would be a brief disruption in the daily routines of close relatives and friends—his brother, Kendra and the kids, maybe Midge and Haley would be shocked and hurt—and, then, things would regress to the mean, tragedy giving way to the inertia of the ordinary.

Memories of him would become a less constant presence in their lives and more of a surprise. While passing through the daily routine, a sudden remembrance would pop up, then the memory would disappear. The space between each one becoming further and further apart, weeks passing between each one, then months and finally years. The progression of grief.

A horn sounded.

Gray was brought back through the looking glass. The man in the delivery truck behind him waved his hands. The driver's face was red in anger. It took a second, but Gray understood. The light was now green, although he had no idea how long he'd been sitting at the intersection. It could have been seconds. It could have been much, much longer.

The elevator doors slid open and Gray stepped into the foyer of Daniels & Bloom. It wasn't an elaborate space. Some law firms spent millions on artwork, modern furniture, and walls covered with rare wood paneling with brass accents. The purpose was to intimidate and impress any visitors or opposing attorneys who happened to come to the firm. Daniels & Bloom, however, was different.

Its location on the upper floor of Met Square, with a commanding view of the river and the iconic Gateway Arch, along with the firm's reputation for navigating the city's fickle bureaucracy was enough. They didn't need anything more. Most of the firm's clients were government agencies and real estate developers. Over the top artwork and decorations would be viewed with suspicion by this clientele. They were focused on efficiency and results.

Gray walked towards the receptionist desk, pretending as if nothing had happened, pretending that his body wasn't stiff from the short drive from his home to the office and hoping that nothing would happen to cause a hallucination or for him to black out. It'd been more than a week since the incident in his living room, and the monster had remained mostly in its box.

"Good morning, Rachel."

She smiled. That was Rachel's talent, and that was why she was hired. It was a natural ability and willingness to make the middle-aged men in the firm feel attractive.

"I'm so glad that you're back Mr. Wendt." Another perfect smile followed with a little wink.

"Right." Gray nodded, "It is very good to be back." He walked past her, embarrassed that, even with full knowledge that it was all an act, he fell for Rachel's performance every time.

Gray swiped his magnetic card on the reader next to the door, waited for the click, and then, when the door unlocked, he stepped back into the firm's maze of offices and cubicles. Gray immediately felt the eyes. People were looking at him, but it wasn't as he had imagined. He wasn't a beautiful conquering hero. He was, instead, a curiosity.

Uninterested in small talk, Gray held his head high, looked straight ahead, and walked to his office. The layout of the firm was no different than others in the city. It was a hierarchy of concentric circles. Lawyers, like Gray, were in the offices along the outside edge with windows. Partners with the most seniority had large corner offices. The inner ring was comprised of legal secretaries and paralegals. Most of them had cubes. A few had offices. None had windows. Then, in the very middle of each floor there was the smallest circle composed of people with the lowest status. It was tech support, delivery guys, and some developmentally delayed kids that the firm hired to process mail and demonstrate how kind and benevolent they were to the less fortunate.

When he finally made it, Gray shut the door, trying to convince himself that it was just another day at the office. He was just punching the clock, nothing more. He took several deep breaths, and then told himself that everything was going to be okay. It was just work. He had given up changing the world a long time ago, just bill the time.

Entering law school, Gray had thought he'd get a job at Legal Aid and represent poor people. That's what most law students thought on their first day. Then their eyes were soon opened up to the caste system within the legal ecosystem as well as an awareness of their ever-growing student loan debt. The steadfast commitment to the poor weakened, just a little. Then, over decades, it morphed from a core value, to a belief, and then to something more distant, almost nonexistent.

It happened to Gray, just like it happened to most of them. Rather than take unpaid clerkships, he participated in on-campus interviews for paid summer associate positions. A short-term decision justified by the need to make rent and pay for a little beer money. Then the summer gig turned into a job offer at a firm, justified by the need to pay-off loans and get a little retirement fund started for a few years. When guilt arose, he repeated the mantra of all the young lawyers who sold out: "Don't worry I'm totally going to do a lot of *pro bono* volunteer work."

Soon, the few hours a week doing pro bono work shrunk to a few hours a month, and then just a few hours a year. When Gray became a partner at Daniels & Bloom, he convinced himself that his experience and intellect was better used on the board of directors at these nonprofits rather than actually providing direct services to their clients. Then, finally, Gray was just too busy to do anything at all. He'd write a check, instead, but even that became more and more irregular.

As he sat down at his desk, Gray looked at the shelf of awards and recognition reflecting more noble pursuits. All of them now more than fifteen years old or more. The Pro Bono Publico Award given to him by the bar association had faded to an awful shade of yellow. An engraved glass plaque had gathered dust, and the Missouri Justice Foundation certificate had curled at the edges.

He felt bad, but not so bad that he was going to do anything different, and that made him feel even worse. Gray looked at his watch, now somehow more depressed than he was when he had gotten up that morning, and calculated how long he'd have to be there until he could go home.

They'd be coming for him soon. As he stared at the door, he knew it, and, sure enough, a few minutes later, there was a knock.

It was Ethan Bloom. The son of the firm's founder and managing partner, Herbert Bloom. Ethan was somebody his ex-wife would likely call, "funny looking." Short and round with a club foot, which affected the way he walked, Ethan was an easy target for jokes and ridicule.

"Welcome back." Ethan waddled into Gray's office and closed the door behind him. "Glad you're okay."

"Thanks." Gray forced a smile.

"I thought about visiting you in the hospital," Ethan said. "But I didn't want to intrude."

"I appreciate that, but I did get the card from the firm."

"A card." Ethan rolled his eyes. "Typical, I told my dad that you should get six months paid time off, but it was shot down, which isn't surprising."

"At least you tried." Gray remained polite. He genuinely liked Ethan, even though Gray wanted him to leave. "It's probably for the best. In the end, I need to keep up those billable hours."

"Unfortunately, that's true." Ethan opened his mouth, intending to say something further, but hesitated.

Gray waited, and the silence grew awkward.

"Speaking of billable hours," Gray said. "I better be getting back to work."

"Me too." Ethan started to stand, but then somehow mustered the courage to make his proposal. "I know that you and Virgil worked really closely together... and, if there's any files that need attention or anything that you need, I'd love to work with you on them, help you out. If it goes well, maybe we could do more of it, you know... like, working together, as new files come in."

Gray didn't know quite how to respond. He certainly needed the help, but he wasn't sure about working with Ethan. This hesitation wasn't a reflection on Ethan's skills as a lawyer. Although others doubted his intelligence, simply because of the way Ethan looked and his limited social skills, Gray knew that Ethan was smart. He wasn't just a partner at the firm because of his father.

Gray's hesitation was more practical. The truth was that he and Ethan were too much alike. Neither one of them wanted to wine and dine clients or attend bar association mixers. Both preferred to sit behind a computer and do research and writing. That was why Gray's relationship with Virgil worked so well. They each had different strengths.

"I definitely have some work for you," Gray said. "I'll shoot you an email when I get a little more settled. Then we can take it a step at a time."

Gray could tell by Ethan's expression that he was disappointed, wanting more of a commitment, so Gray tried to reassure him. "Seriously, I'm open to it, but I'm just getting back to the office. I have a lot to figure out."

"I understand." Ethan didn't look Gray in the eye. "Whatever I can do."

"I appreciate that," Gray said, "truly."

He watched Ethan leave, and made a mental note to find something for him, a little project. Maybe they couldn't be a team, but Ethan could certainly help Gray catch up.

He then spent the rest of the morning sifting through email as another half dozen people filed into and out of his office wishing him well, passing on gossip, and subtly trying to extract more details from Gray about the night that Virgil Hawthorne had died.

On his way home, Gray called Jack Durell. He was the potential client that they had dinner with on the night of the storm. His file was one of the tasks that Gray had considered passing along to Ethan, but Gray didn't want to give it up, entirely. If he didn't see it through to completion, it would almost be like Virgil's death was for nothing, like they had that dinner meeting for no reason at all.

According to the notes in the file, there had been a brief follow-up call between Durell and another partner at the firm, but nothing substantive had happened. Durell still wanted to acquire a triangle of green space owned by the Missouri Department of Transportation.

The triangle was near Union Station, once a magnificent train hub and later converted into a marginally successful shopping mall that seemed to be rebranded every eight to ten years. The triangle's southern border was Interstate 64, still referred to by the locals as "Forty," because Highway 40 was what was there prior to the development of the interstate highway system, and the remaining two sides of the island were pinned by ramps magically transporting commuters in and out of the city.

Excess dirt from the highway's expansion in the 1970s was dumped in the triangle, resulting in rolling hills, and, in the middle, a grove of old trees. Who planted these trees after completion of the highway and how the trees survived fifty years of general neglect and car exhaust was unknown, but, this grove of trees was Jack Durell's primary focus of concern.

Not that Durell cared much about trees. He even quoted President Ronald Reagan who once said in response to an environmentalist who wanted to preserve California's redwood forests, "If you've seen one tree, you've seen them all." It was, rather, what was going on around and under the trees that caused concern.

A note in the file indicated that there were some homeless people living there. Gray immediately knew that was how the transaction got tricky. Legally, it was straight forward: make a bid, draw up the purchase agreement, and buy the property, but, the existence of a homeless population, however small, complicated matters. It added a different element.

Real estate developers were already viewed with skepticism, regardless of political affiliation. By adding the displacement of a homeless encampment into the mix, politicians became nervous. Nervous politicians were unpredictable.

Gray thought about his shelf of old awards for his volunteer work and representation of the poor. Back then, he'd be the one representing the people in the homeless encampment, and now he was the one kicking them out. His mind did the mental gymnastics necessary to justify the work that he was doing as the phone rang and he waited for Durell to answer. Then the line clicked.

"This is Gray from Daniels & Bloom." He forced himself to smile while he spoke, an attempt to manufacture energy and excitement in his voice. "I'm back in the office, now, and I just wanted to follow-up on the Triangle property."

As Durell began a rant about homeless people, Gray built another little box in his mind. He put all the shame and guilt inside and shoved it away, stacking it among the other boxes, including the one with the monster. The conversation continued. Durell did most of the talking, and then they set a time to meet.

CHAPTER EIGHT

In the following days, Gray's body continued to heal although his mind did not. With Thanksgiving just around the corner, his brave facade began to crumble. His carefully constructed boxes, each containing memories and fears that he thought he'd buried deep inside, surfaced and began to open.

In the evenings, Gray lay in bed, unable to fall asleep. Every car that drove by sent a wave of adrenaline. His heart pounded and eyes grew wide at the sound of an engine, anticipating the stocky man and the baby-face kid to somehow appear in his room and finish the job. It wouldn't take much. All that separated him from the wolves were panes of glass, easily broken. This was how it was, night after night.

Hours passed.

It was now Wednesday, the night before Virgil's funeral, Gray got up to check and double-check the locks on all his doors and windows. Outside he saw some movement in the alley. He waited as the hairs on the back of his neck stood on end, but nothing happened. A false alarm, perhaps.

In the kitchen, he opened a bottle of sleeping pills. It was a simple task, complicated by his shaking hands. Gray took out one, put it in his mouth, and then decided to take two more. He had to sleep, desperate to close his eyes and make it all go away. Before the incident, he never knew that it was possible to feel so tired, and yet be so unable to rest. Emotions, ideas, and worries just kept coming at him, relentless.

How many times since he'd been discharged from the hospital had he circled parking lots, waiting for the spot closest to the door to open, because he was afraid to walk more than a dozen yards to the entrance? How many times had he left work early to be home well before sunset, afraid of what would come after dark? How many times would he blame himself for Virgil's death, replaying the argument that night outside the restaurant, insisting on walking back to the office when Virgil had wanted to call a cab?

Maybe he should take another pill?

At some point, Gray fell asleep on the couch, although he had no precise memory of when and how this happened. All he knew was that he was on the couch when his eyes opened, and it wasn't because he was rested. Gray woke up because he was in pain. His neck and back were torqued. His arm was numb, and his head felt like it was in a vice.

Based on the light coming through the window, Gray knew the next day had come, but he was disoriented. Then the phone rang. It took a second for Gray to figure out that his cellphone was on the coffee table. He fumbled with it. "Hello?"

"Gray?" It was Ethan. "I stopped by your office to check-in. The meeting starts in five minutes. Where are you?"

"Meeting?" Gray felt a knot form in the pit of his stomach. Despite all of his efforts to project to others that everything was fine, he was just a juggler, constantly catching plates before they fell and tossing them back up in the air.

"Wait… is this the meeting with Durell?" Gray thought about the conversation that he'd had with Jack Durell on his way home from work. "That isn't until Thursday."

"It is Thursday," Ethan said. "He's really pushing for this thing to move forward."

"Wait…today is Thursday?" Gray's mind was processing information through a fog. He tapped his phone's screen, confirming what Ethan had said. It *was* Thursday, but he didn't see any meeting on his calendar. The only appointment on his calendar was Virgil Hawthorne's funeral that afternoon. "When is it?"

"Right now. Durell is in the conference room, waiting." Ethan paused. "Where are you?"

"At home," Gray said. "There's no way I can get to the office in time." He closed his eyes and leaned back into the cushions of the couch, forced to accept reality. "Tell him I'm sick, apologize, and do your best."

Ethan was unsure. "You want me to handle the meeting, alone?"

"I don't see another option." Gray, then, tried to explain the plan to Ethan. "There are about sixty homeless people in the encampment, maybe more, we're trying to get the city to clear it before any deal is announced, but that takes time. They need to set-up some emergency shelter beds, coordinate with some non-profits."

"He's in a hurry."

"Developers are always in a hurry," Gray said. "It'll take a month or two and the early winter isn't helping, a lot of the shelters are already full."

"That's not going to go over well. He wants to break ground in a few weeks."

"Just do your best." Gray pressed the button on the screen, ending the call, and then began scrolling through his electronic calendar. He knew that he'd put the meeting on his schedule, but it wasn't there. Confused and angry, he clicked through the entire week, and then the coming months. There was no meeting scheduled with Jack Durell.

Gray swore that he had dutifully added the meeting to his calendar. He understood the importance. He regularly checked his phone and depended on those little reminders to pop-up on his screen. Yet, the meeting with Durell wasn't there. One of the plates had dropped.

CHAPTER NINE

Gray took the rest of the morning, slowly. He decided he wasn't going to go into the office at all, but rather go straight to the funeral. At two, he pulled up to the tidy Catholic church on the corner of Dale and Bellevue, the sky was clouding over and the temperature had dropped, again. Another early winter storm was coming. Nobody knew exactly when it was going to hit, but everyone could feel it, especially Gray, and he was anxious to get home.

St. Luke's the Evangelist was just off the highway, located in one of the dozens of tiny cities that bordered the city proper. They were the original suburbs, but now didn't look new or feel much different than the houses in the city itself, less than a half mile away.

Gray finally found a parking spot. It was the only one available, and he considered himself lucky. Those that had arrived just after Gray were now abandoning the lot and prowling the local streets.

After popping a painkiller, Gray got out of his car. A cold wind greeted him the moment he began to walk toward the church. It cut through, as if he wasn't wearing any clothes at all. Gray buttoned up his coat, but even that didn't make much of a difference.

He quickened his pace, but still recovering from his injuries, Gray could only go so fast. Once through the church's heavy oak door, he stopped in the entryway. It was the longest Gray had walked since being discharged from the hospital, and he had to rest.

Standing near a coat rack, an elderly woman walked past him. She shook her head, talking with a heavy southern Missouri accent. "Just doesn't seem right, and doesn't look right, neither."

She nodded toward the front of the church. There was a wooden table near the altar, surrounded by flowers. A large photograph of Virgil Hawthorne was on top.

The family had delayed the funeral because Virgil's body hadn't been released by the medical examiner. There were pictures to be taken and reports to be written as part of the police investigation. A thorough autopsy had to be performed, and, as a result, the body would be cut, dissected. What was left of Virgil's head would be studied for entrance and exit wounds and searched for bullet fragments. No amount of makeup would make Virgil Hawthorne presentable. There would be no open casket.

Gray didn't mind. He'd already seen it in his nightmares, and, even if he hadn't, there was no point. In early America, the open casket was necessary to prove the person simply hadn't disappeared to avoid debts or erase past wrongs. Today, the only purpose seemed to be as a method to traumatize young children.

He still remembered his own mother, handkerchief in hand, pointing at the coffin of his deceased grandmother. Gray's father put his arm around him and slow-walked him over to the casket. "Say goodbye, little Grady, tell Gams you love her." Then his father nudged him a step closer to the coffin. Only seven years old, Gray didn't want to do it, but he did. It was the first dead body he'd ever seen, and the memory of his grandmother — puffed and distorted, laying on a bed of white satin— still haunted him.

Gray took a seat toward the back of the church, surrounded by other people who worked at Daniels & Bloom. The firm had closed the office, and sent a strongly worded email to all employees that their presence was "expected." The firm had also agreed to count the time attending the funeral toward an attorney's annual billable hour requirement, which helped. A client code was attached to the email.

He waited patiently for the service to start, studying the carved stone and intricate wooden screen, called a reredos, behind the altar. A few minutes later, the service began with the priest welcoming all of the people in attendance. A young man followed the priest and sang "Blest Are Thee." Herbert Bloom, then, came forward to give a eulogy.

Bloom was old, but still reveled in his role as the founder and leader of the firm. As expected, his remembrance glossed over Virgil's flaws and filled in the gaps with platitudes.

"Virgil Hawthorne was a lawyer's lawyer," Herbert Bloom declared. "He always demanded the highest standards of himself and others."

Bloom then went on to tell a story about when he and Virgil went to the American Bar Association's annual conference in Miami. Upon arrival, Virgil demanded that the hotel change his room assignment multiple times because the air conditioners were too loud.

This got some chuckles from the crowd, especially among the lawyers who were all too familiar with Virgil's demands. Herbert's remembrance was consistent with Virgil Hawthorne's pedigree, a man accustomed to the finer things in life. Perhaps that was why the next remembrance by Virgil's sister was such a surprise.

Katie Hawthorne was a plump woman, wearing a simple black dress. When she spoke, her voice had a gentle lilt, softer than the woman Gray had heard upon his arrival, but still pronounced. There existed a divide between those who lived in Missouri, pronouncing it with a hard "e", and those who lived in Missouri, and pronounced it, Missour-ah. The latter being more Tennessee than Iowa.

Katie Hawthorne pronounced it Missour-ah.

"I love my younger brother." She dabbed her eyes with a tissue. "I'm so very proud of him. He was always so different from everybody else in the family. Virgil wasn't satisfied.

Schooling was like his way out of the trailer park. We'd all be watching T.V. and he'd be over in the corner, under a blankie, and reading some book."

She paused, sniffled, and then wiped away a tear.

"We were proud when he graduated high school, and moved out. Virgil worked multiple jobs to pay his own way, go to college. He was the first one to do it. He set an example for his cousins and even me, his big sister."

Gray looked around at the other people from the firm, and he could sense the collective confusion. They all had heard Virgil talk about his family's lineage, private schooling, and love for the finer things in life. Within five minutes of meeting the man, Virgil had the tendency to somehow work the fact that a long-dead relative was purportedly part of the official delegation that brought the 1904 World's Fair to St. Louis. There was never any mention of growing up in a trailer park.

His sister stepped to the side, blew her nose, and then continued as her voice faltered. "Although he wasn't around much," she said, "He helped out the family financially, never forgetting where he came from."

She started to cry, uncontrollably. "I'll miss you Virgil. We will all miss you."

Gray made eye contact with Ethan, who was sitting further down the pew. He had the same look of bewilderment, and mouthed, "What?"

They both shook their heads.

When the funeral ended, Gray patiently waited as ushers dismissed one pew after another. Virgil's family stood in a receiving line at the exit, thanking each person for coming and offering their condolences as the organ worked through the cannon of traditional funeral hymns. The tunes were somewhat familiar to Gray, but he could only name "Old Rugged Cross" and "Amazing Grace."

Eventually the usher gestured to Gray, signaling that it was now his turn. He stood, walked down the aisle, and was greeted warmly by Virgil's sister, the one who gave the eulogy. Then he shook hands with a few others who he presumed were uncles or cousins. Behind them, a couple kids played amongst the jackets hanging in the alcove. Then Gray stood in front of Cassie, Virgil's wife, and she began to cry.

"I'm so sorry." Gray reached out and put his hand on her shoulder, but Cassie wanted more.

She put her arms around Gray and rested her head on his chest, still crying, and held him for a long time. When she was done, Cassie raised herself up and lowered him down. Then she whispered in his ear.

"Be careful," she said, then Cassie released him.

Gray took a step back. His eyes were narrowed, searching. His mouth slightly open, on the cusp of asking any number of questions, but Cassie gave a slight shake of her head, warning him off. There were too many people.

"Call me," she said, and then turned away from Gray to receive the next person in line.

CHAPTER TEN

Gray did call later that night, but Cassie didn't answer. He left a message, and then busied himself with household chores, checking every ten minutes or so for a text or call that would never come. As the snow began to fall, he turned on the television. Gray tried to find a show, but he wasn't in the mood for anything in particular.

He stared at the screen. It was filled with hundreds of choices, some purportedly selected by an algorithm just for him, but he wasn't interested in laughing or crying, being scared or thrilled. He was lost. Cassie's warning, perhaps overblown or misunderstood, hung over him. It felt like she had pulled a string and the magical blanket that he'd been slowly constructing since Virgil died unraveled in an instant.

Gray checked his phone another time. He toggled the tiny button on the side to ensure that all of the device's bells, beeps, and tones were not silenced. Then he went to the kitchen, removed the bottle of sleeping pills from the cabinet, and popped a few in his mouth. For something that was claimed to be non-addictive, the pull of that bottle of little white pills was strong.

It didn't take long for sleep to come, deep and dreamless—better living through pharmaceuticals. Perhaps that was what made the morning so surprising. For the second day in a row, Gray woke up in pain, disoriented. His sheets were soaked through, sweat. His eyes wide. His chest was tight. It took a second too long for him to figure out where he was and even who he was.

He looked at the clock, worried he'd missed another meeting, another day of work.

A gust of wind rattled the windows, which reminded Gray of the storm, the funeral, and the words that Cassie whispered in his ear. He took his cell phone off of the nightstand and checked it. Cassie still hadn't called.

It was a little after 5 a.m.

Gray took a few deep breaths, an attempt to loosen the grip of whatever was squeezing his chest so tight. Then he got up, stripped the sheets off the bed, and went down to the laundry. As he shoved them into the washer, Gray committed himself to ending the week on a high note. He'd push everything else aside and focus on the work.

When he sat down at his desk an hour later, Gray was the first to arrive at the office. He logged onto his computer, and then pulled up a program that the firm used to track billable hours. The program was the lifeblood of the firm. Without documented billable hours, nobody got billed and, therefore, nobody would get paid. He typed the name of a client into the program, started the clock, and got to work.

The draft proposal and legal prospectus were already late. It was for a new boutique hotel in the Delmar Loop with a rooftop bar, each room featuring a local artist. The client had wanted it the week before, but, under the circumstances, they were forgiving. "Delivery the following week would be fine," they had said, but Gray didn't want to use all of the allotted time. He wanted to get it done.

Working non-stop through the morning, Gray found his old groove. He glided from file to file, checking off one item on his to-do list after another. There was almost a euphoria every time he clicked the button on the tracker, logging another entry of billable work. The lunch hour came and went. Gray wasn't hungry so he didn't stop. He was in the zone, so focused that he didn't notice the darkening of the sky outside his window or the expected winter storm finally arriving.

At two-thirty, Gray's phone rang. He almost ignored it, but then remembered Cassie. Gray picked it up, hoping to talk and get an explanation, but it wasn't Cassie. It was a client. A developer specializing in senior living facilities.

"Tim, how are you?" he asked, although he already knew the answer by the sound of his client's voice. Timothy Gault was agitated.

"Are you on your way?" Timothy asked. "I thought we were going to meet before the hearing."

Gray didn't know how to respond. "Meeting?" He clicked over to his on-line calendar. It was clear. Just like the day before, there were no scheduled meetings or hearings.

"The planning commission starts in an hour," Timothy said. "We were going to run through my presentation one more time."

"Right." Gray began to scroll through his calendar, another sickening feeling formed in the pit of his stomach as all the confidence he'd built up that morning disappeared. He clicked the days ahead, and then he found it.

"I thought the planning commission didn't meet until next Wednesday."

"No," Timothy said. "It's today."

Gray was confused. He had the meeting and hearing on his calendar for the following week, but he knew better than to argue with a client. There wasn't time.

"Let's talk about your presentation now," Gray shut down the computer, grabbed his jacket, and began walking to his car. "I think you're third on the agenda. If I leave now, I should make it."

They continued to talk as Gray got on the highway and drove west toward Clayton. He was working hard to sound calm and in control, reassuring his client that everything was going to be fine. By the time he exited the highway, Timothy sounded a little more relaxed, but it was hard to tell. It wasn't the level of service that Gray wanted to provide, nor what clients had come to expect.

"I'll see you soon." Gray hung up the phone, and then drove into the parking garage attached to the sprawling office complex that housed various county agencies and boards.

Gray drove up one ramp and then another. His shoulders were tense. He didn't understand how it could happen, again, and his mood darkened even more. He eventually found a parking spot, and then his phone dinged, a text message.

Gray looked at the screen. It was from Kendra:

Where r u???

He swore under his breath, and then called her as he got out of the car. "I'm so sorry," Gray said. "I forgot it was my weekend."

"You forgot?"

"I mean….I didn't forget." He lied. Gray got on the parking garage's no-frills elevator, and pressed the button for the ground floor. "Something came up at work and now I'm headed into a planning commission meeting."

"I've already gotten two calls from the school," Kendra said. "How late are you going to be?"

"I don't know," Gray said. "I can still take them for the weekend. That's not a problem." He looked at his watch. "Can you pick them up right now? I can just go to your house when this is done."

There was silence, as the elevator doors slid open and Gray began to walk across the plaza. The clouds were heavy with snow, and the muscles in Gray's back and neck began to revolt against the sudden burst of movement.

Then Kendra's answer came with a heavy sigh. "I'll get them," she said. "Since you don't know when you're going to be done, why don't you come in the morning?"

Gray knew that the planning commission meeting wouldn't go that late. He hated the idea of missing a night with his kids, but wasn't going to argue. Kendra was showing amazing restraint under the circumstances.

"I'll be there tomorrow." Gray opened the door and walked into the building's foyer. Stepping toward the metal detector and security screening, he offered her an apology.

There was another long pause. Then Kendra sighed. "I know," she said, and then hung up.

CHAPTER ELEVEN

Ethan Bloom called as Gray was driving back to the city after the planning commission hearing. "I stopped by your office and you weren't there," he said. "You around?"

"In the car," Gray said without much enthusiasm. "I was at a meeting in Clayton. What's going on?"

"Two words," Ethan said. "Jack Durell."

"What about him?" Gray took a right on Skinker toward Forest Park Parkway. He decided that he'd take the sideroads back into the city to avoid traffic. It would take about the same amount of time, but at least he'd be moving.

"Well, let's just say he didn't take our advice."

The firm's advice had been to wait. They were working behind the scenes to push the city and state bureaucrats in the right direction. The plan wasn't going to come together in a day, but Gray was confident that the homeless people living in the Triangle would be found shelter elsewhere and Jack Durell would be free to purchase and develop the property. That was the agreed upon plan, but Durell now, evidently, had different ideas.

Durell was convinced he could do it better, faster, and cheaper. Without warning, he had notified local reporters and held a press conference on the edge of the Triangle. He expected to receive glowing praise for revitalizing downtown, creating jobs, and increasing the city's tax base. Instead, he got a protest.

"I've got a couple people with me in a conference room and we're in full damage control," Ethan said.

"Is Bobby there?" Gray asked. Bobby was Robert Cantrell, the law firm's lobbyist. If he was involved, Gray knew that Ethan wasn't exaggerating.

"He is," Ethan said. "Mind if I put you on speaker?"

There was a click, and then Cantrell started talking. "Your man created a helluva mess. At this point, I'm just trying to convince the aldermen and the mayor to not comment. Take no position."

"That's it?" Gray asked.

"Do you know how hard it is to keep a politician's mouth shut?"

Gray could picture the big man shaking his head. Bobby Cantrell was an old school lobbyist who preferred cowboy boots to wingtips.

"Dang near impossible. I had this whole thing wired and then this—" Cantrell stopped. "Hold on a minute....just got a text." There was a pause, and then Cantrell ordered somebody in the conference room to turn to Channel 11.

Gray listened as people argued about how to connect to a live television broadcast on the conference room's large flat screen television. First they couldn't find the remote control, then there was a disagreement about inputs and cables.

Finally, Ethan said, "Hey Gray, I think we gotta get this working here. Can I call you later?"

"You can, but do you need me to come back to the office or what?"

Ethan hesitated. "I don't know."

Gray felt a heaviness in every part of his body, and, after a long day, he didn't have much patience or energy to deal with Jack Durell. "I'm just gonna go home," he said. "Send me links to the newspaper articles and television reports and call if anything new comes up. I don't think we're going to solve this problem tonight."

Gray drove the rest of the way in silence. He turned the ringer on his phone and the radio off, and tried to sort through everything that had happened over the past few weeks. He'd just gotten back to work, and he'd already missed two meetings and forgot to pick up his kids. Meanwhile, Cassie Hawthorne hadn't returned any of his calls to explain herself or her warning.

Gray parked behind his house, reheated some leftovers, and pulled out his laptop. Ethan, as instructed, had sent him an email with the media coverage of Jack Durell's press conference. He skimmed the *Post Dispatch* article, and then he clicked on one of the videos.

A box popped up on his screen, and then there was the image of a reporter standing in front of the Triangle holding a microphone. In a breathless voice, she described the situation.

"For years, homeless men and women have been quietly living on an unused and forgotten piece of land wedged between the skyscrapers of downtown and the highway. They were safe, out of the way, and just wanted to be left alone until now."

Then the video cut to Jack Durell speaking at his press conference, sounding like a pompous rich guy as he boasted of his plan to invest millions. Then, the protesters arrived. There was yelling back and forth, and the hot mic captured Durell telling his assistant to call the cops and referring to the protesters as "smelly bums." The video cut back to the reporter standing in front of the homeless encampment. There were tents and people milling about in the background.

It was then that a man caught Gray's attention. He was just to the reporter's right, over her shoulder. Next to him was somebody short. Gray shook his head, initially doubting what he'd seen. He leaned in closer to get a better look, then the story ended. There were a few quick words by the anchorman, and soon a skinny guy with glasses appeared and began talking about the coming winter storm.

"Could be four inches, could be a lot more," he said. "Let's take a look at the radar after the break."

Gray clicked a button. The news story restarted from the beginning. He watched carefully, and then he watched it again.

Gray watched it with no sound, and then other times he'd press pause, scroll back and play, and press pause, again. Then a full-time through without stopping.

It'd been almost three weeks since the shooting. He'd almost convinced himself that his memory of being shot in the chest was just a high definition dream, but as much as he tried to forget, it felt so real, and now Gray had just seen the man who cradled him in his arms while he almost bled to death.

The picture quality wasn't the best, but Gray knew that the man standing behind the reporter was the same person. He had white hair and looked like Santa Claus. On the night that Virgil Hawthorne died, he had tried to keep Gray calm, talking to him in a soothing Irish lilt. Then he'd said a quick prayer, putting pressure on Gray's chest, while a little person flagged down the ambulance.

In Gray's mind the little person was an elf, but, the more he thought about it, the little person wasn't dressed like an elf. There was no pointy hat. There were no long toed shoes with bells on the tips. The little person wore jeans and a winter jacket. He was just trying to help.

Gray clicked pause, and then he made the image as large as possible in his browser. Gray studied the blurred, pixelated image. It was him, Gray thought as he touched his chest. He had no doubt.

CHAPTER TWELVE

The second winter storm went on for days, dropping over a foot of snow. For the second time in November, the city shut down. It wasn't until Thanksgiving that the side roads had all been plowed, and people were, once again, able to move freely.

Herbert Bloom sat in his large study, seeking a brief refuge from his family. They were all there—his brother, Sal, and his sister, Margie; his wife, of course; his daughter, Miriam, and her husband along with their three children, the eldest of the grandchildren brought her husband along with Herbert's great grandchildren and the youngest grandchild brought his girlfriend; Thomas and his wife and kids; his brother and his wife, alone due to children who went to college on the coasts and never returned—and then there was Ethan, the one that Herbert would rather have stayed home. Herbert's wife always scolded him for such thoughts, but even she would admit that he ruined the picture. He was an imperfection, in an otherwise perfect picture.

When Herbert and Jules had gotten married, neither had much. He went to school on the G.I. Bill, and Jules supported them by selling shoes at the old Stix department store on Sixth and Seventh. They put in long hours, and eventually Herbert understood that "making it" meant more than hard work. Sometimes a man had to play rough and get a little dirty.

Herbert Bloom sat in a large leather chair, a brandy in hand. This was his favorite room in the house. It was on the third floor of a classic Victorian. They had bought it in the 1980s, just as the

Central West End neighborhood was being rediscovered. Now every inch of the house had been restored to its original 1892 grandeur, including a small pipe organ in the corner of the room.

He would miss it when he was gone.

The doctors were vague. It didn't matter how much they were paid, none of them would commit to a specific timeframe. Maybe he'd live to celebrate another Thanksgiving, more likely he would not.

Bloom took a sip from his glass, let the alcohol warm him, and then wandered over to a large picture window overlooking the backyard. His youngest grandchildren and great grandchild were playing in the snow. He watched them while thinking of the coming weeks and months. There was so much to do to prepare, and Bloom wondered if he'd have the energy. Then his son Thomas knocked on the door, opened it, and stepped inside.

"The kids are coming in now, and I think we're all ready for you." Thomas took another step. His face softening, concerned. "Are you okay?"

"Fine." Bloom waved it off, and began walking across the room. "How was your trip?"

"Things are going well." Thomas smiled. "The donation you made to the mayor's church went a long way."

"Figured it would. You're going to do things that I couldn't even dream of," Bloom put his hand on his son's shoulder and guided him out of the study . "No matter how much money I've made. I've always been an outsider, always been working for others—kissing their feet and running their little errands—but you won't have to do that."

"I'm going to try."

Bloom shook his head. "No, son, you've got to do more than try. This isn't just about you. You have to consider your kids and your future grandkids, it's about them too. I've gone as far as I can go, but if you can do this.....if you can pull this off, everything changes." He patted his son's shoulder. "I'm already proud of you, but this would make me very happy."

The entire Bloom family gathered in the large formal dining room, standing around the edge. Each held a glass. The adults had wine, and the children had sparkling grape juice. Herbert Bloom, then, stepped forward. "This won't take long."

Bloom took them all in, savoring the sight of his family, but with a slight pang of guilt. None of them knew his diagnosis. It was pride. He was never one to seek or accept the pity of others, and that would not change. He hadn't even told his wife, although there would come a time that he couldn't hide it any longer, but this day was not the right time. He wouldn't spoil it.

"I can smell the turkey and I think everybody's hungry." Herbert Bloom looked down at his feet to gather his thoughts. "This is Thanksgiving, and it is my favorite holiday—didn't used to be. When I was young, I didn't understand it. There wasn't much to be thankful for growing up. Life was hard for me and Sal and Margie, but over time, this day has become more and more important. Each year, things have gotten better and better and our family continues to grow. We have been blessed, and we need to celebrate that, knowing that next year will be even better." Herbert looked at his son, Thomas. "We will do great things."

Herbert Bloom raised his glass higher. "Cheers."

"Cheers."

Everyone took a sip, and then Herbert Bloom's brother stepped forward.

"Hold on. Before we eat all of Herbie's food—I still get to call him Herbie—I want to say a few words of thanks." Sal looked at his older brother and smiled. "I don't know where I'd be without Herbie. He wasn't just my brother. He was more of a father to me. Got me out of a lot of jams, and he gave me support, too, when I needed it, kicked my butt when I needed that too."

They laughed.

"When I was out of work, Herbie got me a job with the city. That was over forty years ago, and now I've got a good city pension to keep me going in my old age." Sal, then, looked at his sister. "He's been generous with us, me and Margie, and I know he's been generous with all of you, too."

Sal scratched his nose and gave a little sniff. "In short, my brother is the smartest guy in every room. He's tough as nails, and he would do anything for his family. So when I pray—which ain't as often as I should, sad to say—I thank God for my brother. I truly do." Sal raised his glass higher. "To a great man."

"To a great man."

Then they all took a drink, everyone except for Ethan.

CHAPTER THIRTEEN

Gray slept until ten and could have slept longer on Thanksgiving morning, but his need to go to the bathroom forced him out of bed. After breakfast and a long shower, he was finally ready to bake with Haley and Midge. Bread baking was a simple thing in his life that always gave him joy. It had kept him sane during law school, and helped him grieve the death of his parents and process his divorce. Now, maybe it could help Gray get his mind right.

Since being back at work, he'd made mistake after mistake. Nothing like that had ever happened before, and, when combined with Cassie's warning, Jack Durell's behavior, and Santa's appearance in the background of the evening news, Gray felt unsettled. Something bad was going to happen.

As Midge checked the temperature of the oven outside, Gray and Haley worked in the kitchen. This was his domain. It was the place that he always felt the most confident, but, as Gray walked over to the counter to check the dough, there was hesitation. As he lifted the linen cloth covering the ratan basket, he noticed his dough wasn't quite as smooth, and as he gently poked the dough with his finger, his finger trembled slightly, nervous.

Gray stepped back and studied the small indentation.

"How's it look?" Haley was standing near the door. Her cheeks red from the cold.

Her question had brought him back. "What?" Gray turned to her.

"The dough," she said, "how does it look?"

"Good," Gray said. "When the little indentation remains, that means it's ready for the oven."

He quickly poked the other loaves on the counter, each passing the test. "Let's do it." Gray took a large wooden peel off a hook on the wall. It was similar to the wide paddles used in pizzerias, but with a longer handle.

Haley came over and took the peel from Gray, as he opened the cabinet and removed a bag of cornmeal.

"You don't want to put too much on or it'll just burn." Gray set the bag on the counter, it slipped out of his hand. Luckily, it didn't fall on the floor. The bag dropped just a few inches with a thud, tipped, but Gray caught it before too much cornmeal spilled out. He swore under his breath, and then took a step back, giving the space to Haley. "Why don't you take it from here?"

Haley knew something was wrong. "Are you okay?"

Gray automatically responded that he was fine, but Haley didn't accept it. She didn't challenge him, but she didn't move, either. She just waited for Gray to tell the truth.

Eventually Gray lowered his head, a bit defeated. "It was a tough week, but I'm glad I've got the day off and I'm baking bread. Tonight we'll have a great Thanksgiving dinner." Gray, then, decided that was as far as he was going to go. There would be no pity party, no further revelations. "Now I need you to sprinkle the cornmeal on the peel, just enough so that it won't stick, and then get the dough out of the baskets."

"Okay." Haley was reluctant to let the issue drop, but decided not to push for now. She listened to Gray's instruction as she walked over to the sink to wash her hands.

"The worst case scenario, here, is that the dough collapses and we get flat bread with our turkey instead of a loaf, but it'll still taste great."

"Sure you want me to do this?"

"I am." Gray mimed the movement for her to copy. "Gentle and quick."

Haley stood in front of the baskets, paused for another moment, and then picked one up and flipped it over. Nothing stuck and it maintained its shape fairly well. She looked back at Gray.

He assured her that she'd done it right with a nod, amused at how intimidated people were by the process of baking bread. It was something that human beings had done for thousands of years, and, yet, there was a myth that it was incredibly hard.

Haley flipped the second ball of dough out of the basket and stepped back, admiring what she had done. The two balls of dough each had beautiful concentric circles imprinted and highlighted with the white rice flour that Gray had used to prevent the dough from sticking to the baskets.

"Nice." Gray opened a small side drawer next to him and removed a wooden tool with a very sharp razor blade on one end. Bakers called it a, "*lame*," which was French for blade. The lame was used to score the top of the dough, both for decorative purposes and also to control the rise that occurred in the oven.

"Are you ready for this part?" Gray held out the tool for Haley.

"I think so." She took it.

"You want to do something simple for your first one," Gray said. "A couple quick slashes across the top, not too deep. Once you get the hang of it, you can do some more intricate designs." Gray moved next to her and demonstrated the movement. "I'd probably start with three diagonal lines running parallel or maybe four small ones on top in the shape of a square."

"Okay."

"Score both loaves the same, just pretend the first one is practice. Do one right after the other. Don't stop and think."

Haley did just as she was instructed, slashing the tops of the dough.

"That's great. Now let's get them in the oven." Gray began to walk toward the backdoor, but Haley stopped him.

"You do know that we're not done talking, right?" She picked up the heavy peel and carried the loaves across the kitchen. "You can't just tell me that you had a tough week, and then move on."

Gray emitted a little laugh, defensive. "That was sort of my plan."

"Well, I have a different plan," she said. "We'll have plenty of time to talk more while these are baking."

Gray puttered around for the rest of the day. When the sun set and he noticed other guests beginning to arrive at Midge and Haley's house, he removed a small crock of Irish butter from the refrigerator, and then put the loaves that were baked that morning in a cloth bag along with a wooden cutting board and a knife. It was Thanksgiving, and, from the noise and extra cars now circling the street out front in search of a parking spot, it was clear that there was going to be a party.

A sign on Midge and Haley's front door instructed guests to come inside—don't knock or ring—and so that was what Gray did. He stepped into the entryway. There were already about eighteen people milling about, more than half in the dining room and living room. A few sitting on the stairs, snacking on hors d'oeuvres, and the remainder in the kitchen.

"Gray has arrived." Midge had spotted him from across the room and gave the announcement. She was wearing an ugly sweater with a large turkey and snowflakes on the front. Her earrings were two small turkeys with pilgrim hats. "Ladies and gentlemen and those somewhere in between or not at all." Midge tapped her wine glass with a spoon to quiet her guests while she continued to shout. "I want to introduce you to our neighbor Mr. Graydon Wendt. He is a lawyer. He is divorced, and he bakes bread. That is all the information that you need at this time, so let's say 'Hi Gray.'"

Everyone did as they were told, greeting him in unison, as if in some sort of support meeting.

Gray raised his hand and waved. "Happy Thanksgiving everyone." To Midge he said, "And thank you, Midge, for that totally accurate and somewhat sad description of me and my life."

The people gathered laughed, and a man in the corner of the room wearing a purple silk shirt raised his glass for a toast. "To Midge and Haley, they are the hostesses with the most-est-es."

"That almost rhymes, Frankie." Midge then walked over to Gray and pointed at the cloth bag in Gray's hand. "I can take that from you," and then she said, "Haley's busy in the kitchen, so you should circulate amongst the misfits and losers first. I'm telling you that these are your people."

"Thanks." Gray pointed at the bag, which Midge was now holding. "And the bread turned out great, by the way."

"I have no doubt." Midge opened it, lowered her head , and inhaled, deeply. When she looked up there was a big smile on her face. "Intoxicating."

The bread was a hit, and the rest of the food served for Thanksgiving dinner was the best that Gray had ever eaten. Midge and Haley brined and baked two sixteen pound turkeys, everyone else brought sides ranging from the fancy to the classic. Although it was all delicious, he went back for a second helping of the classic green bean casserole from a can with fried onions on top. In theory, a person could make the dish with fresh beans, scratch cream sauce, and onions fried with panko crumbs…but why?

It had been a long time since Gray had a proper Thanksgiving dinner. After his divorce, he had spent several Thanksgivings with his brother's family in California. When that got old, he simply spent the day racking up billable hours at the firm.

He'd forgotten how fun Thanksgiving could be, and he, unfortunately, lost track of the number of drinks he'd consumed during all the fun.

A guy named Tony mixed up a pitcher of his "Tony's T-Day Extravaganza." It was cider, spiked with a disproportionate amount of rum along with pumpkin spices and a splash of orange liqueur. By his third glass, it was almost as if Gray was having an out-of-body experience. He floated near the ceiling looking down at himself in horror. *Who was that man? Why was he talking so loudly? How could he be stopped?*

The party continued. Gray continued to drink as the lights were dimmed when another guest took it upon herself to create a dance party. He spun around the living room turned dance floor, stumbling every so often. If he was in pain, Gray wouldn't know. The combination of alcohol and pain killers had numbed every part of him.

The music slowed. Couples paired off, and Gray wandered up the stairs to the bathroom. A candle burned in the corner, painting the white tiles different shades of orange, shifting with every flicker. Below, the slow dance had ended and the beat quickened. A heavy bass thumped as Gray splashed water on his face. Then Gray felt his chest tighten as the walls turned from orange to red.

"No." He shook his head. "Not now."

The door to the bathroom swung open, and the baby-faced man stood in the doorway. He pulled Gray's daughter from the shadows. One arm around her chest, the other holding a gun to her temple. His gold tooth sparkled as he smiled. "Say goodbye." He pulled the trigger, and Zoe fell to the floor.

Gray crawled to her, screaming. Then the lights turned on.

"Are you okay?" Haley stood over him.

"I have to call Kendra," Gray said. "I have to call her."

Haley knelt down, trying to provide comfort, but Gray would have none of it.

"I need to call her." Gray scrambled to his feet, using the wall to steady himself. "Right now." He left the bathroom, and went down the hall to a spare bedroom. He closed the door, got out his cell phone, and called Kendra. When she didn't answer, he left a panicked message.

"Kendra, listen to me." Gray's words slurred. "It's Thanksgiving and you need to call me back right now. I need to talk to the kids. I need to know they're okay. It's important."

When she didn't call back right away, Gray began to text her, one after another throughout the rest of the night. There was nothing that he could do. Floating above, Gray looked down at himself unable to intervene. He screamed, telling himself to stop, but Gray could only watch as the very intoxicated version of himself below let it all come out.

The monster got out of the box, again.

The anger, frustration, and confusion that he'd kept buried, compartmentalized and pushed aside, broke free. And, although it wasn't fair, the rage was all directed at his ex-wife and it kept coming all night long.

CHAPTER FOURTEEN

Gray woke up naked. How his clothes were removed and under what circumstances were a mystery. A funk rode heavy on his breath with a faint aftertaste of vodka, peppermint schnapps, and vomit. He rolled over and, at that moment, Gray realized that he wasn't in his own bed. He looked around the room. He wasn't even in his own house.

"Thanksgiving." Gray laid back, remembering bits and pieces of Midge and Haley's party, and then remembering their signature cocktail. Every party they threw had a signature cocktail, last night's was something Midge called a "Candycane Martini." That was what had ultimately destroyed him.

Gray's head sank into the pillow as he closed his eyes, willing his brain to function, but it resisted as his memories of the previous night were slow to come back. He was dehydrated, but afraid that any water he drank wouldn't last long before coming back up. Gray hadn't experienced a hang-over of this magnitude since his first year in college.

I'm going to die, he thought, then, n*ever again.*

Gray rolled over into the fetal position. He was about to drift back to sleep when he remembered what had happened in the bathroom, his crazy phone call to Kendra, and the texts, so many texts. His eyes opened wide. His heart pounded, beating faster. Gray pulled back the sheet as the sickness rose up. Panicked, he looked around for a garbage can or a bowl or anything, then he bolted toward the bathroom.

Gray worshiped at the altar for thirty minutes, then crawled into the shower to purify with hot water and steam. When he eventually emerged, the bed was made. His clothes were folded and placed on a dresser by the window. Next to the clothes was Gray's wallet, watch, and cell phone. He walked over. When he picked up his t-shirt, it was still warm from the dryer. Gray slipped it on, and then the rest of his clothes. He felt comfort for a second, but Gray knew that it wasn't going to last.

His hand trembled as he looked at the phone, knowing what he'd done the night before, but still fearful of the confirmation. It was going to be bad, but Gray wasn't sure exactly how bad. He pressed a button. The screen came to life, and then he pulled up his texts.

At the very top of the list of messages was Kendra's name along with a portion of his last text. It was sent at 3:15 a.m., a demand to wake up his children so that he could confirm their safety and threatening to call the police.

He touched it. The full text appeared, and he felt a weight press down on him as he read it all. Gray could hardly believe he was reading something that he had written. He closed his eyes, willing himself not to start throwing up, again. He told himself to pull it together, as he tried to slow everything down. It took a few minutes, maybe more to feel like he was back in control.

Gray opened his eyes, and then he started scrolling through the history.

He must've sent thirty texts throughout the night, maybe more. They ranged from bitter to angry to loving to threatening to suicidal:

> If u don't let me talk to my kids, I don't know what I will do.
> Can't live like this.
> Won't live at all like this, and you will have to deal with that. U did this to me. U will have to tell them what happened to their dad.

Gray set the phone back down on the dresser, then sat on the edge of the bed, frozen. *What had he done?*

There was knocking on the door. "Gray." More knocking. "Gray, are you doing okay in there?" When there was no response, Midge opened the door a crack.

"You decent?" She then opened the door all the way and entered the room. "You okay?"

Gray looked up at her, tears in his eyes. "I screwed up." He wiped his eyes, and then ran his hand through his hair. "I really screwed up this time. Never in a million years would I ever say something like this… But I did."

"Can't be that bad." Midge sat down beside him as Haley now appeared in the doorway, a concerned look on her face as well. Midge put her hand on Gray's shoulder. "You got drunk, and you got mad. It happens to people."

"I threatened her," Gray said. "I told her I was going to hurt myself."

Midge looked at him. Her face softened with sympathy.

"It'll be alright," she said, but didn't sound convinced.

They talked more about what happened and various options that Gray had to repair the damage. Haley wanted him to make the call right away. Midge agreed, but Gray refused.

"Later." He wasn't ready, and he didn't want an audience. If he was going to apologize, Gray wanted privacy, in part because he was embarrassed and in part because he didn't know how Kendra was going to respond.

Haley walked over from the doorway and sat down on the other side of Gray.

"We're your friends." She patted his leg. "And we're worried about you. We want to help you, but you have to ask. We're not mind readers."

There was another long pause. Gray closed his eyes. There was pressure around his throat. It wasn't as if someone was squeezing. It felt, instead, like it was frozen in place, preventing him from revealing to Midge and Haley what he hadn't spoken about since he woke up in the hospital.

He coughed, trying to loosen it, and then a few words tumbled out.

"That night...the night...there's more to it." A tear rolled down Gray's cheek. "It's so stupid, because I know it isn't real, but it feels real. To me it's real. You know?"

But they didn't know. How could they possibly know? But Midge and Haley were patient and kind. After another pause, Gray revealed his secret.

"...I got shot. On the night that Virgil Hawthorne died, I was shot twice in the chest." Then Gray looked up at the ceiling. It wasn't just a confession, he had finally pulled back a curtain that he'd created to hide the fragility of his own mind, his vulnerabilities, and the very real possibility that he may never go back to who he was. "Look," Gray said. "It's complicated."

Then he wiped a tear away, and avoided any eye contact with the two women on either side of him as he told his story. "I got hit in the head, and I went to the ground, and this kid stood over me." Gray felt his throat begin to freeze, again, but he pushed through it. "He was told to pull the trigger, and the kid did as he was told—two shots." Gray tapped his chest. "It burned. I felt it, and there was this guy who found me and held me while the ambulance came, and then when I woke up in the hospital, there were no bullet wounds in my chest. Nothing. The doctor says it wasn't real...." Gray's voice trailed off. "I'm having a hard time accepting that."

He ran his hands through his hair and took a deep breath. "I even thought I saw him—that guy who held me —I thought I saw him on the news the other night, in the background." Haley put her arm around him. Gray laid his head on her shoulder, and the rest tumbled out. "I'm missing stuff at work, messing up, and now these texts to Kendra... I think I'm losing it."

When he got back home, Gray hung his jacket in the front closet, and then he went back to the kitchen. He tended to his sourdough starter and mixed a batch of dough while he collected his thoughts and rehearsed the conversation. Gray tried to anticipate Kendra's responses, and then craft an appropriate reaction. As he kneaded the dough, he worked through every possible approach: joking, contrite, angry, self-righteous, pathetic, tough, reflective, and a combination of everything in between.

For an hour, he must've practiced apologizing hundreds of times. When Gray began to lose his voice, he decided that there was nothing left to do but call. Resigned, Gray washed his hands in the sink, dried them, and picked up the phone. He dialed, and it rang five times before going into Kendra's voicemail.

It was the one scenario he hadn't anticipated, even though, given his behavior, it was the most likely.

After a pause and a stumbling hello, Gray began: "Kendra, this is Gray—well you know it's me—I just want to say that I'm sorry. I drank too much. There's no excuse, and I'm sorry…call me back if you want. I obviously have to take care of myself, and I'm going to reach out to the doctor today." Gray took a breath. "Give my love to the kids. Wish them a 'Happy Thanksgiving' from me."

CHAPTER FIFTEEN

The underwear in her desk drawer was not a surprise. The thong was bright pink, and could best be described as an elaborate eyepatch, consisting of a lacy triangle of bedazzled fabric with two pieces of silk string. Investigator Amy Wirth did her best not to give whoever had put the item in her desk drawer the satisfaction of any reaction. She pretended like she'd seen nothing, just like she had pretended like she hadn't seen the black one or the purple one before that, or the copies of pornographic magazines that had appeared in her investigative files or on the windshield of her car.

Wirth closed the drawer. She wanted to slam it shut, stand up, and scream, but that would just encourage more abuse. Wirth, instead, turned her attention back to the computer. There were two items open on her screen. The first was an image of Graydon Wendt's cell phone records, and the second was a draft report. She'd already entered the basic information into the template, but Wirth had barely begun her summary of the records.

Her mind couldn't focus. *It didn't used to be like this*, she thought. Wirth looked up at the photograph of her father. He was a cop, now retired and living down in Florida with her mother. It was pinned to the fabric wall of her cubicle.

Every investigator in the unit had a cubicle. The lack of individual offices saved the department money and space, although Deputy Commander Shelly Knox, her supervisor and head of the police department's Investigative Services Division, claimed the layout was intended to encourage collaboration. Knox's explanation, however, rang hollow, because Wirth had never experienced such a feeling. There was no collaboration, at least with her. The open space simply provided her tormentors easy access.

A year ago, Wirth wasn't an investigator. She was a street cop, patrolling the north side and chasing 911 calls. She'd had a good start to her career. After three years working the dog shift there were no flags in her file. Wirth got along with everyone, and she even managed the "boys will be boys" moments with grace and minimal conflict.

Then it happened.

There was an incredible outcry from the community. It made national headlines, and the fall-out was immediate. Some cops lost their jobs in the aftermath and Wirth got a promotion, but she knew it was just a set-up. She had violated the brotherhood's unwritten rules, and, therefore, must be punished.

The underwear and the pornography had nothing to do with sex. It was about power—who had it and who didn't. The promotion isolated her while the harassment kept her off balance, regular reminders that she was different and very much alone. Each incident dared Wirth to complain and stir up more trouble, which would cause even more backlash and propel the cycle forward even faster.

It wouldn't be long before her annual review. With no real training and no solvable cases assigned to her, Wirth's "close" rate would be the lowest in the division. A performance improvement plan, otherwise known as a PIP, would be written by Deputy Commander Knox, and the police department would be one step closer to the goal of getting rid of her. Whether Wirth was fired or quit, it didn't matter which one happened as long as she was gone.

As a kid, adults were always saying, "life isn't fair." Somebody gets an ice cream cone or a new toy and somebody else doesn't. That was just the way it was. Get used to it. The equal distribution of goods may be noble, but our flawed and sinful selves make that noble goal impossible. Just ask the pigs in George Orwell's *Animal Farm*.

Few adults, however, will ever say, "life isn't just unfair, it's cruel and there are people who will want to screw with you for no apparent reason, through no fault of your own, simply because they can." In the United States of America, cruelty had become a sport. Kindness, sensitivity, knowledge and experience was a threat, and the mob actively worked to beat that trait out of anyone for any reason or for no reason at all. The goal was not for the implementation of a grand policy or ideal, it was simply to make that person cry, to break them.

That's what nobody ever told Amy Wirth. Her dad never told her that. Her dad just told her that, "cops trust cops." The brotherhood required loyalty to one another. It was advice that seemed so wise at the time, and now felt insulting.

"Done yet?" Doles knocked on the top of Wirth's desk.

She hadn't heard him come up behind her, lost in her own thoughts. "What?"

"I asked if you were done with the report on the phone records." Doles glanced over his shoulder at Sergeant Bird with a smirk. He was the stooge. Sergeant Bird was too smart to get directly involved, but he loved to see his partner rile her up.

"We got a meeting this afternoon," Doles said. "Gotta nice break on this case and we don't have time for daydreams, Miss Sunshine. Evidently that lawyer, Hawthorne, was connected with a bunch of honchos at City Hall and they're pushing down on Knox to show progress in solving it and so now she's pushing down on us."

Wirth nodded. "I'm almost done."

Doles gave a dismissive chuckle and pointed at the computer screen. "Looks like you haven't even started, babe." He put his hand on her shoulder, leaning close to her ear, and then squeezed while looking down at her chest. "Let me know if you need a little help."

A lump formed in Wirth's throat. "I got it." Her skin crawled. "It'll get done."

"Hope so." Doles backed away.

"Let's go get some coffee," Bird said. "Miss Wirth seems to have everything under control." He gave her a long look over. "She's perfect in every way."

"Couldn't agree more." Doles gave Wirth's shoulder another squeeze. "We could learn a lot from her." He whispered. "She could teach us things." Then the two walked away, leaving Wirth very much alone.

She probably shouldn't have called Schmitty, but Wirth was desperate and he was the only one with enough pull to get her into the meeting later that afternoon. The murder of Virgil Hawthorne and the attack on Graydon Wendt was the only high profile case that she'd been allowed to touch, even though Bird and Doles were working hard to keep her involvement minimal and at a distance.

It had taken weeks to get the cell phone company to respond to their warrant, and, once they had the information, it needed to be analyzed. In the meantime, everybody had been waiting for one of the stolen phones to be turned on and ping off of a tower. Once that happened, they'd have a location. Wirth figured that this was what the meeting was going to be about. A phone went live, they needed to decide whether to conduct surveillance or immediately execute an arrest warrant.

Schmitty had suggested that they meet at the Blues City Deli, a neighborhood institution proudly holding down the corner of McNair and Victor for more than a decade. It was early— just after 11:00— and the lunch time rush hadn't quite hit. There were people, because there were always people at Blues City, but it was far enough away from the police station that there weren't going to be any other cops around and that was the point. Schmitty knew when to be discreet.

Schmitty was the nickname for Deputy Commissioner David Schmidt and an old friend of Wirth's father. Recently promoted, he was also one of the most savvy people in the department, a true survivor. Despite a steady rotation of new police chiefs every three to four years, Schmitty remained. He was valued for his advice, but rarely blamed if things went badly.

When Wirth entered, she saw Schmitty right away and gave him a little wave. He was already settled at a table in the corner, which faced the door. Like most law enforcement officers, Schmitty liked to see who was coming and who was going. He nodded his head, acknowledging Wirth, and then continued reading the paper while she walked up to the counter and ordered her sandwich.

Schmitty knew what was going on, because he knew everything that was going on in the department. She wouldn't need to get into the details. For that, Wirth was grateful. If she was forced to recount the weekly, if not daily, attempts to belittle and embarrass her, she'd start to cry and cops weren't supposed to cry.

The cashier took Wirth's credit card, ran it through the machine, and then Wirth walked over to Schmitty's table. "Been here long?"

He folded up his newspaper and set it aside.

"Not too long. Best part of my day, actually." He scanned the pictures of various guitar legends that adorned the wall next to him. "This place is like a little ray of sunshine in a messed up world."

"My dad always said, 'funny thing about the blues is that it always makes you feel good.'"

"Is your pops still playing?"

"He found an open jam session that he goes to almost every week," Wirth said. "It's about forty minutes from their little retirement community. Mom doesn't like him being out that late, but she's also happy to get him out of the house. He bought some fancy new guitar a couple months ago, says it practically plays itself, but my mom doesn't want to hear it any more, bought him a headset for his amp so she doesn't have to listen to him play."

"Retirement sounds nice." He paused as a person emerged from the back kitchen with some baskets. When Schmitty saw that it wasn't his order, he continued. "Well, say hello to that old bastard for me, and tell your pops that I want to see him when he's back in town."

"I will, but it probably won't be until the summer." Then there was an awkward pause in the conversation as Wirth tried to figure out a way to ask for a favor without sounding desperate. Luckily the arrival of their food from the back broke the silence.

"I'll get it." He walked over to the counter and retrieved his chili dog and Wirth's pastrami. They both enjoyed the food and made small talk. Then, when Wirth was about to ask for Schmitty to get her into the meeting, Schmitty took it in a different direction.

"So you're looking for a new job?"

Wirth was stunned. She hadn't told anyone. "What are you talking about?"

"Come on," Schmitty said. "It's understandable."

Schmitty drank a sip of Fitz's root beer, and set the bottle back down on the table.

"It'd be a shame to see you go. You're really good, just happen to be surrounded by idiots." Then he took a bite of his chili dog. "Had any luck yet?"

"I've floated a few resumes," Wirth decided that there was no sense in denying it, "but there haven't been any bites. I don't have enough experience as an investigator to get hired straight into that position at another department, and it'd be sort of a demotion to go back on patrol."

Schmitty considered that for a moment, cutting off another piece of his chili dog with his fork and putting the piece in his mouth.

"Ever think about the feds?"

She hadn't.

"I'm not sure I'd be qualified." All Wirth had ever known was local. The bureau was something foreign, something Wirth had never even considered. She'd been conditioned from an early age to think of the FBI and ATF as snobby bureaucrats rather than real cops. Whenever her father had interactions with them, he'd derisively refer to the agencies as a "bunch of feebs" and its agents as "feebies."

"Unlike a lot of people in our department," Schmitty said, "you've got a real degree from a real university and not just some two-year associates degree from some community college in no-wheresville Missouri. Washington University is top notch, and the FBI gives a crap about education and credentials and stuff like that, because sometimes they want people who can actually think and the crimes they're involved with can be a lot more complicated than a drunk boyfriend knocking his girlfriend around."

Schmitty let the information settle for a beat, and then gave Wirth the first compliment she'd heard in years. "Your brain, as you've already experienced, is not particularly valued within our organization at the moment, which is a shame, because you could be great."

"But when you're chief...."

Schmitty cut her off. "Don't even start. People have been telling me that I'm going to be the Chief of Police for over twenty years. I'm beginning to wonder."

Wirth couldn't argue with that. When Mayor Angela Montgomery fired the last police chief, most expected Schmitty to get the job. He had the experience and he was also supported by the Glass family. Usually being blessed by the first family of St. Louis politics was enough, but, instead, the job went to an outsider.

To bolster her reelection bid and undermine a challenge from her left, the mayor selected a reformer named Barry Kagen.

Kagen had rotated through jobs at various midwestern cities over the past fifteen years, the latest was serving as the Chief of Police for Gary, Indiana. Thus, his nickname within the department quickly became "Barry from Gary." It wasn't clever, but cops were rarely that clever.

Barry from Gary, in one of his first acts, promoted Schmitty from Sergeant to Deputy Commissioner. He abided by the old adage of "keeping your friends close and your enemies closer." It wasn't necessarily a bad move for Schmitty either. Barry from Gary's push for a citizen review of police misconduct, body cameras, and diversity among new recruits had already made him enemies.

With the promotion, Schmitty played both sides, depending on who was in the room. He served as the mediator, bridging the divide between the general and the troops, and, when Barry from Gary wore out his welcome and moved on to yet another city, perhaps Schmitty would finally get the top job.

"This is the contact information for Agent Charlie Matthews." Schmitty opened his wallet and removed a blank card with a handwritten name and number. "I believe he's interested in that lawyer case that you're working on with Bird and Doles. You should give him a call. Make a friend."

Wirth was skeptical. "In theory I'm working on that case with Bird and Doles, but, in reality, I'm doing a bunch of secretarial work."

Schmitty shook his head. "Don't worry about that. It'll be good."

"What am I supposed to say?"

"Just introduce yourself and give him a little update."

Wirth put the card in her pocket.

"I thought that inviting the FBI onto our turf was discouraged."

"It is." Schmitty's lips curled into a tight, clever smile, "but given your current situation, you're not risking too much. There's a job opening there, and once you're in, there's a lot of freedom to transfer anywhere you want. Go down to Florida to be closer to your parents, maybe go out west to the mountains...or stay right here." He shrugged, making it clear that it was up to her. "I'm just saying that there are benefits that might be bigger than just a change of scenery and better cases. That's all."

"You're encouraging me to leave?"

"No. I think you've already decided to leave." He wiped his hands clean with a napkin and pushed himself back from the table. "I'm just helping you find a job."

Wirth wished that she could believe him. Sure, Schmitty probably wanted to see his friend's daughter succeed and be happy, but Schmitty also probably wouldn't mind seeing a potential sexual harassment lawsuit walk out the door, either.

CHAPTER SIXTEEN

Gray hadn't stepped foot in a hospital since his release, and he felt his blood pressure rise the moment he walked through the sliding glass doors. His general anxiety continued through the preliminaries, filling out forms and waiting in the lobby. Then things got worse.

They laid him down on a padded, plastic board. It was narrow by design. The longer he was on his back, the faster his heart seemed to beat. As he waited, a nurse placed a pillow under his legs for comfort, and then she slid a plastic helmet over his head. The helmet surrounded his head, but didn't touch it; similar to what an astronaut might wear on a spacewalk, but open and without protective glass over the face. It all seemed a little ridiculous, epitomizing the absurdity of the American healthcare system: overbuilt and too complicated. Yet, the machine was going to scan his body. Who was he to question it? He was getting an MRI.

After a phone consultation, Doctor Craig thought it made sense to get images of Gray's brain, and, afterwards, they'd talk in more detail. Craig would be looking for damage to the meninges, a thin membrane that held the brain in place, and whether there were certain parts that weren't active.

"Ready?" The nurse asked. "I'm going to move you into the machine now."

She finished securing Gray in place, then she slid the board backwards; Gray went headfirst into the large tube that filled half the room. He closed his eyes as it clicked and buzzed. The nurse had warned him that it would sound a little like a construction site.

Gray felt the palms of his hands moisten with sweat and a lump formed in his throat. He'd never considered himself to be claustrophobic, but, then, he couldn't ever remember being so enclosed. It was like he was participating in some futuristic experiment, waiting to be frozen and shot into space, or, simply about to be buried alive.

There were two large bangs, and then a whistle.

His body jumped at the sounds. In that moment, Gray was sure that all the memories would rush back and the madness would return. If the monster could escape with the drop of a clipboard, in his living room, or after Thanksgiving dinner, surely it would come for him while trapped in a narrow tube. He was easy prey. There was nowhere to go.

Gray waited for it. His eyes darted from side to side as the machine continued to click and buzz. His pulse quickened in anticipation. He wondered, what would happen this time? What horror would he be subjected to? The temperature in the tube began to rise. His sweating worsened, and Gray's throat became dry.

He closed his eyes, tight. Gray now felt himself wanting it to come, just to put him out of his misery and get it over with. The monster, however, never came. There was, eventually, a beep. The odd noises stopped, and the nurse slid him out of the tube.

She smiled as she removed the helmet. "You doing okay?"

Gray wasn't sure how to respond. He didn't know how he felt, a mixture of emotions. He was almost disappointed that he didn't freak out. At the very least, if it happened in a hospital, then everybody would know that he wasn't making it up. That he wasn't being dramatic or exaggerating. He wasn't just some lonely man seeking attention. They would all see for themselves. But, the monster didn't work that way. It didn't perform on command or as part of a particular pattern. That was its power, and that was what made it so cruel. The anxiety attacks, flashbacks, and hallucinations could come at any time.

The nurse led Gray to a small examination room. He was given time to remove the hospital gown and get dressed. Then Dr. Craig arrived.

After squirting his hand with antibacterial foam, he said. They shook, and then Dr. Craig sat down and read a summary of Gray's medical history on a computer screen. "Oh yes….I remember you well." He turned away from the screen. "How's it going, Graydon."

"Please call me Gray."

Doctor Craig smiled. "My apologies. I should've made a note of that when you were here before. Tell me what's going on."

Gray sat frozen, thinking not just about what to say, because there was so much, but also where to begin. Doctor Craig was comfortable with the silence. He didn't press. He waited.

Gray's hand trembled as he finally broke the silence "I thought I could pretend. I thought I could shove it all down, compartmentalize, and things would get back to normal. Just ignore it." Gray shook his head, trying not to put himself through the same emotional ringer that had happened when he had talked to Midge and Haley. "That just made it worse, and I can't do that anymore."

He told Doctor Craig about his troubles at work, his hallucinations, and also his troubles with Kendra, explaining about how he had forgotten to pick up his kids for the weekend, and now Kendra needed her "space" following his Thanksgiving texts, and he even told Doctor Craig about Cassie's warning at the funeral. Then there was the shooting, itself. The trauma from an event that didn't exist, and seeing the Santa on television, a man Gray was now being paid to evict.

It tumbled out. If Gray's daughter, Zoe, were to describe what happened, she'd say, "Daddy spilled his guts." And, Zoe would've been right. It all came out. Even more scattered and emotional than when he'd told Haley and Midge. Theoretically, it should've been easier, but it wasn't.

Doctor Craig didn't bother with questions. He listened, patiently. When Gray had been at the hospital after the incident, the doctor was juggling dozens of patients, anxious to move on to the next person in his scheduled rounds. Now he took it all in, until finally Gray was done.

"What do I need to do?" Gray had been staring at the floor, unable to make eye contact, and now looked up. "I'll do anything you say. I just have to get better. I'm.... I think I've lost my mind."

Doctor Craig took a pen out of a cup. He located a post-it note on his desk, and then wrote on the little piece of paper. "This is a really good psychiatrist." He pointed at the name he'd just written, Samantha Jax. "She works with a lot of veterans coming back, some of them have seen six or seven tours in the middle east, they're dealing with the same things you're dealing with. Some of it is physical—you got a serious concussion and a very real injury to your head—but other parts of it is on the emotional and mental side. Everything is tangled up together."

"I still believe I was shot," Gray said. "It happened."

Doctor Craig shrugged his shoulders. "I've been doing this job for a long time, Gray. I've seen everything, and I've also seen nothing. Every day is different. Every patient is different. What you believe matters. What you think matters, but, physically, there's no indication that it happened."

In a quiet voice, Gray said, "That's a very nice way of saying that you don't believe me." Gray reached out and took the slip of paper from Doctor Craig, and then looked down at the referral. "No magic pill?"

"Not exactly," Doctor Craig said, "I am going to prescribe you an anti-anxiety medication. They often help smooth the edges, but the pill only treats the symptoms. If you want your life back, you need to get at the root trauma. That's the real problem, and Doctor Jax is really good at that, better than any pill." Doctor Craig turned to his computer, typed in a few notes, and then turned back to Gray. "There's usually a long wait before you get an initial appointment, but, if you tell her that I made the referral, she'll move you to the front of the line."

"Why's that?"

Doctor Craig chuckled. "Because she's my little sister."

Gray walked a few blocks north of the hospital to a bagel shop for a late lunch. After ordering, he found a table in a quiet corner. He first called the pharmacy to confirm that they received the prescription, then he called the number of Doctor Craig's sister.

A receptionist answered.

Gray steadied himself, trying to manage the competing instincts of running or fighting.

"Hello?" The receptionist asked, "Is anyone there?"

Gray chose to fight. "Yes," he said, "I'd like to make an appointment."

"Are you a current patient or someone new?"

"New." Gray looked around, nervously, wondering whether anyone was listening.

"Okay," the receptionist said. "Doctor Jax isn't accepting any new patients at this time. I can refer you to someone else, if you'd like."

Gray recognized the opportunity. It was the perfect excuse. If Doctor Craig or Midge or Kendra asked, he could simply tell them that he had called, which was true, and that the psychiatrist wasn't accepting new patients, which was also true. It was a graceful opportunity to move on with his life. He'd take the pills, see if they worked, and then fake it until he made it.

"Sir?" The receptionist asked, "Are you still on the line?"

"I am." Gray sat a little taller in his chair, steadying himself. "I was told that she'd make an exception for me."

"Really?" The receptionist sounded bemused. "Let me guess, you've been referred to Doctor Jax by her brother."

"That's right," Gray said. "He told me that she'd squeeze me in right away."

The receptionist laughed. "I'm sure he did."

"Was he right?"

The receptionist sighed. "Yes, he is."

CHAPTER SEVENTEEN

The headaches continued and a full night's sleep remained difficult over the coming week, but Gray felt like the anti-anxiety medication was working. Daily tasks were getting easier, and he managed to not miss another meeting or hearing. Gray felt a little bit of momentum, like progress was being made. This feeling, however, was short-lived.

At two-thirty on Thursday afternoon, his phone rang. Gray almost didn't answer it, but the Caller ID indicated that it was a phone call from Herbert Bloom, the firm's managing partner and founder. The old man knew everything that was going on, including who was at their desk and who was not. Ignoring the call wasn't an option.

As Herbert Bloom spoke, whatever momentum he had felt at the start of the day, disappeared. The old man expressed his concerns about Gray's performance since returning, and it became clear to Gray that he'd been betrayed by the most unlikely person.

Ethan Bloom had gone to his dad and told him everything.

Herbert Bloom did not say this, but Gray knew it, and he felt like he'd been blindsided. He trusted Ethan. When others had dismissed him or made fun of the way Ethan looked and dressed, Gray had always been kind to Herbert Bloom's misfit son. Ethan was a good attorney. He had no problem working with him, if the project was a good fit, and it now baffled Gray that Ethan would do such a thing.

At the end of their conversation, Gray was summoned to the conference room.

There were four people already there when Gray arrived. Herbert Bloom, Elaine Gregore from human resources, a tall, sharply dressed man in a three-piece suit who Gray had never met before, and Ethan. Gray tried to lock eyes with Ethan, but Ethan wouldn't look at him. He stared at the floor. His shoulders were slumped, and he sat low in his chair.

Gray hoped Ethan felt shame and embarrassment, and he swore he'd never work with him again.

"Let's get started." Herbert Bloom pointed at an empty chair where he wanted Gray to sit. No time was wasted. The meeting had been hastily called, and it was obvious that Herbert Bloom now wanted to get it over with. "I think it goes without saying that everybody at the firm is still shocked about what happened to you and Virgil, and we were happy when you returned to work."

Herbert Bloom, then, nodded at Gregore, passing the baton. She was the one designated to document Gray's lapses and warn him about what would happen if it continued.

"Mr. Wendt," Gregore said to Gray, then she introduced the one person in the room that Gray did not know. "This is Anthony Townes. He is from Western Gate Mutual, our malpractice insurance carrier."

Gray mumbled something about it being nice to meet him, although, in truth, it was never nice to meet somebody responsible for paying claims arising from your legal mistakes.

"We are concerned about what has recently been happening with your performance at work." She looked around the table for agreement, allowing a moment for solemn head nods and affirmation. "We're concerned about making sure our clients have the best representation possible and that the firm's reputation is maintained, but we're also concerned about you, as a colleague. My understanding is that you recently missed a meeting with…" Gregore paused and looked down at her notes. "With Jack Durell, and then more recently you missed a meeting with Timothy Gault and almost missed the planning commission hearing that evening."

Gray confessed. "I remember putting both of them in my electronic calendar, but one was missing and the other was entered on the right day and time, but the wrong month. I don't know how it happened, but it did. With Gault, I did make it to the hearing."

"And the meeting with Mr. Durell?" Gregore asked.

"Like I said....I missed it." Gray looked at Ethan, but Ethan remained focused on the floor. Then he turned back to Gregore. "That was covered."

"Have you spoken with your doctor?" It was the first question posed by Anthony Townes. "I believe you sustained a significant head injury."

"I did," Gray said. "And I have more appointments scheduled."

"Any prognosis?" Townes asked.

Gray wondered whether these questions were appropriate. There were rules about medical privacy and confidentiality, but he wasn't going to argue.

"It's a process," Gray said. "Everybody is different."

Townes appeared to accept that answer.

"We've made a note of these incidents in your file. Our expectation is that you continue to get treatment, and that you inform us if your medical condition continues to impact your ability to represent the firm's clients. Of course we'll make any reasonable accommodations for you, but there are certain elements of your job that must be done at a very high level."

Gregore passed a sheet of paper and a pen to Gray.

"This is a document that memorializes that we had this conversation. I'd like you to read it and sign it."

Gray considered whether or not he should refuse to sign, but that seemed like it would just cause more problems. The language was fairly vague, and there wasn't anything to dispute. Gray picked up the pen and signed. Then the meeting concluded with promises to follow-up in a few weeks.

Herbert Bloom, Gregore, and Townes left the room, but Gray and Ethan remained. When the door closed, Ethan jumped in before Gray could say anything.

"I'm sorry."

Gray resisted the urge to leap across the table and strangle the little twerp. "How could you go to your dad and tattle on me like we're in elementary school? It's ridiculous."

"They already knew. He knew everything."

Gray shook his head, even though Ethan was likely telling the truth.

"They did," Ethan said, still defensive, "and, when they asked me about it, I couldn't lie. I assume a client complained or maybe there was just gossip. Who knows? You know how this firm is. It's like we're in high school."

Gray's jaw clinched as he studied Ethan. He wasn't going to let him off that easily, and he decided to provide an alternate theory. "Or maybe you saw an opportunity to take all of my clients."

"Now that's ridiculous." Ethan shook his head, looking genuinely hurt. "If that's what you think of me, then maybe you are losing it."

Ethan stood, turned toward the door, and began to waddle away. He raised a hand, good-bye. "See you around, Gray."

CHAPTER EIGHTTEEN

With two black vans approaching, Morales knew that he didn't have time. The vans were obviously St. Louis SWAT, even though there were no lights or sirens. When he had arrived, Morales had a simple plan, but it was no longer viable. The police came too quickly. He'd have to figure out a different way.

He turned the key. The engine started, and Morales pulled away from the curb. He drove a few blocks west of Deonte Banks' apartment building and parked. From the glove box, Morales removed a fresh cell phone. He punched in Banks' phone number and gave the young man notice of what was about to happen, hoping he wasn't too late.

"If you get caught, don't say a word, except that you want a lawyer," Morales said. "It doesn't matter what the cops say. You aren't getting out. There is no deal. There is no evidence. Everything they tell you is a lie. The squad is wired. Don't talk to anybody in the squad car or the interrogation room. Just be cool and keep asking for a lawyer, and I'll get you one. Understood?"

Morales waited for the kid's response. Banks told him that he understood, but Morales asked the question again. "So if you get arrested, what are you gonna do?"

"Ask for a lawyer."

"Good." Morales looked around. He saw nothing. The perimeter wasn't secure, yet. "You got a chance now. You need to listen to me. Get out the back and run. I'll meet you on the far side of the soccer fields by the middle school. Get out now. If you're caught, keep your mouth shut."

Morales, then, opened the back of the cell phone, and followed his established routine. He removed the battery and also took out the phone's tiny SIM card. He clipped the card in half, wiped everything down with an antibacterial wipe, and tossed the pieces of plastic out the window as he drove to the meeting point. That's where he would ditch what remained of the phone.

###

The sun had just set as the line of police cars and vans passed the America's Center, formerly the home of the Rams football team before the team's owner abandoned the city and left it with a pile of debt. As they got closer to the house where Deonte Banks had been crashing for the past month, they splintered in different directions. The vans continued straight, a marked squad went up to O'Fallon Street, and Amy Wirth went in the other direction down to Carr.

Those were her instructions. She'd be the clean-up crew. Sitting on the western perimeter, Wirth was responsible for catching runners. It wasn't what she wanted. Wirth would rather be the first one through the door, but it was better than nothing.

Deputy Commander Knox had planned to leave her behind, but Schmitty intervened as he had said that he would. The more she thought about it, the more Wirth appreciated Schmitty's savvy. The favor to Wirth wasn't significant enough to create a rift with Commander Knox and the other detectives, Bird and Doles. It'd probably be forgotten within a few days, but the intervention was enough to show Wirth that somebody cared. If she survived, Schmitty would have her loyalty. If she didn't, there'd be no long term damage to him. That was how Schmitty played the game.

As Wirth sat alone in the unmarked sedan, she took the card that Schmitty had given her out of her pocket. She looked at the name and number for Agent Matthews. It was a graceful path out of the department. Maybe it wasn't the right path, but Wirth knew that she had to do something. If she remained, she'd be neglected and fall just like the crumbling buildings that surrounded her.

Wirth put the card back and studied the old elementary school on the corner. Built in 1908, it was once magnificent; now abandoned and left to rot. Boards covered most of the windows of the Carr School. The windows that remained were broken. The roof had collapsed on itself. The copper and wire likely stripped long ago.

Wirth listened to the radio chatter and continued to wonder whether or not she should call Agent Matthews as she studied the school's fading mosaics. Just being out on the streets where she used to patrol every night, filled her with sadness and loss. What could've been? And now, what could be?

A crackle came over the radio, bringing her back to the present. "Going in."

Wirth heard the sound of the door breaking. The entry team relayed each move over the secure police channel. Three inside. Everyone on the floor.

Wirth sat up straighter. She watched for movement, but the streets were quiet. There was nothing. Although the latest winter storm had passed, it was still cold, keeping people inside.

After a few minutes, Wirth relaxed. It sounded like everything in the apartment was under control. She wouldn't have any role to play, which was disappointing, but that was likely the point. Even though Wirth was on the team, Commander Knox wanted it to be clear that she really wasn't.

Maybe it was for the best. Sleep wasn't coming easy, and her paranoia grew as the harassment continued in waves. Just when she'd think people had moved on, there'd be something else to bring it forward, again and again.

Sitting in the squad car, waiting for the operational lead to give the "all clear," Wirth worried. If she did call for backup, would anyone show up? She'd seen it happen to other cops on the outs. A distress call would come over dispatch, and officers would take their sweet time getting to the scene. It was dangerous. Bad things happened, and it was impossible to hold anyone accountable.

Wirth continued listening to the police chatter. There was the typical chaos following a raid, but, from her position, the street remained still. Nobody walked the sidewalks. No cars drove past. As time passed, the radio chatter died. Updates were intermittent and routine.

She checked her watch and figured that whoever was in the apartment was now under arrest, and it was time to go home. Then she saw it: a person rounded the corner, running.

"Have you identified Banks?" Wirth asked into her radio. "Do you have Banks in custody, over?"

There were a few crackles, then, "Negative."

Another crackle, different voice. "Five in the apartment, still identifying."

"I've got a runner down Carr." Wirth waited. She watched as the young man got closer. "Late teens, medium build, maybe 5'10. No coat. Just white t-shirt and black jeans, over." Then Wirth saw his face as he ran past. "It's him. It's him."

A new voice barked an order. "Hold your position." Wirth recognized the voice. It was Investigator Doles. "Don't pursue."

"He's right here," she said. "I can get him."

"No pursuit," Doles said. "Presumed armed and dangerous. Wait for backup."

Another voice came onto the line. "Dispatching a chopper now. ETA three minutes."

Wirth sat, watching Deonte Banks get further and further away from her. The seconds felt like hours. Muscles tightened and a knot formed in her stomach.

"He's still running." Banks was now three blocks away, only a silhouette.

"Stay where you are," Doles said. "We're coming."

Right, Wirth thought, *you're coming to get the credit for this arrest or blame me for letting him go.*

Wirth turned the key and hit the lights and sirens.

"I'm moving," she said into the radio. "He's getting too far away. I need to keep eyes on."

In the distance she heard the helicopter coming. Deonte Banks snuck a quick glance back at her as he ran down the middle of the road. He maintained a steady pace, but every fifteen feet or so, his foot hit a patch of ice. He'd slide, but he never fell.

Wirth pressed down on the gas pedal, taking only seconds to catch up to him.

She got on the speaker and ordered Banks to stop, which he ignored. Banks cut right as he crossed 20th Street, and then began running across the soccer fields toward Carr Lane Middle School.

Wirth stopped and remained in her squad. Then the helicopter came into view, shining a bright spotlight down on the houses and the street.

"He's on the soccer fields." The helicopter followed Wirth's direction and circled toward the fields. It didn't take long for the pilot to find him. The spotlight shone down on Deonte Banks, alone and running through the snow.

Wirth turned and saw two squads round the corner. Doles and Bird were probably in one of them. Tired of being ignored, Wirth shifted her vehicle back into gear and pressed the gas. She drove over the curb and onto the open fields toward Banks. There's no way he didn't hear her coming.

Banks glanced back, again, and then looked up at the helicopter that was now overhead. He had to know that the end of the chase was coming, but he wasn't giving up.

Wirth accelerated. She didn't want to run him over, but she did want him to stop. She pulled up alongside Banks, pacing him perfectly, and then, when the moment was right, she flung open the driver's side door and slammed on the brakes.

It was as if Deonte Banks ran into a brick wall. His body bounced off the open door and onto the cold, icy ground. He came inches away from being run over by the back tire, but was spared. Wirth killed the engine and jumped out of her vehicle, flipped Banks over, and handcuffed him before he could figure out what had happened.

"Stay down."

Wirth tightened the cuffs, and then looked back. Two officers were running down the field, and another squad had just jumped the curb. She was right. It was Sergeant Bird and Detective Doles.

They both got out and came over to Wirth.

"We would've gotten him." Doles put his hands on his hips and looked down at Banks, now shivering in the snow.

"You put a lot of people at risk with that stunt," Bird said.

"He was getting away."

"Not at all." Bird shook his head. "But now you get the reward of writing the report and maybe getting sued by the family of this piece of garbage for using unnecessary force."

Doles patted her on the back. "You're perfect in every way, Wirth, just perfect."

Morales watched from afar as Deonte Banks was run down by a squad car. He ran his hand through his slick black hair, thinking about another way to eliminate the threat that the young man posed and also figuring out how he was going to tell his employer that Deonte Banks was now in police custody. The news wouldn't be well received. He needed to manage expectations and protect his reputation.

Morales took out a fresh phone, dialed the number, and got to the point. "Things didn't go as expected." Morales watched as the helicopter rose into the night sky, and disappeared to the west. A quiet settled over the neighborhood, again, as Deonte Banks was led handcuffed into the back of a marked unit.

"They have him. I didn't get to him first, and he didn't get out of the house fast enough."

Morales absorbed the frustration, allowing his employer to vent as Deonte Banks was driven off the snowy soccer fields and the other cops dispersed.

"Arrangements will be made." Morales tried to sound reassuring. "The less you know the better, but this will be taken care of."

He ended the conversation. He didn't want or need any further feedback when there was work to be done. He put his cell phone in his pocket, and then opened the glove compartment of his car to retrieve, yet, another phone. It didn't matter how many he used and tossed. $50 a piece was a cheap price to pay in order to keep one step ahead and stay out of prison.

Morales dialed the number for Seamus Sterling. He was a criminal defense attorney of dubious reputation. Around the courthouse Seamus Sterling had the nickname, "Shameless," and it was well earned. He was best known for his prominent advertisements. Originally they ran on the back-page of the *Riverfront Times*, and then Shameless expanded to a website called SaintLouisMugshots.com. From there, his ads began appearing on various billboards around town. The simple ads were just text:

SEAMUS T. STERLING, ESQ.
"Sterling results for a reasonable price"

(314) RESULTS

In the original advertisement, the tagline was the same, but the custom phone number was (314) GET-U-OFF. That advertisement resulted in an inordinate number of calls from men seeking sex rather than legal consultation. The new one worked much better than the original, and Morales could easily remember it.

"Got a client for you," Morales said.

Sterling perked up at the sound of Morales's voice. The lawyer had never met Morales, didn't even know his real name, but Sterling knew he'd receive an envelope with $5,000 cash in the morning. "Who is it?"

"Deonte Banks, just got arrested," he said. "I need you to get down to the jail right now and start raising hell. Demand to see the kid and tell them that they have no right to talk to him. If they question how fast you got there, tell the cops that the family called you and retained you."

"What's the charge?"

"Murder," Morales said, "stupid kid used a gun to rob a lawyer and things went sideways."

Morales waited as Sterling presumably jotted down the information, and then, before Sterling asked for more money, Morales made assurances that it would be worth his time.

"We'll go double the normal fee on this one," Morales said. "I need you to keep this kid's mouth shut. Let him know that things are being taken care of and it isn't in his best interest to cut any deals."

"Of course." Seamus laughed. "Snitches get stiches."

CHAPTER NINETEEN

Deonte Banks sat at a table in a bare interrogation room. Two cops in plain clothes sat across from him, trying to make small talk. The tall, skinny one, Bird, took off the handcuffs and offered Banks a soda. The shorter one, Doles, offered him a cigarette. Banks readily accepted both offers and he was relieved to have handcuffs removed, but otherwise kept his mouth shut and let the cops talk.

Bird made a few accusations, but Banks didn't take the bait. "Naw man, not like that." He leaned back, trying to act cool. He'd spent time in jail before. Handcuffs and a concrete box was nothing new, even though he wasn't much older than nineteen. He knew the routine and how to survive. In his head, Banks kept reminding himself to play it through, even though he understood that this time was different.

He wasn't looking at spending a few months in juvenile detention or a little stint in Boonville, a camp for naughty young men guilty of lesser crimes, like auto theft, check forgery, or drug possession. This time a man had died. Banks was looking at 40 years, assuming they didn't stick a needle in his arm. He'd get out as an old man, and it wouldn't be easy-time, either. A judge was probably going to send him to the maximum security compound in Potosi. Banks had heard stories about Potosi, none of them good.

Sergeant Bird continued with innocuous questions about whether Banks had a job or a girlfriend or kids. Banks knew it was a con. The cop was trying to get him to open up and talk, but Banks kept his mouth shut. As the questions rolled off him, Banks thought about ways to get out, deals that could be cut, but for now, he just needed to be patient.

"Tonight we can help you. I can help you right now if you talk to us." Bird dramatically looked at the closed door and lowered his voice, as if he was sharing a secret. "Tomorrow, when you go in front of a judge," Bird waved his hand as if he was performing a magic trick. "Poof, too late. This opportunity is gone. I can't help you anymore. The lawyers take over and we can't really do anything for you."

Then Doles chimed in. "We know a lot of things about what happened, probably more than you think we know, but the bottom line is that there's another guy. There was another guy with you, and my guess is that he was the one who planned this whole thing. That's my guess, but that's only something you can help us with. That's valuable information to us."

Bird took another crack. "That's right. Can't make promises, but information about that other guy would be something to take to the lawyers. I can say to the prosecutor 'hey, cut this kid a break. He helped us solve this thing.'"

"Otherwise it's just you going down for it." Doles shrugged his shoulders. "The whole thing is pinned on you. That doesn't seem fair to us."

Another tag from Doles back to Bird.

"Your choice," Bird said, "but we got you for sure."

Banks didn't respond to any of it. He smoked his cigarette and drank his soda, as Bird and Doles continued the back and forth. Banks listened and thought. *It wasn't a bunch of lies.* A lot of what the cops were saying was true. He knew that was how it worked. People who cut quick, got better deals. But Banks kept his mouth shut.

He worked hard to give no reaction and no response, but that took energy and he was tired. Banks wished he hadn't smoked a bowl of weed that night as a little bit of sweat formed on the back of his neck.

Meanwhile, the cops kept talking.

His head dropped. His body sank lower in the seat as Bird and Doles wore him down. Banks had been in that little interrogation room an hour, maybe more. He knew that he never should've gotten in that car. He was stupid. All for a couple hundred dollars, a bag of good stuff, and a gun.

"Listen up now." Bird rapped his knuckles on the table. The sound echoed off of the bare walls, and this got Banks's attention. Bird's face hardened. The cop had tried doing it the nice way, and now the situation had turned. "In about thirty seconds I'm going to put these handcuffs back on, and you're going to be taken down the hallway. You're going to be striped. Your clothes are going to go in a little brown paper sack, and you're going to be issued an orange jumpsuit, a pair of orange socks, and some flip-flops. This soda is going to be tossed in the garbage and these cigarettes are going back in my pocket. That's it." Bird stared at Banks, never blinking, and then added, "I'm just being straight with you, because I'm tired and I'm ready to go home. Now do you want to talk to us or not?"

Banks watched as Bird took out the pair of handcuffs and handed them to Doles. Then they waited. Banks expected the cops to keep talking, just as they had been doing, but Bird and Doles just stared at Banks, waiting for his decision. The silence was excruciating.

Bird's eyes narrowed, a predator anticipating the kill. Then Banks opened his mouth and took a little breath, "I—"

There was a knock on the door, and the pressure released. It was as if Banks was awoken from a dream. His body jerked, and the kid shook his head.

Irritated, Bird looked at Doles and then nodded to the door. "See what's going on."

Doles got up and walked to the door. There was a brief exchange of words with the person on the other side, and then Doles turned around with an expression of a man defeated.

"His attorney is here."

"What?" Bird's eyes narrowed, incredulous. "An attorney?" When Doles didn't respond, Bird turned to Banks. "You have an attorney?"

###

Banks followed the guard down the hallway, through two secure doors, and into one of the attorney conference rooms. Seamus Sterling was waiting and ready. He had a thin brown accordion folder on the table along with a yellow legal notepad and a retainer agreement.

Banks sat down in the chair across the small table from Sterling, and when the door shut and locked. Deonte Banks examined Sterling, not quite sure what to think. All his life he'd been told how awful and incompetent the court appointed public defenders were, but his experience with them wasn't too bad. Now he had a "real" attorney, but wasn't exactly comfortable with the situation. Banks knew that a dog was loyal to the person who fed him, and Seamus Sterling appeared to be a well fed dog that was certainly not being fed by him.

"I want out of here," Banks said, "You need to negotiate something. Get me out."

Sterling lifted his hand, gesturing for Banks to quiet down. Then he whispered. "Cops and prosecutors swear up and down that there aren't any microphones in here, but I don't believe it." He looked up at the light fixture above their heads, and then back at Banks. "Do you?"

Banks studied the light fixture, and then he looked around the room, searching for a camera or a listening device. It wasn't hard to convince Banks that the cops were crooked, because he'd certainly seen plenty of shake downs, maybe Sterling was right about that.

"What you want me to do," Banks shrugged his shoulders. "Die in here?"

"Keep your mouth shut," Sterling said. "You know about jailhouse snitches. Well this place is filled with them. Don't talk to anybody in here. It's a trick. If you don't talk, it makes things a hundred times harder for the cops. And don't talk to anybody on the phone. You got a message to deliver, give it to me. All the calls coming in and out of this place are being recorded."

Sterling waited for Banks to agree, and then he continued. "Those cops you were talking to, did you say anything to them?"

Banks shook his head. "Naw man, nothing."

"Nothing?"

"What I say, man? No."

"You're sure."

"Positive."

"Good." Sterling relaxed a little. "I can't tell you how important that is."

"So how you getting me out of here then?" That was the only thing on Deonte Banks' mind.

"Bail," Sterling said.

"Bail?" Banks looked at Sterling as if the man was insane. "Ain't got no money for bail, man."

"Doesn't matter." Sterling sounded confident, because he was. He knew exactly what his anonymous source of referrals intended on doing. "I'm going to get a website going for you, setting it up today."

Sterling told Banks the specific website. It was obvious by his client's expression that he had never heard of it before, so Sterling explained a little further.

"It's like one of those websites where you post a page for free, say what you want, and anybody can donate money to you through the website. Like say, your house burns down. Post it up, and people donate."

"Ain't gonna work, man." Banks slid back down in his seat. "Ain't nobody giving no money for me for that. Gonna die in here, man."

Sterling knew when a client was headed off the rails, and he needed to reel him back in.

"I've been doing this for a long time," Sterling said, "and I'm telling you that you have a lot of friends, more friends than you realize, Deonte, and they want you out of jail. Just be patient and keep your mouth shut. That's the deal, if you understand me."

Banks looked down at his handcuffs, and then back up. "What about offers? What about a plea."

"You're up for murder, Deonte. This isn't a shoplifting case or snatching a cell phone from some chump on a light rail platform." Sterling's words echoed off the bare white walls of the conference room. "If those cops told you that there was going to be an offer, they were lying." Sterling paused. "Did they make you a specific offer?"

"Yeah," Banks shot back, then wasn't so sure. "Says that they gonna talk to the prosecutor."

Sterling pounced. "Exactly," he pointed at Banks. "That's not an offer. That's just talk. They don't have the power to make offers. It was a trick, and you almost fell for it. There's no offers and I, frankly, don't want to hear them right now. It's too early. We don't know what kind of evidence they have and what kind of evidence they don't." Sterling pushed the retainer agreement in front of Banks and handed him a pen. "I got a plan. Just sign this and keep your mouth shut."

"How long?"

"Couple days," Sterling said. "A week at the most."

"Then I'm out?"

Sterling didn't verbally respond. He, instead, looked up at what he had told his client were the hidden microphones in the light fixture. Then without a word, Sterling nodded his head and Deonte Banks signed the retainer agreement.

CHAPTER TWENTY

Although he had an appointment with the psychiatrist, Gray decided that he wasn't going to go when he woke up that morning. He'd been reconsidering his decision from the moment that the appointment was scheduled, doubts increasing the closer it came.

The pills were working. He had kept the monster in its box. He was feeling physically stronger and wasn't nearly as anxious. Besides a few sessions of couples therapy with Kendra, which had failed spectacularly, Gray had never gone to a shrink before. *What would she really do? What would she tell me that I don't already know, other than stir up a lot of stuff?*

He sat in the cozy nook of his kitchen thinking about it. He drank his coffee, and looked out at his brick oven as the dark sky transitioned to blue, signaling that a new day had begun. *People are blowing everything out of proportion*, Gray thought, *it's just going to take some time to heal*. Gray, then, picked up his phone and called Doctor Jax. No one answered, of course, because the office wouldn't officially open for another three hours.

As instructed, he left a message at the beep. "This is Graydon Wendt. I have an appointment today, but a conflict has come up and I'm going to have to cancel. Thank you."

He set down the phone, and then leaned back, closed his eyes, and thought about what he had just done. *People just need to calm down.* He wasn't howling at the moon or wrapping his head in tin foil. *I'm not crazy*, Gray thought to himself, minimizing the hallucinations as simply a product of exhaustion.

By the time he finished his third mug of coffee, the shift from night to day was complete. The entire sky was lit, and Gray decided that the best thing he could do was to go to work. He arrived at the office before anyone else, and he immediately began making lists. It was going to be a full day, he decided, and Gray was going to attack it. No excuses.

When the large box of sandwiches arrived from Pickles Deli for lunch, Gray had already billed the same amount of hours as other attorneys would bill for the entire day.

"Just put it there." Gray pointed at the empty edge of the table, and then waited as the delivery boy set it down and exited the conference room.

The three associates eyed the box, ready for a break, but they made no move for the food. They knew that Gray wasn't done. He had already spent the last thirty minutes berating them about a draft motion for summary judgment, and now he had turned his attention to a research memorandum the associates had done related to Durell's proposed development of the Triangle.

"The quality isn't there," Gray said. "If you were the client, would you pay hundreds of dollars an hour for this garbage. When I was reviewing your billables, I nearly fell out of my seat. This memo is three pages, and it is going to cost Jack Durell over $4,000. When he calls, which he will, how can I justify that?" Gray tossed a copy of the memo on the table toward the associate. When none of the associates answered, he continued. "The truth is that I can't justify it, and, if I tried, it'd be an excellent way to lose a client."

Gray pointed at the box of sandwiches. "I just bought you lunch. Enjoy it, but then get back to work. I want a new research memo on my desk when I arrive tomorrow. It should be about ten pages and contain a proper analysis of the easements related to that property and what you recommend."

Gray stood up, walked over to the other end of the conference table, and then removed his sandwich. "And, when I see your billable hours at the end of the month, I'm cutting anything that has to do with this revision. It seems like you all have already padded your bill the first go around, so just consider this an advance warning." He stared at the young associates, making eye contact with each. "Got it?"

They all nodded.

"Good," Gray said. "In the morning I expect to see a memorandum worth the $4,000 that you already billed." He turned to the door and began to walk out. "Have a good day."

The conference door closed behind him, and Gray felt a rush of satisfaction. Beating on young associates wasn't his style, he was one of the "nice" ones, but it felt good. Unfortunately the feeling didn't last long.

There was a message on his voicemail from Kendra. This was the first time she'd contacted him since the Thanksgiving disaster. Unlike his babbling, apologetic message that he'd left on her voicemail the day after, Kendra's tone was even and her message was clear. She was concerned. She'd spoken with her attorney, and she wanted to talk about parenting time and the kids. She didn't make a direct threat, because that wasn't who Kendra was, but mentioning her attorney was enough to signal that she was serious.

Gray erased the message, set the receiver down, and then got up from his desk. Before he called Kendra back, he wanted to shut the door. He needed privacy as he begged forgiveness and offered various ways to atone for his sins, but the return phone call never happened.

"Hope I'm not interrupting." Ethan Bloom stood in the doorway. "Heard you just ripped some associates. That's a new style for you."

"Yeah, something like that." Gray's tone was sharp. He put his hands on his hips, wanting to make it clear that he still felt betrayed. He and Ethan were not friends. "Listen, Ethan, I was about to make a phone call, do you mind—"

Ethan didn't take the hint.

"It'll only take a minute." He waddled past Gray and over to the chair in front of Gray's desk and sat down. "I know I'm not your favorite person at the moment, but please."

Gray relented. "What is it?"

"It's about your therapy appointment," Ethan said. "Or more like the therapy appointment that you cancelled and haven't rescheduled."

Gray shook his head, baffled. "Are you spying on me?"

Ethan held his hands up in surrender. "Come on, Gray, I'm on your side here. I'm not spying on you, but Gregore is watching you like a hawk. She knows when you arrive in the morning and when you leave. She's monitoring your billable hours, and she knows you cancelled that appointment."

"How?"

"You signed all the releases, remember?" Ethan didn't wait for a response. "She's already had a conversation with the guy from the firm's malpractice carrier and my dad. You need to reschedule as soon as possible. That's why I'm here, to give you a warning."

Gray slowly nodded his head, still not entirely trusting Ethan. He gave Ethan a half-hearted thanks.

"And, you should also know that they're drawing up plans to force you out of the firm," Ethan said, "buy your shares and give you a little severance package. If you don't follow through on treatment or a client complains or you miss another hearing, they're going to do it. They're getting ready, looking for an excuse."

"And you're defending me, right? You're telling them that they're making a mistake."

Ethan was silent, as he considered his words. "I'm doing what I can, Gray." He shrugged. "They don't exactly value my advice."

###

Although it was cold, driving a car to the restaurant that night didn't make much sense. Whether a person was on the northside or the southside of the highway, Grand Boulevard wasn't known for its free and abundant parking. It was easier to simply bundle up and walk the three blocks from the house to the best cluster of international restaurants in the city. So, that's what they did.

When Gray, Midge, and Haley entered, a warmth surrounded them along with the aroma of classic Ethiopian dishes: ginger, turmeric, cardamom and cumin. "I need this." Gray looked around at the happy groups of people sharing a meal. "I really need this."

"Who doesn't?" Midge unwrapped her scarf and unbuttoned her jacket.

"I'll get us a table." Haley walked up to the hostess. They talked briefly, and then she gestured for Midge and Gray to follow. "We lucked out." Haley pointed to a cozy back corner of the restaurant. A simple landscape painting of Ethiopia's golden savannah with spindly Acacia trees hung on the wall. "Just one table left."

They settled in, ordered their food and a round of drinks, and, once the small talk faded away, Midge broached the reason why they were there. To Gray, "You're the one that called this emergency meeting, boss. You wanted to talk about something? So we might as well get to it."

"It's Kendra and the kids." Even though Gray was a private person, naturally predisposed to keep most things to himself, he needed help sorting it all out. Gray rubbed the back of his neck, as if turning a faucet. "She called, and then I called her back. She wants me to take a break with Nick and Zoe, focus on getting better."

"Like," Haley was confused, "as in, like, not at all?"

"Public places or with supervision, as if I'm a meth addict or something," Gray said, "No overnight visits, just two or three hours at a time."

Midge and Haley said nothing.

"She says it's not forever, but it feels that way." Gray felt his hand begin to tremble, and so he hid it beneath the table.

"What happens if you don't agree?" Haley asked.

"Court." Gray sighed. "Kendra is already talking with her lawyer. Who knows what she'll do, and, on top of that, I was told that the firm is looking for a reason to let me go. If Kendra files something that makes me out to be insane or incompetent, it's all public. HR would know about it." Gray took a sip of water, and then closed his eyes. "I'm already on sort of a probationary status at the firm, and then this....It just isn't fair."

"You're getting help, right?" Haley tried to sound comforting. "I mean that's the good part. You went to the doctor, got the brain scan and you're taking the pills and all that. I thought you were on it."

"Yeah." Midge chimed in. "And then, didn't you have an appointment with the psychiatrist today? Maybe she can weigh in on this, tell her that it's all under control."

Gray shook his head. "Afraid not."

"Why not?"

Gray hesitated, and then confessed. "I cancelled the appointment."

Midge and Haley both groaned, and Gray thought there was a good chance one of them would throw something at him.

"That was dumb." Midge had never been subtle, and Gray couldn't dispute the accuracy of the assessment. She pointed at him. "You gotta fix this."

Haley was a little more gentle. "Reschedule the appointment, and—" The waitress arrived with a large platter of injera, spiced meats, and curried vegetables. She set it down in the middle of the table, and, after the waitress left, Haley continued. "Reschedule it. At least it's something for you to talk about. Something in your favor."

Gray didn't respond, and Midge pounced on his hesitation. "Do you want your kids back or not? Do you want to keep your job or not?"

"Of course I do." Gray tore a piece of the soft injera away and then used the Ethiopian flat bread to scoop a pinch of beef tibs and shredded chicken onto his plate.

"Then call the damn psychiatrist."

Gray relented. "I'll call tomorrow."

"Now," Midge said. "Call her now."

His immediate reaction was irritation, but he knew that Midge and Haley were only trying to help.

"They aren't open now," Gray said.

"Doesn't matter." Haley leaned closer with intensity. "Call and leave a message. Apologize for cancelling the appointment and say it's really important to get in right away."

"You want me to call my psychiatrist in the middle of eating dinner?" He looked around. "In a crowded restaurant?"

Midge and Haley looked at one another, and then responded in unison. "Yes."

"Fine." Gray took out his cell phone, looked up the number for Doctor Samantha Jax, and called. "See, I'm doing it. Whatever it takes."

CHAPTER TWENTY ONE

Amy Wirth never thought that it would be like this. She hated her job. Every morning she lay in bed wishing that she'd never become a police officer. It was weird. This was the life that she had dreamed about for as long as she could remember, and, now she was ashamed of the badge.

When she had graduated from the police academy, her father sat in the front row. His chest puffed out. His eyes brimming with tears of joy. She'd made the leap, and she had her whole life to look forward to.

That was the past.

As the elevator doors opened and she walked out into the pen, that little girl's dream was dead and she felt like a fool. Her stomach churned as she walked past her colleagues. Wirth did not see men and women who were there to protect and serve. Any one of them could be her tormentor, maybe all of them. They certainly weren't her family and they didn't have her back. This was a big deal. If things got messy and a situation escalated, it meant she was alone and there was a good probability she'd get hurt or even die.

Walking past Doles and Bird on the way to her cubicle, she hoped that neither would notice. They both had been staring at a computer screen, but Bird noticed. He always noticed.

"Glad you decided to show up today, Ms. Wirth." Bird's face was adorned with a familiar smirk. "We were wondering whether you were going to actually make an appearance, or if this was going to be another mental health day. But you made it in after all. Good for you, sport. You're just late, which shouldn't be surprising, because you're always late."

Doles pointed at his screen. "We were just checking out this fundraising website. Seems like people are pretty upset about how you treated that young man the other night."

"Commander Knox is probably not going to like this." Bird piled on. "It's a shame that our rising star would get smeared in this way…"

Doles completed the thought for his partner. "Beating up on an underprivileged child from the north side. It's all really tragic. Especially since you had such a bright future."

Wirth hesitated, but was curious. She looked at the computer screen, and saw that it was, in fact, a website for the kid that she had chased across the frozen soccer field in a squad car and knocked to the ground. There was a photograph of a young Deonte Banks on the left, a picture taken before the neck tattoo and the gold tooth. He was probably in junior high or early high school. Deonte was wearing a football uniform. Underneath the photograph there was some text about being unarmed, run over by cops during his arrest, and seriously injured. On the right side of the screen was a thermometer. He'd already raised $750.

Wirth decided that she'd look at it in more detail later. She stepped away, arms folded across her chest.

"Friends and family say that you attacked him." Bird pointed at the written request for funds underneath Banks' photograph. "They're raising money for medical bills, his bail, and to hire a lawyer to sue the city for a million dollars. They even say he was headed to college before this."

Wirth turned. "Go to hell." She began to walk away.

Bird stood up. "Not so fast, honey," he said. "Knox wants you to call up the victim and tell him that we have the perp under arrest. The kid gets arraigned this afternoon, and you get to babysit the lawyer if he wants to come to court."

The hatred boiled, but Wirth nodded. "Sure." Then she turned and walked away.

The rest of the pen was pretty quiet. A few officers were typing up reports. After a new rash of auto-thefts and carjackings, it looked like others were working with some beat cops in a small conference room. Wirth sat down at her cubicle, hung up her jacket, and then looked around one last time to see if anyone was within earshot.

It was clear.

Then Wirth did something that she should've done the moment Schmitty had given her his phone number. Wirth took the business card out of her pocket. She looked around, and then punched in the number for Agent Charlie Matthews. After a few rings went unanswered, she was switched over to voicemail and prompted to leave a message.

"Hello," she said. "This is…this is Investigator Amy Wirth from the St. Louis Police Department. A friend gave me your number, and I thought you might be interested in talking about the Virgil Hawthorne case. There's been an arrest made."

She left her number, and then hung-up.

When it was done, she checked, once again, to see if anyone might have overheard her brief phone call. Then her lips curled into a tight smile, sadly comical. The whole situation was ridiculous. *Why was she so scared?* It wasn't as if she was violating a formal policy. She wasn't even sure if Agent Matthews would even call her back, but, if Wirth was honest with herself, she knew that it was more than just a phone call.

Wirth got up and walked over to the breakroom. There were vending machines, and she needed a Coke. As she fed it a few dollar bills, Wirth thought about what Schmitty had said: *you've already decided to leave.* And now she'd actually done something about it.

The plastic bottle clunked to the bottom of the machine. Wirth picked it up and unscrewed the top. *Pick a path and follow it,* she thought as she took a sip. Then Wirth walked back to her desk.

Once settled, again, Wirth pulled up the report she'd written after conducting the photo lineup on her computer. Graydon Wendt's phone number was on the bottom. Usually there were advocates who'd work with the victims of crime, but if Commander Knox wanted her to personally hold a victim's hand, then she really wasn't in a position to disobey an order.

As she dialed the number listed in the report, Wirth started thinking more about the fundraising website. *Maybe it was something Bird and Doles set-up just to mess with her.* She clicked the icon for the internet browser on her computer as the phone on the other end of the line rang in her ear. On the fundraising website, she searched for Deonte Banks's page. It only took a few seconds to find and pull up.

"Hello, this is Gray."

"Mr. Wendt, this is Investigator Amy Wirth." As she spoke, Wirth scanned the page. Unlike before, there were now a half dozen comments of support. "You might remember me. We met shortly after you'd gotten home from the hospital. There have been some new developments in the case."

Wirth looked at the fundraising thermometer. The amount raised had now grown to almost two thousand dollars. Wirth muttered under her breath, "Unbelievable."

"What's that?" Gray asked.

Wirth recovered.

"Nothing, I'm sorry." She swiveled her chair, forcing herself to look away from the computer and focus. "An arrest has been made, Mr. Wendt, and I wanted to see if you'd like to attend the arraignment."

###

Morales pulled into the narrow parking lot outside Comet Coffee. It was a small coffee shop squeezed between a deli and a yoga studio on the ground floor of a new office building on the outskirts of downtown. There was, inside, a businessman scrolling through his text messages and two older women chatting about grandkids.

Morales walked past them. He ordered, paying with cash, and then found a table near the window overlooking the highway. He took a quick hit of caffeine, and then got to work.

His computer booted up, and Morales immediately opened a program that allowed him to mask his identity. This was an important precaution. In order for websites to function, there needed to be an internet address connected to the computer so that information could be sent back and forth between a website's server and an individual's personal computer. If Morales was shopping for shoes or reading the *New York Post*, that wouldn't be of any concern. On this morning, however, Morales needed anonymity.

With a few clicks, his proxy software generated a false address for his computer, making it virtually impossible for others to trace his actual geographic location. If law enforcement attempted to identify who was responsible, they'd think he was logging onto the internet somewhere outside of Warsaw, Poland.

Morales, then, took a thick envelope out of his bag. He reached inside and removed a paper spreadsheet of fake names and email addresses. He set it aside. Then Morales took out a stack of prepaid Visa credit cards, which were all purchased with cash at different times and locations all over the country with different amounts ranging from $20 to $200. Morales made a habit of purchasing a few of these cards whenever he was on vacation or traveling for other jobs, just to have on hand for situations like this.

After a few sips of coffee, he pulled up Deonte Banks' fundraising website. Seamus Sterling had done a nice job. The fundraising request was short and sweet. The photograph was also a nice touch, although it may not have actually been Deonte Banks. Morales wondered where he got it. Maybe a family member gave it to him, or maybe it was just some random photo Sterling found on the internet.

Morales entered one of the names from the spreadsheet as well as the corresponding email address. Then he typed in an account number from one of his prepaid credit cards and picked an amount. With another donation made, Morales took a sip of coffee and then continued to shower the young man with support.

###

The City Justice Center was on Tucker Boulevard in downtown. It was an Orwelian name for a six-story, stone and glass building. The city jail held over eight-hundred people. Overcrowded and understaffed, riots had become common. Toilets were flooded. Windows were broken, and somebody usually ended up injured or dead. The conditions were so awful that a lot of men pled guilty and, rather than wait for a later sentencing date, asked to be sent to prison immediately just to get out of the place.

Gray passed through the metal detectors. Investigator Amy Wirth was waiting for him on the other side.

"Welcome to paradise." She offered a little smile, they shook hands, and then they walked down the hallway. "Ever been here before?"

"Never." Gray's eyes adjusted to the harsh fluorescent light. "I do real estate. It's usually contracts and drinks, certainly nothing like this. Smells like they hose it down with chemicals every night."

"Probably." Wirth stopped in front of the bank of elevators, then she pressed the button to go up. "I think they use the same stuff on these hallways as they do to sanitize the holding cells. You get used to it."

When the doors slid open, they walked through a crowded hallway toward the arraignment courtroom. The hallway was filled with parents wrangling children, lawyers huddling with clients, and others just staring off into space. The smell of disinfectant, so prominent in the Justice Center's entryway, now mixed with body odor and stale marijuana.

Wirth opened a door marked private, and the two entered a small room with a table. A television monitor hung in the corner that broadcasted the proceedings in the courtroom, and then there was a large one-way mirror. Gray walked over to the mirrored glass, and watched the swirl of activity on the other side.

The arraignment courtroom was even more crowded than the hallway. The benches were filled with a motley crew of humanity. The majority were people who lived on the margins of polite society. They were neither sociopaths nor serial killers, most were just men and women dealt a poor hand in life who consistently put themselves in the wrong place at the wrong time. Others lived in a different world entirely, spaced out and mentally ill, and then there were always one or two rookies. It was clear that this was a new experience. Their demeanor was tense, and they were dressed in their Sunday best.

"It should take a little while. The judge will do the people held in custody first, and then do the out of custody people." Wirth pointed at the chairs, and then she sat down in the one that was closest to her. "Feel free to sit. It's going to take some time."

Gray thought about it, and then declined. "I really don't mind standing. I sit all day." Then he turned his attention back to the courtroom and silently watched the parade as one case was called after another.

Every person accused of a crime was entitled to see a judge within 72 hours of their arrest. At the arraignment, a judge either sets bail, releases the defendant with conditions, or awards the golden ticket home, meaning that there wouldn't be any requirement to check in with a release agent—no drug tests, no curfew, nor any other requirements beyond just showing up for the next court appearance. Everybody wanted a golden ticket, but few won the prize.

Gray watched as a metal door opened, which separated the courtroom from the secure holding area. Arguments were made. The judge made a decision, and the next court date was set. Then the next man or woman walked into a bulletproof box. They wore orange jumpsuits. Often their hands were shackled. Each processed through the law factory in a matter of minutes.

It didn't take long for Gray to figure out that the most persuasive information was not what came out of the mouths of any attorneys, but rather the "risk score" and information printed on a sheet of paper that was given to the judge by the court clerk. Prior to the hearing, the defendants had apparently been interviewed. Information was gathered about housing, employment, failures to appear for past court hearings, and prior convictions. This information was entered into a computer, and that computer spat out a risk score that indicated whether or not the defendant was likely to show up for their next court appearance or commit another crime while released.

99.9% of the time, the judge did what the computer recommended.

The algorithm was intended to mitigate bias and decrease racial disparities, but as one black man after another was sent back to jail, it didn't appear to be making much of a difference. It was an illustration of systemic bias. Whether it was a judge or a computer, the information relied upon to hold or release had the disparities baked-in.

Deonte Banks was eventually called midway through the calendar. As soon as he stepped into the box, Gray's heart beat faster. Cold sweat formed. He felt it in the palms of his hands and the back of his neck. He looked over at Wirth, and saw that she had been watching him.

"You okay?"

Gray nodded. "I'm fine," he said, although he wasn't. It was hard to reconcile the person on the other side of the mirror with the huge figure that disrupted his life, pierced his reality, and

haunted his dreams. The memory flashed: gun pointed down—
"Just clap him"— two shots. It was all so clear, even though Gray's
rational mind resisted, reminding him that it never happened.

He closed his eyes. Gray put his hand on the glass, and
leaned forward as his breathing became more shallow. Fragments
of that night circled back on him, again and again, until Wirth
touched his shoulder.

"Maybe you should sit down."

Gray turned toward her. His body felt twice as heavy, moving slowly. When his eyes came into focus, he could tell by
Wirth's expression that she was concerned.

Gray shook his head. "I'm fine." He turned back to Deonte
Banks.

Bank's lawyer, a bulky man, was making an impassioned argument for his release. Gray recognized him from the billboards,
although he was older and thicker in real life. It was Seamus Sterling. Gray had read an article about him in *Missouri Lawyers
Weekly*. He had been admonished, again, by the Board of Professional Responsibility. Something about mishandling a client's
retainer fees.

"Is that him?" She nodded to the other side of the mirrored
glass toward Deonte Banks.

"That's him."

"You're sure."

"I'm sure," Gray said. "Positive."

Gray sat in his car for ten minutes, maybe longer, after the
hearing. The radio was never turned on, neither was the engine
for that matter. The only sound came from the periodic swells of
cold air, some strong enough to shake the car.

Gray stared ahead as he listened to his breath coming in and
out. It wasn't a formal exercise. He wasn't trying to take in deep

breaths or shallow. None of it was timed. It was simply being aware and letting his heart slow.

Gray hadn't been sure what he was expecting to happen at the arraignment. When Wirth had called, he wasn't even sure he wanted to go, but he'd gone anyway. He'd give almost anything to sit in a room alone with the kid, and ask the biggest question on his mind, "Did you really shoot me? Did you fire two shots into my chest?" It burned, and continues to burn.

A chill ran through Gray's body, and he realized the windows of his car were steaming up. He turned the key, and the engine roared to life. He pumped the gas a little, hoping to more quickly warm the engine.

A vibration came from his pocket. Gray removed his phone and checked the screen. It was a reminder he'd set for himself to call his lawyer about Kendra and the kids. Gray started to dial the number, but stopped. Instead of calling his lawyer, he pulled up the contact information for Kendra and called her instead.

Much to his surprise, Kendra answered.

"Hey," Gray said.

"How are you?" Kendra asked.

"I'm…I wasn't really…or maybe I was. I don't know." Gray ran his hand through his hair, gathering himself. "I was just at court, and I wanted to talk to you. They arrested one of the guys who killed Virgil. It kind of shook me up. I'm just sitting in my car…I don't know."

"You need help." It wasn't meant to be a scold. Kendra was sincere, but it still hurt.

"I am," Gray said. "I've been to the doctor. I'm going to a psychiatrist. I'm trying to take care of myself."

He ventured into a topic of conversation that Gray knew he shouldn't have gone. "I don't want to lose the kids. I can't lose them."

"I'm not trying to take them away," Kendra said.

"It sure feels like it," Gray said.

"Well, I'm not. You can see them whenever you want," Kendra said. "I just want them to be safe, and I want you to get better."

CHAPTER TWENTY-TWO

That night Gray had difficulty falling asleep, and, even when he did, the sleep wasn't easy. He rolled and wrestled, then woke, not much later, his racing mind picking up where it had left off. The future forked off in infinite directions. His professional life and family on the precipice as the paranoia grew thick below.

The next night wasn't better, and the third was even worse. On the morning of the fourth day, Gray's low-grade headache was a constant along with sunken eyes and nausea. Standing in front of the mirror, Gray studied himself as the water coming from the faucet took its sweet time to warm. He considered his appearance in light of his first appointment with Dr. Jax later that day.

"Well," Gray rubbed his stubbled chin, "I've definitely got the crazy look down." *Maybe I should go in a bathrobe and slippers?* He smiled at the thought. In his best Groucho Marx impression, "You wanna see crazy, I'll show you crazy."

Gray tested the water and it was finally ready. The old boiler in the basement had done its job. Gray rubbed the cream on his face and began the process. After a close shave and shower together with his best suit, the transformation was complete or, at the least, the disguise was in place. He'd pretend to be normal at the office in the morning, and then pretend to be normal at the doctor in the afternoon.

As Gray drove into downtown, Ethan Bloom called. "You got anything on your calendar this morning?"

"Hold on." Gray pulled off to the side of the road. He'd been so focused on not missing his afternoon appointment, that he hadn't thought much about the rest of his schedule. "Do you know something I don't know?" Gray still didn't trust him.

"No," Ethan said, "it's not like that."

"That's good." Gray felt himself relax a little. "What's going on?"

"It's about Virgil Hawthorne." Ethan said, "and it's a little odd."

"What about him?" Gray's curiosity peaked.

"There are some files missing from the firm," Ethan said. "Stuff you both worked on together, like five or seven years ago. We're trying to scan all the old files and store them digitally rather than have a physical records room."

"Well, I know that I don't have them," Gray said, "if that's what you're asking."

"I'm not," Ethan said. "The log says they were checked out by Virgil about six months ago. They're not in his office, so I figure he brought them home. Do you know anything about that?"

"No," Gray said, which was the truth. "Do you have the names? Maybe that'll help."

Ethan told Gray the names of the parties involved, and Gray vaguely remembered the transactions, but he didn't remember anything significant and, certainly, he didn't remember a problem or reason Virgil would need to bring the files up from the archives. Gray listened as Ethan continued.

"Virgil's wife won't return my calls," Ethan said. "So I thought maybe you could try."

"I don't think I'd have any better luck than you." Gray thought about her warning, and that she hadn't returned his calls, either. He started to get a little worried about her. "Maybe I should just go out there. Check on her and see about the files."

"That's what I was thinking," Ethan said. "Our records department wants the files back. It'd be great if you could get them, and make sure she's okay."

The trip west to Creve Coeur wasn't bad. It was opposite the flow of the morning traffic into the city, and the ride didn't take too long. He arguably had better things to do with his time than retrieve files, but, truth be told, Gray didn't want to go to work. Although he didn't say it to Ethan, Gray was actually thankful for a mindless task.

Although dressed for success, Gray knew that he'd get little done that morning, just as he'd gotten little done the past few days. The lack of sleep had taken a toll. Thoughts tethered to either his kids or the young man who fired two imaginary bullets into his chest, anchors that wouldn't allow him to come back to the surface. Gray couldn't focus. A simple email took more than an hour to compose. He'd type a word or two, and then descend into the various warrens and rabbit holes of the internet. At least the errand gave him a legitimate excuse to talk to Cassie and, depending on the file, he might even be able to bill for his time.

Gray turned off of Ladue Road and onto a winding, narrow street with no sidewalks. It was the opposite of urban density. Each lot was more than an acre, with the homes set far back from the street surrounded by a curated selection of trees. Although covered with snow, Gray imagined that in the summer all of the lawns were manicured and a bright shade of chemically-enhanced green.

Kendra would have loved to live here, Gray thought.

After a couple loops, Gray found Cassie and Virgil Hawthorne's house. It sat with the others on Beacon Hill. It was a standard issue 3,500 square foot, five bedroom home, just one of many that made the suburb one of the area's most sought after places to live.

Gray turned into the driveway, drove up to the house, and parked. He wondered whether he should call. As Gray reached for his phone, he noticed one of the window shades open. It was just a sliver, too narrow to know whether it was Virgil's wife or one of his kids. Gray decided the best thing for him to do was reveal himself rather than try and find her phone number. He stepped out of the car and waved with a forced, friendly smile.

The shade closed.

Gray stood still and waited, as if he was approaching a feral cat, and then walked to the door and rang the bell. For a moment, he was sure that nobody would answer, but then Gray heard the deadbolt turn and Cassie appeared. She was always thin, but now too thin and still in her bathrobe with no makeup, her hair strayed and tangled.

"Hey Cassie." Gray's voice was soft. Her appearance strangely comforted him. She looked how he felt. "Sorry I didn't come sooner. I've been a mess."

Cassie examined Gray's tailored suit and red Ferragamo tie. "You don't look like a mess."

"I'm pretty good at faking it." When he saw a little of the tension leave Cassie's face, Gray asked, "Can I come in for a minute or two?"

She looked back into her house. "I'd rather you not."

"It's nothing I haven't seen before," Gray said. "I'm a bachelor, remember?"

Her shoulders dropped and she sighed, resigned.

"Fine," Cassie turned around, leaving the door open for Gray to follow. "But Bucky is asleep for his morning nap, and so you're cutting into my morning mommy time."

She led Gray through the open entryway and living room toward the kitchen. "Do you want something to drink? I've got coffee, and I've got plenty of stuff that's stronger."

"Coffee's fine," Gray said. "Where are the others?"

"I sent Timmy and Charlotte to my mom's house for a few weeks." Cassie pulled a mug off the shelf and placed it on the counter. "I just couldn't handle them. How are yours?"

Gray took a second to consider how real he wanted to be with her, whether he'd keep it superficial. He looked around. The sink stacked high with dirty dishes. The garbage can filled, a full bag sitting nearby. A couple laundry baskets on the floor, with clothes scattered around somewhere in the process of being sorted and folded.

"Like I told you, I've been a mess, a total mess," Gray said. "Kendra's worried about me....she might file a motion or something in court if I don't get better." Gray picked up the mug of coffee, simply because it gave his hands something to do. He held it, taking in the warmth, and then told Cassie everything that had been going on with him and at the firm. Halfway through, Gray realized he'd been talking about his feelings and emotions more in the past month than he'd ever done in his life. His stoic German ancestors would not be happy.

They sat on the stools at the kitchen island for an hour, and then moved onto the couch in the living room, exchanging stories, laughing and crying. They probably would have continued all day, but then Bucky woke up. The sudden appearance of the toddler forced them back to reality.

"Snack," Bucky said.

Cassie put her hand on Gray's leg, and then stood.

"Well, that was nice while it lasted." She walked over to Bucky, lifted him up, and gave the boy a hug. "Of course you can have a snack, little guy."

As she walked to the kitchen with Bucky trailing close behind, she told Gray that he could take a look for the files in Virgil's office, and then she gave him directions on how to find the room.

"I haven't touched anything," she said. "If Virgil had them, they'd still be in there."

"Thanks."

###

An hour later, Gray loaded two bankers boxes of documents into the back seat of his car, and then went back up to the house to say goodbye. While Gray had been in Virgil's office, Cassie had gotten Bucky his snack and set him down in front of the television. So the house was quiet, again, as Cassie and Gray stood alone in the entryway.

"Thanks for your time this morning," Gray said.

"I'm glad you came." Cassie smiled, but the smile didn't entirely mask her sadness.

"After the funeral, I called, just like you asked, but you never called me back."

She looked away, tears beginning to form, again.

"I know," she said. "I'm sorry."

"At the funeral, you told me to—," Gray stopped when he noticed Cassie subtly shake her head. She looked up and put finger to her mouth, silencing him.

Before Gray could ask for an explanation, Cassie began, formal: "It was really nice to talk to another adult." She paused and cleared a lump. Then, she put her hands on Gray's chest, flat, and came even closer.

"Will you hold me?" Her voice faded, vulnerable. "Just hold me." Her hands moved from the front around to his back, and she pressed her head against Gray's body as she wept.

Gray didn't know what to think or do. It'd been a long time since he'd been embraced by a woman. So he just stood there, frozen, and that seemed to be more than enough. After a minute or two, Gray whispered. "It'll be okay, Cassie, you'll be fine."

He felt her body tremble as the crying lessened. Cassie pulled his head down toward her, just as she had done at the funeral, and whispered in his ear. "Keep the boxes. Don't return them." Then she released Gray, and took a step back. After clearing her throat, she said, "Bucky's show is going to end soon, so you better go." Cassie's voice, again formal, was now an impersonation of normal, faked for whoever she believed was listening. "Take care of yourself, Gray." Her eyes narrowed and hardened as she nudged him out the door. "I mean that, because nobody else will do it for you."

She shut the door and turned the lock. Then Cassie watched as Gray walked to his car and drove away. When Cassie was sure that he was gone, she took out her cell phone and called Ethan Bloom. He answered on the second ring.

"Hey." There was no emotion in her voice. "It's done."

"Good," Ethan said. "Any problems?"

"No." Cassie glanced back in the direction of the television room. Bucky seemed to be content for the moment with a never-ending stream of shows about an animated dog and a grown man who asks a lot of questions.

"He wanted to talk, but I shut it down." Cassie shifted her weight from one foot to the other. "When can I get the money?"

"A courier should be arriving within the hour."

"Cash?"

"$50,000 in cash," Ethan said. "That was the agreement."

CHAPTER TWENTY-THREE

The sun spent fewer hours in the sky as the calendar flipped deeper into December, coming ever closer to the new year. Although the first official day of winter was still a week away, there was a harsh chill in the air. A few flakes fell as the streetlights around the City Justice Center came on, but it was unclear if the flakes were fresh or just blown from the tops of nearby buildings.

Morales watched as Deonte Banks walked out of the jail in what appeared to be the same clothes he wore on the day he was arrested: a white t-shirt and black jeans, no jacket. There was a MetroLink not too far, and Morales figured that was where Banks was headed. There was never anybody checking tickets, and the light rail car would, at least, be warm.

He waited, and then Morales pulled away from the curb and circled the block. For a few seconds, Banks would be out of his view. He didn't like taking the risk, but there wasn't really a choice. There were too many cameras. He needed to be patient. Give the line a little slack, before setting the hook.

Morales turned onto Spruce, confirmed that Banks was, indeed, walking toward the light rail stop at the Civic Center, and then sped past him. Morales found a place to park. He waited, and then perfectly timed his exit so that he could come at Deonte Banks from behind. His intention wasn't to frighten the boy, but he wanted control of the interaction.

When the light changed, and, as Banks stepped off of the curb, Morales put a hand on Banks's shoulder. The boy was startled, but Morales greeted him with a smile.

"You're out," Morales said, and then he lied. "My plan was to meet you at the CJC, but they were a little too efficient when releasing you from jail. I'm parked over there. I got a jacket, some food, and a little bit of cash to get you settled."

Banks's eyes narrowed. In the distance, there was a bell, Morales could tell the gears in the kid's head were spinning, working the angles, and deciding whether to run. The train was coming. At that moment, surrounded by a dozen other people, there wasn't anything stopping Banks from continuing on his way.

"Who do you think posted your bail?" He kept his hand on Banks's shoulder, and then tightened his grip, still smiling and being friendly. "I might be the only person in this world that wants you to get out of St. Louis even more than yourself."

Banks cooperated. He began walking toward the car, but stopped.

"You say got money."

"I just told you that." Morales forced a laugh and shook his head. "I got a little now, enough to make you comfortable," he said. "Tomorrow, I can get you enough to go anywhere you want and do whatever you want."

A gust of wind cut through them, and Morales felt the kid shiver.

"Florida," Banks said. "I want to go to Florida."

"Don't blame you." Morales nodded, another smile, and a little nudge toward the car. "This thing I'm driving, it's a beater, but it'll work. In the morning, you can take it. We'll fill it with gas, get some more cash in your pocket and you'll be on your way." Morales opened the door, and ushered Banks inside. "Before you know it. You'll be sitting on the beach, surrounded by women in tiny bikinis."

Banks nodded. "I'm down with that."

"I bet you are." Morales shut the door, went to the driver's side, and a few minutes later they were out of downtown.

The house was in Bellefontaine Neighbors, a small inner-ring suburb with little houses on winding loops. The city was a product of the post-World War II building boom. Bellefontaine Neighbors was the future. It wasn't ever a place for the rich, but it was paradise to thousands of working class Germans and Italians who wanted to escape the grit, pollution, and density of St. Louis.

Then white flight carried them west in the 1970s, and Bellefontaine Neighbors, like most of north county, diversified. A recent wave of foreclosures hit the little neighborhood off Lilac Drive hard. Most had become unlicensed rentals, either by the week or by the month. A few remained empty. Everybody kept to themselves. It was a perfect place for Morales to finish the job.

"This is it." Morales pulled the ten year old Buick into the driveway. "Stay here while I get the key and unlock the place."

Morales turned off the engine, and he got out while Banks continued to eat the burger and fries that Morales had bought beforehand. The kid didn't really care that the food was cold. It was amazing compared to the food they served in jail.

Morales went through the back, turned a few lights on in the house, and then opened the front door. He stepped out onto the small concrete stoop, and he waved for Banks to come.

Deonte Banks took the last remaining bites of his burger, and then got out of the car and walked up to the house. The warmth of the car and the food had settled him. He was starting to adjust.

Morales could tell that Banks was feeling more comfortable and relaxed, even though both of those feelings were misplaced.

What Banks hadn't seen was that Morales had put on a pair of gloves, broke the window at the back of the house to gain entry, and removed his gun. If Banks had, maybe things would've turned out differently. Instead, the young man came into the house, clueless. The door was closed, and he was shot in the head.

CHAPTER TWENTY-FOUR

Gray arrived at the psychiatrist's office in the Central West End confused and a little scared, unable to stop thinking about his visit with Cassie earlier in the day. He moved the boxes from the backseat to his trunk. He knew that wasn't that much more secure, but it was better than nothing. Then, Gray walked over to a tan, old brick, two-story building.

The door was on the side, and Dr. Jax was listed on a wooden plaque along with a therapist, a wedding planner, and a photographer. Gray was about to press the buzzer to be let in, but checked his watch and decided he was too early.

He walked down the street to Left Bank Books, wandering the aisles and reading the little notes taped to the shelves, written by employees about books they loved. When he was done, he walked back and killed the remaining time in an antiques shop that occupied the entire lower level. The back corner was filled with old LIFE magazines, national geographics, tattered paperbacks and a random assortment of cookbooks.

Gray flipped through the old magazines, and then moved to the cookbooks. Near the bottom of the stack he found one about baking "frontier" bread. It looked like it was associated with a long-forgotten 1950s television show that was about lumberjacks and gold prospectors. In the back of the book, there was an envelope glued to the page. It was still sealed and purported to contain "genuine Alaska sourdough starter."

A sticker on the cover stated that the book only cost three dollars. Gray decided that this wasn't a bad price to find out if the packet of sourdough starter was any good. It'd be a fun experiment. He could try it with Nick and Zoe the next time he had parenting time, whenever that was going to be.

At the counter, Gray paid for the book. As he put it in his briefcase, he noticed a little sign on a large piece of furniture crammed between a lamp and a dresser. He pointed at the sign that said, "Trick Cabinet: $150" and asked the cashier.

"What's so tricky about it?"

The old man with a bushy white mustache smiled. "It's got a fake back. Built in the 1920s during Prohibition." He walked out from around the counter, pulled the cabinet away from the wall, and began to demonstrate. "There's a little button right here that releases the latch." He ran his hand along the side, feeling for it. He pressed the button, there was click, and a narrow door opened. "It's to hide the booze." He shut the door, and then went to the other side. "Same thing over here, but this side is much bigger. You can put all sorts of stuff in there."

"For bootleggers," Gray said.

"That's what I think," the old man shrugged, "but who knows?"

Gray thought about the boxes now in the trunk of his car. If he wanted to keep the boxes, Gray didn't think he could. The firm was looking for the files, and Ethan knew he went out to Cassie's house to get them. He could lie, but didn't see why he'd do that. If he got caught, that'd give the firm a reason to fire him.

Gray decided he'd split the difference. He'd return the originals and keep a copy for himself. The cabinet would be a safe place for storage, and it'd look nice in his living room.

"I'll take it," Gray said as he checked his watch, realizing that he was now in danger of being late for his appointment. "Do you deliver?"

"Of course," the old man said. "For a fee."

He didn't have time to negotiate. Gray surrendered his credit card again, and wrote down his address and slid the piece of paper back across the counter. The old man promised to have it delivered later that day as Gray hustled out the door.

"I know this is going to sound crazy…." Gray must've prefaced his statements with that phrase a dozen times, maybe more, even though his hour with Dr. Jax wasn't even done.

He knew full well that "crazy" was not the appropriate term. It'd fallen out of fashion years ago. Each time he said the word, Gray noticed Dr. Jax flinch a little, but she worked hard to remain open and not correct him. It was an effort that Gray appreciated, even though he didn't understand who he was offending, because the crazy person he was referring to was himself.

Gray was mostly truthful, but kept some of the details to himself, especially about Cassie. "It's just that….It's all tangled up and I can't seem to separate what's real and what's not. There's more going on, but maybe that feeling is just a trick, like how I *think* I got shot, but I really didn't."

"Have you ever thought about going to this encampment?" Dr. Jax asked. "I think you called it the Triangle?"

"I have," Gray had thought about it a lot since seeing the Irish Santa in the news report. "But I'm not sure it's such a good idea."

"Why not?

"I don't know." Gray shrugged his shoulders, and then looked out the window. All the leaves had fallen from the tree, but a fat squirrel remained, staring back at him. It was clear that the squirrel didn't have an answer, either. "For one, I'm the guy trying to evict them, but I'm also afraid…"

Jax finished the thought. "That he doesn't know what you're talking about."

Gray bowed his head. "I'm not sure how I'd feel about another person telling me that there was nobody there to comfort me. That I laid on that cold sidewalk alone."

"Or maybe it might give you closure," Dr. Jax said. "It's just something to think about." A little bell rang, signaling the end of their time together. Jax continued, "On the other hand, if he tells you that he was there, it might confirm that other aspects of your memory are real, a validation, while other aspects are not."

Gray considered it, but didn't commit.

The sun was setting when the cabinet was finally delivered. Gray gave a generous tip, and then ushered them out the door. After taking a moment to admire his new purchase, Gray walked over to it and pressed the button. There was a click, and the panel opened, just as the old man had showed him earlier in the day. Gray looked at the compartment and smiled.

It would be perfect.

The afternoon had been different than he'd planned. Rather than going back to the office, Gray went home after dropping the two file boxes off at Campus Copies near Washington University. He had needed some time to think, and he also wanted to avoid Ethan and anybody else who may be wondering where he'd been and what he'd been doing.

As he had waited for the scanning to be completed as well as the delivery of the cabinet, Gray baked a few loaves of bread while replaying his conversation with Doctor Jax. He considered the possibility of visiting the Triangle and searching for Santa. It was an interesting idea, but making progress in therapy wasn't his primary concern. It was the fear in Cassie's eyes, her warnings, and the old files. None of it made any sense to him, and, for someone who was usually detached and in control, that was the scariest part.

Gray put on his jacket, grabbed his wallet and keys, and then left the house. Campus Copies had a high speed scanner, just like his law firm. Everything, by now, should have been run through the machine, converted into a digital image, and put on a small jump-drive. By morning, Gray figured he might have some answers or at least some direction as to where he was going.

CHAPTER TWENTY-FIVE

Wirth was in her cubicle when Schmitty called.

"Have you talked to Matthews yet?" There was a conspiratorial sound in Schmitty's voice.

Wirth looked around to make sure that nobody was going to overhear their conversation. "I called him, but I haven't gotten a call back."

"Okay." There was a moment of silence, and Wirth could imagine Schmitty weighing his words carefully. "Call him again. Tell Matthews that they found Deonte Banks dead in a house over in North county."

"When?" Wirth was surprised, although she shouldn't have been shocked that Bird and Doles weren't keeping her in the loop. "I thought he was in custody."

She clicked the "IL" short-cut on her computer. "IL" was an abbreviation for "inmate locator," and in less than a second, it was confirmed. Deonte Banks was no longer in custody at the City Justice Center.

"He made bail some time yesterday," Schmitty continued. "They found his body this morning. This is a good opportunity to do Matthews a favor. I don't think too many people know yet. He'll return your phone call this time. I guarantee it."

"And you're sure I should do this?"

"You want a new gig, right?" Schmitty asked. When Wirth didn't respond immediately, he took her silence as agreement. "Go over to the scene. Take a look around and get some more information about where the investigation may be headed. Then when you meet up later with Matthews, you'll be able to talk a little more in depth."

"Okay," Wirth said. "I will."

Wirth exited onto Chambers Road and then eventually arrived at the house. For a murder scene, the area was relatively quiet. There was an ambulance, a squad car, and a few other unmarked cars, but the cold kept gawkers inside.

The media hadn't yet mobilized, and Wirth wondered whether they would even care. Finding a dead body on the northside was hardly spectacular news. St. Louis had more murders per 100,000 than any other American city. It has held the title of "Murder Capitol of the United States" for five years in a row; Baltimore a close second.

Since the front door was sealed and generously adorned with yellow police tape, Wirth walked around to the back of the house. It was obvious that this particular area of the crime scene had already been processed. There were little markers on the ground near various footprints, as well as markers around the open back door. Each had a number, which would be logged and documented. There were also several markers, just inside, by what appeared to be broken glass.

Around the doorknob, there was grayish powder. The first team that processed the house had obviously hoped to find some latent fingerprints. Wirth didn't share that hope. Nothing about the murder of Deonte Banks suggested that it was random or unplanned. If the person who did it was sophisticated enough to scout out and lure Banks to an empty house in a quiet residential neighborhood, it seemed obvious they'd wear gloves to avoid leaving fingerprints behind. Wirth, however, didn't blame the investigators for looking. They were being thorough, and even the absence of evidence was sometimes evidence itself. It also avoided insinuations by an aggressive defense attorney that the police were lazy, incompetent, or hiding something for failing to check.

Wirth stepped over the glass and went further into the house. A patrol cop stood in the pantry, not far away, trying to stay warm. She flashed her badge, and he nodded.

"Ain't pretty," the patrol cop said as Wirth continued toward the front. "Fresher back here."

Before the cop had even finished giving his warning, the air soured. When she rounded the corner and entered the living room, she saw Banks in the front entryway. The smell stopped her from getting any closer.

When a person dies, a body goes through five distinct phases. Upon death, the first phase was sometimes referred to as the "chill." The chill was when the body temperature dropped from 98 degrees to room temperature, *algor mortis*. It doesn't take long to pass through this stage.

The second phase began within two to six hours after death. Without blood circulating, it coagulates in the veins and the entire body stiffens, *rigor mortis*. The third phase was decomposition, meaning that bacteria were given time to grow and break down the cellular structure of the body. Without the aid of microscopes, the bacteria itself can't be seen. If left undisturbed and uninterrupted, however, the bacteria's activity causes the body to bloat. The dead body is filled with gas and the color of the body shifts, turning from green to purple to black. Eventually the internal gas pushes the tongue out and pushes the eyes out of their sockets.

Wirth put her arm over her nose and mouth, a futile attempt to dampen the smell, and looked at the body one more time before stepping back. Deonte Banks's face was blown off, so the identification must've been done by fingerprints. Wirth also concluded that Banks must've been shot within an hour or two of being released. The bacteria was already breaking him down. His body had begun to bloat and the smell was putrid.

She heard people talking in a back bedroom. Wirth recognized two of the voices as Bird and Doles, and she walked down a hallway toward them. They were in the midst of ranking the various forms of snack cakes. Twinkies and Moon Pies were near the top, but there was now a fierce debate about whether a Ho-Ho and a Hostess Cupcake were actually the same thing just in a different shape.

"It's about the frosting." Bird held up the Hostess cupcake with the distinctive white loops across the top. "Look at this frosting."

"It's the same as a Ho-Ho, just a thicker coating." Doles face reddened, exhibiting more passion for snack cakes than his actual job. "Same chocolate cake, same white filling, and same frosting. It's just the shape that's different. The shape is tricking you into thinking it tastes different."

"It isn't tricking me." Bird was about to explain why when he noticed Wirth, and the argument dissipated.

In a normal world, he'd have invited Wirth to weigh in on the controversy, but there was nothing normal about this world. The two just stared at Wirth, like she was a kid who'd interrupted an adult conversation.

Then Doles said, "What are you doing here?"

"Sergeant Knox wanted me to talk to that lawyer, Graydon Wendt, tell him what we found." Wirth could tell that they were trying to formulate a snide remark or make a joke, but they weren't fast enough to poke any holes in her lie. "Thought I'd take a look and see if there's more information before I give him the update. Any idea when the DNA from the scene will be processed?"

An investigator that she'd never met from Bellfontaine Neighbors answered her question. He was on the other side of the room quietly scrolling through his text messages.

"A week," he said. "DNA is on file because of priors. Just need the lab to confirm."

"Thanks." Wirth was happy to get the information, something that Bird and Doles would have never provided. She was sure that'd be a question Agent Matthews would ask her, and now she had an answer. "What about the neighbors, did they see anything?"

The cop looked up from his phone and shook his head.

"A lot of the houses are vacant. The ones we talked to weren't much help." He shrugged, as if expected. "We'll do another canvass tonight."

Matthews didn't hesitate to meet with Wirth. She parked in the small lot next to Maggie O'Brien's. The Irish pub was a survivor. It had navigated the ups and downs of the area around it for decades. The key appeared to be keeping it simple and staying open late. When she went inside, the tables were already half full. Most of the customers were St. Louis Blues hockey fans, even though the puck wouldn't drop for another four hours.

Agent Matthews was in a booth in the back corner with a burger and chips. He was not what Wirth had expected. About the same height as her, Matthews was wiry with a military style haircut and an intensity in his eyes. He definitely wasn't the strongest person Wirth had ever met, but she wouldn't bet against him in a fight. He looked like a guy who'd never quit no matter how many times he was dropped to the floor.

"Thanks for meeting with me." Matthews held out his hand, and the two shook. "Schmitty speaks highly of you."

"He's an old friend of my dad." Wirth sat down. "They worked together for years."

"Your dad was a cop?" Matthews asked, and Wirth nodded. Then Matthews flagged a waitress passing by. "I'll take a black and tan." Then he looked at Wirth. "What do you want?"

Wirth paused, and nervously glanced at her watch. "I don't know."

"Well," Matthews said. "If it makes you feel any better, you should know that I took a couple hours of vacation for this meeting, so I'm technically done for the day and free to drink whatever I want."

"Then I'll do the same." To the waitress, "I'll have a Guinness."

After the waitress confirmed the order and disappeared into the mass of hockey fans, Wirth and Matthews exchanged the expected information when first meeting anyone from St. Louis, beginning with where they went to high school and then a quick summary of family and jobs leading to the present. When that was over, Matthews leaned in.

"So," he said. "Deonte Banks is…. dead."

"Afraid so," Wirth shook her head. "I figure it happened shortly after he made bail."

"Not surprising," Matthews said, "but frustrating. I wish I would've known he was going to be released so I could've caught him on the outside."

"You knew something was going to happen to him?"

Matthews took a bite of his burger, and then set it back down in the basket.

"I didn't know for sure," Matthews leaned back, "but I knew that kid was in over his head. He was a loose end, and, frankly, I thought he might get killed while he was in-custody, shanked with a toothbrush or something."

"So you don't think Virgil Hawthorne was killed in a botched robbery."

"Not at all," Matthews said. "And I don't think you do either."

"I'm not sure what I think," Wirth said. "It was just a feeling I had from the beginning, but the two guys assigned to lead the investigation are lazy. Now that Banks is dead, my guess is that they'll write up a couple more reports and then close the file. Since the kid wasn't killed within the city's boundaries, it isn't their problem. There's no benefit to being curious. The case is solved, but with no conviction."

The waitress delivered the beers, and took the empty glass in front of Matthews away.

Wirth, then, made a guess, "Was Hawthorne into gambling or drugs?"

"I don't think so." Matthews took a sip of his black and tan. "But that might be part of it."

Matthews set his glass down on the table, obviously considering how much information to share. Wirth was patient, giving him space while he considered.

"We got an anonymous tip about a developer and a law firm. The developer was called Bevo and the law firm was Daniels & Bloom," Matthews said. "The CEO of Bevo also happened to be under investigation for inflating appraisals and tax evasion. It was a coincidence, I think, but we'll never know."

Matthews picked up a french fry and popped it in his mouth. "So we pressed the developer first, because that's where we had the leverage. Didn't get much, initially, but then the guy's lawyer calls and offers up a deal, says his client can deliver some much bigger fish, if we're interested in showing his client a little mercy on the tax stuff."

"So you start investigating the firm." Wirth said.

"Not exactly. The developer begins to meet with me and the prosecutors and outlines a general scheme, but he doesn't give any names, dates, or times. No documents or proof. He won't give us anything until a deal is signed and he gets immunity." Matthews takes a few bites of his burger, wipes his mouth, and continues. "The lawyers go back and forth, and the prosecutors are growing impatient. So, finally, a deal is struck, but the CEO never shows up to the meeting. He never signs the papers."

"What happened to him?"

"May have fled the country or is hiding somewhere," Matthews said. "I think it's more likely the guy is dead."

"So you never got any details?" Wirth asked. "No names?"

"Just one name," Matthews said. "Virgil Hawthorne."

CHAPTER TWENTY-SIX

Gray spent all night reviewing every piece of paper in the two boxes retrieved from Virgil Hawthorne's house, but, when morning came, he had nothing to show for the effort. There was no revelation and no breakthrough. It was just a file.

The only amazing thing was, in retrospect, how little it mattered. He had spent hundreds of hours working on a series of real estate transactions for Bevo Development, staying late at the office while his marriage unraveled, friendships faded, and his kids hit big and small milestones that he'd never see. The work, at the time, seemed so important. He was proving himself, and focused on ultimately making partner.

Gray looked down at all the paper now spread out in front of him on his kitchen table. He considered all that he'd lost, and concluded that it was a bad trade. The work itself was so insignificant. It wasn't as if he was defending an innocent man, falsely accused; patenting a miracle drug; or fighting for an immigrant seeking asylum from a brutal dictatorship. It was just a real estate deal, and its lack of conflict or nuance was also what made it so confusing as to why Cassie believed it put him danger.

She had warned him for a reason. She told him to keep the files, which suggested that they were important, containing some secret, but there were no secrets that he could discern. It was just thousands of pages of memoranda, correspondence, contracts, and invoices for his time. It was no different than the hundreds of other transactions that he'd worked on over the years.

Gray gathered the papers, put them back in the boxes, and set the cardboard top in place. Then Gray picked up the envelope from Campus Copies. He opened it and looked at the flash drives that contained a digitized version of all the paper he'd just spent the night slogging through. Then he thought about his new "trick" cabinet. It seemed like a good idea at the time, but now a waste of money.

Nonetheless, Gray put the flash drives back in the envelope, got up, walked over to the cabinet, and pressed the small button. A latch clicked and the panel opened. Gray, then, put the envelope inside, unable to stop laughing at the ridiculousness of hiding something so banal. Gray checked his watch and decided to take a shower. It was a quarter after eight, and he needed to go to work.

Victor Morales sat in his car and waited. Eventually Graydon Wendt emerged, dressed like a lawyer in a suit and tie and carrying a box. The box was put in the car's trunk, and Morales watched as Gray went back inside and retrieved another. When he was done and drove away, Morales did not follow.

He picked up the phone, dialed the number, and sought confirmation. "It's clear to go in. You're sure he made a copy? Looks like the original is in his car."

Morales listened, and decided that he wouldn't rehash the argument. A decision was made, and he was expected to execute it.

"When it's over," Morales said, "I'll call it in. Whether I find it is another matter."

Gray met the firm's record clerk in the garage. He had a cart and loaded the Bevo Development boxes onto it. Then the clerk handed Gray a clipboard. "You need to sign these in." He handed Gray a pen.

Gray filled-out the information about the date, time, and file number, and then he initialed and signed the form. "All set?"

The clerk looked at it, nodded, and put the clipboard on the cart. "We're good."

The phone rang at emergency dispatch a little after 11:30 in the afternoon. "911, what is your emergency?"

There was no answer, just background noise. It sounded like wind or maybe heavy breathing. The dispatcher repeated the question.

"Hello? 911, what is your emergency?"

Another pause, then, "Yes, I was just walking my dog and I seen 'dis door open, wide open....and, uh, I waited, and nobody was like comin' or goin'." The man's speech was slow and a little slurred.

"Where was this? Where did you see this?"

The questions were ignored.

"Then I seen 'dis glass...bunch of glass on the porch. Some of the other windows got knocked out too. Person who did it might still be inside, probably send an ambulance or something."

"Where are you calling from sir?"

A pause.

"The house is at...." A longer pause, then the caller gave the address.

"I'm sending some officers now." The dispatcher typed the information and address into her computer. "I'd like to ask you some additional questions. Okay?"

"Huh?"

"I'd like to ask you some questions, sir," the dispatcher said. "Can you please give me your name."

A pause.

"What?"

"Sir, can you give me your name?"

Just the sound of wind and muffled conversation.

"Can you give me your name and provide the best phone number to reach you?"

The dispatcher heard more muffled conversation, although couldn't make out any of the words, then the phone call disconnected. She tried to call back several times, but there was no answer. According to her computer, the call came from a little park on Olive Street, but the purported break-in occurred a couple miles away in the Tower Grove neighborhood.

In addition to the squad car in route to the address, the dispatcher sent another car to where the phone call originated. She doubted that the officers would find anyone, but it was a slow afternoon and there were resources available.

As the dispatcher scrolled down her screen, she noticed that the address had been flagged. Although she'd originally classified the call as a Category 2, the dispatcher quickly reclassified it as a Category 1. The electronic note at the bottom of her screen stated:

The address is associated with an ongoing investigation, contact Investigator Amy Wirth.

It didn't take Gray more than fifteen minutes to get from the office to his house after the police called, and when he arrived there were two squad cars and a few curious neighbors milling about on the sidewalk. As he walked up to the front door, an officer emerged.

"Mr. Wendt?" he said. "I'm Officer Hansen. Why don't we chat a little before we go inside."

Gray agreed, and, as he walked up the porch steps, small pieces of glass crackled under his feet.

"How bad is it?" He looked past Officer Hansen, trying to get a glimpse of the inside and shaken by the violation.

The cop was steady and calm, experienced enough not to answer the question. "We'll need you to walk through the house and note anything that's missing."

They talked about when he left that morning, whether or not he had been robbed in the past, and if Gray had seen anything suspicious. When Officer Hansen was finished collecting the initial details for his report, he stepped to the side, allowing Gray to enter.

"I'm sorry, but there's quite a bit of damage, Mr. Wendt."

Gray didn't say anything in response. He looked at the living room, everything tossed. Cushions had been cut open. The sofa was overturned. Drawers pulled. A lamp lay broken on the floor. Gray then went upstairs and encountered the same scene.

His bedroom was trashed. The mattress lay on the floor, cut open. The dresser drawers were emptied, clothes dumped. His closet pulled apart. Then he noticed the mirror. Gray walked over to the mirror, and felt a wave of nausea rise up. He choked it back down, but a little taste of what had crept up remained in the back of his mouth.

Someone had drawn a knife with the initials BMP on the handle in black marker on the mirror.

The memories of that night hit Gray hard and pushed him back. He felt like he was lying on the ground, fat snowflakes falling from the night sky. He saw the kid standing above him: his baby face, his wispy mustache, the gold tooth, and that same image tattooed on his neck. Then he felt a gentle hand on his shoulder.

Gray turned, but it wasn't Officer Hansen. Amy Wirth was studying him, concerned.

"Let's go back downstairs," she said. "I think we need to talk."

They walked together, slowly, through the living room toward the back of the house. The kitchen wasn't in much better shape than the rest of the house. The refrigerator door was open, the shelves emptied onto the floor. There was a pool of milk, souring among broken eggs and a package of sandwich meat. Gray ignored it at all and went directly to Old Betsey. She was, remarkably, untouched. He'd left the crock in a discrete corner of the counter. While everything else was in chaos, Old Betsey survived.

Gray picked up the crock, removed the top, and inspected his sourdough starter. A few tiny bubbles rose to the top of the mixture. *Life,* he thought. Then Gray put the top back on and walked to the little breakfast nook, carefully avoiding the debris and keeping the crock cradled in his hands.

After they had sat down, Wirth looked at Old Betsey. "Is she going to be okay?"

"Probably the only thing that's going to be okay." Gray's mouth formed into a sad smile.

Behind his eyes, Wirth saw a brokenness that was familiar to any cop, a look she'd also sometimes seen in a reflection of herself.

"That symbol on the mirror," Wirth said. "It's the same one as on the neck of Deonte Banks."

"I know," Gray said, "which is probably why you're here." He took a second to rub the tension out of his neck.

Wirth let the comment slide past without confirmation or denial.

"We think we found Deonte's body in a vacant house up in Bellefontaine Neighbors. I was intending to contact you anyway, and then this happened." She looked around the room, and then back at Gray. "I'm worried about you, Mr. Wendt. It's possible that this is all a coincidence, simple revenge, and it's also possible that there is something far bigger going on. Something you haven't told me."

Wirth didn't elaborate. That wasn't the plan that she and Agent Matthews had discussed. She'd take it slow, wait and see what Gray would offer on his own. Then press hard, if it looked like there was an opening. She waited as instructed, then went direct.

"Virgil Hawthorne was murdered," she said, "and you were not. Why was that?"

Gray looked at her, thinking. Wirth's tone had changed. Underlying the question was an accusation, which unsettled him. Gray opened his mouth, about to protest his innocence, but stopped short. He thought about Cassie and the Bevo file. He thought about the magic bullets that entered his chest and then disappeared, the markings somehow erased. She wouldn't believe him, even if he told her. So Gray told Wirth none of it.

"I have no idea."

"No idea?" Wirth looked Gray in the eye. She didn't know what Gray was going to tell her, but Wirth knew he was holding back. "Is it possible that these people weren't trying to threaten you or steal from you? That symbol above the bed, just a misdirection. Is it possible that they were looking for something here? That you may be involved in something more than just a botched robbery."

He looked away, and Wirth sensed an opportunity.

"You worked more closely with Virgil Hawthorne than any other person at that firm," she said. "What aren't you telling me? Because I think I can help you. I think you're in trouble and I can help you."

"I—" Gray, at that moment, should've told Wirth everything, but he didn't. The jump drive containing the file was still safe in the back compartment of his cabinet. He should've gotten up, taken it out, and given the file to Wirth. He should've told her how he got it and explained how, after he looked at it, the Bevo Development file meant nothing to him. Gray, instead, held back. He didn't know why, but it was a mistake he'd later regret.

"You're sure you don't have any idea what's going on?" Wirth asked one more time.

"I'm sorry," Gray said. "I haven't got a clue."

CHAPTER TWENTY-SEVEN

After Wirth and the police left, Gray immediately called Cassie, but she didn't answer. When prompted to leave a message, Gray gave a brief summary of what had happened and ended with a plea. "We need to talk, Cassie, right away. Please call me."

He hung up the phone, and, once again, surveyed the destruction all around him. Gray was frozen, unable to decide where or even how to begin. He closed his eyes, took a breath, and decided to just leave. He walked out the front door and kept on going.

Gray wandered through Tower Grove Park, and then through the Missouri Botanical Garden, losing track of time. He later figured he was gone for almost two hours before his head cleared and he was in a space to wind his way back home. He'd handle it, just as he always had, by breaking everything down to the smallest task. For his house, Gray decided, he'd pick one small area and ignore the rest before moving on. As for the danger and the file, Gray focused on Cassie. He just had to connect with Cassie. He couldn't think of any other moves, just the incremental steps in the moment.

He focused on the plan as he walked the final blocks, blocking out the rest. If he'd been paying attention, Gray would've noticed an unusual number of cars parked on the street along with several service vehicles as he approached his house. When he turned onto his walkway, Gray realized something else was going on. His house was filled with people.

His brick oven in his backyard was fired. A man and woman who lived three houses down from him stoked its coals under Haley's direction. At the back of the house, two men installed a new door, and Midge was yelling something out the window at a woman taking a bulging plastic bag to the garbage. He recognized another two from the Thanksgiving party.

Then Midge noticed Gray.

"Welcome home, sunshine." She smiled. "Glad you decided to finally come back. We've been working hard in here."

Gray felt the kindness, and his shoulders relaxed. He took it all in, and then began to cry.

###

It was about eight o'clock before the broken windows had been boarded, and the house was put back together enough to be habitable. Everyone had left, except Midge and Haley. They lingered, reluctant to leave Gray alone.

"I'll be fine." Gray sat down at the small breakfast nook with a glass of ice water. "You don't need to babysit me."

"No offense, bud," Midge said. "But we kinda think you do need a babysitter."

As the more diplomatic of the two, Haley continued her wife's thoughts. "If you want to spend the night at our place, we don't mind the company."

"With everything that's happened, nobody's going to think you're weak," Midge said. "If you don't want to be alone."

Haley, then, walked over to the table and sat down across from Gray.

"You're our friend." She leaned over and took hold of his hand. "You're in real danger."

Gray looked at her and then at Midge. He nodded his head, acknowledging all that had happened and what was continuing. Gray looked out the window toward the oven. A little fire still burned in the back.

"You don't know the half of it." He turned back to his friends. "That kid who got arrested is dead."

"I thought he was in jail," Midge said.

Gray folded his hands in front of himself, and then told them about Cassie and her warnings. "But I looked at the file, and I didn't see anything. I thought it was a joke or maybe she's been struggling just like me." Gray looked around the room, free of debris, but only a fraction of what it once was. "Then this happened."

"Why didn't you tell us about this?" Haley asked.

Gray shrugged his shoulders. "After thinking I got shot when I didn't, missing meetings, drunk texting Kendra, and seeing a shrink....I guess it just seemed like more crazy." Gray sunk. "It wasn't as if you could do anything about it."

"Of course we can't *do* anything about it, but that's not the point," Midge said. "Friends aren't there to just do favors, we're here to lean on."

"Now I feel even worse."

"That's not what Midge was saying," Haley said. "We're here to support you."

"Thanks." Gray looked at his watch. "I should be getting to bed, and you two should be getting to bed too."

Haley looked out the back window at the oven. The flames had now broken down into coals. "Bake bread tomorrow?"

"Definitely," Gray said as they all stood up. "I'd like that a lot."

"I'll throw in some more wood and put on the door so it'll be ready."

Gray's nose filled with the smell of fresh paint as he changed into his pajamas. There was no hesitation to take a couple pills to help put an end to the day, and so it didn't take long after his head hit the pillow for Gray to fall into a deep sleep, but it was a false sleep. Although his body was still, parts of his brain were still awake, processing everything that had happened.

His location jumped from one place to another: at the park with Nick and Zoe; in front of the brick oven, flames dancing as the dry oak popped; Cassie's driveway, a figure up in the window; the hospital's claustrophobic tube searching for abnormalities; the antique store; alone in the elevator at Daniels & Bloom, rocking back and forth as it descends, its doors open and Gray was now at the river. He steps outside, still in his pajamas, but warm.

The moon was blood orange. The sky was a deep purple, whisps of clouds were carried west on a wind that also bent the brittle grasses poking up from the hard, icy snow. Gray walks towards a bridge. It's an old metal structure built over a hundred years ago for trains. Up top, the little man waits for him. The same little man who waved down the ambulance as Gray lay on the sidewalk, while the old man with a white beard and the Irish lilt held him.

He wore a long, dark green, velvet jacket with a subtle pattern that suggested various woodland creatures. The clasps were silver, intricate in design. The collar was fashioned from a beaver pelt. The little man took a long draw from his cigarette and tossed it aside. "You're late."

"I didn't know I was supposed to come."

He shook his head, then rubbed his nose, as if Gray's statement physically hurt him. "You knew what you were supposed to do." Then he looked around, as if confirming that they were alone. "Suppose it doesn't matter." He examined Gray, top to bottom, then a shrug. "You're here." He, then, reached into his pocket. "Big man wants you to have this."

"What is it?" Gray stepped forward.

He held it out, and Gray took the object and examined it. Warm in his hand, the object was a white rabbit's foot on a long silver chain. Confused, Gray asked, "What am I supposed to do with this?"

"Use it." The little man smiled and laughed so hard he began to cough. This carried on for some time, initially intermittent, but never settling. His warm breath in the cold night air clouded the space around them, and it smelled of stale cigarettes and whiskey.

Gray was confused. "Use it?"

The little man's eyes grew wide, still working through a fit of coughs, and he stretched out his arms as if the answer was obvious. "Of course," he shouted, then bent his legs and sprung himself backwards, laughing, just as the bridge shook and groaned and a train appeared from nowhere with a roar.

Gray lunged forward, reaching out to stop him from being hit, but it happened too fast. The train never stopped, and Gray fell to his knees on the bridge's thick wooden slats, still holding the rabbit's foot in his hand, searching for the little man. Then, there was darkness as a heavy blanket covered him. It pressed him down, surrounding his body. The blanket becoming a bag.

He kicked and punched at it, searching for an opening, but this only made it tighten. Soon there was no space to move. Gray was forced to be still, to be quiet and calm. His breathing slowed as the inside of the bag grew comfortably warm.

Then fragments surfaced, a new carousel of images, eventually settling on one.

Amy Wirth was in his kitchen. She was talking, asking the questions she had posed earlier in the day. Gray watched himself answer, but he could tell that he wasn't there, still in shock from the robbery and destruction of his home. Kendra used to describe it by saying, "you're here, but not listening to me."

Now, as the fragment played on a loop, over and over, Gray had no choice, but to listen to Wirth and pay attention to everything in a way that he hadn't at the time.

Wirth said, "Virgil Hawthorne was murdered and you were not. Why was that?" Longer and shorter versions of the fragment replayed, over and over, it felt like there was something more.

Each time Gray watched the scene play, he felt like he kept missing its significance, so it rewound and played, again and again, until his mind grew tired of the exercise and it faded.

Deep sleep crept closer, then eventually came now devoid of dreams. He tried to exert control, keep searching, but his body and mind had different ideas. It wanted to rest. It needed to heal. He drifted, until it came to him from the darkness.

Gray's eyes popped open. He sat straight up, realizing what he'd missed. Poker players called it a "tell." A slight movement or change in expression that revealed the truth. Gray's heart pounded. The hairs on the back of his neck stood on end. His body was coated in a thin layer of cold sweat, and he turned on the light.

It wasn't her words. It was a slight crinkle at the edge of her eye when she suggested that something bigger was going on and pointed out that Virgil was murdered, yet he was saved. Wirth had tensed when she said those words, trying to keep her tone casual, hiding a conclusion had already been made.

It was not that Gray knew more information than he was revealing. There was more to it. What lay behind Wirth's questions was the fact that he was a suspect.

He needed to call Cassie. He needed to talk to her. Gray turned to his nightstand to see what time it was. The clock stated that it was 5:30 a.m., and next to the clock there was a rabbit's foot on a long silver chain.

CHAPTER TWENTY-EIGHT

Wirth met Matthews at a smoothie and juice shop on New-stead, a convenient location not too far for either of them. After ordering and settling in, Matthews listened as Wirth described what she'd seen at the house and Gray's responses to her questions.

When Wirth finished, Matthews got to the point, "What's your gut tell you?"

"Did he arrange for or know what was going to happen to Hawthorne? I don't see that," Wirth said. "I even have a hard time believing that he was in on the bribery scheme. From what you told me and what I've read in the file, Virgil Hawthorne was a spender. He liked money and status, the finer things. I don't get that feeling from Graydon Wendt."

Matthews considered this.

"Makes sense," he said. "Mostly these white collar guys are narcissists, always thinking that they're the smartest guy in the room. They truly believe that they found the loophole that no-body else can see. They're entitled and arrogant. It's not until their back is against the wall that they admit anything, and even when they do, the guys believe they're a victim of overzealous prosecution. They don't view themselves as criminals at all."

Matthews paused. "But I've been doing this a long time. And I've realized that there are some white collar criminals that maybe have mental health issues or they are gambling addicts or addicted to drugs. They don't fit the mold of the slick Wall Street operator. They commit the crime for some other reason or maybe he stepped over the line, just a little, and then got sucked in. Before he knows it, the guy is in too deep."

"And you think that happened to Graydon Wendt?"

"Maybe," Matthews said. "The guy strikes me as a dreamer. One of those people that has this secret dream to run away to an island with a bundle of cash and just sit on the beach and do nothing, running away from the failed marriage and the boring job. Maybe that's his motivation. Maybe that's what is really going on. He's got a secret bank account somewhere, socking away the cash and waiting to hit a certain number before he pulls the plug and disappears."

The explanation was too convenient for Wirth, too easy, but decided it was best not to challenge him. The whole point of reaching out to Matthews was to make a connection and possibly get a new job, and getting argumentative wasn't going to foster that relationship. So, she bit her tongue, and hated herself for it. She was tired of biting her tongue.

They talked a little more about Hawthorne and Gray, and then Matthews asked a few questions about Deonte Banks and the anemic investigation into his death. "Wondering about whether there's any tape from when he was released, like from the jail or the street cameras. You told me that you think he was killed pretty soon after that happened, maybe we can get lucky. Do you think it's already been pulled?"

Wirth shook her head. "Doubt it. That'd require Bird and Doles to do some actual work. Those two hate that stuff. They don't like looking at documents or videos. They'd rather drive around and bang heads."

"Can you do it without....you know, creating problems for yourself?"

"I can do the tapes," Wirth said with confidence, although she'd never done such a thing.

"That's great," Matthews said. "That's the difference between cops like them and cops like us. I hate banging heads. I hate going around and beating down people who've already been beaten down their whole lives. Going after criminals wearing suits and ties rather than baggy pants is more of a challenge. It's righteous work, and Schmitty says you're good at it."

"Thanks."

Matthews finished his smoothie, then stood and picked up his coat. "I know that Schmitty told you there's an opening at the bureau." He fastened a few of the buttons, and then took the scarf out of the pocket. "But you aren't going to get the job if you don't put your application in."

She entered a large room on the upper floor of the police headquarters. It was called the RTCC, which stood for Real Time Crime Center. In addition to being the department's digital information library, it was also filled with a half dozen officers who each monitored live feeds from over 600 cameras scattered around downtown St. Louis on multiple screens.

RTCC's manager noticed Wirth from across the room. His name was Charlie Hoop. Once upon a time he was a popular beat cop in the Benton Park neighborhood, but, after twenty years, Hoop was happily off the streets. He was safe in his little room, surrounded by toys.

"Investigator Wirth," Hoop held out his hand and they shook. "Do you want to get to work or would you like a little tour?"

Wirth wanted to get to work, but Hoop's enthusiasm and friendliness made her agree to a tour. "I guess a quick tour would be okay."

Hoop smiled. "Wonderful."

Hoop clapped his hands together, and they started to walk around the room. They watched one of the people monitoring the 8th and Pine light rail station. Something had caught the technician's eye. Wirth watched as she took control of the camera. With a small joystick, she turned the camera to a place at the far end of the platform and zoomed in.

"That guy." She looked away from her screen and up at Hoop. "I'm pretty sure he's been trespassed from the MetroLink a bunch of times. Want me to call it in?"

Hoop considered the request.

"Might as well. Let the patrol decide whether they're going to do anything about it." Then Hoop turned to Wirth. "Let me show you where I've got you set up."

Hoop led Wirth to the far end of the room where there were three identical doors that led to three windowless rooms. Hoop opened the middle door. There was a chair and a desk inside, and on the desk there was a computer with two screens.

"This is it." Hoop puffed up with a fair amount of pride. "It doesn't look like much, but all you have to do is log onto that computer and pull up whatever video surveillance footage you want."

"How far back does it go?"

"90 days," Hoop said. "After 90 it isn't accessible on these terminals. It goes off-site and the footage is stored on a separate server for a year. After a year, it's deleted."

"Sounds good." Wirth stepped into the room. "I just punch in the date and time?"

"That's right," Hoop said. "And then you can pick your camera." He pointed at the desk drawer. "There's a book in there," Hoop said. "It has maps and the cameras that are at each location. Each camera has a number and that's what you type into the terminal."

"Pretty slick."

"I think so," Hoop said, "Sometimes it takes a little while to load the video, but, if you're patient, it should all come up within thirty seconds or so…just don't keep clicking the button. That'll make the whole thing freeze and you'll have to reboot."

###

It took Wirth about 45 minutes to get comfortable with the process. It wasn't complicated, but the program was a little more buggy than she expected. Even though Hoop warned her, Wirth still had hoped that the program would work as quickly and seamlessly as the billion-dollar websites and apps that she used daily on her phone. Not long ago a low resolution graphic of a dog barking the "happy birthday" song on a crude website was a revelation. Now expectations were higher.

Wirth flipped through the book of maps with camera locations. Just as Hoop had told her, the maps were of the downtown streets and also had the locations of the various cameras. Each camera had a fifteen digit code assigned to it. When she wanted a piece of footage, she needed to type in the camera code, date, and time.

Wirth started at the Justice Center. There were a lot of cameras around the building. Wirth had hoped that somebody was waiting for Banks right outside, but she wasn't that lucky. She watched the video, and it showed Banks walk out the back door of the jail alone. Then she pulled up the footage from two other cameras, but the result was the same. If someone was waiting, they were smart enough to keep their distance.

Wirth flipped the page and looked at the maps around the jail. She needed to decide what direction Banks walked after his release. There were really only two choices. He either went North on Tucker, looking for food or maybe a ride, or he went South on Tucker. There wasn't anything south that would provide comfort, but there was a Greyhound bus station and the light rail. Getting out of town seemed like the most likely priority for Banks, so Wirth located a camera at the intersection of Tucker and Clark, punched in the details, and waited for the video to load.

When images eventually began to play, the resolution wasn't as crisp as she expected. It was getting dark and the cameras were a few generations out of date. Wirth leaned in close. She studied the people walking on the sidewalk, stopping and rewinding

164

several times. Then she found Banks. He was the only one who didn't have a jacket or anything, and he was still all alone.

She continued to watch segments of Banks' journey, sometimes lasting less than a second. Each picked up by a number of different cameras, always hoping that she'd see something or someone suspicious. As Banks paused at an intersection, waiting for the light to change, Wirth held her breath. She imagined a car pull-up and Banks get inside, but that didn't happen. He took a right, walking West on Clark, and then Banks went out of view.

Wirth watched another 15 minutes of video, but nobody followed behind. She began to wonder if she was just wasting time. Perhaps Bird and Doles had already done this same work and found nothing, but her gut told her to keep watching.

She pulled up the next video. It was a camera on Spruce Street. Wirth, once again, located Banks and he was alone. She checked the map, now certain that Banks was going to the station. If he got on a bus or on a light rail train, things would get complicated. That video would no longer be on Hoops' system. She'd have to get a warrant, and hope that Greyhound or the Metrolink hadn't deleted any of their security footage.

The grainy images from the camera at 14th and Spruce now had more people. Banks stood on the corner, surrounded by commuters. Underdressed and out of place, he was about to cross the street when he stopped and looked back. Someone was talking to him. Wirth paused the video. She pressed a button, enlarging the image, but it was difficult to see the face of the person that had Banks' attention.

It looked like a man, but Wirth wasn't confident about even something that basic. Whoever it was, Banks followed him or her. Wirth noted the direction they walked and referenced her map. As the two left the frame, Wirth tried to figure out if there was another camera that recorded the rest of their journey.

She considered their direction, and then found the camera that would be in the best position to capture them. Her hand shook as she typed in the number assigned to the camera. Her screen flashed. Then the video played as Wirth allowed herself a brief moment to dream, imagining what it would be like to find the crucial information to solve the case, and then hand in her resignation letter to Commander Knox. What would it be like to work with Matthews every day?

CHAPTER TWENTY-NINE

Gray arrived at Virgil and Cassie's house a little after seven in the morning. After the dream, he couldn't fall back asleep. It was frustrating. Every time Gray thought that he was making progress, something happened to remind himself that he wasn't well. The rabbit's foot was locked in the trick cabinet with the flash drive, hidden away. He'd tell nobody. It was too bizarre. He had no explanation, and didn't even know where to start.

Instead, Gray focused on what he knew was real. He knew that Virgil wasn't killed in a botched robbery. He was not a random victim. He knew that it had something to do with the firm, and he knew that Cassie was playing games. She had information that he needed. She had information that could help him regain at least some of what he'd lost, revert back to the normal, boring life he'd taken for granted, a life without guns, migraines, hallucinations, blackouts and flashbacks. A life where he could fall asleep on his own, and wake up in the morning without pain or feeling like he'd lost his mind.

On the drive out, Gray texted his neighbor, Haley, and told her that he had some errands to run. The oven was hot and ready. They'd bake when he got back around nine.

As he pulled into the driveway, Gray surveyed the house. There were no lights on. Unlike his last visit, there was nobody watching from the window. He got out, and began to walk toward the door when a neighbor called out.

"You a realtor?"

Gray turned and looked at the man on the other side of the street. He was at the end of his driveway, still in his pajamas, but wearing a winter coat and boots. It looked like he had only ventured outside to retrieve his morning newspaper. A copy of the Post-Dispatch, safe from the elements in a blue plastic bag, was in his hand.

"No," Gray said. "I worked with Cassie's husband. Just wanted to check on her. What's going on?"

The man shrugged his shoulders. "Not sure. Couple days ago, a truck came and loaded up a bunch of stuff and they were gone. Thought you might be a realtor, hoping to get an update."

"Sorry," Gray said. "Any idea where she is or how to get in touch with her?"

The man shook his head.

"Didn't say good-bye or anything, not that we were close." The man glanced over his shoulder toward his warm house. His attempt to gather some neighborhood gossip had failed, and now he was ready to get back inside. "Lived next to them for ten years, but can't say I knew them too well. Sad about her husband, though."

He turned and began to walk away.

"If you don't mind," Gray reached into his back pocket and removed his wallet, "I'd like to get in touch with her." Gray removed one of his business cards. "Can you tell her that I dropped by?"

The neighbor turned and took the card.

"My cell phone is on there," Gray said. "She can get me anytime."

"Okay." The neighbor nodded, eyes narrowed. "I'll put it with the other one."

"What other one?"

"A guy from the FBI was looking for her, too." The neighbor wasn't particularly shy about sharing this information. Probably one of the most exciting things to happen in Creve Coeur in years. "Did the same thing you just did. Asked the same questions, and I gave the same answers."

Back home, Gray stood in front of his oven, preparing it for baking with Haley. Although the majority of wood had now turned to ash, the oven still radiated a calm warmth. In addition to the heat that had been absorbed into the stones, there were still some sizable coals in the very back.

Gray put on his pair of large, leather welding gloves, and then picked up his 6 inch wide, iron ash hoe, which was actually sold as a manure spreader. He, first, worked the front of the oven, pulling the powdery ash into a narrow slit at the front. After that was cleared, Gray worked the back. The larger coals burned a bright orange every time they were touched, and softly chimed as they cooled, again.

His movements fell into a rhythm, like he was pushing little stones around a Japanese sand garden, and, as he worked, Gray's head began to clear. He had to get answers from Cassie, and, when his trip out to her house was unsuccessful and he left without talking to her, Gray felt like he wasn't any further to understanding what was going on than when he had woken up from his dream.

As he spread the hot coals into an even layer across the oven's floor, his frustration faded and he was finally able to recognize that he had, in fact, made progress. He had learned that the FBI was involved, and this alone confirmed his suspicion. Amy Wirth's questions weren't casual or routine. She was asking on behalf of the FBI, and Gray knew that the federal government didn't get involved in street crime, even if a botched mugging resulted in someone's death.

He set the ash hoe aside, and then Gray lifted the oven's high-temperature concrete door back into place, trapping the heat inside. *The federal government doesn't get involved in street crime.* It had been just a musing, but there was something more, a tiny string that could be pulled, if he could find it.

Gray put his hands on his hips and took a deep breath. With the oven now sealed, the cold morning air filled his lungs with a little burn. He closed his eyes, and then he felt a surge of warmth and adrenaline when the answer came: jurisdiction.

That was the string that he needed to pull.

Every government agency, whether local, state, or federal, was just a box in a gigantic organizational chart. After a career of dealing with bureaucrats, Gray had heard the refrain thousands of times, "That's not my job" or "That's outside our scope" or "You'll have to get approval from this—insert whatever acronym you want here— first and then come back to us." In many ways, it was just the government being difficult, but, at its core, these interactions were rooted in jurisdiction. Every box in the gigantic organizational chart had a prescribed list of work that it was empowered to do, and couldn't legally do anything beyond that list.

Although there was a mystique about the Federal Bureau of Investigation and a belief that it could do whatever it wanted, the truth was that the days of J. Edgar Hoover and Roy Cohn were over. Congress and the courts had reigned them in, and now the FBI had rules, too. So, Gray flipped the question on its head.

If the FBI could not investigate ordinary street crime, what could it investigate?

Gray took out his phone and looked-up the number for a law school classmate in his contacts. They had been in the same study group, and stayed in touch over the years. Daniels & Bloom had season tickets to the Cardinals, and Tad Hankerson was always willing to catch a game on short notice as well as buy the first round of beer. It was an excellent excuse for Hankerson to escape the small house where he and his wife lived with their six kids. For this reason, Hankerson owed him a favor.

Gray dialed the number, and his old friend answered on the second ring.

"A little too cold for baseball." Hankerson said. "What's going on?" Gray gave him the short version, and Hankerson agreed to drop by after work. He was a criminal defense attorney, and would have a much better idea of how and what the FBI investigates. "I'll bring our new puppy," Hankerson said. "He's at the groomer this morning, and I'll pick him up on my way to your place. We can walk and talk."

Gray spent the afternoon baking bread with Haley, thankful for the distraction, and Hankerson arrived shortly after five. He was still wearing a full suit and wool trench coat, but his tie was gone, his wingtips were replaced with winter boots, and, in his hand, Tad Hankerson held a leash instead of a briefcase.

Gray looked down at Hankerson's dog.

"He's cute," he said. "What's his name?"

"Atticus." Hankerson reached into his pocket, removed a treat, and gave it to the dog. "Named him after the lawyer in *To Kill a Mockingbird*."

"The kids have to love him."

"My wife says she's going to nominate me for father of the year." Hankerson gave the puppy a quick pet, "but then she immediately had second thoughts—didn't want me to get too cocky."

"Can't say I blame her." Gray looked up at the sky, checking. It was overcast, but still. The absence of cold gusts of wind was unusual for this time of year. "Just give me a second, and I'll be right out." Gray grabbed his coat, hat and gloves from the front closet, and soon Gray and Hankerson were walking toward Tower Grove Park with Atticus happily sniffing the terrain along the way.

They made small talk for a few blocks, catching up on what they'd heard about their law school classmates: who switched firms, who got appointed to the bench, and who disappeared without a trace. "Remember Peter?"

"The crazy German?"

Hankerson smiled and nodded. "The one and only."

Gray hadn't thought about Peter in decades. He was there on a full scholarship, perfect LSAT score and obviously brilliant, but strange. He was suspended a week for breaking the thermostat in one of the library's study rooms and turning it into a sauna. He probably wouldn't have gotten caught, except another student walked by and noticed through the small window on the door that Crazy Peter was naked, wearing only a towel, as he studied Constitutional law.

"So my wife and I went to this improv show out in St. Charles last weekend with a group of people from our church." Hankerson paused, waiting for a car to pass, and then continued his story when everybody had safely walked across Arsenal and began down a looping path through the large rectangular park and past its many intricately carved, Victorian pavilions, fountains, and statues.

"Anyway," Hankerson said. "We get settled in, have a few drinks, and the host starts talking about the evening and how improv works and that there will be two teams competing against one another. Then he begins introducing the performers, and out runs Crazy Peter. I couldn't believe it."

"How was he?"

"Crazy," Hankerson laughed. "He looked and acted exactly the same as he did in law school." The conversation faded as they walked westward toward the bandstand pavilion, with its curved, red tin roof. Then, Hankerson transitioned to the real reason he was there. "Been thinking about what you told me," he said. "And if the FBI is involved, it could be a lot of things, but I figure it's related to one of the big four: guns, drugs, taxes, or government corruption."

"Guns and drugs doesn't seem like Virgil," Gray said.

"You never know." Hankerson stopped walking as Atticus sniffed a nearby tree, "but I agree with you for different reasons. Your law partner is dead, so if the FBI was really going after him, then their case ends when he dies. You know? They've got hundreds of investigations going on, and they generally don't keep investigating people who are dead."

Gray understood where Hankerson was going. "But if it was bigger than just Virgil and it involved a lot of other people."

"Then it makes sense why they are still poking around. In fact, his death might've made it an even higher priority."

"So if it isn't drugs and guns," Gray said. "That leaves taxes or corruption."

"Or both," Hankerson said. "The two often go together, not always, but sometimes a prosecutor can't prove the quid pro quo, but they can certainly prove that a person got money and didn't pay taxes on it. They use the tax charge as leverage to get people to talk."

"Like mobsters?" Gray asked.

"Doesn't have to be the mob," Hankerson said. "Although it got Al Capone, it applies to lots of other people and situations."

Gray thought about the firm's track record of successfully shepherding real estate development deals through the city and county, securing government contracts for clients, and securitizing municipal bonds worth millions.

"It's possible," Gray admitted, "But, even if it's true, I'm just not sure what that has to do with me."

Hankerson waited for Atticus to finish his business at a tree, and then continued to walk. "It may not have anything to do with you, but the FBI doesn't know that. From the outside it looks like you and Virgil were working together, closely. Now your house gets broken into, and that confirms some suspicions. None of it is admissible in court, but in their mind it pulls you in deeper."

Gray thought about all that had happened and his conversations with Cassie.

"I got warned," he said, but stopped himself before going any further. "Can we classify this as attorney-client privilege?"

"Of course."

"Okay." Gray told Hankerson about what Cassie had said at the funeral, and then told him about the file that he went to get for work. "She was acting weird when I left and she told me to keep the file."

"Did you?"

"Not exactly," Gray said. "I took it to a copy shop and had it scanned first, then I returned it to the firm's record department."

Hankerson was trying to keep track of the chronology. "Was this before or after your house got broken into?"

"My house got broken into after I got the file and made the copy."

"So that's what they were looking for?"

"Maybe," Gray said, "But I don't understand why, looked at every page of that file and didn't see anything."

"When this investigator was here, did you tell her any of this?"

Gray shook his head. "No."

Hankerson rubbed his chin, thinking. "None of it."

"Nothing," Gray said.

"That could be another problem." Hankerson turned and began walking back to Gray's house. "I'm not trying to sound harsh, you're a friend, but you should've never talked to that cop, never."

Gray got a little testy. "I know that. I'm a lawyer, just like you."

"But unlike me, you talked to them," Hankerson said. "Cops and the FBI love to play this game where they ask you questions, and if you don't answer or tell a half-truth, they blow it up into an obstruction of justice charge."

"Intellectually I knew that," Gray said, "but it's different in real life. I thought I could just make it go away."

"Because you're an educated white guy, you thought the advice didn't apply to you," Hankerson said, "but that isn't how it works. Never talk to a cop."

"Do you think I should call her now?"

Hankerson shook his head.

"No," he said. "Wait a little bit and let's see how it plays out. Maybe it'll go away."

"And if it doesn't?"

"Call me first," Hankerson said, "and don't say another word to them. I'll poke around, and then I might have to call in some backup. I do mostly state stuff. This is federal. I don't think the feds will respect me, and I know for a fact that they won't fear me. We're just little ants that they have no problem stepping on while on the path to get to wherever they're going."

Herbert Bloom gave his keys to the valet and walked into the Missouri Athletic Club. The old man was still filled with pride every time he entered the historic building. The "MAC" as its members called it, had occupied the corner of Washington and Fourth since 1903. As a boy, the MAC seemed like a midwestern version of Buckingham Palace. It was a place for the powerful, a place that he desperately wanted to belong. This was where deals were made, and the rich got richer.

After toiling for years, Herbert Bloom was eventually given a chance. At that time, it wasn't a matter of simply paying a fee online for a yearly membership. The Missouri Athletic Club was exclusive. A gentleman needed to be invited to apply by a current member, and then approved by the club's executive committee. Once accepted, there was a probationary period and then, eventually, a full membership.

Bloom still remembered the first day he walked through its front doors. It was as memorable to him as his wedding day, and, although such clubs were now somewhat out of fashion and in no position to deny admission to anyone willing to pony-up the fee, he still loved the place.

Herbert Bloom strolled through the entrance, greeting most of the employees by name and randomly giving a nice tip to this person or that. He, then, rode the elevator up to the third floor, and walked down a hallway to his private office. The MAC was known for its gym, restaurant, bar, hotel and grand ballrooms, but there were also a few private offices tucked here and there. The office Herbert Bloom used had once belonged to the brewing magnet Adolphus August Anheuser Busch. Now it was Bloom's refuge. A quiet place to work without disturbance.

The sun was setting as Bloom opened an electronic folder related to his son's political campaign. It contained draft speeches, polling data, and, of course, financial information. Thomas, his eldest, was doing well, but he thought that he should be doing better. They were burning through money, and they'd need more to get the remaining players on board.

Herbert made it a priority to know and understand the community organizations and charities favored by nearly every local politician and party leader. He strongly encouraged Thomas to be present at any fundraising gala or year-end party, showing support and interest. If the politician or party leader was a high priority target, Bloom made sure his son also provided a generous donation. Herbert Bloom didn't need everybody to know where the money came from to fix up the community center's gymnasium, recarpet a church's community room, or provide new uniforms and equipment for a neighborhood baseball or football team, but it was important that the person on his list knew what they had done.

In addition to the political files, the computer was also linked to the law firm and all its accounting and administrative files. Herbert Bloom may have been old and dying, but his mind was still sharp. He began clicking through the law firm's accounting and administrative files when there was a knock on the door.

"Who is it?" His tone was sharp. Staff were instructed to never disturb him, and he didn't appreciate the interruption.

"It's me."

The old man recognized the voice. He shut down the computer, returned the security fob to its box on the mantel, and then opened the door. Herbert looked at Ethan with disdain. "This better be important."

"It is." Ethan shuffled into the room, like a dog. "I wouldn't have come if it wasn't."

CHAPTER THIRTY

There were no further incidents at Gray's house, windows were replaced and the house reverted to its previous form. There were also no more answers or explanations. Cassie never called, and neither Amy Wirth nor the FBI knocked on Gray's door. That did not, however, mean that the days were quiet and uneventful. In fact, Gray's professional life spiraled.

It began with his magnetic key card. The card had somehow become demagnetized and had to be replaced. Gray's computer was then infected with malware, causing the screen to freeze and random websites to pop-up, selling everything from Viagra to desktop air conditioners. After the fourth time that the malware was removed and his software reinstalled, Gray's contacts, which contained the addresses and phone numbers for his clients, disappeared and couldn't be recovered.

He fell behind as deadlines approached. He tried reviewing and approving his associate's billing records as well as the final invoices sent to clients, but had trouble concentrating. He noticed that Jack Durell was charged for more time on an associate's research memorandum for the Triangle file, even after he'd declined to authorize the bill and had told the associate that they couldn't bill the file for it, but Gray forgot to follow through with accounting. The invoice was sent.

At night, Gray had trouble sleeping, took a pill, and then had trouble waking up, and so he took a different pill to wake himself up. The amphetamine came from a small stash of

Adderall for his daughter, Zoe, who had ADHD. There was hesitation, at first, but, as things continued to get worse, he rationalized the behavior, knowing it was wrong, but not sure what else he could do.

Gray called Doctor Craig and Doctor Jax multiple times. Emergency appointments were arranged, which took him out of the office and pushed him further back. The stress continued to build and mistakes continued to occur. Emails purportedly sent by clients never arrived. Changes to documents weren't saved, and Gray was late for three client meetings in two weeks. If he was a boxer, he'd be the bloodied man, stumbling around the ring. It was only a matter of time before he was knocked cold.

As he sat in his office, the door closed and lights off, Gray vacillated between anger and depression. He searched for answers and explanations, but never found clarity. Nothing made sense. He had thought that he was healing. The medication for PTSD that Dr. Jax had prescribed was working. He thought that he was getting better. Yet, all of a sudden, the number of mistakes and missteps increased, one after another, a snowball.

The phone interrupted his self-loathing. Gray looked down at the Caller ID. It was Herbert Bloom, and Gray knew exactly why the old man was calling. There was no need to delay the inevitable. He picked up the phone and was summoned to the conference room.

Just like the first meeting, there were four people present. Herbert Bloom, his son Ethan Bloom, Elaine Gregore from human resources, and Anthony Townes from Western Gate Mutual. And, just like the first meeting, Gray was in trouble.

He decided to take the lead. "I'm sorry." Gray looked around at each of them, hoping to see a sympathetic face. The closest was Ethan Bloom, but he looked more embarrassed than sympathetic. "I know that there have been a series of incidents over the past two weeks. I'm working on it, but, at the end of the day, the only person I can point the finger at is me. Ultimately I'm responsible."

"Obviously we have to respect your privacy, Mr. Wendt," Gregore said. "But it'd be easier to make accommodations for you, if we had a better understanding of what's really going on."

"I've seen my doctor and I went to a psychiatrist. I've got another appointment next week with her. I've already told you about the diagnosis for PTSD and maybe some of this is due to the concussion." Gray felt his heart beat a little faster, panic rising. "I'm trying."

"I know," Gregore said. "We've discussed it internally and with Mr. Townes from our insurance carrier, and we think it's best if you take a medical leave of absence from the firm."

"A leave of absence?" Gray sat up on the edge of his seat. "You're firing me?"

Gregore began to respond, but Herbert Bloom interrupted her.

"We're not firing you, Mr. Wendt," Herbert Bloom said. "We're protecting the firm and, most importantly, we're protecting you."

"We want to give you time to heal," Gregore added. "Obviously if your condition doesn't improve, then we'll have to figure out some mutually acceptable terms of separation."

"There are clauses in your partnership agreement related to situations such as this." Herbert Bloom folded his hands in front of him, and he outlined the plan to get rid of Gray just as Ethan had said. "By a simple majority vote of the executive committee, the firm would buy back your shares." Bloom flicked his hand as if it would be nothing but a stroke of the pen, which wasn't far from the truth. "Of course there may be further severance if you agree to waive any claims you may or may not have as well as sign a confidentiality agreement."

Gray leaned back. "Sounds like this is already a done deal."

"That's not true, Gray," Ethan said. "You're a good lawyer."

Ethan's comment was met with a harsh look from his father. With a shake of Herbert Bloom's head, Ethan was silenced. His father's control over the meeting was restored, and the protection of his beloved law firm was achieved once again.

"As my son was trying to say, but perhaps a little unartfully, was that you've always been a valued member of this firm," Herbert said, "And we wish you the very best in your recovery, and hope that you can return."

Gray felt he had no choice, but to nod his head and accept. Arguing with them wouldn't do any good, and maybe they were right. This wasn't working. "How long?"

Gregore looked at Townes. Then to Gray, "Ninety days. You can submit any information that you would like to the executive committee after ninety days, and then they will vote."

Gray sunk a little lower in his chair. The weight pushing him into dark corners. He wondered how he would explain this to Kendra and the kids, his family and his friends. Gray tried to look Gregore in the face, but couldn't muster the strength. He stared at his hands. "Anything else I should know?"

"Just one thing," Herbert Bloom said, and when Gray looked up he saw a tiny, cold smile form on the edges of the old man's mouth. "Your keys."

"You want the keys to my office?"

"Yes," Gregore said. "And the magnetic pass card and your computer will need to remain here."

"It's standard practice," the old man said. "While you're on leave, your remote access to the firm's files will also be frozen and you're not to contact any of the firm's clients. Ethan will be handling the day-to-day in your absence."

Gray looked across the table at Ethan Bloom, but Ethan avoided eye contact. He was looking down at a fresh legal pad, scribbling notes, as if the details of the meeting needed to be recorded. At the outset, Gray suspected that Ethan wanted his clients. It had seemed a little farfetched at the time, a desperate accusation, but now that was exactly what had occurred.

###

His car was filled with boxes, inside them were the framed diplomas, pictures, books, and conference giveaways collected over the years at Daniels & Bloom. His hands gripped the wheel, rigid and tight. Gray's mind was somewhere else as he drove past the intersection where he'd usually turn south, then past another. A light flashed from yellow to red, but he didn't stop. Cars honked, another screeched to a halt, avoiding a collision by inches.

Gray was oblivious. The noise barely registered. The car kept going. His mind was underwater. Nothing was automatic. The electricity in his brain that normally carried a command from one synapse to another was shut off. It was all broken. The color of his hands, still tightly gripping the steering wheel, had turned a light shade of purple.

He didn't even know where to begin. The thought of sorting through the aftermath overwhelmed him. Supposedly it was just a ninety day medical leave, but he knew that was just a ruse. The leave of absence gave human resources time to paper his file, document his failures, and mitigate the firm's exposure to a wrongful termination or discrimination lawsuit. It was over. His career had ended in a meeting that lasted less than ten minutes.

Gray's mind sunk further into a fog, like he was just drifting down a river, gentle waves carrying him and his buddies through the Mark Twain National Forest. His body becoming even lighter as old memories rushed beneath him, lifting him up. Those times may not have been simpler, but peace was easier to come by: a lazy day on the water under the bright Missouri sun, an innertube with a few friends and a couple pretty girls, along with a smaller tube with a cooler of Bud tied with a rope, dragging behind. Gray took another breath and everything went dark, until he heard the Irish lilt.

"Wake up, son." The voice was comforting, and had the opposite effect. Gray fell deeper. "Come on, boy, wake up." This time is was harsh. Then there was a scream, and a slap across his face. "Wake up boy."

Gray opened his eyes. His car barreled toward the intersection of Market and 18th at fifty miles an hour. The traffic light in front of him was red, and Gray was seconds away from T-boning a large white delivery truck.

Both feet slammed the brakes. The back of his car slid into a slow spin, as the tires screeched. The boxes, which contained all of the personal items from his office, flew off the back seat. Some hit the back of his head and the dashboard, other items fell onto the floor. Horns sounded from all around him, and Gray pulled the steering wheel back, like it was the reins on a horse, but the car kept going. It kept sliding, and Gray was sure that he was going to die.

Then it stopped. Everything stopped.

The side of the truck was close. Gray thought that the front of his car and the side of the truck might actually be touching. He peeled his hands off of the steering wheel. His fingers sore, and the palms bloodied from where Gray's nails had cut through.

He unbuckled his seatbelt and stepped out of his car as the other driver emerged from the delivery truck's cab. The driver spewed all manner of cuss words that Gray didn't register, just a barking dog. Both of the men looked at where the two vehicles kissed. There was no damage.

A woman unrolled her window and screamed. "Get outta the road."

The truck driver looked at her and told her to shut up, and then to Gray, "You drunk or something?"

Gray shook his head. "Bad day." Gray rubbed his bloodshot eyes. "Got fired"

The truck driver snorted, but his edges smoothed. "Been there."

He took his big hand and put it on Gray's shoulder as traffic backed up even further and horns continued to sound. "If you'd-a-gone hit me, then you'd-a had a really bad day, know what I mean?" Then he took a step back. One hand formed a fist like a mallet and he rubbed that fist into the palm of the other, an exaggerated movement, like a 1920s silent movie villain.

Then the trucker smiled. "But I got no damage. So better get while the gettin's good, 'fore the cops show up and start giving everybody tickets."

Gray looked, one more time, at where the impact would've been. It didn't take much to imagine the damage. The hood would've given way as his car would've continued to slide forward. Momentum would have pushed his car under, shearing off the roof and probably Gray's head, before the trucks large back tires crushed him.

Maybe that was what Gray wanted.

An uneasy calm settled upon Gray on his drive home. He wasn't sure of what he was going to do, but he couldn't stop thinking about the large assortment of pills in his kitchen cabinet. They were calling him. Their attraction was in the simplicity, and he felt the idea taking hold, so easy and clean.

As he crossed the highway, Gray thought about how many he'd have to take to do the job: twenty, forty, sixty? Could he do that? Was it possible to take too many, certainly people had, but could he? Gray didn't want to screw up his own suicide just like he'd screwed up everything else in his life. If he was going to do it, he needed to be certain. How pathetic would it be for him to Google such information?

Gray wiped a tear from his eye. He was, now, less than a half mile from his house. He pulled the car to the side of the road and pressed a button on the dash. Hazard lights came on with a steady, hypnotic click every time they flashed.

He took a deep breath, trying to process, but his mind was scrambled. Then Gray got out his phone and called Doctor Jax. It was a long shot, but he was still disappointed when she didn't answer.

"The office is currently closed. If this is an emergency," the recorded message began, "go to the hospital or call 911."

Gray thought about that, driving himself to the hospital and checking himself in. Barnes Jewish wasn't far. St. Louis University's hospital was even closer. Surely they'd take him. Blacking out, almost dying in a car accident, hearing voices, believing an elf gifted him a rabbit's foot, and wanting to ingest a handful of pills certainly seemed to qualify as an emergency, but Gray wasn't convinced. Emergencies were a sudden circumstance that put a person at risk, but this was more like something that had been building over time.

He had never been a happy guy. There was always darkness in his mind, and now that darkness just eclipsed everything else. All he knew for sure was that if he went home and went to sleep, he'd never wake up. So Gray resisted the urge.

He just drove around. Hours passed. Somewhere along Manchester Road he stopped at a Sonic for a burger, onion rings, and a chocolate shake. The combo meal went down fast and easy; gone in minutes, but the smell of grease lingered in his car as he continued to drive. The food had settled him, a little, and he decided that he'd go to the Triangle.

There was activity in the camp. A couple police officers stood by the fence. News trucks from the local stations had illegally parked on the street, and not particularly well. A gaggle of reporters huddled together, gossiping while one smoked. In the distance, there was a camera crew following city employees around as they handed out pieces of paper and talked to people about what would happen in the coming days.

Gray didn't need to see the piece of paper to know what it said. It was an eviction notice that he and the lawyers at Daniels & Bloom had drafted. Gray also didn't need to hear the conversations to know what the city employees were saying, since he was the one who had created the plan and set it in motion.

Whether voluntarily or by force, everybody would be gone by the weekend. There was space in an industrial area near the river, north of downtown. The land itself was probably toxic, but that didn't matter. It was where the city had ultimately decided to set up temporary shelter for the displaced residents of the Triangle.

When he had proposed it, the bureaucrats and politicians were excited. The location was perfect. Out of sight and far away from any voters who may complain about their new neighbors. Like most rust belt cities, the St. Louis riverfront wasn't set aside for the rich and famous. The Mississippi was a polluted working river. Going all the way back thousands of years to the native Americans who lived at Cahokia, it was the original superhighway, albeit a much prettier one.

The plot of land designated for the homeless was between an abandoned battery factory and a ten acre lot used to store, load and distribute thousands of shipping containers from Asia that arrived in St. Louis by barge, train, and truck. After some negotiations, Daniels & Bloom had arranged for containers of a different kind to fill the space. Fifty FEMA trailers on loan from the federal government until the next hurricane season—surrounded by six foot high cyclone fencing— awaited their new occupants.

A prison for the unwanted.

Gray got out of his car and walked across the street to the fence. The homeless encampment looked just like it did on television, except bigger and much colder. There were well over a hundred tents. Each pitched wherever there was space. It wasn't a clean grid, like a park campground. There were no clear paths or roads leading to a particular destination. It was more organic, like refugees gathering on the edge of a war zone.

Maybe they were, thought Gray. Although there may not have been a war, they were certainly refugees of some sort of conflict, a broken health care system, perhaps, or just an economy that's left them behind.

When the wind changed, Gray was hit with a sweet, sour smell. It was like rotting fruit. He walked toward the opening in the fence where he'd seen others coming and going. Somebody had cut the steel fencing and pulled it back. Gray ducked through the hole, looked both ways, and then crossed the on-ramp to the other side.

Gray didn't know how he was going to find the Irish Santa among the jumble of tents, but he felt pulled toward the grove of trees in the distance. He kept walking, stepping carefully around garbage and tent poles. Gray looked back over his shoulder. It didn't take long to disappear. Where he had come from was no longer visible. He was immersed.

The intermittent smell that he caught as he entered was now constant and thick. The further he went into the encampment, it also got louder. In addition to the city workers handing out leaflets, there were radios playing, generators humming, and babies crying.

Gray walked through another series of tents. A woman brushed snow off the top of a large blue tarp that covered her tent even further, while a group sat around a small fire. Each were covered with multiple blankets. They were passing a joint from one to the other.

When the woman saw Gray, she smiled. "Got any food coming?"

Gray stopped, a little unsure how to respond. She must've assumed that he was a volunteer. In the Durell file, it indicated that there were some local churches bringing soup and sandwiches out to the encampment every day. "Not right now," Gray stuttered. "I think it's coming."

She looked disappointed.

Gray took a step away, but stopped. "I'm looking for an older man. He has a white beard, Irish accent."

She smiled, a couple teeth missing. "Everybody knows him, makes things happen." She pointed toward the grove. "Lives up there in the big green tent. You're going in the right direction, can't miss it."

The woman was right. Gray couldn't miss it. The big green tent was like a castle, four times larger than the others. It was a sturdy Army tent with green canvas and a wooden frame rather than light metal poles. It sat at the top and in the center of the grove, looking down at the rest of the Triangle with the lights of the St. Louis skyline as a dramatic backdrop.

There was a line out the door. Gray assumed that they were all people waiting to see the same man he was looking for, people wanting him to make something happen.

Gray stood near the back of the line, watching as others were allowed to enter the tent only after someone else left. The man guarding the door was large, built like a bouncer. His hair was black and pulled into a ponytail, and his dark eyes scanned the people in front of him, alert for trouble.

A few minutes later, Gray felt a poke. He turned, didn't see anyone, and then looked down. It was a little person, he wasn't much over four and a half feet. Gray recognized him, immediately. This was the man who flagged down the ambulance, who he'd seen in the background of the television news report, and who he met with on the bridge and gave him a white rabbit's foot. Except, he wasn't dressed like an elf or dressed in a fancy velvet jacket. He was tired and dirty. His winter coat was thin and ripped, and his eyes were sunken.

If the little man recognized Gray, he didn't show it. The only expression on his face was one of skepticism. "What do you want?" His brow furrowed. His eyes filled with contempt. "He already met with you guys, and we're not leaving."

"What?"

"You're here to try and convince us to leave, right?" He put his hands on his hips. "Well the answer is the same one you all got this morning—we ain't leaving."

Gray didn't know quite how to respond. "I'm not with the city. I'm not really…"

The little man folded his arms across his chest. "Not really? What's that supposed to mean?" He shook his head, as if it all made sense now. "You're some do-gooder, come to see how you can help the less fortunate. Is that it?"

"I….," Gray searched for something coherent to say. "I bake bread. You're right. I'm a do-gooder, and I have this big oven and I thought maybe I could bake some bread."

The little man considered this, skeptical.

"The food that's served here is distributed by Redeemer Church, they get it from all sorts of different places. Call them. They'll take whatever you got." He turned and began to walk away. "Now go."

"The older man with a white beard and an Irish accent." Gray followed him, put a hand on his shoulder, and then took a twenty dollar bill out of his wallet. "I'd like to talk to him."

The little man looked at the cash and smirked.

"Is this like some type of bribe?" He laughed. "I don't think so."

"Listen," Gray said. "It's important that I talk with him."

"Well he's busy," the little man said. "Look around. We're all busy. It isn't a good time."

"I only want to talk with him, briefly." Gray lowered his voice. "It's a personal matter."

"I thought you just baked bread." The little man's eyes narrowed, and he stepped closer. He examined Gray closely. "Or was that a lie. If you come on behalf of the developer, you can forget it. Ain't no private deals. You'd be wasting your time if you think you can buy him off. He isn't going to abandon all these people. They need him."

"I don't want to buy him off. I'm..." Gray looked around for help, but there wasn't anyone who was going to intervene. Gray tried, again, to plead his case. "I really need to talk with...."

"Well it ain't happening, buddy, get lost." The argument had escalated now, and people were beginning to notice.

Gray, now frustrated, took a step toward the tent.

"I wouldn't do that." The little man's voice was loud and strong, and it caught the attention of the bouncer. The giant eyed Gray, ready to intervene. "You're going to get yourself hurt."

"I just...." Gray struggled to find the words, then took a step back. "You're right," Gray said. "I shouldn't be here."

"Now you're getting smart."

"I apologize." Gray held out his hand to shake, like a little kid at the end of a t-ball game. "I didn't catch your name."

"I didn't offer it." The little man looked at Gray's out-stretched hand, but refused to accept it.

"Well, I'm Gray." He crouched down so that they were at eye level with one another. "And I think we've met before."

The little man shook his head. "Don't think so."

"I don't blame you for not recognizing me, but I recognize you." Gray lowered his voice, as if sharing a secret. "It was the night of the big snowstorm just before Thanksgiving. You and the man in that tent were downtown. My friend was killed. I was on the ground bleeding. And *you* flagged down an ambulance while he held me in his arms."

The little man didn't say anything, but his eyes betrayed the truth—a blink, a quick look to the side, and then back, again. Gray didn't understand why he was so hesitant to admit where he was and what he'd seen, but he wasn't talking. Perhaps, as a homeless man, he knew better than to admit that he was at the scene of a shooting, a high probability that he and the man in the tent would become suspects, easy targets to take the blame.

Gray held out another twenty dollar bill. "You both saved my life."

The little man took it from Gray and put the money in his pocket with minimal examination. His eyes scanned his surroundings the whole time. It wasn't safe to be seen with cash. He, then, took a step back.

"Well, you ain't getting in now," he said. "Come back some other time."

Come back some other time, Gray thought about the bottle of pills waiting for him. He didn't have time. He needed to talk now, but there was no way. The giant at the door continued to stare in his direction, and looked as if he was eager for a fight.

After some hesitation, Gray stepped back. "Sure." He bowed his head, slightly in surrender. "Some other time."

Gray must've looked like hell when he appeared on Midge and Haley's doorstep long after midnight, because neither hesitated when he asked if he could, "crash at their place." Haley's eyes softened, and she put her arm around his shoulder as she guided him through the door and up the steps.

"Do you need anything else?" Midge asked.

"No," Gray said, nearing the top step. "I just can't be alone right now."

"Well," Haley said, "You know where we are."

"Thanks." Gray entered the spare bedroom, closed the door, and took off all his clothes except his undershirt and boxers. He walked into the bathroom—the same one he'd sullied after the Thanksgiving party— splashed warm water on his face, and then climbed into the sturdy old bed. The springs creaked as he rolled over on his side and he turned out the light.

He decided that he didn't have to figure everything out. He just needed to survive, one day at a time, as his heavy eyelids closed. When they opened, again, it was the next day.

Gray laid in bed for about an hour, thinking, and then he heard a car on the street below. The engine stopped, one of the car doors opened and shut with a creak, and then he heard knocking. The person wasn't knocking on Midge and Haley's door. The person was next door, at his house.

Gray flipped off the sheets and walked over to the window. It was a man, wiry and strong, and he was wearing a suit and long overcoat. He knocked, again, on Gray's front door, then the man in the overcoat went over to the window and looked inside.

He waited another second or two, and then removed something from his pocket. He stuck it on the door. It was probably a business card, thought Gray, as he watched the man step down from the porch and walk back to his vehicle.

Gray watched as he drove away, and then Gray picked his clothes up off the floor and got dressed. Midge and Haley were in the living room, reading the newspaper and drinking coffee. Gray held out a finger, preempting any inquiries or small talk. "I'll be right back."

Gray went out the front door and walked over to his house. In the doorframe, the man had, as Gray had guessed, left a business card. Gray noticed the official seal first, and then read the name:

Agent Charlie Matthews
Federal Bureau of Investigation

CHAPTER THIRTY-ONE

By the time the doorbell rang the next morning, Gray had five freshly baked loaves of bread and a notepad filled with notes and questions. Gray got up from the kitchen table, walked to the front of the house, and opened the door. It was Tad Hankerson and he'd brought a friend.

"This is Naomi Moyo." Hankerson introduced the woman standing next to him. She was a tall, thin woman. "Like I said before, you need somebody with federal experience. Naomi used to work for the Department of Justice in D.C., and I think she's in a much better position to help you then I ever will."

Gray held out his hand and introduced himself. "Please call me Gray." They shook hands, and then he stepped to the side so that Hankerson and Moyo could come inside the house. "Let me take your coats, and thank you both for coming on such short notice."

"Not a problem." When Moyo spoke, she had a faint accent. As she handed Gray her coat, she examined the living room. "You have a beautiful home."

"I love the woodwork and it's a great neighborhood." Gray hung the coats in the front closet. "Please have a seat. Would either of you like some coffee?"

"I'd love some coffee." Moyo walked over to one of the chairs in front of the fireplace and sat down.

"Coffee sounds great for me too," Hankerson said. "And I'll never turn down your bread, if you have any."

"Of course I have fresh bread." Gray disappeared into the kitchen for a few minutes, and returned with a french press filled with coffee, sliced bread, and several small jars filled with jam, butter, and honey. They talked a little about their backgrounds.

"I worked for the Department of Justice in Washington, then my husband was offered a tenure track position at Washington University," Moyo said. "Those have become increasingly rare, and my extended family is in Nashville, so this is a little closer to my parents than D.C.. It'll make it easier as they get older and might need me more."

"Well, I appreciate your willingness to help. I'm not a criminal lawyer." He passed Agent Matthews's card to Moyo. "When I got this, I followed Hankerson's advice and called and left a message that I was represented by counsel."

"That is good." Moyo smiled, trying to be reassuring. "You were under no obligation to call right away, but there may come a point when you need to talk to them."

"The problem," Gray said, "is that I'm not exactly sure what they're investigating. I'm worried that...." He felt his thoughts cascading from one to the other, but bit his tongue. "I don't know where this is going."

Moyo held out her hand.

"It's okay." She sat up a little straighter, taking control. "Law enforcement and prosecutors are mostly hard-working people who are trying to do the right thing, but they get fixated on a theory of the case, and, once they have their mind set, it is difficult to get that original theory to change. Part of it is ego, and part of it is that, nine times out of ten, their theories are correct." She looked at Tad Hankerson, briefly, and then turned her attention back to Gray. "When I talked with Tad, it sounds like they're probably investigating bribery or money laundering, and, if that's true, it's unlikely that Virgil Hawthorne was acting alone. It's only logical for them to think that you would be involved as well."

"I know it might be logical," Gray said, "but it's not true. I didn't even talk with a …"

Moyo held out her hand. "I'm not the one you need to convince. This is where we have to develop a plan. First, I'm going to follow-up with Agent Matthews and let him know that I represent you. Usually when an attorney gets involved it slows things down, and I can also try and get more information about the scope of their investigation and their targets."

"Won't that make me look guilty?" Gray asked.

"To be frank, Mr. Wendt, we're way beyond that," Moyo said. "You have to assume that they've been watching you for a long time. You have to assume they have every email, text, and cell phone record from the last year, perhaps longer. You have to assume they have all of your bank records. For Agent Matthews to come to your house, in the manner he did, that isn't something the FBI does at the beginning of an investigation when they may be worried that documents or other evidence will disappear. It is more likely that they are now at the end of their investigation, and the prosecutor, if he or she hasn't already, is about to convene a grand jury and obtain criminal indictments."

Gray absorbed the information as his stomach churned. To hear someone confirm that he was, in fact, on the precipice of being arrested and losing what little he had left.

"Mr. Wendt." Moyo noticed that Gray's focus had become more distant. "Do you want me to continue?"

Gray nodded his head, slightly, and so Moyo continued.

"Good," she said. "We need to think strategically." Moyo pointed at Gray's notepad. "When I talk to Agent Matthews, I am also going to ask for a meeting with them and I'll want you at that meeting."

"I don't think I want to go."

Moyo smiled, comforting. "It's ultimately your choice," Moyo said. "But I really want you to hear what they say, rather than rely on me to summarize it. There may be an off-hand comment that I don't think is important, but you know is significant. This is not a meeting where you talk. This is a meeting where we listen. Hopefully it will give us some clarity about the crimes that they believe have been committed."

Gray looked at Hankerson, and his friend nodded his head. "You're paying for her advice," he said. "You need to take it."

"Okay," Gray said, "and then what?"

"We try and figure out a way to prove your innocence," Moyo said. "And, in the process, we need to gather so much information and evidence related to this scheme that Agent Matthews and the Department of Justice offer you immunity in return for your cooperation. That's the goal."

"I've only got one file," Gray said. "It was at Virgil's house, but I've already looked at it, and there's nothing there."

"Then you need to look again," Moyo said. "And you need to pull the other files that you and Virgil had worked on over the years. The proof has to be in those files."

Gray shook his head. "But I don't have access to them anymore." Hankerson and Moyo exchanged looks of confusion, and so Gray explained. "They put me on medical leave," he said. "They took my pass card to get into the building, my laptop, and my remote access to the law firm's computer network was also suspended."

Moyo's eyebrow raised. "When did this happen?"

"A couple days ago."

"And then Matthews came to visit," Moyo said.

Gray nodded.

"Convenient," Moyo said. "Very convenient."

CHAPTER THIRTY-TWO

Although it ran counter to his frugal nature, Gray cashed out a large portion of his retirement account. If he was going to fight, he needed a good attorney and Moyo was impressive. Every time he spoke with her, Gray felt a little of her strength transfer to him. She gave him hope, and the idea of solving his problem with a handful of pills became less and less attractive, although he still considered it an option.

As promised Moyo had spoken with Agent Matthews, and then with the Assistant United States Attorneys that had been assigned to the case, Colton Steele and Amber Brenner. Neither provided her with meaningful information, but Agent Matthews agreed to meet with them in a week. Moyo and Gray had also discussed Cassie at length, and Gray decided that he'd hire a private investigator to track her down. Moyo recommended a firm from northern Virginia on the outskirts of Washington D.C., a mix of former military and law enforcement agents that used to work for an alphabet soup of federal agencies. They were expensive, but Moyo was confident they'd be able to find her.

"Because they're no longer law enforcement," Moyo said, "they have more tools at their disposal. Less rules."

Gray had no reason to disagree, and, because his second and third review of the Bevo Development file was just as unenlightening as his first review, he was getting desperate.

"Let's talk a little bit more about the files," Moyo said. "I need you to make a list of every client and development deal that you can remember, then see if you can recall any details, particularly interactions with inspectors or politicians. We need names. In the meantime, we can pull newspaper articles and any filings related to those properties from the city."

Gray agreed, but was doubtful. "I push that information out of my mind as quickly as I can once the deal is done."

"Well," Moyo said, "You're going to have to try. We don't know what will be helpful to Agent Matthews, and, even if it's just a confirmation that the firm was involved in a deal in some way, that could have value for them as well as the prosecutors."

"Okay," Gray said. "I get it."

"And I need you to make a copy of the electronic Bevo Development file and bring it to me," she said. "After the break-in, it's not good that you have the only copy. And really think about whether there are any other papers or documents related to anything in your possession. Anything."

"Like I told you," Gray said, "it's been all electronic for years. They took my laptop when I went on leave, but I'll look around."

The FBI offices in St. Louis were located in a modern three story building not far from Union Station. Although there was some effort made to make the room feel like a regular conference room, because it had wood paneling, padded conference chairs, and a heavy oak table—it obviously wasn't. There were no pictures on the wall. There were no plants. There was no phone, and no windows. Gray, then, saw a small camera in the corner, and he wondered who all was watching and listening.

"Bottle of water?" Matthews asked. "It wouldn't be a problem."

"No, thank you," Gray said, and Moyo also declined.

"Okay." Matthews took a small digital recorder out of his pocket. "Do you mind if I record this?"

A lump formed in Gray's throat. "I don't mind."

"Good." Agent Matthews pressed a button on the recorder. "This is Agent Matthews of the Federal Bureau of Investigation." He gave the date, time, and location. "I'm meeting with Graydon Wendt this morning along with his attorney Naomi Moyo." Matthews looked up at Gray. "Mr. Wendt, I spoke with your attorney not long after I had dropped by your house and left my card at your door. I have some questions for you, informally, but your attorney indicated that you both would rather have a more formal meeting, is that right?"

"Yes," Gray said, "we discussed it."

He and Moyo had also discussed the slight chance that he would be leaving this meeting in handcuffs and not returning home, but Gray pushed that scenario away and kept his answers short and to the point.

"Okay." Matthews continued with a paraphrased Miranda warning. He was trying to keep the tone casual and friendly, but a recitation of one's Constitutional rights generally did not lower an individual's blood pressure. "And you're a lawyer, so you understand that you have a right to remain silent and that any statements you make could be held against you and that you also have a right to a lawyer, correct? And, in fact, you have retained a lawyer to represent you."

"I understand my rights." Gray looked past Matthews at the door. "As well as my right to get up and leave at any time, correct?"

There was a long pause before Matthews answered. "Of course." He removed a pad of paper from his briefcase as well as a pen. On the top of the piece of paper, he wrote Gray's name. "Do you know why I came to your house?"

"I can only speculate," Gray said.

"No idea at all?"

This was a trap. If they can get Gray to admit to anything at all then they can paint a picture of Gray's involvement.

This was when Moyo intervened. She put her hand on Gray's arm, protecting him.

"As we talked about on the phone," she said to Matthews. "My client and I have some general ideas, but we're actually here to listen to you and figure out how we can be of assistance to your investigation. I'd hate for anything my client may say to be misinterpreted, because we don't actually know what you're investigating or who you're investigating."

Agent Matthews did a good job of hiding his disappointment. Usually he was able to get a few more questions answered before a defense attorney put a stop to it, but he took it in stride. This was expected.

"The FBI was provided information related to an alleged bribery of some city officials, and we were in the process of investigating those allegations when Virgil Hawthorne was killed." Matthews paused, and then looked at Gray. "You worked closely with Mr. Hawthorne, and so it stands to reason that you may have knowledge about what was going on."

Gray wanted to say something in response, defend himself, but Moyo tightened her grip on his arm. They had a plan, and she was going to stick to it. "I know you can't or won't provide me with details, but certainly you can narrow the scope of abstraction. My client and Mr. Hawthorne worked on hundreds of files over the years."

"Okay," Matthews said. "Bevo Development."

Gray's heart sunk, and he remained silent as Moyo continued to press. "What about it?" She asked. "As I stated on the phone, my client is eager to help your investigation."

Matthews looked over his shoulder, as if he was about to do something he shouldn't do, but both Gray and Moyo knew it was an act. He was too experienced to make mistakes. Matthews said, "The FBI has been requesting the file for months. I'd like to know why Mr. Wendt had it in his possession and wouldn't disclose it to us, and what, if anything, he removed from the file."

Gray almost sprung out of his seat in protest, but he controlled himself, keeping his mouth shut as his anger grew. The only reason he went to get the file was because Ethan Bloom had asked him to go. He didn't even know it was missing, and certainly didn't know that the FBI had subpoenaed the firm to produce the file to them.

Moyo said, "I'm sure the client, Bevo Development, would have all the information in that file and would be in a position to waive any attorney-client privilege. You could've gotten it from them."

"I'm afraid not," Matthews said. "The CEO has been missing for some time and he must've taken the paperwork. His whereabouts are unknown. We don't even know if he is alive." Before the bombshell had time to settle, Matthews turned to Gray, "Were you aware that your client was under investigation at the time you took the file?"

Matthews waited for an answer, but Gray remained silent, so he pressed forward. "And that he was looking at going to prison for quite some time, but his attorney had made us an offer." Matthews looked at Moyo. There was an intensity in his eyes, a hunter staring at his prey. "The offer was a reduction in his sentence if he provided evidence of bribes and money laundering facilitated by Virgil Hawthorne as well as yourself."

"No," Gray shook his head, "I didn't know that, and I think this meeting is done."

"I agree." Moyo stood. "We'll talk soon."

"Obviously you can leave," Matthews said, "but you're in trouble, Mr. Wendt, and if you cooperate now then I can help you."

"I've got to go." As Gray turned and walked toward the door, he put his hands in his pockets, so that Matthews wouldn't see them shake.

"Think long and hard about what happens next." Then Matthews hit Gray with a final jab. "What happened to Cassie Hawthorne?" he asked. "Where did she go?"

Gray paused a half second, but wasn't able to respond. Moyo had her arm around him and ushered him out the door.

###

Amy Wirth sat in a small room down the hallway from where Agent Matthews, Gray and Moyo met. Video was relayed via a closed circuit system to a large flat screen television that had been mounted on the wall. Wirth took down some notes, but she wasn't particularly interested in the content of the discussions or answers to the questions. Wirth, instead, studied Gray's body language and demeanor. She tried to observe everything, regardless of how seemingly insignificant. Agent Matthews was certain that Gray was a key player in the bribery scheme, but she wasn't so sure.

She'd largely kept her doubts to herself. It ran against her very nature to hold back, but she didn't want Matthews to think that she wasn't on the same team. She was so close to escaping the harassment and marginalization, and she didn't want to jeopardize her chances to get out. Her application had been submitted. Wirth knew she was a finalist for the position at the bureau, but, even if she got it, at what cost?

Wirth watched as the meeting abruptly concluded, as Gray was led by his attorney out the door as Matthews tossed out allegations. He looked genuinely shaken. Although she'd seen the sworn statements of co-conspirators, as well as the files and billing statements implicating Gray, Wirth couldn't shake the feeling that she was looking at a unicorn. Could it be that Graydon Wendt was an innocent man?

In a few minutes, Matthews would want to talk about the interview, and she couldn't just stand-by and allow a potentially innocent man to be indicted for something he didn't do. There was a difference between right and wrong. There were no shortcuts or compromises. Wirth knew this, and knew that doing the right thing wasn't always rewarded. Having principles sometimes meant that it cost you. She had learned that the hard way.

Less than two years ago Wirth was just a cop on patrol. It was one of those classic summer nights in St. Louis. The day was hot and humid, and, even after the sun went down, there wasn't much relief. The heat hung tight to the asphalt, refusing to surrender to the night, like an invisible ceiling.

A call came across the radio from dispatch. She responded. Nothing spectacular, Wirth was just a backup for another officer's jump search at a bus stop near the corner of Garfield and Grand. As she had driven west across the city, the dispatcher relayed information, which appeared on the laptop mounted to the squad's dashboard. The suspect was only twenty years old, but already with a lengthy record of police contact and a couple felonies.

When she arrived the other squad had its lights flashing and the area was lit by its spotlight. Officer Timmy Cruz was in the thick. The suspect wouldn't stop talking, most likely high on something, so Cruz got impatient and a little rough. There was nobody else around except Cruz's partner, who stood about ten feet back and watched. His hand was on his side, ready with the taser if Cruz needed help.

There were a couple hard pushes into a brick wall, and then Cruz kneed the kid in the stomach, bringing the young dealer to the ground. Once the kid was face down on the sidewalk, still talking, Cruz pinned him hard and cuffed the kid tight. Wirth didn't approve. She wouldn't have done it that way, but she hadn't seen everything leading up to the interaction, just the end.

Her dad used to tell her, "Cops give cops the benefit of the doubt. Remember that, Amy. Trust in one another is all we got keeping us alive sometimes."

Wirth radioed her position to dispatch, informing them that the scene was clear, and waited for further instruction on where she should go next. In the meantime, she watched as Cruz put the suspect in the back of his squad, and then talked with his partner. She didn't hear what was said, but Wirth saw the two smile and laugh. Then Cruz retrieved a small cloth bag from under the squad's front seat.

She watched with some confusion as Cruz took the bag over to where the confrontation had occurred with the dealer. He crouched down, removed a small Taurus 9 millimeter, and put the gun in the suspect's backpack. With that, a small-time drug case, probably a misdemeanor, turned into something far different: an "ineligible felon in possession of a firearm." The firearm charge came with serious jail time, maybe prison.

It was a set-up.

When Officer Cruz stood, he noticed Wirth standing to the side for the first time. He stared at her and his face hardened. If it would've been a year earlier, maybe there would've been a different reaction, but times had changed. What gave Officer Cruz pause was the black box attached to Wirth's patrol uniform. It was one of only ninety body cameras issued by the department as part of a new pilot project. The whole thing was recorded on her body camera, and there was no way for the video to be deleted.

Even though Wirth hadn't volunteered to wear the camera, she had proof that a wrong had been committed. She saw what she saw, and notified the night-watch commander, providing him with the recording. The public outrage was swift and immediate, and the feeling among most in the Department was she had betrayed the brotherhood and would have to pay the price. The promotion to investigator was the set up for her to fail. Everybody knew it. Even officers who were sympathetic to Wirth's situation chose to stand aside out of fear of being brought down with her. Then the harassment started.

That was what Wirth was thinking about when Matthews entered the room.

"That guy is guilty," he said. "I can feel it." Matthews looked at Wirth, waiting for her affirmation, but it never came.

"I don't think so," she said, but with hesitation.

"What's that?"

"I'm not sure he's guilty," Wirth said. "The whole thing is off, like it's a set-up…. Too easy."

Matthews raised an eyebrow, surprised and a little taken aback. "You said that when we first met, but I didn't think you still believed that."

"I do," she said. "I talked to him right after he got home from the hospital, and he's just not a person who would get involved in something like this. You've gathered a lot of evidence, but it's all circumstantial."

Matthews looked a little offended. "You can indict and even convict a guy on circumstantial evidence," he said, "but the prosecutors are leaning hard on a couple developers and politicians. If one of them flips and agrees to testify, the case gets a lot stronger."

"So these people have independently said Graydon Wendt was orchestrating this thing?" Wirth shook her head in disbelief, unwilling to concede, "or are they just willing to say it in order to save themselves. There's a big difference. You could be convicting an innocent man." And with that little bit of defiance, she was certain that a potential job with the FBI had just vanished.

In the parking lot, Gray leaned against his car as Moyo tried to cheer him up.

"I know that was difficult," Moyo said, "but I'm glad you were there. I can explain some of these things, but nobody can truly understand until they experience it for themselves." Moyo looked back at the squat building filled with federal agents. "None of those people are getting rich. Agent Matthews is a true believer. I've heard he's a decent guy, but he's tenacious. If you say you're innocent, he wants proof."

Gray's shoulders sagged and he looked down at the ground. "I thought I was innocent until proven guilty."

"You know they don't think that way. We've talked about this." Moyo put her hand on his shoulder. "I'm sorry."

Gray looked up at her, resigned. "What's next?"

"Our plan stays the same," Moyo said. "I'll keep in touch with Matthews and the prosecutor."

"And me? What do I do?"

"Get me something that I can use to negotiate with them," Moyo said. "Anything. If I were the prosecutor on this case, I'd let us stew on this meeting for a few days, then I'd call, framing it as a courtesy. I'd casually let the defense attorney know that a grand jury was being summoned and an indictment was coming any day, and then leave it open. Say something like, 'if you've got anything to make me change my mind or analysis, now is the time.'"

Frustrated, Gray felt his hands ball into fists. "But they don't have anything, because I didn't do anything."

"The prosecutor, Colton Steele....he has a reputation as a risk taker," Moyo said. "Just given your relationship with Virgil Hawthorne, he can get an indictment even though the evidence is thin. He can paint a damning picture."

"Just because I worked with Virgil Hawthorne?"

"You've gotta understand," Moyo said, "This isn't like a civil case that goes directly to a judge and there's an opportunity to immediately challenge the complaint. Here, we have a grand jury proceeding and it's stacked in favor of the prosecution. There is no judge. There are no defense attorneys. There's nobody making the counter-argument or cross-examining the witnesses. It's just a prosecutor in a room with those jurors, alone, completely one-sided. If Colton Steele wants an indictment, he can get it. Trust me. It isn't hard, even with the thinnest case. Then, he'll be hoping to flip a developer or somebody like that who will point the finger at you."

"It doesn't seem very fair."

"Because it isn't fair," Moyo said. "That's why you need to give me something to try and stop this."

"I can't prove a negative," Gray said, "I feel like I'm just thinking about the same things, and doing the same things over and over again. I'm stuck."

"Why don't you try this," Moyo waited until Gray met her eye. "If *you* needed to bribe somebody to get a development deal done, how would you do it? Forget Virgil Hawthorne. Forget the files. Think about ways that you would do it, test it out. Maybe things will look differently."

"An envelope of cash," Gray said, only partially joking.

Moyo, however, didn't take it as a joke. "Could be, but what if the amount of money we're talking about is so large that it doesn't fit in an envelope? Based on what Matthews has said, Hawthorne was laundering it some way, moving money in a way that appeared normal and perfectly legal. "How would *you* do that?"

"And if I don't come up with anything?"

"Then just start making lists of names," she said. "Anybody you can remember. Give me lists of clients, attorneys, politicians, anybody who you regularly dealt with at the city. Those can be more valuable than you may think. It would give us something."

CHAPTER THIRTY-THREE

Gray made the lists as Moyo instructed. He sat in the breakfast nook of his kitchen for hours, scribbling notes. He could remember the names of eight large real estate development companies that he had done work for over the past twenty years, but he knew that was just a fraction. There were many more.

He tried to think of where the projects were located, hoping to spark a memory or two, but most of the projects ran together, specifics elusive. Developers were constantly researching properties, acquiring properties, and selling properties. Thousands of dollars were spent on architectural renderings and inspections for projects that never happened.

Gray had an even harder time with the names of people. He and Virgil Hawthorne had a pretty clear division of labor. Virgil did client management, not him. It wouldn't be uncommon for Gray to bill hundreds of hours on a matter, but never speak to the client.

He set his coffee cup down and pushed the paper to the side, realizing that if pieces didn't click into place fairly soon, Moyo wouldn't have much to offer in exchange for a deal beyond the electronic copy of the Bevo Development file. Nothing in it proved his innocence, and its value was unknown. An indictment would follow, and then jail.

Gray thought about that: custody, trial, prison. It was simultaneously both absurd and, yet, very real. Then he thought about the newspaper headlines, and the impact everything would have on his kids. They would know. Kendra would do her best to shield them, but it couldn't be hidden.

Nick and Zoe were still young, and Gray wondered if they'd forget a time when he was ever just a normal dad, grilling on the barbeque as they played in the sprinkler, sipping beer and laughing with their mother.

Gray, then, decided that he had to call her. Kendra was the last person he wanted to talk to, but she had little idea of what was going on and what may be coming in the near future. There was a time when they were very much in love. She was the one who supported him during law school. She was the one at his bedside after Virgil was killed, and, even though they were divorced, he didn't want to hurt her.

Gray took out his phone and pulled up her number, but stopped before pressing the little green dot on the screen. She probably wouldn't answer if his name popped up on her caller ID, so Gray decided to text first. He tapped out an initial draft, deleted it, and started, again, trying to get the tone right. It was urgent, but he didn't want to scare her. He kept it vague, and thankfully Kendra responded a few seconds later.

Kendra and her husband's house was built in a style that Gray often referred to as a "Fancy Ranch." It shared many of the same features of a typical ranch-style house—one story, open floor plan—but, in this part of the St. Louis suburbs, they supersized them on huge wooded lots. They didn't resemble their poorer cousins to the north in any way.

Gray pulled into the driveway, and it didn't take long for Nick and Zoe to notice his arrival. Zoe ran out the door without a jacket, but somehow did manage to get a pair of snow boots on her feet. Nick followed, and Gray greeted them both with huge bear hugs. He felt a surge of happiness, and never wanted to let them go.

"Are you staying for dinner?" Zoe asked.

Nick offered more incentive before Gray could respond. "5 cheese Mac and Cheese."

"Sounds delicious." Gray put his arm around Nick, and they walked up to the front door. "But we'll have to see what your mother says."

Kendra was waiting. She opened the door for them, and all three walked into the entryway. Before Gray could even say hello, Nick began to pester about dinner. "Can dad stay? Can he?"

Kendra exchanged a look with Gray, unsure of what her response should be. When Nick didn't stop, Gray put his hand on his son's shoulder.

"Why don't you let us talk first, and we'll see what happens. I might need to get a raincheck for another time."

Nick looked a little disappointed, but soon recognized the opportunity that had just presented itself. Children had an innate ability to sense chances to exploit their parents.

"Can Zoe and I play on the computer while you talk?"

Zoe also seized the moment. "Nick can do the iPad, and I can go on the laptop."

Kendra shrugged. "Fine," she said, "but only until dinner, and then all of the devices go back on the desk."

An instant cheer came from the kids, and they scattered as quickly as they came. Both Kendra and Gray watched, bemused, and then Kendra ushered Gray into the living room. It was modern and clean, a lot of white and black that appeared to be straight out of an Ikea catalog only it was likely from a place three times more expensive.

"Have a seat by the fireplace," Kendra pointed, "I'm going to get a glass of water. Do want anything?"

"Water would be great." Gray sat down. "Thank you." As Gray watched her in the kitchen, he asked about her husband.

"Working. He's always working, but he's got some resumes out. They don't pay him enough for what they expect." She began filling up the glasses. "We'll see where it goes. The grass isn't always greener."

A few seconds later Kendra was back in the living room. She set the glasses of water down on a coffee table, and then sat down on the sofa across from Gray. "So what's going on?" She asked. "Must be pretty serious if you were willing to come here."

She was right, of course. Gray hated driving out to Creve Ceouer and actively avoided coming into Kendra and Gary's house.

"It's a lot of things." As he thought about how to begin, Gray picked up the water glass, took a sip, and put it back down on the table in order to buy himself some time. "Mostly it's related to work."

"What about it?" Kendra asked.

Gray paused, and then told Kendra the first of what would be a series of revelations.

"I got placed on medical leave." Gray, then, told her about the warning he'd received from HR and the missed meetings. "The saddest part of the whole thing was that I genuinely thought I was getting better, you know? I was going to the doctor. My headaches weren't happening as frequently, but then it all sort of fell apart again."

"But they have to bring you back, right?"

"I don't think so," Gray said. "Ethan told me they'd been planning this for quite some time, and Herbert Bloom made it pretty clear that the executive committee can buy me out. He even told me there would be a nice severance package, if I go quietly."

"Can they do that?"

Gray nodded. "Pretty much. I think they can."

Kendra's face scrunched into a knot, a look of concentration and fight that Gray used to find adorable. "What about those laws, the ones that are supposed to protect people with medical conditions?" She genuinely cared, and Gray felt a little sad that he had assumed she wouldn't, a by-product of divorce that tainted his perceptions. He'd spent years rationalizing, and settled into a narrative: She was shallow and he was deep. It wasn't, however, that simple.

"The Americans With Disabilities Act requires accommodations, and they'd argue that showing up to meetings and getting work done on time are essential components of the job. It's not like building a ramp for somebody in a wheelchair who can still otherwise do the job," Gray said. "Plus, I don't even think that law applies. I'm not an employee of Daniels & Bloom. In theory, I'm a part owner, so I guess I'm discriminating against myself."

"It's not right," Kendra said. "You should fight it."

Gray took a deep breath, knowing that the potential loss of his job was probably the least of his problems. "I don't think I'm in much of a position to fight."

That's when he told Kendra that there was a very high likelihood that he'd be charged with a crime, and that ultimately he might end up in prison.

###

Gray stayed for dinner. For all he knew, he may wake up the next day to pounding on his front door, led away in handcuffs. He needed to take the opportunities to spend as much time with his kids as possible, even if it meant sitting around a dinner table with his ex-wife and her new husband.

When all the kielbasa was eaten and most of the Mac & Cheese was gone, Gray thanked Kendra and pushed away from the table.

Zoe said, "Don't go yet."

"I don't want to go, sweetie," Gray said. "But it's getting late."

"I want to show you my new house." When Gray looked puzzled, she giggled. "In Minecraft." She dashed from the dinner table, ran down the hall, and then returned with a laptop computer. "I've been working on it for weeks. It has a pool and everything."

Zoe booted up the laptop, opened the program, and was soon flying through a virtual world made of blocks. Minecraft was like a Lego-set with an infinite number of electronic blocks as well as ghosts, zombies, and dynamite.

"Here it is," she said, and Zoe began giving Gray the grand tour. "Look at all these cats. And I've got sheep too."

"In your living room?"

"Why not?" Zoe smiled. "In the game they don't poop."

This made Gray laugh as well as everybody else.

"It's perfect," Gray said. "Where'd you learn how to do all of that?"

"YouTube."

"Of course," Gray said. "Why didn't I think of that?" Gray exchanged looks with Kendra, and then checked his watch. "It really is getting late, sweetie. I better go."

Both the kids whined in response, but were out of ideas to further delay. Then, Kendra held out her hand, "And the laptop."

Zoe shut down the computer, walked over to her mother, and gave it to her. That's when Gray noticed the sticker. On the top of the laptop there was a small sticker that had a barcode and device number. He knew immediately what it was.

Three years earlier the law firm upgraded all of the firm's computers, printers and scanners. If an attorney wanted to buy their old laptop, the cost was minimal. Gray bought the laptop and gave it to the kids as a present, and never really gave it much further thought after that. In his mind, the laptop would maybe last a year before it was obsolete or broken, but it evidently still worked.

"Kendra," Gray said. "I think I might need to borrow Zoe's laptop for a little while."

CHAPTER THIRTY-FOUR

Gray sat in his kitchen with the shades drawn as he opened the old laptop. It took awhile, but eventually the screen flashed to life and a small fan began to whirl. While he waited, Gray fiddled with a small plastic stick with a metal USB port on one end. It was a jumpdrive, and he intended to get a copy of everything on the laptop.

When it had finished loading, Gray went to the computer's directory and scrolled through hundreds of old briefs and memoranda. It was still unclear what he was looking for, but Gray spent hours pulling up documents, reading a little of what was written, and then saving it onto the flash drive. On a notepad, he made a list of all of the individuals and companies involved in the transactions.

He never saw anything peculiar or criminal, mostly it was just sad how often a letter he wrote or a motion he drafted coincided with a birthday, holiday, or anniversary. These faint or forgotten legal matters, which were so important at the time, always took priority over his relationships.

And now he was alone.

It was past midnight when Gray finished reviewing and copying the computer files. His back was sore and his eyes were bloodshot, but he still had one thing to do. He couldn't go to bed. Since he'd hired Moyo, they'd had multiple conversations. She didn't want to scare him, but, Gray could tell she was worried. She had emphasized, repeatedly, that he needed to take precautions. He needed to be safe.

So, Gray got up and retrieved a plain white envelope from his junk drawer along with his roll of stamps, the documents on the old laptop were consistent with at least one of Moyo's theories. She had told him that his medical leave was just an excuse for the firm to get Gray out of the building, confiscate his computer, and deny him access to files. Given all the information he'd just gathered—even if he didn't understand its value—Moyo's theory now made more sense to him.

Gray wrote a note, folded it, and put one of his flash drives and the note in the envelope. He put three stamps in the corner, just in case the letter needed extra postage, and then addressed the envelope to Moyo. If something were to happen to him, he wanted her and Tad Hankerson to have those files.

Outside, the temperature had dropped, again. Gray sat behind the wheel of his old car, and hoped that the engine would start. He looked in the mirrors, wondering if someone was watching him, and then he turned the key.

The car gave a little groan, but kicked over. It was so cold that Gray could see his breath. He pumped the gas in an attempt to get the heater going, and then pulled out of his back driveway. The local post office wasn't that far away.

It was located in a two-story brick building on the corner of Grand Avenue and Wyoming. Gray didn't have any problem finding a parking spot. Although the pizza place next door to the post office was still open, nearly all of the other restaurants and small businesses were closed for the night. Gray kept the engine running. He got out of the car, ran up to the blue mailbox, and slid his letter into the slot. Then, he ran back to the safety and warmth of his car.

That simple act of precaution gave Gray some comfort. Even if he returned home to broken windows and his old laptop stolen, the information was preserved. He had a growing suspicion that the information was important, but still wasn't sure why.

As he drove toward Hartford Street, instead of going home, Gray decided to take a drive. He was now wide awake. Adrenaline was pumping. He sensed that the tide may be turning. If he just went home, he wouldn't be able to sleep anyway.

Driving around might break him out of a mental rut. As he started down Manchester Road, Gray tried to identify what he knew, what he didn't know, and possibly figure out a few things that he didn't know that he didn't know.

An hour later, Gray found himself on the corner of Chestnut and 6th Street. It was quiet and cold, just like the night that the Chevy Tahoe seemingly came out of nowhere and changed his life. Virgil Hawthorne died on that corner, but there was no sign, flowers, or memorial. It was a street corner, just like any other, except for him.

The images of that night replayed in Gray's mind, again, but, unlike the past, this time he was in control. He thought about the dinner with Durrell, the disagreement about whether or not to walk back to the office, and then hitting the ground hard, his head snapping back against the concrete as the kid stood over him with a gun. A shudder rolled through Gray, and then he thought about the Triangle, not far away, and then a feeling. It was another tiny string, so small it was almost imperceptible, but it was there. Gray couldn't see it, but he felt it.

The string had always been there, niggling at him, forcing him to return over and over, again, not understanding why. Now he understood. It was a connection, ever so tenuous, but important. If he could find that string, the fractured ideas, theories, and memories may just come together to form a picture.

Gray pulled away from the curb and drove to the Triangle. He was supposed to go back and talk to the little man, who might give him access to the Irish Santa or the King or whatever his name was. Agent Matthews had interrupted that plan, but he thought that maybe tonight it would happen.

When Gray arrived, however, it was obvious that they wouldn't meet. The Triangle was alive with activity. More than a dozen people were walking around with flashlights. The engines of at least five skidloaders, which some people called bobcats, hummed and growled. Every thirty seconds, a high pitched beep pierced the night when they went into reverse. Each bobcat also had a light bar on its roof, which shook as it lowered its bucket to remove tents and other debris from the site and moved it to a series of dumpsters.

This was the last stage of the eviction process. The fact that it was occurring late at night and in the dark wasn't an accident. It was by design. During the day, social workers, cops, and advocates try to cajole the homeless residents to leave. The more they resist, the better the incentives. Then, in midafternoon, the incentives start to get worse. Finally, the only incentive offered is that they get to keep their stuff before its destroyed.

Most reporters disappear after the sun sets. They have filing deadlines, which means the stories have to be written before the dirty work begins. The darkness also makes it less likely and more difficult to get quality images of the government plowing over someone's home and few belongings, which is the one aspect of the relocation plan that most local government officials appreciated the most.

Gray stood and watched. Twenty yards away they had cut away the fence to allow people and equipment to easily enter the Triangle. Gray saw a man with a clipboard walk back and forth a few times, and then there were some other people, who Gray assumed were former residents. A few had old plastic suitcases, and the rest had large backpacks with sleeping bags attached. They each took a final glance over their shoulder, and then they got into a waiting van that was likely going to take them to the temporary trailers on the other side of downtown.

The ends of Gray's toes grew cold. He stomped his feet a few times, forcing the blood to flow, but he remained. He watched one van leave, and then another arrive to be loaded with another group of people. Gray watched for the little man, but he especially looked for the man with the white beard. If he did see them, Gray didn't know what he was going to do. Perhaps he'd buy them a meal or get both of them a hotel room, but it ultimately didn't matter. He never saw them.

The bobcats continued to remove tents and debris, and vans eventually stopped coming. Everybody was gone. If Gray had wanted to talk with the Irish Santa, he should have come back sooner. He knew this was coming. He was the one who had written the plan. Gray wanted Durell to wait until after Christmas, but Durell was in a hurry. Durell wanted them out, and he paid Daniels & Bloom a ridiculous amount of money to make it happen.

$5,000 for a memorandum. Gray laughed at the absurdity, and then he felt the tickle of the string as the connection came into focus.

CHAPTER THIRTY-FIVE

Gray pressed a few buttons on his old laptop, and then clicked on one of the billing statements. He'd seen and reviewed hundreds of them. As he thought about the $5,000 memorandum for Durell, the more he became convinced that this was the key.

If a bribe was going to be paid, the firm had to be in the middle of the transaction for two reasons. First, the developer and the government official wouldn't want the money to directly transfer from one to the other. Both would want distance and deniability. Second, the firm would want a mechanism to get paid for its risk and facilitation of the illegal transaction. As an intermediary, the firm could take a cut, and then wash the money through different accounts.

Gray looked at an old summary of all of his billable hours for the month. It was fairly straightforward. At the top was his billable rate, and then below there were three columns: date, description of activity, and time spent on the activity. If he were to falsify some work, nobody would really know. The cost of legal research and a memo could easily be $2,000; add a few emails and teleconferences and the bill could be one or two thousand more. That wouldn't be a bad bribe, but the dollar amounts seemed too small for the risk. It needed to be bigger. It needed to be hundreds of thousands of dollars.

Gray kept thinking, then he got up and walked to the kitchen and began getting out his bags of flour and mixing bowls. As Gray picked up his crock of sourdough starter, he thought about when the most money flowed through the firm's trust accounts.

"Settlements," he said to himself. When somebody sues somebody else and they reach a settlement agreement, the settlement amount was electronically sent to the firm. Then Daniels & Bloom would distribute it.

The problem with his theory was that settlements needed to be approved by a judge. Gray thought about it some more as he removed an electronic scale from the drawer and set it on the counter.

If a judge was involved, that seemed like it could be a problem. A lawyer didn't control who was assigned to any given case, the assignment was random. One or two crooked judges wasn't impossible, but it was unlikely that they were all on the take.

Given the money involved, it'd be unlikely to be left to chance. It needed to be guaranteed to work. Gray put the bowl on the scale and filled it with 600 grams of flour, then went to the sink to wash his hands. As he squirted a little soap on his palm, Gray focused his thoughts on the various settlement negotiations and agreements that he had been involved in over the past twenty years.

Most of the disputes were settled informally without any lawsuit ever being filed. One lawyer wrote a nasty letter to another lawyer alleging something horrible, and the parties eventually worked it out. Informal settlement agreements were never reviewed by a judge and rarely made public.

He left everything on the counter and went back to his old laptop computer. Gray looked down at the list of cases and clients that he had written on his notepad earlier in the evening. He clicked around and soon identified six companies who had threatened litigation against one of his local clients, but the disputes were resolved out-of-court.

On its face, there wasn't anything unusual. One company had sold a developer five hundred windows, and it hadn't received the final payment. Another company purchased land from a real estate speculator, and, allegedly, oil tanks were found while a foundation for a new apartment building was being dug. The company wanted payment to remove the oil tanks and any environmental cleanup. A third company was an architectural firm that alleged that one of the law firm's developers had copied their designs, which they had drafted for a different building in Florida.

When Gray dug a little deeper, however, a pattern emerged: none of those companies existed. Although a few had incorporated in Delaware, they were inactive and their licenses had expired. None had a web presence, owned any property, or were ever mentioned in any newspaper article or trade magazine. Although Gray had corresponded with the general counsel, the names of the opposing attorneys weren't unique. So, for example, when Gray had attempted to look up the background information for an attorney named Gregory Jackson, hundreds of lawyers popped up, none having any apparent connection to the company threatening litigation with one of Gray's clients.

In the morning, Gray called Moyo. They decided to meet with Hankerson later in the afternoon, and he happened to arrive at Moyo's offices at the same time.

"She told me you found something," Hankerson said. "Can't wait to hear about it."

"I have a little bit of hope for the first time in a long time," Gray said as the elevator door slid open. "But I don't know how far it gets us."

"We'll soon find out."

A bell chimed, and they arrived on the third floor of an old rope factory that had been converted into office space. The foyer looked more like an advertising agency than a law firm, exposed brick and thick wooden beams. Moyo's office was down an open hallway overlooking the atrium below. At her door, Gray pressed a button and a receptionist buzzed them inside.

Gray introduced himself, and she smiled. "You can go on back to the conference room, Ms. Moyo is waiting for you."

When Gray and Hankerson entered, Moyo was at the head of the table along with two beefy men and a person Gray assumed was one of Moyo's associates or a paralegal.

"Please sit and I'll make some introductions." She looked at the woman to her left. "This is Vanessa Ahern, a young prosecutor who I stole from the State's Attorney across the river in St. Clair County." Then Moyo turned to her right. "And this is Malcom Shore and Benny Weah, these are the investigators who are trying to find Virgil Hawthorne's wife."

"I thought they were in D.C.," Gray said.

"Their offices are in D.C., but it's gotten to the point where they need to be here to follow through on some leads."

This was good news.

"So you've found her?" Gray looked at Malcolm, and then to Benny, for a response.

"We have some leads," Benny said. "Nothing is for sure, but it's a good lead."

"Great." Gray, then, opened his briefcase and removed his old computer. "I got this last night. I already copied the files and mailed a jump-drive to you, but now I'm thinking that you should just take it. It'll be safer with you."

Moyo's eyebrows raised.

"Wow," she said. "Should I ask how you got it?"

"Sure," Gray said. "I got it from my daughter." He told them the story about how he'd gone to Kendra's house, and then how he'd given his kids the laptop when the firm issued new devices. "I knew it was important, but I still didn't know how it would help me at the time, just like I didn't understand how or whether the Bevo Development file could help me."

"But, based on your message this morning, I'm thinking that you've now figured it out."

"Right," Gray said. "I think so." Gray shared his theory about how Virgil Hawthorne was likely creating fictitious legal disputes with fictitious companies to launder money through the firm to pay bribes.

"Based on the Jack Durell invoice, I'm pretty sure that legal bills were padded, too," Gray said, "but the fake settlements were how the big money was transferred."

Moyo had been silent, listening the whole time, while Tad Hankerson asked questions and Vanessa Ahern scribbled notes.

Finally, Moyo said, "And you have proof?"

"On the laptop," Gray said, "I have correspondence and settlement agreements. I haven't researched every file, but, so far, none of these companies are real." Gray continued. "After one of our client's paid a settlement agreement and its placed in the firm's trust account, Daniels & Bloom is under an obligation to distribute it to the plaintiff, but if that plaintiff didn't exist then that money went somewhere else."

"And that 'somewhere else' is eventually into the pockets of government officials." Moyo paused, thinking it through a little further. "It's clever." Then she leaned forward. "When we get the call, I'd like to have a nice typed list of all the clients involved and also if you can go back and figure out what other business dealings that client was having with the city at the same time, perhaps we can provide a link to a specific politician or government employee. That could be valuable."

Gray felt a wave of relief, but it didn't last long.

"The problem," Moyo said, "is that we don't know the extent of the FBI's investigation. You know the scope is wide, but they may or may not know this. If they already have all these names and all of this information, then it won't be of much value."

Gray said nothing as Moyo continued with an even more deflating analysis. In Gray's excitement of figuring out the law firm's scheme, he'd lost sight of the most important goal: proving his innocence.

"This information doesn't absolve you of any crime, unfortunately," Moyo said. "In fact, if your name is on these letters and correspondence and if you drafted all of these fictitious settlement agreements, then it places you right in the middle." Moyo rubbed her chin. "If I were the prosecutor, these would be the documents that I would use to indict *you*, not Virgil Hawthorne or Ethan Bloom."

CHAPTER THIRTY-SIX

Despite Moyo's pessimism and his own doubts, Gray continued to press. If he couldn't prove his innocence, then he'd bring them all down. Every day Gray got up and went to Moyo's office. There was a file room where she had set up a table for him to work. Gray spent hours mining the old laptop for documents and information. He made lists of clients and shell companies. He generated flow charts, and then dug through city records on who approved the building permits, who inspected the buildings, and who voted in favor of a variance or a subsidy.

The names of government officials and employees were all, then, given to Malcolm Shore and Benny Weah to investigate. Moyo told Gray that they'd pull property records and credit reports to determine if any of the government employees or politicians were living beyond their means, and, if necessary, dig deeper into their background.

When the investigators found anything promising, Gray went back through the documents, again, to see if he'd missed another transaction.

Three weeks later, Moyo called Gray into the conference room. "We need to talk," she said. "I'm worried about you."

Gray rubbed his eyes. "That's kind," he said. "I'm worried about me too."

They sat next to each other, and the receptionist followed with a tray.

"Help yourself." Moyo pointed at the small plate of cookies, and then picked up a cup and saucer. "We often discuss important things over tea where my family comes from." She selected a small packet, placed it in her cup, and then filled it with hot water.

She looked at Gray expectantly while waiting for her tea to steep, and, although Gray preferred coffee and lots of it, he understood what Moyo wanted and obliged. He owed her that. Gray knew the time that she'd been dedicating to his case, and most of those hours weren't appearing on his bill.

"Let's begin with honesty," she said, "I honestly don't mind that you come into the office. It's unusual for me to allow a client such access, but I don't mind."

Gray selected a small spoon from the tray and swirled the tea bag. The color of the water deepened. "Well, as long as we're being honest." Gray set the dirty spoon aside. "I think I'd have otherwise gone insane. It's given me an excuse to leave the house."

"Good." Moyo nodded. "But you look worn. You've lost a lot of weight." She picked up her cup, took a sip, and set it back down as she weighed each word, carefully. "I also think you're reaching a point of diminishing returns. Shore and Weah aren't cheap. Every name you're giving them is costing you thousands of dollars."

Gray thought a moment about his ever-shrinking retirement fund, but it wouldn't matter if he was in prison. "I can pay it, if that's what concerns you."

"It is *part* of what concerns me," she said, "but every example you've found over the past three weeks simply pulls you in deeper. It's like quicksand—the more you move, the deeper you sink. You're involved in every matter. Although you say Virgil was the one interacting with clients, it's your name on every letter. The loop is never broken. Do you understand?"

When Gray said nothing, Moyo continued. "When I've spoken with the prosecutor, that's what he wants. If he is going to grant immunity, then the loop must be broken, but we can't do that. We don't have that kind of proof which exonerates you." She paused, and then approached Gray from a different angle. "I believe that Virgil Hawthorne had a lawyer and he was going to cooperate with the U.S. Attorney's office. I don't know this for a fact, but I believe that Virgil was going to minimize his role, and you and everybody else were going to go down. I'm assuming the prosecutor had some indictments already in hand, but when Virgil was killed they had to reassess."

"You think Virgil was setting me up?" Gray looked away. It was so obvious, and he'd been so naive. Of course he was being set up, Virgil Hawthorne may not have been a great legal mind, but he was savvy. He knew how to protect himself, if things went wrong.

"That's what I believe. I haven't gotten into specifics and no specifics have been provided," Moyo said, "but, given this and our current situation, I've thrown out some hypotheticals, agreements that could be struck." Moyo waited for Gray to look her in the eye, making sure he heard her and understood. "The prosecutor doesn't want ten or twenty or thirty or fifty new leads on *potential* cases. He wants one solid, air-tight case, which requires you to testify that there was a quid pro quo. He wants you to testify that these developers knew about the deals that were being made and funded those deals, and he wants you to testify that the politicians knew the deal when they took the money and voted in favor of the project. That's it."

"So if I lie, like Virgil was going to do," Gray said, "then I'll get immunity?"

Moyo shook her head. "Unfortunately," Moyo said, "I don't think immunity is on the table. Colton Steele would reduce your sentence, but absent some hard proof that you truly had no knowledge of what was going on, I think that is the best they will do."

"Well," Gray said, now frustrated. "I don't have an email that says, 'let's keep Gray in the dark about this whole scheme.' It doesn't exist."

"I understand," she said. "but, perhaps, if you reflect a little more, maybe there were warning signs or conversations that, in light of what you know today, could be helpful to the prosecution. At least in the sense that you'd be able to be a strong witness against these other people."

Gray's eyes narrowed. "Are you asking me to lie?"

Moyo sat up straighter and set down her cup of tea. "I absolutely am not asking you to lie."

"Well I can't and I won't," Gray said. "I can't admit to something that I didn't do. I can't testify as to conversations that I didn't have." Gray ran his hand through his hair, and then began rubbing the back of his neck. "What about Cassie? Where is she? I thought they were close to finding her?"

"They're working on it, Gray," Moyo's voice softer, deescalating. "She slipped away, but I have confidence in them. They'll find her."

They sat in silence as Gray processed everything he'd heard "I'm sorry," he said. "I know how this looks, and I know sometimes a lawyer isn't just a cheerleader, but I am innocent."

Moyo was patient. She gave Gray space to finish his tea and process, comfortable in the silence.

"It's actually pretty brilliant when you think about it," Gray said. "Virgil sets me up to protect himself, and then they kill Virgil so there's really nobody left to incriminate the person who's really in charge."

"And who's that?"

Gray could only think of one name. "It has to be Ethan Bloom." Gray shook his head. "I had actually felt sorry for that guy and he was playing me the whole time."

"Herbert Bloom's son?"

"There's no way that Virgil came up with this on his own," Gray said. "At first, I thought Ethan was just trying to get my clients, but the more I think about it. I think he was setting me up. He was the one who sent me out to Cassie's to get the Bevo file, and he knew everything that was going on with Jack Durell and the Triangle. And, he was the one who told HR about my memory problems and missing meeting. It has to be him."

CHAPTER THIRTY-SEVEN

It was late when Gray heard the noises. After meeting with Moyo, he'd stopped by Midge and Haley's for a glass of wine, which soon turned into three or four glasses. He commiserated with them until the bottles were empty, and his neighbors were satisfied that Gray's mood had sufficiently been lightened. Then Gray had sat alone in his living room, flicking through apps and websites for an hour before going upstairs. He was in the bathroom when he first heard it.

Gray dismissed the noise as just the wind, continuing his routine. He flossed and brushed his teeth. There was a deeper shake as he began to wash his face. It was like the house's foundation moved. All the windows and doors rolled as the aftershock flowed from the basement to the roof. The solid walls merely pieces of fabric.

He turned off the water. Gray didn't leave the bathroom. He waited for another sound to come, but it was silent, unsure of what to make of it. The noises weren't that of a person kicking a door open or prying a window. It wasn't the ordinary creaks and squeaks of an old house, neither quirky nor endearing. There was no comfort.

Gray stood frozen. His heart beat a little faster as a lump formed in his throat. He waited some more, but there was only silence. Perhaps it was over. Gray waited a minute longer, and then shook his head, dismissing it all as too much alcohol. He dried his face, now scolding himself for drinking too much. The combination of prescription drugs and alcohol of any kind was a bad idea, and Gray wondered when he was going to learn that lesson.

He stepped out of the bathroom and was walking down the hallway, when another sound filled the house, less defuse. It came from the kitchen. Gray looked around for something he could use as a weapon, but he had no baseball bats or golf clubs. He had nothing. Gray thought about calling the police, but, given his situation, had no desire to interact with cops. He'd rather die.

Gray walked down the staircase, pausing with each step. The noise continued, but not as intense. It was like someone or something was trapped behind a door. They were trying to get out, but couldn't. The handle remaining locked in place, growing discouraged.

Like every character in a horror movie, Gray could've simply run out the front door and escaped, but Gray didn't. He continued walking, slowly, toward the increasingly intermittent sound. In his head, he could hear the audience in a theater groaning with each step, shouting at him to stop, marveling at his stupidity. An odd smile emerged, incongruous with the situation, and Gray began to laugh. It was absurd, not just his behavior in that moment, but everything—once upon a time he had been a divorced real estate lawyer and now he'd become….whatever *this* was.

A warmth washed over him as he entered the kitchen. External sounds became muffled beneath a soothing pulse, comforting. He felt safe as he walked toward the pantry door. His fear replaced with curiosity. It could be a monster, blood and death, a tableau of loved ones sacrificed, but Gray thought it unlikely. This time was different.

A narrow strip of light shown from the crack beneath the door. The handle vibrated, and turned a glowing amber. Gray hesitated, and then reached. He was confident that no harm would come to him, but Gray was wrong.

The moment his hand touched the handle, it burned. He tried to pull away, but it stuck. His palm blistered as the handle became even hotter. Gray screamed. He tried to yank his hand free, but it didn't release. The pain grew even more intense. He felt himself about to lose consciousness. His knees buckled, and then it was as if a switch had been turned off.

His hand released, and Gray crumpled to the floor as the door opened.

There was a grunt, and then Gray felt himself being picked up by two gigantic hands and pulled into the pantry. The light was bright. It took a few seconds for his eyes to adjust, and then everything came into focus.

Gray was in a large army tent. On the far end, a woman in a colorful dashiki, a West African dress, fed a piece of wood into an old iron stove. There were three cots, neatly made with crisp white sheets and a green wool blanket. The walls were lined with books. Behind Gray, there was a giant, presumably the man who picked him up and brought him inside, and at a small table sat the two men who had saved his life. There was the little man who flagged down the ambulance, and the big man with a robust, white beard and the comforting Irish lilt.

"My goodness." His eyes sparkled as he examined Gray while stroking his whiskers. "What has happened to you?" When Gray didn't answer, he turned to the woman at the stove. "Some tea, please."

The woman nodded and filled a pot of water, although her expression was one of skepticism. Gray was an outsider. He did not belong, and she did not like the intrusion or the extension of hospitality. As the water began to heat, she voiced these concerns. "Why did you let him in?"

"I allowed him in, because he was outside." The man's eyes twinkled, bemused. "I thought it would be a friendly gesture. One we are called upon to do, love your neighbor and all that crap." Then, to the giant, the big man said, "Douglas, please help Mr. Graydon Wendt to the table."

The giant did as he was told. Gray was lifted to his feet, like he was a child, and guided to the table and plopped down in the empty chair. They sat in silence for a moment, and then Gray said, "You know my name."

"I do." The man leaned back like a professor, evaluating a student. "Does that surprise you?"

Gray thought about this. It should surprise him, because they had never formally met, but it didn't. "Not really, no."

The man nodded, approving of the answer.

"But I don't know your name," Gray said.

"Sure you do." His eyes darted to the others in the tent, checking to see if they were enjoying themselves as much as he was. This was fun. A game was afoot. He, then, turned to the woman at the stove. "How's the tea coming?"

She was still annoyed, putting a hand on her hip. "It takes a moment."

"Very well," he said. "Take as long as you need. I shouldn't be in such a rush, 'tis rude, indeed." Then he turned his attention back to Gray. "Where were we?" He touched his temple, then flicked his hand away. "I lose my focus sometimes, distracted. There are so many things and people to keep track of, it can be overwhelming, a burden, but it is also a tremendous gift. The duality of life."

"I asked your name," Gray said.

"Did you?" A grunt. "I don't believe such a question was posed. You merely stated that you did not know my name, to which I disagreed. At any rate, such things are not important. I have and had so many names, I've quite frankly lost track. Call me whatever you want." He then pointed to the Giant. "He, as you know, is Douglas." Then to the little man. "This is Peter." Then to the woman at the stove. "And that is Ms. Mary." He dipped his head in a slight bow, leaned in, and then whispered. "She is my true love."

He laughed, and Gray laughed with him. All pretension was gone. There was lightness in Gray that he wasn't sure he'd ever felt in his entire life. If the big man had asked him to stay in the tent forever, he'd have done it, but such an invitation never came. Gray knew it was an impossibility. He was not one of them, nor had he totally lost his grip on reality. This was surely a hallucination or a dream that he'd wake up from, just like the others. Deep down, he knew this truth, though he still wanted to stay.

"Tell me about your family," the big man said. "Please, I want to know everything…from the beginning."

Gray did as requested, starting with the little house where he and his brother were raised. The tea arrived, the cups were filled, and the stories continued. They drank and laughed for a long time, until the entire pot was gone.

"It looks like we are almost done." The big man finished his cup. He set it down on the table, and then looked at what remained for Gray.

"But you haven't told me anything about yourself," Gray said, realizing that their time was running out. "I want to know about you."

The big man shook his head. "Another day, perhaps."

"But that night, the night that Virgil Hawthorne was killed," Gray said. "You were there. You saved me."

"Is that what you believe?"

"I don't know what I believe," Gray said.

"Then I'm not sure I can help you."

The ease that had wrapped around and comforted Gray began to unravel, and he felt himself become agitated, again, scared. "You can tell me I'm not crazy." Gray felt the giant step away from the tent's door, closer to him, ready to intervene. "You can tell me what happened."

"That's what you want?" The big man cocked his head to the side, his normally twinkling eyes dimmed. "And what does that give you? What does my confirmation and validation actually provide to you? It doesn't change anything."

"It changes everything."

"I'm not sure about that." The big man pointed at Gray's cup. "You should finish up, and we may continue this another time."

Gray felt himself begin to breakdown. A tear rolled down his face. "Did you heal me?"

The big man, whom Gray called the Irish Santa, reached over and put his hand on Gray's shoulder. "Tell me," he said, "Do you feel healed?"

Gray stared into the big man's eyes. Finally, he whispered, hesitating. "I have no idea."

"Then neither do I." He released his grip on Gray's shoulder, and leaned back. "Perhaps I am just as confused as you are, but you have to have faith in yourself. You're stronger than you think."

Gray wiped the falling tear from his cheek, and finished his tea.

A phone rang and vibrated. It took some time, but Gray eventually opened his eyes. It was dark, but he knew where he was even in the darkness. He could feel it. Gray was in his own house, in his own bed, and wearing his own pajamas. His body was sore, as if he'd run a marathon. His head was cloudy, and Gray was tempted to roll-over and simply go back to sleep. The phone, however, didn't stop.

Gray reached for the light on his nightstand, groped for the switch, and turned it on. He took a deep breath, and, with his other hand, attempted to pick-up the phone, but could not. It was bandaged, wrapped in a thick layer of gauze.

The phone kept ringing and vibrating.

Through the fog, Gray remembered— the pantry door, its knob turned a deep amber, the pain, excruciating pain — he tried to sort it out, but couldn't. There were parts that were clear, but others slipped away every second he was awake. That was the way dreams worked, but, as he stared at his hand, Gray knew it wasn't a dream, at least not entirely.

The phone continued.

"What?" He picked it up, without looking at who was calling, just to shut it up, angry. "Who is this?"

It was Naomi Moyo. "They did it," she said. "It's on the front page of the paper. I wanted to call you right away so that you wouldn't be surprised."

"What?" He still wasn't entirely awake.

"The indictment," Moyo said. "We have an arraignment this afternoon. You'll be served with a written copy of the charges at the hearing. I'll waive a formal reading, and then the magistrate will set conditions of release."

Moyo continued, but Gray had a hard time concentrating, reconciling his experience that night in the tent with the day's reality. He stared at his bandaged hand as Moyo spoke, catching bits and pieces. They'd, of course, been anticipating and waiting for weeks, but he'd always held out a small kernel of hope that the criminal investigation would all just go away. His lawyer brain understood that would never happen, but the denial was there, nonetheless, a stubborn belief that everyone would recognize their mistake and let him return to his former life.

Gray surfaced, just enough. "Did you just say I might be taken into custody?"

"It's a possibility," Moyo said. "You can never say never."

"And if I'm taken into custody," Gray played the scenario forward, "and if I'm held for trial, and then I'm found guilty….I'd go directly to prison, and so this could be my last day as a…." Gray didn't finish. His thoughts jumped to Zoe and Nick.

Moyo, sensing Gray's rising panic, did her best to talk him down. "It's possible," she said, "but very unlikely. Federal agents arrested the others last night, and their homes were searched. You, obviously weren't arrested, which tells me the prosecutor is trying to play a little nice with you."

"I thought you told me that he doesn't need me," Gray got a little testy, but he had nobody else to lash out at. "You told me that the case was solid, and that's why they won't offer me immunity."

"All of that is true," Moyo said. "We've gone over this many times. Immunity is one deal, which is not happening at this time, but a lesser sentence is still a possibility. They certainly can follow the money and prove their case against the politicians and the developers, but your testimony would guarantee a guilty verdict. There probably wouldn't even be a trial. Once their defense lawyers find out you're cooperating, they'd all plead."

"I'm not confessing to something I didn't do."

"And I'm not asking you to do that." Moyo remained calm and patient, her cadence steady. "You asked why I didn't think they were going to take you into custody, and that's the reason. I also hinted to them about you having the names of others, and that may be another reason for treating you a little differently."

Gray didn't have anything more to say. "Okay," he said, what little fight he'd just exhibited had left him. "We can talk later. I have to think."

Gray sat in his living room, alone, scrolling through the early media coverage. It was sensational news. Local television led their morning broadcast with it, including video of the developers being led from their fancy houses in handcuffs. All of the stories were damning, and sounded even worse than Gray had imagined, which didn't seem possible. There was even an article in the *Washington Post*, due to one of the aldermen being the son of a United States Congressman.

He watched and read it all.

The headline across the top of the *Post-Dispatch:* Six Charged In Bribery Scheme. Moyo had done her best, but she had no magical powers. Gray was guilty until proven innocent, and he had no proof to dissuade the U.S. Attorney's Office or Agent Matthews that he was simply a pawn. The eventual indictment was inevitable. Still, it was a shock to see his picture along with the pictures of three city alderman and two real estate developers on the front page of the newspaper.

After Gray had cycled through several times, he even, briefly, made a foray into the comments section. None of the readers were kind.

They all look like pedophiles.

Can we just agree that these losers should be taken to the public square and flogged fifty times.

Scum.

Crooked politicians. Crooked lawyers. No surprise.

Cousin robbed a store and took a couple hundred dollars, twelve years in prison. What'll these white guys get? Slap on the wrist?

I say hang 'em high.

If he went to trial, these were the people who would be sitting on the jury. If he was found guilty, which based on the media coverage and comments appeared to have already happened, the sentence would be at least twenty-five years, and he'd probably die in prison. Gray doubted there would be much sympathy.

He tapped his phone with his unbandaged hand, and called Kendra to see if he could visit the kids before the hearing.

Gray spent the late morning at the Science Museum. Zoe and Nick had been there many times, running ahead to their favorites with minimal consultation as he trailed behind them. Then they watched an Omnimax movie about South American caves, before it was time to go. When he passed the kids to Kendra, he gave both an extra hug and kiss before driving back downtown.

He arrived at the parking ramp at noon. Across the street from Bush stadium, it was a massive structure built for the thousands of baseball fans who came to the games in the summer, but it sat mostly empty in the winter. Because of this, Gray had no trouble finding Moyo at their designated meeting spot.

She had a large black SUV, and was the sole vehicle parked on the third level. Gray pulled into the space next to hers, got out of his car, and then stepped up into the passenger seat. "I made it."

"How were the kids?" Moyo asked.

"Okay," Gray said. "Kendra kept them home from school, worried about the bullying, so I spent some time talking with her. We came up with a plan as to what to say, and then she left us alone for the rest of the morning." Gray wiped a tear from his eye. "It was tough, really tough."

When Gray handed Moyo his car keys, she noticed the bandage. "Something happen?"

Gray brushed the question aside, just as he had when Kendra asked. "I'm a baker. Sometimes baker's get burned." He, then, reached into his briefcase and removed an envelope offering no further explanation for his injury. The envelope contained his passport and extra keys to his vehicle.

Moyo, focused on the hearing, didn't ask any questions. She took the envelope and put it in her own briefcase. They intended to surrender Gray's passport at the hearing, the keys were a precaution if he was taken into custody. Her assistant would need to move his car.

"Midge and Haley can give you access to my house if you need it." Gray nodded toward the backseat of his car. On a hook, there were clothes. "I picked out a couple suits, shirts and ties for trial, just like you asked."

"Thank you," she said, "but hopefully you'll be driving yourself home today." Moyo checked her watch, and decided that it was time to go. They both got into her SUV, and a few minutes later were at the courthouse. News trucks were in front. Reporters were already setting up.

Moyo drove past them, circling the block. They had no intention of entering the courthouse through the front door. Moyo knew a discrete side entrance by the building's loading dock that was primarily used by employees and administrative staff. It was an official, public entrance, just not an obvious one.

She found a spot on the street not too far away. They parked and made it into the building without being noticed. The criminal arraignments were going to be held on the seventh floor and handled by Magistrate Judge Bonnie Rack that afternoon. While most judges detested the arraignment calendar, she loved it, developing the nickname "Judge Rack and Crack" for the speed and zealous delight she took gathering all the defendants, like pool balls on a table, centering them, and then lining them up to later be broken by a federal judge.

Moyo and Gray took the elevator up, where Judge Rack and Crack had her chambers and courtroom. Off to the side, there were a series of small conference rooms. Gray and Moyo took the one at the furthest end of the hall and then waited.

An hour later, the proceedings began. Moyo and Gray watched the politicians and real estate developers be led into the courtroom in orange jumpsuits and shackles. Their heads were down, eyes glazed. Gray almost felt sorry for them. He'd had months to try and come to terms with the sharp, downward turn his life had taken, whereas most of the people standing in the front of the courtroom were still in shock. Twenty-four hours ago they were rich, powerful, and free. Now all of that had been stripped away, leaving them looking quite small.

Judge Rack and Crack peered down. Her half rim glasses perched on the very tip of her small nose. She heard from the U.S.

Attorney, and then from the defense. Judge Rack and Crack spent a few moments to shame each one. She went on about the allegations and breach of public trust. "I hope, for your sake, these allegations are not true, because, in my mind, corrupting our system of democracy is treason and should be punishable as such."

She paused, hoping her dramatic statement (likely rehearsed) hit with sufficient force and giving adequate time for it to be properly documented by the attending reporters. She raised her posture to its fullest height, took a deep breath, and then set a future hearing date.

In the end, however, Judge Rack and Crack's harsh rhetoric was mitigated by her actual order. She granted the defense attorney's request, and allowed the developers and politicians to be conditionally released and placed on house arrest.

Moyo exchanged a look with Gray and a little smile. The fact that Judge Rack and Crack conditionally released the others meant that Gray was unlikely to be taken into custody. The odds shifted further in his favor. The possibility, however, still made Gray nervous as the other defendants were led out of the courtroom.

"The people of the United States versus Graydon Wendt." The clerk took a breath, then she noted the case file number for the record.

Judge Rack and Crack called Moyo and Gray forward. "And you must be the other one." Her head bobbled, eyes hardening. "The lawyer, whom if the allegations are true, should've known better." She looked away from Gray to the prosecutor as if she could no longer bear to look at Gray a moment any longer than she already had. "What do you have to say, Mr. Steele?"

"Thank you, your honor." Colton Steele buttoned his jacket, straightened his tie, and proceeded to lay it on thick. "Although you are correct that the idea that an attorney, a member of our esteemed profession, could be at the heart of this corruption scheme is disturbing, we have no objection to Mr. Wendt being treated similar to his co-conspirators."

Moyo opened her mouth to begin a counter-argument, but Judge Rack and Crack held out her hand. She wasn't going to waste time. "That is fair, and that is what I will do." A clerk gave the judge a slip of paper and she signed it. "Mr. Wendt, you are to surrender your passport and report to our pre-trial supervision office on the second floor. You'll be assigned an officer, and you are to comply with all of the rules and regulations. The monitoring bracelet should not be removed for any reason without permission."

"24 hour house arrest, your honor?" The prosecutor knew the answer, but he wanted to rub it in.

"Yes," Judge Rack and Crack said. "You can go to church, doctor's appointments, meetings with your attorney, and I'll give you two hours for errands and exercise a day."

And that was it.

CHAPTER THIRTY-EIGHT

The charges and arraignments dominated the news for a few days. Then, like all sensational news, the story faded away. To the public, the case was over. They were all guilty, and it was only a matter of time before the machinations of justice confirmed this fact. For Gray, it was something entirely different. He was no longer waiting for Agent Matthews or the prosecutor to absolve him of any wrongdoing and issue the golden ticket back to the before times. The indictment happened, and it wasn't going to disappear.

The wheels of justice moved forward at a slow, deliberate pace. There were motions and objections, and pre-trial maneuvering. Gray wanted Moyo to give notice of their intention of raising the affirmative defense of 'alternate perpetrator,' otherwise known as "the other guy did it."

Moyo, however, refused. Even though Gray was sure that he had been set-up, and Ethan Bloom was to blame. Gray had no proof. Unlike on television and in the movies, where a defense lawyer can surprise the prosecutor by suddenly accusing someone else of committing the crime, real life didn't work that way. In order to present the alternate perpetrator defense to a jury, Moyo would first need to prove by clear and convincing evidence to the judge that Ethan Bloom was guilty, not Gray. This was a nearly impossible task, and Moyo was not the type of attorney who went on a suicide mission. Judges trusted her, and that level-headed credibility was her greatest strength.

As the winter turned to spring, the others began to plead guilty. First, there was Kyle Hitchens. He was the youngest of the three city alderman who were indicted. Hitchens was married and had three young kids. Publicly there were no details about what, if any agreements had been reached, but Moyo had sources. She'd been told that his prison time would be capped at two years, if he testified against the others, including Gray.

He'd never met Hitchens. It was possible that they'd spoken on the phone, but Gray doubted it. Virgil Hawthorne was the one who attended meetings and political fundraisers. He knew everybody, and Gray struggled to think of anything damning that Hitchens could testify that Gray had done.

"At this point," Moyo had said, "the truth doesn't matter as much. The guy is drowning, and he'll say anything to save himself."

Gray understood, but he wished that Moyo would soften the blows just a little every once in a while. After all, they were all drowning, and, of the five of them, Gray was probably the deepest under water.

The second alderman pled guilty in February, and then both of the developers pled guilty a few weeks after that. Like Hitchens, the details released to the public were scant, but the deals were getting worse. Alderman Marcus Perry, according to Moyo's sources, was offered a max of four years in prison. The developers were offered a maximum of ten years in prison. All contingent upon providing the prosecution with information and documents as well as their truthful testimony.

Gray's morning walks had now become much longer. He used the time to think of a way out, but nothing ever came. The only people left were him and Council President Barbara James, a woman who famously blocked the defunding of her local recreation center via filibuster by talking for thirteen hours. When asked how she was able to talk that long, President James claimed it was a toughness learned by growing up poor in a household of eight kids as well as putting on an adult diaper before the hearing so that she wouldn't have to take a bathroom break.

James was now his co-defendant. Despite Moyo's objections, Judge Espinoza decided that Gray and James would be tried together rather than each being given a separate trial. It was a huge win for the prosecution, because it meant that Gray would be guilty by association.

A week before the trial was set to begin in late April, Gray stopped at the Missouri Botanical Garden. He read the newspaper by himself, drank a cup of coffee, and then began to walk back home just as he had done almost every day for the past several months. Each time he lingered just a little longer, pushing up against his two hour limit, savoring the days. Then he got a text from Moyo.

Barbara James, President of the St. Louis Board of Alderman, had pled guilty.

Gray was the only one left.

The prosecutors, Colton Steele and Amber Brenner, called the meeting. It occurred in a large conference room at the U.S. Attorney's Office. Their offices were in the federal courthouse, just a few floors below where Gray and the others had been arraigned many months ago.

Gray and Moyo sat on one side, and the rest of the seats were occupied by the prosecution. In addition to Steele and Amber Brenner, there were two young prosecutors who looked like they had just graduated high school, and several paralegals. There was also Agent Matthews.

"Let's begin," Colton Steele ran his hand through his thick, perfect hair. "I know that everybody is busy, but I also know that the first thing Judge Espinoza is going to ask us is whether we made a legitimate offer and talked about settlement. God help us if the answer to his question is 'no.' " Steele smiled. His confidence was ridiculous, but Gray understood that he had every right to be confident.

Amber Brenner, the other prosecutor, added, "I know you've insisted on immunity in the past, which we've rejected, but I think circumstances have changed."

"How so?" Moyo, of course, knew the answer to the question, but she wanted to hear their take and Steele was more than happy to oblige.

"When we charged this case, we had the basic facts and documents," Steele said. "We also had the cooperation of the law firm."

Gray thought about Ethan Bloom, and Moyo asked, "Did you subpoena them?"

Brenner shook her head. "We deemed that wasn't necessary. There is so much privileged information at a law firm that, although we could, we concluded that the firm was being more than forthcoming and a subpoena was unnecessary."

"You mean Ethan Bloom was more than forthcoming," Gray said, but neither Steele nor Brenner responded. The silence became uncomfortable, and Moyo intervened to keep the meeting on-track.

She put her hand on Gray's arm, and then spoke slowly, deliberating on her choice of each word. "*I* believe that the higher levels of the law firm were fully aware of what Virgil Hawthorne was doing." By stating that it was her belief, rather than Gray's belief, Moyo was protecting Gray. Although settlement negotiations were supposed to be confidential, a good attorney knows that nothing is confidential.

"Great," Steele said. "That is definitely information and testimony we'd want to hear."

Brenner was less kind. "But we'd need actual proof."

"And if my client could provide that proof along with information related to other bribes involving other companies and government officials," Moyo said, "is immunity even a possibility?"

"We weren't offering immunity before," Steele said, "and our case against your client has only gotten stronger. All of the co-defendants are ready and willing to testify against him at trial."

Gray's emotions had been building, and finally it burst. "But I didn't do anything."

"You did plenty, Mr. Wendt." Brenner pointed at him. "Your name is all over these files, and your name is all over these emails and correspondence. And, now, we have your co-conspirators who will testify that you were orchestrating it."

"I didn't know the cases were fake, I thought——"

Moyo interrupted, attempting to take back control. "Well you have to be offering him something, so let's hear it. He's not just saving you the time and risk of a trial. My client is offering you additional information and perpetrators that you do not have."

Brenner locked eyes with Gray. "But you still don't have direct evidence that the top levels of Daniels & Bloom knew about these bribes, right?" Brenner, then, emphasized the most important requirement. "*Direct* evidence."

Gray knew the answer to that question was no, but he didn't answer. Such an admission would undercut what little leverage they had.

"What if we did?" Moyo asked. "Assume we have that information, theoretically."

Brenner looked at Steele, and Steele looked back at her as if they were communicating telepathically. Then, Steele leaned forward. "If you had that type of information. We'd likely cut the prison sentence down to three years."

Moyo countered without even asking Gray.

"What about a cap of three years, no higher, and the judge can decide?"

Colton Steele started to reject it, but Brenner cut him off. "That's a possibility. Depends on how good the information is."

Steele, Brenner, and Moyo leaned back. The attorneys relaxed a little bit, considering whether they had just reached an acceptable agreement or not. Then Gray blew it up. "This all assumes that I plead guilty, but I can't do that because I'm not guilty. I didn't do anything wrong."

Amy Wirth waited for the meeting to end in a small conference room down the hall. It had been months since she had received the form letter from the bureau informing her that she did not get the job. The time between phone calls and meetings with Matthews had also become fewer and far between. She figured Matthews extended the invitation in an effort to be nice, sort of a consolation prize, but Wirth couldn't help but feel bitter.

She deserved to be in the room with the others. Instead, she was still suffering the daily indignities meted out by Bird and Doles. Despite a few decent assignments arranged by Schmitty, Wirth knew her annual evaluation was going to happen and the end would become that much closer.

The door opened. "Sorry about keeping you waiting." Matthews sat down at the table. They exchanged some pleasantries, talked about future vacations, and then Matthews summarized the meeting with Graydon Wendt and his attorney. "If I was going to bet, I'd say this is going to trial. He isn't taking any deal."

"That doesn't surprise me," Wirth said. "But, then again, I'm not sure I'd be able to resist the temptation. Getting out in a few years, guaranteed, verses what would essentially be a life sentence is a pretty stark choice. I wouldn't be willing to take that gamble."

Agent Matthews smiled. "You still believe him. Don't you?"

Wirth wasn't interested in having this conversation, again. "Come on, man, give it a rest."

But Matthews pushed, anyway. She folded her arms across her chest.

"We've got the documents with his name on them and five people that are going to testify under oath that he was right in the thick of it with Virgil Hawthorne the whole time."

Wirth rolled her eyes. "Of course that's what they're going to say. Just like Graydon Wendt might plead guilty, even though he probably didn't do it. Just like the thousands of other people that are churned through the system." Wirth pushed her chair back from the table and stood. "I better get going."

"Come on," Matthews said. "Don't go, yet. I'm just pushing your buttons."

"Well I'm tired of people pushing my buttons." Wirth began walking toward the door, but stopped. "Just because we get the conviction doesn't mean we're right. I want to get it right."

"I know that." Matthews held out his hands in surrender. Then he took a step forward. "I apologize. You're a good investigator, and you're righteous, which I respect."

Wirth waited for Matthews to follow the compliment with a snide put-down, but it never came. With reservations, Wirth accepted the apology. "Thanks."

"There's another opening here," Matthews said. "You should apply for it. That's why I invited you here, I wanted to keep you up to speed on the case, but I also wanted to tell you about the job in person." He took another step closer. "I feel bad about you not getting the last one. I should've pushed harder for you. No guarantees, but I want you to get it."

CHAPTER THIRTY-NINE

The trial judge assigned to his case was Reginald C. Espinoza. Judge Espinoza was the first Latino appointed to the federal bench in Missouri. As a former federal public defender and Obama appointee, senate Republicans were wary of his bleeding-heart background and were quick to tag him with the nickname "Judge Catch and Release."

In practice, however, Judge Espinoza handed out the harshest sentences of any judge in the Eighth Circuit, which included district courts in Missouri, Iowa, Minnesota, North Dakota, South Dakota, and Arkansas. When asked by a reporter about this incongruity between his background as a criminal defense attorney for the indigent and his reputation as a "hanging judge," Judge Espinoza simply stated, "I spent over twenty years listening to their sob stories, and I've sadly come to the conclusion that 99% of the time they're b.s."

The judge looked down at the attorneys from his perch. Just as Steele had predicted, he asked the question. "Have the attorneys attempted to resolve this matter?" The question was a simple one, and, if someone were to read a court transcript in the future, it would seem innocuous. Judge Espinoza's tone, however, was piercing. It was obvious that he was skeptical that any case couldn't be resolved with a plea agreement, and that, anyone who wasted his time with a trial, would pay a price. After all, everyone was guilty.

"We have, your honor," Steele said.

Judge Espinoza's eyes narrowed, then turned his attention to Moyo. "Is this true?"

Moyo stood. "It is true, your honor," she put her hand on Gray's shoulder. "My client maintains his innocence, and all of the offers are premised on a plea of guilty."

Judge Espinoza grunted. He began to say something, but thought better of it. "And your client understands the risks in going to trial?"

"Of course, your honor," Moyo said. "We've had many discussions and if you'd like me to put anything on the record, I'd be happy to do so."

"That's not necessary." Judge Espinoza checked his watch. "Let's get started."

###

It took three days to seat a jury, and, when it was all done, there were fourteen people seated in the box. There were twelve jurors and two alternates, evenly split between men and woman. Some more eager to serve than others.

When Colton Steele stood and delivered his opening statement, Gray felt like he was having an out-of-body experience. It was as if his mind couldn't accept the present and sent him far away, back into those childhood woods, leaping across the narrow creeks, and dodging behind trees. When that escape played out, Gray's mind sent him to the prairie, a kite in hand, chasing an unreliable breeze.

Eventually, Colton Steele brought him back to the present. "And after you've heard all the evidence," Steele said, waiting for Gray to acknowledge, willing Gray to meet his eye. And when he did, Steele finished. "You, members of the jury, will find Graydon Wendt guilty beyond a reasonable doubt."

Moyo was on her feet before Colton Steele had sat down. She and Gray had talked about whether or not to reserve her opening statement until after the prosecution had rested, but decided against it. The jurors expected a response, and Gray didn't want Colton Steele's opening to linger unchallenged in the minds of the jurors.

"As instructed by the judge at the outset of this trial," Moyo walked a little closer to the jurors, "these opening statements are not evidence. Mr. Steele can say whatever he wants, but, in the end, your decision must be based upon the evidence. And, I will tell you right now, that the evidence isn't there. Certainly, you will be given evidence of a crime, a bribery scheme. You'll also hear testimony from the people who actually committed these crimes and pled guilty. Neither myself nor Mr. Wendt have any problem with that."

Moyo turned toward the door leading to the jury deliberation room. "But when you leave this courtroom and go back there, when all of the evidence is done being presented. When you are sitting around a table in the deliberation room, you will realize that there is not only a lack of evidence to convict Mr. Wendt beyond a reasonable doubt, I don't think you'll have much of any evidence at all. And for that reason, you'll return a verdict of not guilty."

When Moyo sat down, Judge Espinoza announced a recess, and when they returned Amber Brenner and Colton Steele got to work. Over the next five days the two prosecutors traded witnesses, interspersing forensic accountants with the testimony of developers and politicians. There were over two hundred exhibits entered into evidence, and every time Gray's name was mentioned, the prosecutors would look at him with disdain.

"And who sent you this email?" Steele had asked, and then, he'd offer another exhibit. He'd hold it in his hand and raise it up, as if it was a letter of confession. "And who drafted this document?"

Each time the answer was the same. "Graydon Wendt." Over and over, again, the witnesses said his name, and as the trial rolled into its sixth day, Gray began to feel the harsh stares of the jurors. Not only was he guilty, Gray was also wasting their time, requiring a trial when none was necessary. He was guilty and it was obvious.

The only thing that made Gray a little hopeful was that, on cross-examination, Moyo had gotten every witness to admit that they'd never spoken directly with Gray about the bribes and money laundering, and most of the witnesses had never even met Gray. It kept the door open, and he only needed to keep it open a crack for a reasonable doubt.

That was his hope.

Unfortunately, the prosecution's last witness wasn't afraid to lie. Barbara James was promised a significant reduction in prison time, and she was going to earn it. The former President of the St. Louis Board of Aldermen arrived in a dark blue, tailored suit, and a red silk scarf around her neck. She was poised and articulate, listening with attention and then delivering her answers in soundbites.

James took responsibility for her mistakes, but, as a practiced politician, she easily pivoted the blame with each response.

"Let's talk about the Columbus Square project." Brenner projected the minutes of a board meeting up on the screen. "Do you remember this day?"

"I can't tell you everything that happened at the meeting," James said. "But I can tell you about the subsidy that the city awarded to Bevo Development."

"Okay," Brenner enlarged the exhibit, zooming in on the second to last agenda item. "We are looking at Item 13 on the non-consent agenda, correct?"

"That is correct."

"And tell us what happened?"

James nodded. "We awarded Bevo approximately $5 million in forgivable loans—if they met affordable housing goals—, and $15 million in low-interest loans, and a $2 million grant."

"And who first reached out to you related to this project?" Brenner asked.

James looked at Gray, nodded in his direction, and then told the jurors his name.

"Just so the record is clear," Brenner said. "Let the record reflect that the witness identified the defendant as the person who first reached out to her." Brenner looked down, removed a piece of paper from the stack, and then asked, "What did he offer you in exchange for getting his client the loans and grant?"

"$50,000," James said.

"Let me get this straight," Brenner pretended to be confused. "You arranged to give Bevo Development millions in government subsidies for the Columbus Square project and all you got was $50,000."

In a flat tone, James delivered the punch line. "I guess I wasn't a particularly good negotiator." A few of the jurors laughed, and even Judge Espinoza cracked a smile. Gray couldn't believe it. The witness was perjuring herself, and people thought it was hilarious.

Brenner waited a moment, and then shifted back to become quite serious. It was all an act, but the sudden change was enough to ensure that jurors were now paying attention to the most important part of James's testimony. "But this was what the Defendant, Graydon Wendt, offered you?"

"Yes," James said.

"And this is what you accepted?"

"Yes," James said.

"And what about Virgil Hawthorne, did you have any interactions with him?"

"I did," James said, "but Graydon Wendt was who set this up. Fifteen days after the vote, I got an envelope filled with cash in the mail."

Moyo tried to mitigate the damage on cross-examination, but James deflected, evaded, and minimized. After ten minutes, Moyo determined that she was doing more harm than good. She passed the witness back to Brenner, and Brenner wisely chose to quit while she was ahead. A lesser prosecutor would've tried to score a few more points, but good prosecutors resisted asking that one additional question, which, at best, simply diluted the power of earlier testimony.

Brenner watched as Barbara James stepped down from the witness stand. After James had left the courtroom, Brenner straightened her posture, standing tall with chin raised, and concluded. "Your honor, the prosecution has no further witnesses at this time but reserves the right to call rebuttal witnesses if appropriate."

Judge Espinoza nodded. "The prosecution rests?"

"Yes, your honor," Brenner said. "The prosecution rests."

CHAPTER FORTY

It was a Friday afternoon, and Judge Espinoza allowed the jurors to go home a little early. The juror's relief and happiness with the judge's announcement was obvious. They filed out of the courtroom with a little spring in their collective steps.

When the jurors were gone and the federal marshal had closed the door, Judge Espinoza turned his attention to Moyo. "Have you had an opportunity to discuss the jury instructions with Mr. Steele and Ms. Brenner?"

Moyo stood. "A draft was circulated a few times, and we should have a joint proposal to the Court by Monday."

Judge Espinoza didn't like that plan. "How about you get that joint proposal to me tonight so that I can review it this weekend?"

Moyo knew better than to argue with a judge. "Very well."

To Steele and Brenner, "And you?" Judge Espinoza's body appeared to tighten in anticipation of a fight. "I assume you two don't have any problem with that."

"We don't have any problem with that timeline," Steele said. "We'll get it done."

Judge Espinoza took great pleasure in squeezing attorneys, looking delighted with himself, but he only reveled in his power for a moment before moving onto the next issue. "We also need to discuss your client's right to testify or not testify." Judge Espinoza looked at Gray, and then to Moyo. "Have you had such discussions with your client?"

Moyo stood back up. "We have had lengthy discussions, your honor, and, as you know, my client is also an attorney, so he is very aware of his right to remain silent and the burden of proof in this case."

Judge Espinoza nodded. "And has he made a decision?"

"No, your honor," she said. "Of course we've had discussions, but given the importance of the decision, I think it's best for my client to think about it this weekend."

Judge Espinoza didn't like that answer, but knew better than to interfere. Their conversation was on the record, and he didn't want Gray to later claim he was pressured by the Court to make a decision. So, he let it go. "Any other witnesses that you intend to call?"

Moyo, again, avoided committing to anything.

"This is also something I need to discuss with my client," she said. "The prosecution has our witness list."

"As a professional courtesy," Judge Espinoza said, "I think it's appropriate for them to have a little more notice as to who will or will not testify before Monday morning."

"Of course," Moyo worked hard to be respectful, "I was a prosecutor myself, and I never appreciated being surprised by undisclosed witnesses or evidence, but sometimes that's unavoidable." She widened her stance and put her hands on the podium. "But I can't tell them something I don't know. I need to talk to my client and make sure he's comfortable with my decisions. I can promise the Court, however, that there are no secret witnesses. We've disclosed all of our potential witnesses."

Steele didn't let that pass. "Their witness list has over twenty people, your honor, including a statement that they reserve the right to call anybody on our witness list. Certainly they are not going to call more than twenty people. They should rule some of these people out now, so that we don't waste our time preparing for someone who is definitely not going to testify."

Moyo countered. "I think you are fully aware of the theory of our defense and should have no problem cross-examining anybody we call."

Judge Espinoza had heard enough. He raised his hands. "I hate bickering lawyers, and I think Ms. Moyo understands that I hate surprise, gotcha tactics even more than bickering lawyers, so think carefully." To Steele, he said, "If either you or Ms. Brenner need extra time to prepare for a witness next week, then I'll grant it."

Once a draft of the jury instructions was emailed to Steele and Brenner, Moyo joined Gray. He was waiting alone in the conference room, lost in his thoughts, surrounded by bags of Chinese take-out. Moyo attempted to shake him out of his trance.

"We need to resist jumping to a conclusion or making a decision, and then trying to rationalize it," Moyo said. "We need to be methodical." She handed Gray one of her printed copies of the jury instructions. "Read this, and, when you're done, we'll go through the testimony of every witness. We need to see where they're weak and where there might be an opportunity for us."

Gray glanced at the jury instructions, but showed little interest. He set them aside and reached for one of the containers of food. "Do you want sesame chicken or General Tso's?"

"I'll take the sesame," Moyo said. "And did you get egg rolls?"

Gray found the right container and handed it to Moyo, and then gave her the egg rolls after taking one for himself. "Can I be honest right now?" Gray took a bite of his egg roll, and then pushed the draft jury instructions back across the table to Moyo, resigned and defeated. "I wish I would've pled guilty."

He worked hard to control his emotions, and he noticed that his hand was shaking, again, ever so slightly, despite trying to maintain his composure and not embarrass himself. "There are no weaknesses. There are no opportunities. I should've just lied and told the judge I did it, taken the deal, and moved on. In a couple years, I'd get out and reinvent myself."

Gray closed his eyes and took a jagged breath. "I didn't really like being a lawyer anyway," he said, almost in a whisper. "But I was stubborn and stupid, just like when I insisted to Virgil that we walk back to the office in the middle of a snowstorm." Then Gray sat up, opened his eyes, and looked at Moyo. "I'm going to die in prison. This jury is going to find me guilty, and I'm going to die in there."

"Our strategy was good," Moyo said, trying to lift Gray's spirits without sugar-coating anything. "Barbara James testimony hurt us. We have to overcome that."

"But was it really unexpected?" Gray shook his head. "I mean…you know, why would I think that?"

"Because the statements that the prosecutors disclosed to us were just like the other witnesses. They were vague, nothing specific, but there isn't anything we can do about it now."

"What about Cassie?" Gray asked. "Have they found her?"

Moyo pursed her lips, a rare display of frustration. "No. She's not using credit cards. She's not using a cell phone that we know of. She's not with relatives. She's disappeared, and I'm beginning to wonder if she's even alive."

"Can you call Shore and Weah tonight?" Gray asked. "I will pay anything they want to find her, anything. I'll sell my house. I don't care."

"Okay, I will," Moyo said, "but I think you've paid them enough already."

They talked more about the trial, witnesses, and polished off the remaining food.

"Is Ethan Bloom on our witness list?" Gray asked.

"He is," Moyo said.

"I want to call him as a witness." Gray folded his arms across his chest. "He set me up."

"That's a bad idea," Moyo said. "We've talked about what it takes to accuse another person of the crime, and we don't have the evidence for an alternate perpetrator defense. And, if I tried without the express permission of Judge Espinoza, he'd likely toss me in jail for contempt."

Gray didn't respond. He had a constitutional right to defend himself, but the rules made it illusory.

Moyo waited for the idea to pass. "And you?" She looked at Gray. "What do *you* want to do?"

"Call Steele and see if the offer is still on the table to plead guilty?"

"Maybe I should've been more specific," Moyo said. "Do you want to testify or not?"

"I'd like you to ask about a plea deal, first," Gray said. "Seriously, will you do that?"

"I can," Moyo said, "but I can guarantee you that the answer will be no."

"Then I'll go down swinging," Gray said.

"You'll testify?"

"I don't see how it can make matters worse."

Even though it wasn't his weekend, Kendra dropped the children off in the morning. She understood that time was running out. Gray didn't have to remind her. The case was winding down, and these were likely his last few days before he was found guilty and sent to prison.

Since the indictment, Gray had seen his kids more than he ever had in the past even though he was under house arrest. This fact did not make him happy. It was a reminder of opportunities lost. This was how it could've been, if he'd made different choices and had different priorities. Gray swore if given a chance that he'd never go back to the life he led before.

He now called them every night. He helped them with homework. He showed them how to bake bread, and introduced them to a series of films released in the 1980s that Gray believed encapsulated what it meant to be a kid: inventive, at times mischievous, and able to do remarkable things in the absence of appropriate parental supervision. He even attended activities at their church, despite his hatred of the rock band and the slick preacher.

On Saturday, Gray and the kids spent the two hours permitted for him to be out of the house at the new nature playscape at Forest Park followed by burgers and root beer floats at Fitz's on Delmar. On Sunday, Gray made pancakes, and then they walked from his house over to Tower Grove. They engaged in a prolonged game of monster tag. Gray was, of course, the monster, growling and generally making a scene as he chased them up and down the slides and through large plastic tubes. Technically they were getting a little too old for monster tag, but, once it got going, Nick and Zoe forgot.

Then it was time to go. Kendra would be picking them up soon, and Gray couldn't hold back his emotions. On their walk back home, Zoe noticed the tears. "Are you okay, daddy?"

Gray patted her on the back. "I'll be fine. Don't worry about me."

Nick didn't notice the exchange. He'd run ahead and was peering through the window of a vacant one-story building with a "For Sale" sign taped to the window.

It was on Morgan Ford Road. Although it was a stretch to call it a commercial district, the vacant building was in the middle of a small cluster of funky businesses, including a tea house, a Ramen noodle shop, and a taproom. All were built in the early 1900s.

Gray had walked or driven past it hundreds of times. He always liked the building's brick facade, painted white with bright red windows and doors and green inlaid tiles along the sides. It reminded him of some of the small shops on the western coast of Ireland.

Originally the building was a small grocery store, but, over the past forty years, the property had been home to an accountant, several barber shops, a yoga studio, a florist, and, most recently, a purveyor of candles and hand creams. None of them lasted long.

Gray and Zoe joined Nick. They cupped their hands, pressed their faces against the glass, and tried to get a decent look inside. It was a little dirty, but wasn't too bad. The windows provided a lot of natural light. The floor was oak. There were white plaster walls topped with intricate crown molding. The very back looked like it was some sort of a kitchen. Originally, it was probably where they butchered and sold meat.

"That place is cool, dad," Zoe said. "You should get it. You could open a bakery."

Gray nodded. "It's very cool." He put his arms around his kids as they walked away. Perhaps in a different life he'd buy a building like that and bake bread, he thought, but likely not in this one.

On Monday morning, Gray woke up extra early. He wandered around the living room with a mug full of coffee and interrogated himself, practicing his answers to various hypothetical questions. The pressure building every minute that passed. He felt the weight pressing down upon him. This wasn't simply testimony. It was his life.

It was 7:00 a.m. when he showered, shaved, and put on his best suit and tie. In front of the mirror Gray gave himself a pep talk, then he went downstairs. Walking toward the kitchen, he stopped in the living room and looked at the trick cabinet he had purchased at the antique shop. It felt like that was decades ago.

He checked his watch, and then walked over to the cabinet, approaching it with caution. He pressed the little button, and the panel clicked open. Gray had done his best to ignore what he had put inside, pretend it never happened. There were long periods of time when he'd forget it was even there.

All of it was subject to alternate and equally plausible explanations, which proved he wasn't insane. The firing of two bullets into his chest did not happen. The memory was the result of a concussion. The knob on the pantry door that burned his hand and subsequent conversation with a group of homeless people in an army tent did not happen. It was a hallucination from a combination of prescription medication and alcohol. The burn occurred during a blackout, likely while he was attempting to light his brick oven. And, this…

Gray took the white rabbit's foot out of the cabinet. Its silver chain hung down as Gray touched the soft fur in his hand, feeling each of the little nails. He was supposed to use it, when he made "the great leap of faith." Gray looked up at the ceiling. He'd convinced himself the rabbit's foot belonged to his kids, left for him as a present. That's what he told himself. That was his explanation.

He was about to put it back in the cabinet, when he stopped. "Why not?" Gray loosened his tie, unbuttoned his shirt, and then put the rabbit's foot around his neck. He checked his watch, and now was in danger of being late. So Gray pulled himself back together—the rabbit's foot hidden beneath—and hustled out the door.

Gray met Naomi Moyo at the side entrance to the courthouse. Moyo handed her briefcase to the federal marshal, and then walked through the metal detector. "You're going to do great. Just answer the questions, like we talked about and you'll do fine."

Gray removed his watch, wallet, cell phone and belt. He put them into a plastic container, and then followed his attorney through to the other side. For whatever reason, the rabbit's foot around his neck did not set off any alarms, which was a relief. "I promise you that I will not talk about miracles, Irish Santas or little elves."

He collected his things, and then they walked toward the elevator.

Moyo hit the elevator button and a bell rang. "I think you also mentioned a horse sticking its head out of a car or something as well." She gave Gray a sideways glance with a smirk. "Unless directly asked, I think that should remain amongst us."

"Good catch."

A few seconds later the elevator doors slid open and Gray walked into the hallway. He felt the stares as he walked toward the courtroom, feeling more sick to his stomach with every step.

He leaned over and whispered to Moyo. "I'm assuming that when you talked to Steele that he agreed to dismiss all the charges and drop the case against me?"

"Not quite," Moyo said. "They politely declined to engage in any further negotiation."

"I figured that when you didn't call." Gray opened the door.

They went inside, walked down the center aisle, and settled in at the defense table. Steele and Brenner arrived a few minutes later, and then Judge Espinoza took the bench.

"Let's get started," Judge Espinoza said with a smile, "shall we?"

They discussed the proposed jury instructions, placed an agreement related to the final instructions on the record, and then Judge Espinoza placed Gray under oath and questioned him related to his decision to testify. "And you understand that this is your decision and your decision alone to make, regardless of the advice of your attorney?"

"I do understand that," Gray said. "And I choose to testify on my own behalf."

"Very well." Judge Espinoza summoned the jury, and they soon filed in through the side door looking rested and happy after the weekend break. When the jurors were seated, Moyo stood and called Gray to the witness stand.

Gray stood, and came forward. He felt the jurors evaluating him, curious. His every movement scrutinized. When Gray was at the witness chair, he did not sit down. Instead, he looked at Judge Espinoza and raised his right hand.

The judge began. "Do you swear to tell the truth, the whole truth, and nothing but the truth, so help you God?"

"I do," Gray said.

"You may lower your hand and then please state and spell your name for the record."

Gray did as he was told, and, when he was done, he sat down in a large leather chair. He tilted the microphone so that it was at the proper height, and then took a moment to orient himself.

Gray looked at the jury box. Although the ultimate decision would be decided unanimously by twelve jurors, with the alternates there were fourteen people staring back at him. Then Gray took in the full courtroom. There were probably fifty people in the gallery, and it was hard to tell whose side they were on. In the back, Gray saw Amy Wirth and he thought about the first time they met and how much had changed.

Judge Espinoza asked, "Are you ready to proceed Mr. Wendt?"

Gray turned to him. "I am, your honor."

Moyo stood and walked over to the wooden podium. At first glance, the podium didn't look like anything special, but it was actually a very expensive piece of trial equipment. Built into the podium was a computer and a myriad of devices that could display digital images, play video files regardless of format, and project paper documents onto the screens that were placed throughout the courtroom.

"Good morning, Mr. Wendt." Knowing the rule of primacy, Moyo didn't begin softball questions about Gray's background. There were no questions about family or kids or where he grew up. She had warned him in their trial preparation that she liked to "start hot" while the jury was actually paying attention.

"Are you a criminal?"

"No," Gray said.

"We heard from several politicians since this trial began," Moyo said. "Did you bribe them?"

"No," Gray said. "I didn't have any idea that Virgil Hawthorne was doing this."

"But your name is all over those emails and documents, right?"

"That's correct," Gray said, "but Virgil Hawthorne did the client contact. My strength was writing and legal research. He'd tell me what we needed and I'd do it, just a division of labor."

"So you don't deny drafting settlement agreements or correspondence to opposing parties?"

"I don't deny that," Gray said. "If I signed it, I don't have any reason to suspect that my signature was fake, but I didn't know the truth."

"The truth, meaning the truth about the files and conflicts themselves?" Moyo led him a little more, hoping not to draw an objection from the prosecution. "What about those?"

"I learned that they were fake after Virgil Hawthorne was killed," Gray said. "It took some time, but I figured out what he was doing."

"And did you report it to the FBI?"

"They already knew," Gray said. "I was being set-up."

Steele was immediately on his feet, shouting. "Objection, your honor," Steele said, and then, for the benefit of the jury, he added, "Mr. Wendt has absolutely no proof that anybody 'set him up.'"

"Sustained," Judge Espinoza said with a growl. "You are cautioned, Mr. Wendt, consider yourself warned."

Moyo didn't let the reprimand linger any longer than it had to. She moved to a safer topic, allowing everything to settle down. "Tell me what type of lawyer you are, Mr. Wendt?"

"I'm a real estate lawyer, which also included zoning and land use issues related to larger developments," Gray said. "Like new apartment buildings, shopping malls or the expansion of hospitals or universities."

"And where did you work?"

"I worked at Daniels & Bloom." Gray looked over at the jurors and spoke to them. It felt awkward, but Moyo had encouraged Gray to not just look at her during the questioning. She wanted Gray to try and make a connection with the jury.

"I started as an associate at the firm after law school, and then I became a partner in the firm."

Moyo waited until Gray was finished, then she pressed a button on the podium and a document popped up on the screen.

"I'm showing you what has previously been marked as Exhibit 85. Do you recognize this document?"

Gray looked at the screen that was on the witness stand. "I do," he said. "It's a research memorandum for Apex Development." Moyo projected five more documents up on the screen, and asked Gray the same questions related to each one.

"And who is Apex Development?" Moyo asked.

"They are a real estate development company that works primarily in the St. Louis area and also does some work on the Illinois side, like Alton and Edwardsville."

"They are a client of the firm?"

"Yes," Gray said. "I did a lot of work for them."

"These documents, Exhibits 85 to 91, tell me about them? What do they pertain to?" Moyo asked.

"They are related to a dispute with IRT Capital from New York," Gray said. "IRT is a finance company that provides developers a bridge loan, essentially they provide a line of credit that a developer can draw down as they build, then once the construction is completed there is an understanding that the developer will refinance and pay IRT back its money. Often there is an agreement for the finance company to retain some ownership interest in the property for a period of time. So IRT gets interest on the loan, and then once it is paid off, they continue to get a percentage of the development's revenue for a certain period of time."

"Could you be more specific about this dispute?"

"Yes," Gray said. "IRT purportedly claimed that Apex wasn't paying them enough. They thought the revenue was higher than what Apex was claiming."

"You used the word—purportedly," Moyo said. "Why did you use that word?"

"Because there was no dispute," Gray said. "It was made up."

"At the time, did you know that?"

"I did not," Gray said. "Virgil Hawthorne told me about a new issue that had come up on a student apartment building that was built near Washington University, provided me the details, and I got to work."

"Did you ever talk to anyone at Apex?"

Gray shook his head.

"No," he said. "Virgil did."

"Did you ever talk to anyone at IRT?"

"No, I did not," Gray said. "I just did some of the legal research, reviewed the financial information provided by Apex, and then wrote a memo with recommendations. I was told there was a successful mediation, and drafted a settlement proposal."

"And were you there for the mediation?"

"No."

"And were you there when the settlement proposal was signed?"

"No," Gray said.

"And what was the settlement amount for?"

"$1.7 million," Gray said, "which was then deposited into the firm's escrow account for Apex and was supposed to be paid to IRT."

"But that didn't happen?"

"As we heard in this trial," Gray said, "the money was paid, but siphoned to an off-shore account, laundered, and then that cash was paid to various government officials as bribes related to another Apex project pending before the St. Louis Board of Aldermen."

"Did you get any of that money?"

"No," Gray said. "I had no idea."

Moyo pretended to be a little surprised, and softly challenged Gray. It was an attempt to mitigate the prosecutor's inevitable attack on Gray's credibility.

"You are a senior partner at this firm and you want the jury to believe that you were out-of-the-loop?"

"It seems weird that I wouldn't be at these mediations or meetings, but when you charge over $400 an hour, clients don't want extra lawyers involved. They'll think a law firm is just padding its bills. So, the legal team makes a decision as to who is necessary to avoid writing off billable hours. Billing a client is only good for the firm if you can actually collect the money."

Moyo moved on. She projected a new document on the screen, and spent the next hour going over fifteen examples of work that Gray did related to legal disputes that never existed. It was the same scheme related to legal disputes where lawsuits were never filed in court with quiet settlements.

The defendants were always real companies that wanted to bribe a local government official, and the legal disputes were always fake. The only real difference was that sometimes the plaintiffs were real, and sometimes the plaintiffs were off-shore companies created by Daniels & Bloom for the sole purpose of laundering the money.

Gray could tell that the jury had lost interest about halfway through his testimony, but Moyo needed him to address every allegation against him. When Moyo finally finished, she wisely acknowledged the juror's boredom.

"I think we've seen enough documents." Moyo smiled, and a few of the jurors chuckled. "Let's turn our attention to November of last year." The majority of the jurors wrote down the date on their little notepads as Moyo turned back to face Gray. She asked, "What happened last November?"

"Virgil Hawthorne was murdered," Gray said. "And I was with him when he was shot."

"Do you remember the date?"

Gray told the jurors the specific date. "It was the night of the big snowstorm."

"You said that you were with Mr. Hawthorne when he was killed," Moyo said. "Where were you?"

"We were downtown, walking back from dinner," Gray said. "We had finished meeting with a potential client, and, as we were walking back, a vehicle approached, a man got out of the vehicle, and Virgil was shot."

"And what happened to you?"

Gray looked at Amy Wirth, and then said, "I was beaten by another person."

Moyo asked Judge Espinoza for permission to publish a photo, and Judge Espinoza agreed. Ordinarily it wouldn't be published to the jury until after foundation had been laid, but the photographs of Gray in the hospital had been stipulated by the parties to automatically be allowed into evidence.

"I'm showing you Exhibit 318." Moyo pressed a button and a grotesque image appeared on the screen. Some of the jurors visibly flinched. For hours they'd been looking at black and white legal documents, and now they were hit with a full color image of Gray in a hospital bed.

Tubes ran into his arms. A cord was attached to his finger, tracking his pulse. Another tube fed oxygen into what was his nose, although the swelling made it difficult to discern. One eye was swollen shut. The side of his head was bandaged, but blood had soaked through. The hair on his head spiked in every direction, and the rest of his face was a mottle of colors, blotches of black, blue, and yellow.

"Is that you?"

It took a moment for the question to register. Gray stared at the photograph. A lump formed in his throat making it hard to breathe, speak, or swallow. He knew that Moyo was going to show some photographs that were taken of him at the hospital, but he'd actually never seen them. He wasn't even conscious when the police had documented his injuries. Perhaps it was an oversight, or, more likely, Moyo wanted the jurors to see Gray's honest reaction.

The courtroom was silent.

"Mr. Wendt?" Moyo tried to get through, but Gray didn't respond. He sat frozen, unable to speak or move. Moyo tried to get his attention, again, but still no response.

"Can you go forward, Mr. Wendt?" She asked, but Gray said nothing.

Moyo looked at the judge, unsure of what to do, and Judge Espinoza called a recess. The jurors were excused. As they filed out of the courtroom, Gray remained silent and still. Judge Espinoza studied him, skeptical that it was all an act. Then the clerk banged the gavel, and the judge exited out the back without another word.

When it was Colton Steele's turn, he didn't waste any time. "Have you ever heard of Occam's Razor?"

The question took Gray by surprise. Moyo had prepared him for many things, but a pop quiz on a fourteenth century philosopher had never come up in their preparations for trial. As Gray struggled for an answer, Moyo stood.

"Objection, your honor," she said. "I fail to see the relevance."

Steele offered the judge an impish grin.

"A little leeway, your honor." He smiled at the jurors as if they were in on the gag. "This is cross-examination after all."

Judge Espinoza was not amused. "Get to the point, Mr. Steele."

"As you wish," Steele bowed his head. "Occam's Razor is 'the simplest answer is the most likely.' At least that's my crude paraphrase of a problem-solving theory developed by a Franciscan theologian."

Moyo stood, again. "Same objection, your honor."

This time Judge Espinoza didn't wait for Steele's response. "Sustained."

Steele played along, because his mission was already a success. His intent was to present the jury with his theory of the case, and his theory was that the simplest explanation was the correct one. In short, was it more likely that Gray and Virgil Hawthorne were working together or that there was a grand conspiracy to set Gray up to take the fall? The latter hypothesis, Steele would likely remind the jurors during closing argument, was only supported by the testimony of the defendant, himself, and no other evidence of any kind.

"You are not currently working as an attorney," Steele said. "Is that correct?"

Gray nodded. "Correct."

"Medical leave, is that right?"

"Yes."

"You weren't put on leave because you were charged with a crime, is that correct?"

Gray paused before answering, and this was a mistake. It provided Colton Steele an opportunity to make it seem like Gray was withholding information from the jury.

"Mr. Wendt, you are under oath and you have to answer my questions."

Moyo objected, but Steele didn't wait for Judge Espinoza. "Answer the question," he said.

"I was put on medical leave," Gray said.

"Because of your erratic and unreliable behavior, right?"

Gray thought about the fact that he had a dead animal's paw hanging around his neck, but managed to stay on message. "No, I was put on leave because…." Gray paused again. Under the rules, he could not name an alternate perpetrator without proof. This was the subject of voluminous pre-trial briefs and arguments. "They were setting the stage."

"Right." His smirk had returned. "And as for all the settlement agreements, billing statements, emails and letters that have your name on them," Steele said. "You admit that these are true and correct documents that have not been altered in any way."

Gray looked at Moyo, but there was nothing that she could do.

"That is correct," Gray said. "I had no idea a fraud was being committed." His frustration finally grew. "I had no idea the issues and disputes that I was working on were fake, because these were real clients of the firm." His frustrated outburst sounded more like panic, and Gray stumbled in his attempt to repair the damage. "These were… actual real estate developers with whom we also did real legal work, but these other things were made up to launder money and….I had….no, no idea that—"

Judge Espinoza intervened, mercifully.

"That's enough, Mr. Wendt." The judge leaned forward. "There is no longer a question before you."

Gray apologized and Steele continued, obviously pleased with himself for getting under Gray's skin. "I think I've heard enough," Steele said. "No further questions."

Moyo tried to rehabilitate Gray on her re-direct, but it was obvious, even to Gray, that the damage was already done. The jurors didn't believe a word that he had said. He felt like a fool.

CHAPTER FORTY-ONE

When Judge Espinoza adjourned for the day, Moyo asked if he wanted to debrief in one of the conference rooms before going home. Gray declined. There was nothing to debrief. He knew his testimony wasn't even close to enough. At this point, Gray wasn't even hoping for a "not guilty" verdict, he just wanted one juror to believe him. One would be enough to avoid a conviction and trigger another trial.

"What bothers me most is that Colton Steele is right," Gray said. "The simplest explanation is usually correct and I don't have a shred of evidence that Ethan Bloom orchestrated this whole thing or that there's some vast conspiracy out there intending to set me up."

Moyo put her hand on his shoulder. "It's not over, yet," she said, "and we've still got closing arguments. Luckily, I'm a pretty darn good advocate."

"You are a *great* advocate," Gray stood and put on his jacket, "but you are not a miracle worker." Gray turned and walked out the door. Midge and Haley had invited Gray over to dinner that night at their house, and he was looking forward to what may be one of his last home-cooked meals for quite some time.

In the parking garage, Gray called Midge. "Are we still on?"

"Of course," she said. "Haley's got a sheet pan dinner prepared and she's about to pull it out of the oven."

"Perfect." As Gray drove home, he pushed back a feeling of total hopelessness. There had to be something more that he could do, but short of kidnapping and torturing a confession out of Ethan Bloom, Gray couldn't think of anything.

He parked his car in back and walked over to Midge and Haley's house. When Gray entered their home, it smelled like butter, garlic and chives. The dining room table was already set, and, as Gray sat down, Haley emerged from the kitchen with a large platter of food. In the center was a chicken. Its skin baked golden brown. On one side, there was roasted cauliflower and Brussel sprouts. On the other, Haley had prepared four Hasselback potatoes, a classic dish from the 1950s that had become trendy once again. Gray had little doubt that Haley had seen the potatoes—sliced like an accordion, smothered with herbed butter, and topped with crunchy Panko crumbs— on Instagram and decided to give them a try.

With his mouth watering, Gray realized that it had been a few weeks since he had eaten a real homemade dinner. Cooking for one was never that enjoyable, and so he'd primarily subsisted on cereal and toast. With the kids, he ordered delivery.

"I think I could eat that whole thing," Gray said. "Absolutely all of it."

"Good." Midge opened a bottle of wine. "We need to fatten you up."

Glasses of wine were poured and Gray felt himself relax as the dinner progressed. Their conversations focused on the neighborhood, who's moving, who's remodeling, and whether or not there had been an uptick in petty crime.

As Haley brought out a plate of cookies for dessert, she and Midge tried to draw Gray into a disagreement they'd been having about summer travel plans. Midge wanted to take the old Route 66 to Los Angeles, while Haley wanted to go down to the Gulf Coast.

Everybody had done a good job of acting normal, but Gray knew Midge and Haley were just being polite.

"I know you want to hear about the trial," Gray said. "Giving you an update is the least I can do after that great meal."

Midge laughed. "How about a nightcap?"

"Sounds good," Gray said.

Their glasses were topped with the remaining wine, then they all got up from the table and walked over to the living room. Gray sat down on the couch. Midge and Haley sat down in chairs across from him.

"So?" Midge asked.

Gray took a deep breath, and then recounted his testimony and his conversation with the prosecutors. "We're going to rest tomorrow. Then closing arguments and jury deliberations." Gray finished his wine and set the glass aside. "I don't think they'll be deliberating very long. We're not going to win."

"You don't know that," Midge said. "It's not over."

"That's how it feels." He was a dead man walking. Best case scenario, Gray figured he had until Friday. The jury would likely begin deliberations late Tuesday or early Wednesday. It would look bad for them to only deliberate for a few hours, so somebody on the jury would require them to look at the hundreds of exhibits one last time, and then they'd reach a verdict on Friday afternoon. They'd been stuck together for two weeks, missing work and family. There was no way any of the jurors would want to return the following Monday.

He left Midge and Haley with a round of hugs, and then began his nighttime routine of brushing and flossing with the stupid rabbit's foot still around his neck. Gray made a list of all the things he needed to do and wanted to do in the coming days. Although there were times when his undoing had been painfully slow, as if God had simply pressed pause on the heavenly remote control, Gray recognized the end would come quick. When he was found guilty, the jurors would exit the courtroom, and Judge Espinoza, with a flick of his hand, would direct the federal marshals to take Gray into custody.

He spit out a mouthful of toothpaste, rinsed his mouth, and then walked back into his bedroom. He studied the furniture, considering whether or not he should rent a storage unit or sell it all, then his phone rang.

He looked down at the number. The caller was unidentified. Gray, initially, figured it was a robo-call—somebody trying to sell him an extended car warranty or congratulating him on winning a three day, two night, all expenses paid trip to Las Vegas— but given the time, it was too late for that.

Gray decided to answer. "Hello."

A woman started screaming at him, and Gray smiled. He lifted the rabbit's foot to his mouth, and gave it a kiss.

Cassie Hawthorne had been careful. She'd been moving every month or so, likely waiting for the trial to be over before settling down in one place. The investigators, Malcolm Shore and Benny Weah, knew she was still in the general area, never more than a four hour drive from St. Louis, likely because she was leaving her kids with relatives, but they were always a step or two behind.

Shore and Weah had tracked the location for months, primarily through where she used her credit cards. If it looked like she was falling into a pattern, like shopping for groceries or going to a coffee shop at similar times and days of the week, they'd set up surveillance. If a cancelled check to a landlord was posted to her account, they'd track down the landlord. None of their efforts had been successful.

When a closing was scheduled on the sale of Cassie's house, Shore and Weah were confident that they'd get her, but only the buyers had appeared at the title company. Cassie signed all of the documents electronically. Then they got lucky.

Through methods that Gray would never know, Shore and Weah got access to one of Cassie's social media accounts. The social media account had been dormant since Virgil Hawthorne's funeral, providing little information, but it was linked to an app that arranged for short-term vacation rentals. Rather than requiring a separate username and password, the vacation rental app allowed people to simply use the social media account to log-in. If Cassie made a reservation, Shore and Weah would know. The problem, however, had been that Cassie hadn't used the rental app in months.

Then a reservation popped-up for a small brick house near Old Town St. Charles, and that was all they needed. When Gray arrived forty minutes later, Cassie's mood had not improved. She looked as though she was about to start screaming, again, but Gray cut her off.

"I don't have a lot of time to mess around."

She shook her head. "So you hired two thugs to hold me hostage?"

Gray exchanged looks with Shore and Weah. They were giving Gray some space, but not too much space. If Cassie made a move, Gray had no doubt that they would bring her down. Given her crazed look, wild hair, and torn shirt, chances were good they'd already took her to the floor multiple times before Gray had arrived.

"I know you've been hiding from me and everyone else," Gray said. "So let's not pretend that I could just shoot you a text and we could meet for breakfast." He waited for a snarky response, but Cassie remained silent. Her arms folded across her chest. "In the next few days, I'm going to prison unless you help me."

Cassie shook her head. "There's nothing I can do."

"What do you mean there's nothing you can do," Gray said. "You know that I didn't do this. You can testify."

"Is this the moment where you get me to blurt out everything I know?" Cassie put her hands on her hips. "And then, when I'm done, you pull a little black box out of your pocket with a microphone and shout, 'Surprise, it's all been recorded!'" She shook her head and looked away. "I'm not dumb, Gray. That's the problem with lawyers. You always think you know the answer or that you have the perfect plan figured out, but you don't."

Cassie took a step back, and stared at Shore, and then gave a hard look at Weah. "They can't make me and they won't make me." She turned back to Gray. "I'm not going to testify, and if you, somehow, make me testify, then you're not going to like what I have to say. I will swear to tell the truth, and I will swear that you knew everything. That is what I will say. This is as far as it goes."

"They killed your husband," Gray said.

Cassie's eyes welled up, but she wouldn't allow a tear. "The cops say that a street thug named Deonte Banks killed my husband," she said. "That's all I know."

"Then why did you warn me?" Gray asked. "At the funeral and when I picked up the file, you warned me. Why did you warn me if you didn't want to help me?"

There was a long pause. Then Cassie's face hardened. "I don't know what you're talking about, Gray. You need to leave."

"I have kids, Cassie, just like you," Gray said. "If you don't help me— those kids are going to grow up, graduate high school, graduate college, get married and have kids of their own without a father." It took everything in his power not to simply break-down. "I may not be dead, like Virgil, but, if I go to prison for the rest of my life, I might as well be." Gray ran his hand through his hair, focusing his mind on what could be his final argument. "You're the only one who can help. I want to be a dad, a father, and I also see how stupid I've been. I see, now, how much of my life I've wasted at the office when I could've been living."

Gray waited, but Cassie said nothing. He could tell that she wanted to help, but he also understood the danger that she was in. She had her own children to protect. Cassie kept her lips sealed tight, refusing to speak. Gray waited, hoping that she'd give him something, but nothing ever came. His shoulders slumped. De-feated, Gray turned away from her and walked toward the door.

Benny Weah opened it for him, and then stepped aside. Cool night air filled the room, and then Cassie said, "Talk to Ethan."

Gray turned, baffled. "Why in the world would I talk to Ethan Bloom?" He asked. "Ethan set me up."

Cassie shook her head. "Talk to him. Not me."

Gray looked at his watch. It was now past midnight, and tried to calculate how many minutes he'd been gone and how much time he'd have left before violating the conditions of his house arrest. "I'm not sure that's going to happen."

Cassie hesitated, then said, "There's a downtown bar that he likes. I don't know what it's called, something, something, dog. I just know that 'dog' is in the name."

"You're going to call him?"

"Just go."

It took Gray a few passes before he found it. Hair of the Dog was a small, narrow place tucked amongst the trendy restaurants and shops that had sprouted up along Washington Avenue. A long bar ran the length of the right side; mismatched tables and chairs on the left with neon beer signs hung above.

The bartender, a young woman with various piercings and tattoos, asked him if he wanted a drink. Gray studied the long row of taps, mostly brands he'd never heard of. "Just give me a Schlafly."

The woman smiled. "I knew it. As soon as you walked in the door, I figured you'd order a Schlafly. All the old guys order it." She poured him a pint and set in on the bar. "Five bucks."

Gray paid, and, as he took a sip of beer, looked around. The bar was mostly empty. Not surprising on a weeknight. A couple hipsters were deep in conversation, another two were watching a replay of a spring training game on the television. A few more were playing foosball based on the sounds coming from the backroom.

Gray walked toward an empty table tucked away, partially obscured by a popcorn machine at the far end. Given what he wanted to talk about, Gray thought it would be the most private spot in the bar. He set his glass down on the table, filled a paper tray with popcorn, and then settled in for the wait.

Even if Cassie called Ethan, there was no guarantee that Ethan would come. Then, he'd have to figure out a different plan. Gray could talk to Moyo about options, but Cassie was right. Forcing her to testify would be a very bad idea.

Gray waited for forty minutes, thought about giving up, but he had no better place to go. He thought about his conditional release, but figured that he was going to prison regardless. What was the worst thing they could do to him?

He ordered another beer and then walked back to his table. As time passed, the bar kept filling up. Hair of the Dog was open until three, so it caught people as they left other establishments that had closed for the night.

Whenever the door opened, Gray's hopes rose only to fade at the sight of another kid in skinny jeans and clunky glasses. Gray was on his third beer, when Ethan finally came. Gray had never seen him in casual clothes and almost didn't recognize him. Still short and overweight, Ethan didn't look cool, but, unlike at the firm, he didn't look out of place in his black jeans, Timberland hiking boots, and a flannel shirt.

It forced Gray to make a reassessment. At Daniels & Bloom, Ethan was always nervous and awkward. As Gray watched Ethan chat briefly with the bartender while she poured him a drink, Ethan looked comfortable. As he walked toward Gray, acknowledging some of the regulars as he passed, Ethan even looked a little confident, but then, when Ethan sat down and began to speak, he seemed to revert to his old self. As if talking to another lawyer was his personal kryptonite.

He fidgeted with a coaster, avoiding eye contact. When Ethan began to speak, his posture worsened. "I don't know why I'm here. I shouldn't have come."

"It's a cool place," Gray said, trying to keep it casual, even though his life hung in the balance. "Cassie says that you're a regular."

There was an involuntary twitch, and then, "I like Shari." Ethan glanced back at the bartender. "I know she's paid to be nice to me. I'm not naive, but I still like her." It was as if Ethan had this conversation with others in the past, or maybe with himself. "She's good to me."

"Ever ask her out?"

Ethan made a little snort as he puffed out some air. "No."

He picked up his glass, took a sip of beer, and then looked at Gray. He opened his mouth, as if he was about to elaborate, but then stopped.

Neither one of them spoke, and finally Gray decided he would break the awkward silence, by simply being direct.

"I know it was you," Gray said. "It took some time, trying to untangle everything, and then, the pieces came together."

Ethan shifted in his seat, looking around. "I didn't set you up, man. You don't have any idea. You don't know me."

Gray wasn't surprised at the denial.

"Enlighten me," Gray said. "Because it seems like you set me up by sending me to get the Bevo file, so the prosecutors have a record of me being in possession of it and supposedly taking and destroying critical documents, and then you allow me to miss some meetings and get me put on medical leave, and now you've gotten all my clients and cases." Gray finished his beer and pushed the empty glass away. "It's all worked out pretty good for you."

Ethan raised his hand. "Lower your voice," Ethan said. "You got it all wrong."

"Really?"

"Yes," Ethan leaned in. "I've been working my ass off to help you, but there's only so much I can do. I told Cassie to warn you at the funeral that you were in danger, which she did, but things were already in motion. At the time, I thought there was just a mistake. I thought they were going to kill you, like they did Virgil, and then I realized they couldn't do that."

"Who?" Gray asked. "Who's they?"

"My dad," Ethan said. "He couldn't just kill you, because it'd look suspicious and result in even more scrutiny of the firm. He needed you alive, so that you could be prosecuted and once you went to jail, everybody could talk about how shocked they were and pretend that you and Virgil were acting alone."

"But you sent me to get that file from Cassie."

"I sent you to get that file, because I had to. My father told me to send you to get the Bevo file," Ethan said. "Then I called Cassie and told her to warn you not to return the file to the firm so that you wouldn't sign that stupid sheet of paper documenting that you had it…but you did it, anyway."

"I had it scanned," Gray said.

"That wasn't the point," Ethan said. "They wanted the signed file return slip when you gave it back to the records department to show that you and Virgil were trying to hide incriminating files. He wanted to create more suspicion. And then my dad started messing with your calendars, deleting appointments and hearings or moving them to the wrong date. All that helped to create this narrative that you're unstable and unreliable, in addition to getting you out the door."

"So, I really was getting better?"

Ethan nodded. "The first few times were on you. You really missed the Durell meeting and that committee hearing. Then, when that didn't happen anymore, my dad started messing with you."

Gray tried to process this. He'd been so angry and suspicious of Ethan for so long that it was difficult to pivot. "The bribes." Gray wanted details. "How long has your dad been doing this?"

"A long time, but not on this scale." Ethan took a few big gulps of beer, beginning to relax. Getting started had been the most difficult part. "It's my brother. He's running for senate and that requires money, millions, and it has to come from somewhere. This scheme gives my dad a lot of cash, and it also gives my dad leverage over a lot of powerful people."

Gray thought about this for a moment. "And you're jealous of your brother?" Ethan didn't respond, so Gray continued with a different question, "Were you the one cooperating with the FBI?" Gray tried to read Ethan's reaction. "That's my theory. You were the anonymous tip, and then Virgil dies and you keep telling them things. That's how they got to these other developers and politicians. You thought that Virgil would flip on your dad, but that didn't happen because he got killed. You didn't expect that."

Ethan changed the subject. "What do you want from me?"

"I want you to testify," Gray said. "Tell the jury everything that you just told me."

"No," Ethan said. "I can't do that. As much as I'd love to see my dad go to prison, I love my mom even more, and she'd never forgive me. It'd destroy her."

"So you're going to let me go to prison, instead?"

"Not necessarily." Ethan leaned in close and lowered his voice. "I've been thinking about this, and I know you need proof that you were set up, and you need proof that my dad did it." Ethan took a pen and began making a little sketch on a napkin. "This is what you need to do."

CHAPTER FORTY-TWO

Since the Missouri Athletic Club was also a hotel, it was always open. Gray didn't have the luxury of contemplating the perfect time to try and get into Herbert Bloom's office. He couldn't wait. In the morning, closing arguments would be made and he'd have no opportunity to present additional evidence. It was now or never.

Gray pulled into the surface parking lot next to the club, and touched the white rabbit's foot underneath his shirt after he had parked. He, then, paid the attendant his money, and walked toward the ornate brass entrance, holding his leather briefcase firmly in his hand. Gray straightened his posture, and stuck his nose a little further into the air. This was how important people acted, he reminded himself, important people who were in a hurry.

Gray stole a backward glance, confirming that Ethan Bloom was still parked across the street, acting as a lookout. Gray had given him two numbers. The first was for him to call Moyo, in the very likely event that he was arrested. The second was for Amy Wirth in case there was trouble of some kind. Of all the cops he'd interacted with, she was the only one he felt had the slightest bit of empathy.

He had his doubts about Ethan. Gray was not completely sure this wasn't a larger set up, but in the end he rationalized that he wouldn't lose much, he was going to prison anyway. But, if Ethan was telling the truth, he might be able to save himself.

There was a tall man at the door with a long black coat and tails. He tipped his top hat as Gray approached, and then opened the door. "Evening, sir."

Gray didn't say anything as he walked past, just a slight nod in acknowledgement. He kept a brisk pace as he moved through the lobby and underneath a series of crystal chandeliers. He was noticed by some of the staff, because they were paid to attend to the whims of the club's members and hotel guests, but Gray kept his eyes forward, never pausing to ask a question or appear in doubt as to where he was going.

A bell rang. The doors of a small elevator, ten yards away, slid open and a couple got out. Gray quickened his pace. He stepped inside just as the doors began to close. Ethan had told him the office was in room 325, and so Gray pressed the button for the third floor.

When he got off the elevator, the floor was empty except for a woman vacuuming. She was to his left and so Gray went to his right. He didn't wander. Gray kept his head straight, scanning the numbers on the doors out of the corner of his eye while pretending to know exactly where he was going.

Then he found it. As expected, no light came from underneath. Gray took out the napkin from the bar. On the bottom, Ethan had written a six digit code. Gray looked at the door. There was the original ornate handle with a modern electronic lock above it.

Gray looked around. Nobody was watching. Then he punched in the code. There was a click, and he slipped inside and turned on the lights. Everything was exactly how Ethan had described. Gray walked over to the rolltop desk, removed a butter knife he'd stolen from the bar, and pried the wooden panel up.

Gray checked his watch. There was no time to be selective. Gray yanked the laptop's power cord out of the socket and shoved the cord and the laptop into his briefcase. Then he rummaged through the drawers, one after another. There were notepads and bills and random scraps of paper. Gray grabbed what he could, and, once his bag was full, he went to the mantel.

Fastened to the mantel was an old black metal box that used to hold matches. As Ethan had told him, the box now contained a small fob with a screen that displayed twelve numbers. Every thirty seconds those numbers changed, and this was the security key to access the contents of Herbert Bloom's laptop.

Gray stuck the fob in his pocket, turned off the lights, and left.

In the hallway, he heard the woman with the vacuum say something, but he ignored her. He took the elevator down to the first floor, and walked out the front door. He was certain that at any moment a police officer would tackle him and he'd be placed under arrest. Adrenaline pumped so hard that Gray had to fight every impulse to run.

He looked across the street, but Ethan was gone. This was concerning, but there was nothing he could do but go faster. Gray turned and began to jog down the sidewalk to his car.

I'm going to make it, Gray thought as he opened his car door, got inside, and put the briefcase in the passenger seat. Then, he started the engine and checked his rearview mirror as he shifted the car into reverse. That was when he saw him.

A man was in the back seat holding a gun.

Victor Morales didn't introduce himself, but he didn't need to. Gray recognized him from the night that Virgil Hawthorne was murdered.

Ethan watched Gray enter the club. He had hoped the simple plan would be enough and be free of complications. Every second that passed, however, the unease grew. He knew his father, and knew that taking down the old man wouldn't be easy.

Then Ethan saw him. From the shadows, Morales emerged

and gained entry to Gray's car. It looked as if he had his own key. Ethan wasn't sure if his father's thug had been following Gray, or, perhaps the surveillance was much broader. Ethan thought he'd been careful, but everything left a trail. Perhaps, his father knew that he was the one who had started it all with a simple tip to the FBI. He wondered if his father knew that he had tried to protect Gray, or that he was paying to hide Cassie and her kids from him.

If he didn't, Ethan figured that his father knew the truth now. There weren't that many people aware of the private office or how to get in. His father wouldn't hesitate in killing him. The old man had always considered him the weakest link, an embarrassment, and very much disposable. His brother would soon become a United States Senator, and Ethan's branch would simply be pruned from the family tree with one swift cut.

Ethan looked at the front of the hotel. Gray would be coming out soon, and, if he waited too long, it'd be too late. Ethan took his phone out of his pocket. The plan had fallen apart. It wasn't supposed to be like this. He had intended to simply hold his father accountable, put his father in his place, humble him. Nobody was supposed to die. An innocent man wasn't supposed to go to prison.

He looked at the cell phone number for Amy Wirth's business card. Then Ethan took a breath and told himself to stop being a coward as he dialed the number.

Amy Wirth's evening didn't go as she had planned. After changing clothes and grabbing a beer from the refrigerator, Wirth settled down for the night in front of the television with a few slices of leftover pizza. She tried to decompress by binge watching the latest, loose adaptation of one of many of Philip K. Dick's science fiction novellas. It wasn't too bad, but, by ten o'clock, Wirth was ready to go to bed.

She stood up, carried her dishes to the kitchen, and went into the bedroom. She fell asleep, but her ringing phone pulled Wirth out of it. She looked at the clock, and it was well after three. Her thoughts immediately jumped to her parents in Florida, maybe her dad had another heart attack.

She answered.

"Ms. Wirth," came the voice, "you don't know me, but our friend Graydon Wendt is in trouble and he needs your help."

With a gun pressed against the back of his head, Morales instructed Gray on how to drive and where to go. They didn't go on any of the main boulevards in the core city. Morales, instead, took Gray on a winding path of backstreets that led out of downtown, through the hollowed neighborhoods of north St. Louis, under the highway, and to the industrial waterfront.

This was the original city. Millions of people lived in the St. Louis area, but few ever set foot on the old cobblestones or walked past the empty factories. It was a step back in time to another era, one that's dirty and gritty, and even in its prime had never been polished.

"Go down that street." Morales poked Gray's head with the barrel of his gun. "Then stop."

Gray did as he was told, turning onto a narrow side street and past two boarded up warehouses. Besides his headlights, the only light came from Merchants Bridge just a hundred yards north. The 130 year old railroad bridge carried freight three miles across the Mississippi River between Missouri and Illinois. Gray had been there before. It was where he was given his white rabbit's foot.

Gray stopped the car when he couldn't go any further. There was a large wooden barrier. The boards had been painted white, but most of the paint had peeled away over the years. In front and behind the barrier were steel drums filled with concrete.

On the other side of the barrier, there was the bridge, built high above the riverfront. When the snow melted in the spring, the Mississippi would rise and the whole area would often flood, but the flood didn't come this year. The land remained dry and desolate. It was a place that Gray now figured that he would die, unless he did something. He needed to take a leap of faith.

"Kill the lights and turn the car off. I gotta make a phone call."

Gray nodded his head, thinking.

Morales took out his phone and gave an update. "I got him. Got your stuff too. It's still in his briefcase.... We good?" There was a brief moment of silence when Gray assumed Morales got his answer, because he hung-up the phone. Then to Gray, "Take out the keys and toss them in the passenger seat."

Although he was scared, everything sharpened. It was the adrenaline, heightening his senses. Gray could smell his own perspiration, a salty musk, and the spearmint gum chewed by the stocky man. He felt the tiny beads of sweat form under his arm, occasionally rolling down his side, and the tiny permutations of the steering wheel that he gripped so tightly. He heard his own heart beating faster than it had ever before, and he now saw the faint outline of steps leading up from the riverfront to the bridge.

That was where he would go.

"I told you to toss the keys onto the passenger seat." The command was sharper. The man was losing his patience.

Gray saw through the rearview mirror that the stocky man had a gun in one hand and a syringe in the other. He didn't have much time. "Onto the passenger seat?" Gray's voice trembled. "The keys." He glanced to the side, and slowly took his hand off the steering wheel and pulled the keys out of the ignition. "You want them over there?"

When Morales answered, that was the moment.

Instead of tossing the keys in the passenger seat, Gray threw them as hard as he could, over his shoulder and back. It caught Morales by surprise. Instinctively, the stocky man flinched. He dropped the syringe as he raised his arms to block the keys from hitting his face.

It was just enough time to get out of the car. In one simultaneous movement, Gray ducked down to avoid getting shot in the head, while one hand unbuckled his seat belt and the other pulled the handle and pushed open the car door.

He spilled out onto the ground, and noticed the back door begin to open. While still down, Gray gave a two-footed mule kick to the back door as hard as he could. The door caught Morales with one leg out. The man screamed as it smashed into his shin.

Gray kicked the door closed twice more, causing Morales to scream again, but, the third time, Morales was ready. The stocky man threw his shoulder into the door at the same time, blocking the impact and jolting Gray back.

Time to run.

Gray rolled away to get a little distance, got to his feet, and began toward the bridge. He went as fast as he could, but the ground was so dry the dirt was like running in sand. With every step, Gray was sure that he'd soon be shot in the back, but Morales never fired the gun, likely because he didn't have to.

Morales gained on him. He didn't need to look for confirmation. Gray could hear him coming. The footsteps growing louder.

There may have been a time that Gray could have outrun Morales, but not anymore. Although they appeared to be roughly the same age, Gray had spent too many years sitting behind a desk. Morales also had the advantage of not having to blaze a trail. Morales directly followed Gray's path. His strides easier and more natural because Gray had compacted the loose dirt.

Ten yards from the staircase that led to the top of the bridge, Gray felt a hand on his shoulder, then his feet were kicked out from under him.

"I don't understand what you're telling me," Amy Wirth said. "I need to know your name. I need to be able to contact you again."

The man, however, didn't give his name. "I can't do that." His voice was steady, but there was also a trace of fear. "You need to hurry. You need to get here now. Do you understand that?"

When Amy didn't respond, the caller made it clear.

"He will die if you don't come." Then the line disconnected.

Amy pulled up her history, and immediately called the number back. It rang and rang, but he didn't answer. She put the phone down and looked around her apartment, hoping that someone would magically appear and tell her what she should do. She even considered doing nothing, but that ran counter to everything that she was ever taught and believed.

She considered the possibility that the call was just a prank. *How could some random guy get her personal cell phone number?* Perhaps Bird and Doles had somehow set-up the call, thinking that she'd panic and call 911. Yet another prank to remind her that they could still get to her.

It was unlikely, but possible.

Amy Wirth decided that she'd go herself. Graydon Wendt wasn't supposed to leave the house. He was on electronic home monitoring. If she found him, she'd call Agent Matthews and they'd arrange for his arrest. If he was in trouble, as the caller had suggested, she'd call for backup.

Wirth went to the closet. She grabbed her coat, purse, and gun. Traffic at night was sparse, and it only took about five minutes to get back into downtown. She slowed, a little, at intersections, but wasn't afraid to roll through stop signs and red lights.

Amy Wirth was a half-block away from the Missouri Athletic Club when she saw a car leaving the parking lot. She wasn't sure, but Wirth was fairly certain that it was the same make and model as the vehicle owned by Graydon Wendt. She picked up the phone and called Agent Matthews.

He didn't answer. The ringing stopped and rolled her over into his voicemail. "Matthews. Call me right now. Graydon Wendt is out and he may be in trouble."

Wirth followed the car from a distance, waiting for Matthews to call her back. There were so few vehicles and people downtown, if she got any closer, Wirth knew that there was a high likelihood that she'd be spotted.

She tried willing the phone into ringing. "Come on, Matthews, give me a call." She then watched as Gray's car passed by the convention center and the attached Dome, a professional football stadium without a team. The car was leaving downtown, but Wirth couldn't figure out exactly where it was going. It hadn't taken the usual routes that fed into the various highways that wrapped around the city.

She thought about where Deonte Banks was killed. Perhaps that was where he was going.

When Gray's car stopped at 9th and Cass, Wirth decided she could no longer wait for Matthews. She needed to take a chance. Wirth called dispatch as she pulled up behind the car. When the light turned green, she followed it as it turned. It was then that, she noticed for the first time, there were two people in the car. The person was directly behind the driver. From a distance it only looked like one person, but now she knew there were two.

Her call was answered.

"This is Amy Wirth," she said. "I'm an investigator with the St. Louis Police Department." She rattled off her badge number, knowing that the call to dispatch was being recorded, because all 911 and dispatch calls were recorded. If things went sideways or ended up in court, Wirth knew that she needed to make sure everything was legitimate.

"I think I spotted a man in violation of his home confinement, and I'd like a plate checked."

Dispatch, replied, "Yes, ma'am. I'm ready."

Wirth relayed the license plate to dispatch, and, just as she finished, the car suddenly turned right without signaling. She didn't follow, because Wirth didn't want to draw their attention.

"They just turned onto 16th. Going north. I'm turning around. I lost sight of them."

There was silence, except for the sound of the dispatcher tapping her keyboard. Then came the confirmation. "The car is registered to Graydon Wendt."

"Thanks." Wirth turned right on Hogan, accelerated, and then took another right on Mullanphy Street, to circle back and, hopefully cut them off.

"Notify any squads in the area," she said. "I'll keep looking. This is part of a murder investigation. It's a high priority."

Wirth hung up the phone, and then drove north to Florissant Avenue. She slowed down at a gas station. None of the cars were what she was looking for. That would've been too easy. Wirth drove four more blocks, and then stopped. If she didn't find them soon, they'd get away and, if her anonymous caller was right, Gray would be dead.

"When you are lost in the woods, stop," Wirth told herself. She, then, pulled over to the side of the road, closed her eyes, and thought about where they could be going. Everything that she'd seen suggested that they were staying off the highways and off the major roads. Gray or whoever was in the backseat of his car was being careful. Wirth put herself in their situation. If somebody was going to kill Gray, then they wanted someplace quiet. Otherwise, it would've already happened.

Wirth put her car back in gear, and turned west toward the riverfront. It was their most likely destination. As she drove under the highway, Matthews called.

"What's going on?"

"I found him," Wirth said. "Then I lost him."

"Graydon Wendt?"

"Yes." As Wirth looked for Gray's car, she tried to explain. "I got a strange call on my personal number, and I was told that he was at the Missouri Athletic Club and he was in trouble." This was the part where she lied, just a little. "That's when I called you, but, when you didn't answer, I decided to go down myself. When I arrived, I thought I spotted his car leaving. I called dispatch, confirmed it was him, and now we're all out here looking for him. I think they know people are looking because the driver took a sudden right and shook me off."

"Them?" Matthews picked up on the plural.

"There are two people in the car. I'm assuming one is Graydon Wendt. I can't even say that for sure, but I've got no idea who the second person is."

"Where are you now?"

"On 9th, heading north, just went under McKinnley. I figured the regular patrol cars would be looking in the neighborhoods, and so I headed to the waterfront."

"Hang on," Matthews said. "I'm getting my coat. I'm coming out to join you."

"You really don't have to, I mean we're doing everything—" At Angelica Street, Wirth spotted a car. It was a couple blocks away, but it looked like the right vehicle. "I think I might've spotted it." Wirth pressed the gas, and her engine groaned. "There's a bunch of warehouses down here. I've gotta catch up."

Wirth hung up on Matthews, and then slowed just enough to call dispatch without crashing into a lamppost. "This is Amy Wirth, again. I think I spotted his vehicle on Angelica near the riverfront....hold on." Wirth watched as it disappeared into an alley. "Just lost sight of it, trying to catch up. Send some cars over."

Wirth was now going over eighty miles an hour past the storage facilities, warehouses, and a brickyard. Then Angelica Street ended. Four concrete barriers prevented her from going any further. She turned around, and, slowly went back. Then she saw a narrow alley that eventually led to Ferry Street. Wirth turned right on Ferry, going west, again, toward the river.

As she went the road grew narrower, the pavement transitioned to old brick pavers, and then to gravel. Wirth decided to turn off her lights. If they were ahead, she didn't want them to see her coming.

Creeping forward in the darkness, if there was an obstacle, she wouldn't see it. Her heart thumped as she slowly pushed forward. If she hit something, there wouldn't be any damage. Her slow speed, however, wouldn't help if she went into a ditch.

As Wirth passed under one of the two elevated railroad tracks that eventually merged overhead to go over the Mississippi River, there was literally a fork in the road. One road led to Merchants Bridge and the other to a large, dilapidated warehouse. Wirth guessed that they would've taken the road to the warehouse, but she thought it'd be safer to go toward the bridge. From the bridge, she'd have a better sightline, and, if she didn't see anyone, Wirth figured it'd be safer to approach the warehouse from behind rather than from the front.

She drove her car to the very end. There were five concrete barriers, about four feet high, dropped in the middle of the road that prevented her car from going any further. She stopped, got out, and climbed over the barriers. From there it was another twenty yards to a narrow staircase that led up to the bridge and railroad tracks.

It was quiet, and Wirth didn't see anything. There was no sign of life, except the cold wind coming off of the river. It shook the branches of several, large trees near the warehouse and pricked her face. She could feel her cheeks turn pink and then red.

As she got closer, Wirth wondered if she'd made a mistake. Perhaps she was so desperate to prove herself and impress Matthews that her mind was playing tricks on her. When she got to the staircase, her phone vibrated just as she took her first step. She stopped and looked at the screen. It was Matthews, and she almost didn't answer. She didn't want to tell him what she now felt was certain—Gray got away, again.

She pressed the button as she navigated the steps, holding it to her ear with one hand as the other tightly gripped the railing. In a whisper, "Hey."

"Where are you?"

"Ferry Road." Wirth paused and looked at the riverbank and then over at the warehouse in the distance. "I may have lost them, again." Wirth figured she might as well break the bad news right away. "I thought I saw the car head down here, but I haven't seen it since."

"I'm on Broadway now, just passed Mallinckrodt. I've got the map up on my screen. Looks like I'm about three blocks away from Ferry Road."

Wirth kept climbing. "If you follow the road east, then you'll get to a fork. The one on the right goes to a warehouse and the other follows the elevated train tracks to the bridge. I went to the bridge, figuring I could get a good view. Unfortunately, I think that's all I'm going to get."

"No worries," Agent Matthews said. "I'll be there in about five minutes. We can keep looking together."

Wirth hung up the phone as she reached the top step. It was, indeed, a breathtaking view. The river looked like black stone, reflecting the moonlight. Lights dotted the riverbank, highlighting the river's gentle curve.

She looked at the warehouse. Wirth didn't see anything or hear anything. She stood on the bridge for a few more minutes, watching, but the wind had grown harsher. The cold seemed to cut through her jacket and clothing, straight to the bone.

She carefully stepped down from the bridge, and began walking back to her car. Wirth was almost there when she heard a scream. Then she heard another. Wirth unholstered her gun, took off the safety, and ran back to where she had just come.

###

Gray lay on the ground. Morales stood over him with a gun pointed at his head. "Roll over." Morales removed a plastic zip-tie from his pocket. "Then put your hands behind your back."

Gray didn't move. "Just shoot me."

Morales smiled. "No," he said. "It's not going to be that easy."

"Just shoot me." Gray's tone hardened. He wanted it over. "I said just shoot me."

"And I said that ain't gonna happen," Morales said. "You're going to cooperate with me."

Gray shook his head. "I don't think so."

"Perhaps you should reconsider." Morales took his cell phone out of his pocket. While keeping the gun pointed at Gray's head, he touched the screen and the phone came to life. "Let me show you something. Hold on, it might take me a minute to find it." Then Morales touched the screen three more times and a picture came up. "There it is." He held it out for Gray. "See that."

Gray looked and it was a picture of his little girl, Zoe. It was a picture taken at her school. She was on the playground with her best friend Tristan.

"If you don't cooperate, I'll kill her," Morales said, " and then I'll kill that great little son of yours, too." Morales slid the picture of Zoe off the screen, and another photograph popped up. This photograph was of Nick. "Too bad it won't be quick, if you make me do it the hard way. I know what you're thinking, why should you trust me?" Morales shrugged his shoulders. "Truth is that you can't, but, at least when you die—and you are going to die tonight—you'll die believing that you saved your kids. And that's gotta count for something, am I right?"

Gray didn't respond.

"I'm not some sick whack job," Morales said. "I'm a professional, and I don't take pleasure in that kinda stuff, try to avoid it if I can." He gestured for Gray to roll over with his gun. "Now cooperate and don't make this difficult."

At a certain point, a person had to admit defeat. Gray was at that point. He started to move onto his stomach, and then he heard a woman shout.

"FBI, get your hands up in the air."

On the ground, Gray couldn't see who it was, but recognized the voice coming from the direction of the railroad tracks. He was wrong. Ethan hadn't betrayed him. He'd made the call to her like they had planned.

"I think there's been a misunderstanding." Morales still didn't turn. "Perhaps we can talk about—" His eyes narrowed. Morales, then, turned and fired six shots in the direction of Amy Wirth. She got off two.

Recognizing another opportunity, Gray got to his feet and jumped on Morales's back. He wrapped one of his arms around his neck, and squeezed. It was the sleeper hold, but Gray wasn't trying to put Morales to sleep. He was trying not to get shot.

Unable to shake off Gray, Morales did the opposite. With his free hand, Morales reached behind him. He grabbed Gray's hair. He pulled it hard, and then flung himself backward, sandwiching Gray between himself and the ground.

Gray grunted in pain. The impact knocked the wind out of him, and his grip around Morales's neck loosened enough for Morales to break free.

It only took a second, but now Gray was back on the bottom. Morales, breathing heavily and his face red with anger. Morales straddled Gray's torso and punched Gray two times in the head. "I wasn't supposed to leave any marks," Morales, punched Gray in the head a third time. "But sometimes things happen. By the time they fish your body out of the river, there shouldn't be much left to find."

Morales pointed the gun at Gray. "Now get up and we're going to walk to the bridge, and you're going to jump into that cold water and die. It'll be a sad day for everyone, but people will certainly understand why you committed suicide. People will understand why you didn't want to go to prison."

Morales led Gray over to the bridge. As they began to climb the stairs, Gray saw Amy Wirth laying on the ground. A gun was in her hand. Her jacket, near her shoulder, was stained red.

"Get going." Morales poked him with the gun. "It's over, and I'm cold."

Gray took another step, and then stopped. "I'm not jumping. When they find my body, I want them to find that bullet hole. I want them to know I was murdered. So let's do it."

"And when you're done with him then you're going to have to kill me too, son." The voice with an Irish accent came from the shadows under the train track, and then the big man with the long white beard emerged.

Morales smiled, assessing the threat as minimal. "Gladly."

But Gray didn't hesitate. He jumped down on Morales, the stairs having given him leverage and position. He drove his shoulder into Morales's chest, and then knocked the gun out of his hand. Gray didn't know where he found the strength, but it was enough to pin Morales to the ground.

The stocky man, however, thrashed and fought, and just when Morales was about to break Gray's hold, there was another voice.

"Enough." With a gun in one hand and a large flashlight in the other, Agent Matthews commanded them to stop. "FBI."

CHAPTER FORTY-THREE

It was unclear to Gray whether he was under arrest. Unlike Morales he was not placed in handcuffs, put in the back of a police car, and driven away. He was, instead, checked out by a team of paramedics, and, once cleared, taken by somebody who he didn't know to the FBI headquarters. The woman gave him a bottle of water and put him in the same little conference room where he had first spoken to Agent Matthews, which now felt like a lifetime ago.

That was where he sat, alone. Gray looked around the room, trying to find the hidden cameras and recording devices. He fiddled with a plastic bottle filled with water while his leg bounced, involuntarily. There was a combination of anxiety and anticipation.

Thirty minutes passed, then an hour.

The fidgeting stopped, and his leg became still. Gray hadn't mastered the art of mindfulness, nor had there been anything that occurred to put him at ease. He simply couldn't maintain it. The rush of adrenalin only lasts for so long. He was slowing. His mind dulled, as all of the events over the past eight months began to come down on him, hard.

Gray decided that he couldn't let that happen. He stood and began to pace the room, deciding that the movement would keep some momentum going. He needed to organize his thoughts. He needed to sort out what had happened and try and make sense of it, while he still had some energy left. He began with the phone call from Weah and Shore and the conversation with Cassie, then

Ethan and the office, and finally ending with the stocky man, Amy Wirth, and, of course, the Irish Santa.

Was he really even there?

Perhaps it was Agent Matthews, and his mind was playing a trick. Gray paced around the room a few more times, and then stopped at the door. He tried to turn the handle, but the door was locked, answering at least that question—he was not free to leave.

Gray knocked on the door. "Anybody out there?"

"Hang on," came the response.

Gray heard someone's keys jingle, and then the door opened. The woman who had driven him from Merchants Bridge to the FBI headquarters appeared in the doorway. "Do you need anything?"

He asked, "How long is this going to be?"

"Your attorney is here," she said. "When they're done talking, she'll come down here and explain."

"Can I have a notepad and some paper?"

The woman thought about the request, but didn't commit. "Why don't you just go back and sit down. You've created enough chaos tonight."

Two hours later, Naomi Moyo entered the room. Even though it was the middle of the night, she looked perfect, wearing a tailored suit along with meticulous hair and makeup. She appeared to be ready for court, despite the fact that, like him, she hadn't gotten any sleep.

Moyo pointed at the scraps of paper that Gray had on the table. "You've been busy." She sat down across from him. "Heard they gave that to you because you wouldn't shut up."

"That's true." Gray picked some of the pieces of paper up, clearing the space in front of his attorney. "Just trying to figure it out, but I don't think I'm doing a particularly good job." He pushed the paper aside and set down the pencil. "What can you tell me?"

"The other man," she said. "His name is Victor Morales and he is in custody. He isn't talking, but Agent Matthews thinks that he's just waiting to learn what the prosecutors know. He knows the game, and he isn't going to tell anybody anything that they don't already know. And then there is the laptop computer and papers that were found in your briefcase."

"I took it from Herbert Bloom's office at the MAC," Gray said. "Supposedly it has information on it that proves I'm innocent."

"I know you broke into his office," Moyo said. "That has complicated things on multiple levels. First, we can't get into the laptop because it's encrypted. Second, even if we could get into the laptop. There are some issues about whether there's probable cause to access the information and whether it'd be admissible in Court, and, third—"

Gray interrupted. "How many complications are there?"

"Many more," Moyo said. Her face severe. "Probably the biggest being that you violated your house arrest and you committed a felony."

"I was already going to prison," he said, and bit his lower lip. "I didn't have much choice."

Moyo's demeanor softened a little. "I know. That's what I've been trying to explain."

"What happened to that investigator?" Gray asked. "I saw her go down. She was shot."

"I don't know," Moyo said. "She's in the hospital, probably saved your life."

Gray nodded, looking down at his folded hands. "I owe her and I owe Ethan, too." Then he looked up at Moyo. "Has anyone talked to Ethan? He can verify everything. He knows everything. He knows I'm telling the truth."

Moyo put her hand on Gray's arm. "They're talking to him now," she said. "He's in the room next door. We just have to wait."

Gray was about to say something, and then stopped. "I know....be patient."

"I better get back." Moyo stood and walked over to the door. She knocked, and then waited for the female agent on the other side to unlock it.

As Moyo was about to leave, Gray remembered what was in his pocket. "Wait." He smiled. "I've got something for you." Then he reached in, removed the fob, and tossed it to Moyo. "For the laptop," he said. "That might help with at least one of the complications."

CHAPTER FORTY-FOUR

Judge Espinoza summoned the parties to the courthouse at 8:00 a.m. His law clerk made it clear that nobody should be late. As a general rule, judges did not like to receive calls in the middle of the night. Judge Espinoza had received three. He was called to issue a warrant when Gray violated his house arrest. He was called to provide permission to open and search Herbert Bloom's laptop computer, and he was called, a third time by the attorneys with a request to delay the remainder of the trial.

When he entered the courtroom, Judge Espinoza held a large cup of coffee in his hand as if it was providing him life-extending properties. His eyes were puffy, and, from the expression on his face, he was skeptical of everything that had happened in the last twelve hours.

"Be seated." He set his coffee down on the bench, and sat in his large black, leather chair. Then to Colton Steele, Judge Espinoza said, flatly, "Jurors will be arriving in about forty minutes for what we all expected would be closing arguments. Do you want to enlighten me as to what is now going on?"

"Yes, your honor," Steele exchanged a look with Brenner, but she offered little support.

Seated as far away from Steele at the prosecution table as possible, it was obvious that they were in disagreement. Brenner wanted nothing to do with her colleague or what he was about to say, but Steele pressed forward.

"There have been some developments." He puffed, filling himself with self-righteousness. "As you know, the defendant has

305

maintained his innocence from the beginning. With the trial coming to a close, he took it upon himself to obtain potentially exculpatory evidence by breaking into the private office of Herbert Bloom and taking a laptop computer and some other papers. The information obtained puts the prosecution and, quite frankly, the Court in an awkward position." Steele paused. "While we certainly seek the truth," Steele turned and pointed at Gray. "What he did was and is unacceptable, and, being a lawyer, the defendant was also fully aware that there are legal mechanisms to obtain this information. We simply cannot condone running around and putting people's lives at risk, as the defendant has done. An FBI agent almost died last night because of his actions."

He turned back to Judge Espinoza, the scolding complete. "For that reason," Steele said, "whatever so-called evidence obtained by the defendant should be excluded. We should finish our closing arguments as planned, and then submit this matter to the jury without further delay."

Steele paused, wanting to emphasize the point, knowing that finishing the trial would definitely please the judge. Then he concluded. "While the jury is deliberating, I believe the defendant should be sanctioned and found in contempt of this Court."

Judge Espinoza folded his arms across his chest. He took a long draw from his coffee. Without saying a word, he rubbed his face, debating in his own mind whether to comment or ask a question. He opened his mouth, but then glanced at the court reporter. Her hands hovered, at the ready, over the stenographic machine. Then he thought better of it and closed his mouth.

Although he didn't know everything, Judge Espinoza knew enough to understand that this was a critical juncture in the trial. Every word he spoke would likely be scrutinized by the appellate courts, and, thus, he knew to minimize thinking out loud or making an unnecessary comment. "Ms. Moyo," he turned to the defense table, "your response."

"Your honor," she said. "Let me be clear, I had no idea what my client was doing and I, in no way, condone his behavior, but I think that you and I as well as the prosecution know how difficult it is to overturn a conviction. There are countless examples of men who have served ten, twenty, thirty years in prison for crimes that they did not commit. There is DNA evidence, obtained after the trial, that proves that they did not commit the crime. Yet, they remain in prison, because the court system is not designed or intended to relitigate and review facts once a jury renders its verdict. Certainly we are good at debating technical legal issues and whether or not a judge made a proper ruling, but not the facts. Facts and evidence are the sacred province of a jury."

Moyo put her hand on Gray's shoulder. "My client, as Mr. Steele pointed out, is a lawyer. He knew this better than anyone. Time was running out, and he understood that it would be highly unlikely for the prosecution to be eager to seek information that undid their own conviction in the future. We like to say that we are searching for the truth, but we are more often searching for finality, regardless of whether it is right."

Moyo, poised and not showing a hint of weariness, continued. "I also want to be clear about something that Mr. Steele didn't truly address, if at all. The evidence that we are discussing is not 'potentially' exculpatory, it is exculpatory. It proves my client did not commit this crime. It proves it, and if this Court excludes this evidence, goes forward with closing arguments, and the jury renders a guilty verdict, which, quite frankly, we all expect, then an innocent man will go to prison."

Judge Espinoza shifted in his chair, weighing his options.

Moyo allowed him to struggle with two choices that were both flawed in their own way, and then offered a third option. "Perhaps, your honor, I could suggest a process that would provide you with some additional time to consider what to do as well as provide the defense an opportunity to ensure that there is a proper record."

As Moyo described what she wanted to do, Gray held his breath. Time again slowed. The palms of his hands moistened. His heart pounded and his stomach tightened. He could hear nothing as Moyo's words faded into a soft slurry of background noise and Judge Espinoza took another sip of his coffee, adjusted his tie, and tapped his pen on his legal pad.

This was the moment. This was all his idea. As Gray paced the interrogation room at the FBI headquarters, he designed a trap and Moyo had set the trap better than he had imagined. All Judge Espinoza had to do was take the bait, and everything else would fall into place.

CHAPTER FORTY-FIVE

Judge Espinoza swore in the witness. After stating and spelling his name, Ethan Bloom sat down in the witness chair. He was just like all of the other witnesses that testified before him, but no jurors would hear his testimony. Moyo had argued that in order for Judge Espinoza to rule on whether to include or exclude Herbert Bloom's laptop computer, the defense was entitled to make an offer of proof.

Legally, the evidence was obtained improperly, and Gray should be sanctioned. Gray understood that, and, in the abstract, Judge Espinoza had ample grounds to punish him. However, for as flawed and unhealthy as the legal system was, no lawyer or judge wants to send an innocent man to prison. And, Gray was convinced that if Judge Espinoza heard the testimony of Ethan Bloom, he would do the right thing, assuming that Ethan Bloom told the truth.

A trial lawyer's golden rule was to never ask a witness a question when you don't know how the witness is going to answer. Moyo was a good lawyer. She understood that rule, and, as she stood behind the lectern, she knew that she was going to be violating it not once or twice, but with every question she was about to ask.

Things had happened so quickly that Moyo didn't have an opportunity to interview Ethan Bloom, herself, or see any reports or review any prior statements. Moyo was trusting Gray's word. That's all she had.

"So," Moyo reviewed some scribbled notes on a pad of paper, "we'll start slow." She cleared her throat. "You are related to Herbert Bloom, is that right?"

"He is my father."

"And you work at Daniels & Bloom?"

Ethan Bloom nodded. "I do. I'm a lawyer. I'm on the executive committee, and I do quite a bit of administrative tasks."

Moyo was quick to see the opening that Ethan had made for her, and she followed it. "Tell me more about the administrative tasks. What are three or four administrative tasks that you did?"

"Sometimes I had to babysit summer associates," Ethan said. "These are law students who are hired for the summer, sort of like an extended job interview, if we like them, then we will extend a job offer before they return to school in the fall. There's an expectation that we take them to Cardinals games, the theater, concerts, and bar association events. It's a perk for them, and also an opportunity for the firm to observe them in social settings."

"And you were one of the people who did that, did the observation?"

"Right," Ethan said. "I'd also interview support staff, like paralegals, IT guys, and receptionists. Then, if there were performance issues, I might meet with them about that or just terminate their employment."

"Anything else?"

Ethan thought for a moment. "Not really," he said. "Sometimes my dad would send me on errands, just grunt work."

"How did you feel about that?"

Ethan shrugged. "He is the boss."

Moyo repeated the answer as she wrote it down on her notepad. "Let's talk about that for a little bit. Was there a second in command at Daniels & Bloom?"

Ethan shook his head. "No. My older brother sort of was, but nothing official and he took a leave of absence last year to campaign full time."

"Your brother is Thomas Bloom?"

"Correct."

"And he is running for the United States Senate?"

"Yes," Ethan said.

"When you hired somebody, did you make that decision?"

Ethan shook his head. "I just did the preliminary interview with the firm's director of human resources, but my dad made the final call."

"And when someone was terminated?"

"My dad would make the decision to terminate."

"How would you describe your father's management style of the law firm?"

"Management style," a little smile came across Ethan's face. "He was a micromanager. He was constantly monitoring billable hours, clients, and money. He'd have reports generated every week related to how much revenue the firm generated and questioned every request for reimbursement."

"Your father is over sixty," Moyo said, "have you seen him operate computers, phones…otherwise use technology?"

"Yes," Ethan said. "He hates it, because he says that, 'the government is always watching.'"

There would ordinarily be objections and arguments related to the form of questions, relevancy and hearsay, but, without a jury, there wasn't any point. Colton Steele and Amber Brenner were silent, listening.

"Let me ask that question in a slightly different way," Moyo said. "Is your father proficient with technology?"

"Yes," Ethan said. "He's always reading about it and whenever there is new software installed at the firm, he gets trained on how to use it and also how to use the administrative functions."

"Administrative functions?"

"In addition to the IT people, my father insisted on also having administrative rights."

"Why?"

"So he could poke around."

Steele objected, but struggled to come up with a basis. "Foundation?"

Judge Espinoza waved off the objection. "Continue Ms. Moyo."

"Had you ever seen your father access other attorney's email or documents?"

Ethan nodded. "I have. He thought it was fun."

"Did your father have the ability to manipulate the calendar for attorneys? For example change the dates and times of meetings or hearings."

Ethan nodded. "He could do whatever he wanted. Like I told you, he was the boss. There wasn't anything that happened at the firm that my dad wasn't aware of."

Moyo looked at Gray, and then said, "Let's get to why you are here. Was your father aware of the bribes being paid to local politicians?"

"Aware?" Ethan considered the question. "He wasn't just aware of it,. He designed the whole thing. It'd been going on for years, but recently the scope of it grew. My dad became more aggressive."

"For what reason?"

"My brother was running for the senate and he needed money and favors," Ethan said. "He needed my brother to win, and he couldn't wait around. He was dying….he hadn't told anybody. I don't think he knows that I figured it out, but I knew." Ethan took a breath, and then he looked at Gray. "I knew what he was doing was wrong. That's when I called the FBI."

It only took another twenty minutes for Ethan Bloom to destroy the prosecution's theory of the case. The testimony was detailed and precise. Ethan explained what he had done and what he didn't. He accepted responsibility for not coming forward sooner, and described how he had tried to help Gray, both indirectly and directly.

Colton Steele asked a few follow-up questions, but it was clear that he no longer had a stomach for the fight. When Ethan Bloom stepped down from the witness stand, Judge Espinoza looked at the prosecutors and held out his hands. "I can't in good conscience keep that information from the jury. Regardless of whether the computer and other documents from that office are allowed, the defense has not rested. They have a right to call witnesses and put forward any evidence favorable to them. I can't imagine any appellate court affirming a decision by me to keep it out as a sanction."

There was, again, a long silence as the judge's words were absorbed by everyone in the courtroom. Judge Espinoza didn't continue. He was obviously waiting for one of the attorneys to make the next move, and that was when Moyo stood.

"Your honor, we could call in the jury and we could call Ethan Bloom back to the stand and also offer the contents of Herbert Bloom's laptop computer into evidence," she said. "But for the sake of judicial efficiency, the Defense moves the Court for a directed verdict of 'not guilty' and the defense hopes the prosecution would not object to such a motion."

Judge Espinoza turned his attention to Colton Steele and Amber Brenner. Steele was looking down at his notepad, and it was obvious he was done. He knew he'd lost, but he wasn't able to admit it.

"Mr. Steele?" Judge Espinoza inquired. "Ms. Brenner?"

Amber Brenner looked over at her colleague, and then she stood when Steele didn't respond. "Yes, your honor," she said, "I think it is clear that the prosecution can no longer meet its burden of proof beyond a reasonable doubt, and we have no objection to a directed verdict."

Judge Espinoza nodded. He'd been a judge for over ten years and he'd never granted such a motion. As a defense attorney, he'd also never been granted one or even heard of such a motion being granted. The preference was always to let the jury decide, even if the prosecution's case was weak, but, here, the motion was uncontested.

"Very well," Judge Espinoza said. "The motion for a directed verdict of not guilty is hereby granted, and you, Mr. Wendt, are free to go."

Gray, however, did not go. It wasn't over. There was still one more matter that needed to be addressed. He waited in the courthouse for hours, and, as five o'clock approached, Gray wondered whether it was ever going to happen.

Then he saw him.

Herbert Bloom stepped off the elevator, flanked by a half dozen tall men in dark suits. They walked toward Judge Espinoza's courtroom. Their expressions tense and ready for a fight.

Gray stood up from the wooden bench as they came closer. He ignored the stiffness in his body, and stepped in front of the doorway, blocking Herbert Bloom from entering. Gray locked eyes with the old man. His hands balled into fists.

One of the lawyers told Gray to get out of the way, but Gray didn't move. He stared at Herbert Bloom searching for any sign of remorse or regret, but there was nothing. "Why? Why me?"

Bloom cocked his head to the side. "Sometimes sacrifices have to be made for the greater good."

Herbert Bloom, then, attempted to step around, as if his words had settled the matter. He was a man used to this. Herbert Bloom had grown accustomed to people accepting his reality and logic without question.

Gray did not.

He grabbed the old man by the lapels on his jacket and slammed him against the wall.

"In case you haven't figured it out," Gray tightened his grip and gave Herbert Bloom a hard shake. "I'm not somebody you can just sacrifice." Then he let go, and stepped back as the old man crumpled to the ground. "Good luck in there, because that judge is never going to let you go. You're going to die in jail."

THE MERCHANTS BRIDGE

The bakeshop closed at 6:30 p.m., and there was still a line out the door. That wasn't saying much, since only about five customers could fit inside the little bakery at one time, but Gray knew that it was enough business to keep the lights on. Over the past three months, he'd developed a system.

In the evening, a young baker fresh out of the Culinary Institute of America arrived and mixed several large batches of dough. Two would be a master sourdough formula, which could be turned into multiple different kinds of bread: basic country white, cinnamon raisin, rosemary, and the Everything Loaf, which was Gray's version of an everything bagel along with sunflower and pumpkin seeds. The other batch would be enriched with butter for scones and other sorts of pastries. All of it would be ready to bake in the morning when he arrived.

The days at the bakeshop were long, but Gray was happy. Unlike practicing law, the work was tangible. There was a beginning, middle, and an end. He saw exactly what he had created, and enjoyed the looks on people's faces when they walked into the little storefront and smelled the aroma of freshly baked bread.

Gray signed the lease for the hundred and twenty year-old building on the day he surrendered his license to practice law. It was a voluntary resolution negotiated by Moyo with the Board of Judicial Standards related to breaking into Herbert Bloom's private office and stealing his computer. There was a chance, if he had fought harder, to simply be suspended for a year or two, but Gray didn't want that. He didn't want the future temptation to ever return to the life of a lawyer, however unlikely such a temptation would be.

Gray didn't know why he thought a bakery would be successful at a location where every other business that'd occupied the spot had failed, but the possibility had stuck in the back of his mind from the moment he had peered through its window with his children while walking back to his house after playing in the park. It called to him, plus he needed to make a living somehow.

It took effort to bring everything inside the building up to code and be ready to open in the late fall. Gray had done most of the remodeling himself, but Midge and Haley lent a hand when they could and the kids loved painting the walls. He took out a second mortgage on his house to buy commercial ovens and an espresso machine, and when it was done, the Morgan Ford Bakery was born.

Gray wrapped two french baguettes in brown butcher paper. He fastened the paper with a piece of twine, and then handed the tidy package to the last customer of the day. She was an older woman with a handkerchief tied on her head.

The woman's eyes lit as she examined the bundle. "Perfect." She turned to the door. "Can't wait to get home and eat it. My daughter and her family are coming for dinner."

Gray stepped around the counter, escorting her out. "Well enjoy and have a great night. I appreciate your business."

At that, the woman turned and took in the bakery's space once more. "Who would've thought that we'd have something like this in our little neighborhood?" She blew a kiss. "Just fabulous."

If Gray would've been closer, he was sure she might have reached out and pinched his cheek. When she was out the door, Gray turned off the "Warm Fresh Bread" sign in the window and locked up. He had about forty minutes, before Amy Wirth would arrive and he needed to clean the shop for the next day.

Amy Wirth arrived exactly on time. Gray had just finished wiping down the huge Hobart mixer and washing the shelves. "Just a few more things on my list, and then I'll be done."

"The place looks great." Wirth followed Gray into the back of the shop, and she waited as he gathered up all the used rags and towels. He tossed them into a large laundry bag, and then he took off his dirty apron and put it in with the rest of the linens. He cinched the bag closed and threw it over his shoulder. "I have to wash these tonight." As he walked toward the back door, Gray pointed at two large cloth sacks on a stainless-steel table. "Can you grab those?"

Amy picked up one of the sacks and peeked inside. It was filled with two dozen loaves of bread. "These look nice." Then she picked up the other sack and they went out the back door together.

Gray had traded in his old car for a large white delivery van. Morgan Ford Bakery was painted on its side along with an address, website, and phone number. Gray set the dirty laundry down on the pavement, unlocked the van, and then hoisted it inside. Amy Wirth, then, put the sacks of bread down next to it.

"This thing has been a lifesaver." He patted the side of the van. "I knew I'd be baking a lot, but I didn't anticipate hauling everything everywhere." They got inside, Gray turned on the engine, and then said, "Tell me how things are going with the new job."

"It's been nice," Wirth said. "The FBI isn't perfect, but I feel like I can be myself. They respect me, and Matthews is a good partner."

Gray grunted and rolled his eyes. "I bet."

"Really," she said. "He's a good guy."

"A good guy who almost sent me to prison for the rest of my life." Gray shifted the van into gear and pulled out of the parking lot. "How about we talk about something else? How about Durell, what's going on with that guy?"

"With Jack Durell?" Wirth nodded. "It was pretty easy. We found the invoice with the charges for that research memorandum that you tried to waive, added them up, and the amount just happened to be the same as a deposit that a city inspector put in his bank account just a few days after the Triangle was cleared."

Gray nodded. "I wasn't sure, but I figured it was something like that. The more I thought about it, everything just happened too quickly and too smoothly."

"So," Wirth said, "the Triangle development is on hold and we're negotiating with Durell's attorneys."

Gray drove east, and then north toward downtown. They rode most of the way in silence, but, as they got closer to Merchants Bridge, Wirth began biting her nails, nervous.

Gray noticed. "Sure you want to do this?"

Wirth hesitated for a moment. "You think I'm crazy."

"I definitely do not think you're crazy," he said. "In fact I know exactly how you feel."

"It never goes away, does it?"

Gray stopped at a light, and, while waiting for the red light to turn green, he looked at Wirth and their eyes met. "It never does." He touched the white rabbit's foot, hanging from his neck on its silver chain, hidden under his clothes. "It's weird not knowing what's real and what's just in your head."

The sun had begun to set by the time Gray turned down Ferry Street toward the river, he began to feel anxious as well. Although it wasn't as desolate in the fading light of day—in one of the lots a truck loaded up gravel, in another two guys in hardhats pumped a tanker with fuel——there was still an eeriness about the place, a sense of loss. Both he and Amy Wirth came close to losing their lives—Gray for the second time in less than a year—and it was hard to shake the realization of one's own mortality and lasting fragility that comes with that experience.

When the gravel road narrowed, Gray slowed and stopped when there was no longer any road left to travel. They were surrounded by overgrown brush and buckthorn. Wirth stared out the window, her mind was obviously flooding with memories as well.

"Let's do this." Gray got out of the van, walked around to the back, and removed the two sacks filled with bread. "They'll appreciate this."

Wirth closed the doors to the van, and then they walked under the rusted iron railroad trusses. On the other side of Merchants Bridge was a new homeless encampment. "Patrice Umutoni from the Beumont Street Mission will be up in that big tent in the middle," Gray said. "She knows everything and everyone, but I really don't think he's around anymore. I've come by a half dozen times delivering bread and nobody has seen him since that night."

"I just need to know," Wirth said.

She had never told Gray exactly what she thought had happened to her by the bridge, but when Gray had visited Wirth in the hospital, he'd told her about the man he'd seen in the darkness, a man with a white beard and an Irish lilt. He told her that it was the same man who'd cradled him in his arms the night Virgil Hawthorne was killed, and who he believed healed him. Gray figured she'd seen, heard, or experienced the same thing.

"Why now?" he asked.

Wirth stopped. "I couldn't get it out of my head. Then I kept thinking about the hospital and you. So I called a friend in the department, and he let me go down to the evidence locker." Wirth hesitated, but continued. "They had a plastic bag of all your clothes. The ones you were wearing that night when Hawthorne was killed, collected them at the hospital. I took out the shirt. It was stiff, covered in blood ….then I flattened it out, and I saw two little holes in the front."

She stepped closer to Gray. "One here." Wirth pointed at Gray's chest and tapped it with her finger. "And one here."

Pre-Order The Second Book in the Dark River Series Today:

Dealing Justice

Coming Fall 2023

www.jdtrafford.com

ABOUT THE AUTHOR

J.D. Trafford is the winner of the National Legal Fiction Writing Competition for Lawyers, has been profiled in Mystery Scene Magazine (a "writer of merit"), and written multiple bestselling legal thrillers. This includes the "No Time" series featuring Michael Collins, which was selected as an IndieReader bestselling pick, and Little Boy Lost, which has sold over 100,000 copies worldwide and spent over three weeks as the #1 overall bestseller on Amazon.

In addition to graduating with honors from a Top 20 law school, J.D. Trafford has worked as a civil and criminal prosecutor, an associate at a large national law firm, and a nonprofit attorney for people who could not afford legal representation.

Prior to law school, J.D. Trafford worked in Washington D.C. and lived in Saint Louis, Missouri. He worked on issues of housing, education, and poverty in communities of color.

He now lives with his wife and children in the Midwest, and bikes whenever possible.

Contact him through his website, www.jdtrafford.com

CPSIA information can be obtained
at www.ICGtesting.com
Printed in the USA
FSHW021736070222
88151FS

9 798985 652918